Leverage

Fortress Security, Volume 17

Rebecca Deel

Published by Rebecca Deel, 2023.

LEVERAGE

First edition. November 29, 2023.

Copyright © 2023 Rebecca Deel.

ISBN: 979-8223301165

Written by Rebecca Deel.

To my amazing husband. You make life worthwhile. I love
you.

Chapter One

Poppy Reynolds sat up with a strangled gasp, threw her blanket and sheet away from her body, and scrambled to her feet. Shoving trembling fingers through damp hair, she glanced at the bedside clock and scowled.

When would the nightmares stop? Several months had passed, and her body still woke at two in the morning, convinced she was in the hands of a man who enjoyed inflicting pain on innocent women and children. Although Poppy's counselor assured her she was improving, the process wasn't happening fast enough to suit her.

Too bad she couldn't snap her fingers and change instantaneously. That's what she wanted, what she needed. Everything depended on Poppy believing she was safe. If something didn't change soon, her secret would come out.

She had to figure this out quickly, or her family and friends would never give her time alone. For this writer, a crowd of well-meaning people was the path to true madness.

Poppy shuddered. People in her face and space all the time? No. A thousand times, no. She liked people well enough. On her terms. On her time line. Not all the time and not in groups over five or ten. Brief spurts, too.

And no media. Ironic since she carried press credentials. So, she was a part-time journalist. Very part time.

Enough. No use dwelling on her problems at two in the morning. She wouldn't solve those or come up with a solution for world peace, either.

Since sleeping was out of the question now, Poppy went into the bathroom to splash cold water on her face, happy to erase evidence of sweat and possibly a few tears from her skin. She could admit the tears to herself.

Not for the first time, Poppy was thankful she lived alone. Bad enough to have a weakness. At least no one witnessed her implosion in the middle of the night. Knowing her happily married sister, Sage, slept soundly a mile away in her own secure home gave Poppy a measure of peace.

She turned off the bathroom light. First order of business? Leave her bedroom and reduce the stress of not being able to sleep.

Poppy left the room without her shoes and stopped, remembering a deep male voice telling her to always wear shoes and socks. Just in case, he said. She rolled her eyes. "Whatever," she grumbled, but took a minute to obey Logan's repeated warning, snagged her laptop on the way out the door, then descended the stairs.

She couldn't sleep? Fine. The middle of the night was prime time for work. Who was here to bother her? No family or friends. No pets. No coworkers. The world around her slept. Nothing but quiet.

Poppy clutched the laptop against her chest. Try to work, she qualified. Nope. Don't do it, she warned herself. Don't jinx yourself. So what if the almighty page had remained blank, a death knell for most writers? She wasn't most writers.

Wow. She sounded like a pompous jerk. Good thing no one heard the thoughts circling in her brain.

The conversation with herself wasn't designed to boost an inflated ego but to stave off a total meltdown. She couldn't afford to panic. Panicking reinforced and perpetuated the cycle. After all, Poppy had finished the true-crime novel under contract when she'd been kidnapped along with Sage plus the book after that since it, too, was under contract. She had never defaulted on a contract and never missed a deadline. A point of pride for her. Since she'd finished those two books, her motivation to work and her creativity had crashed into a brick wall. Hard.

Three contract offers from her publisher lay on the desk in her office, and her creativity froze the moment she opened the envelope two months ago. No progress. No ideas. Nothing. Poppy never signed a contract unless she had at least a vague idea of what the contracted book was about. She didn't mind surprises along the way, but a starting place was an absolute necessity.

For the past eight weeks, she had felt like a rookie writer. Every time she looked at the blank white screen, the cursor mocked her. She felt sick, broke into a cold sweat, and prayed for an idea, even a bad one. She could edit bad ideas into good ones or, better yet, spark good ones.

Poppy blew out a breath. Right. So far, that plan was a bust. She had written nothing, even an email to her parents. She'd been absent from life. The cycle couldn't continue. Her mother would sniff out the truth soon, and that would lead to disaster.

Writing true crime was her livelihood. If she didn't write, she didn't eat. Simple as that. Moving in with her parents wasn't happening. Ever.

Living in Washington, D.C.? The stuff of nightmares. Poppy refused to live in the fishbowl of the political elite. Her parents, Vice President and Second Lady of the United States, were born for politics. They loved political bargaining and state dinners and were perfect in that role. They also had their eyes on the top political office in the land.

She shuddered. Who in their right mind wanted to be president? She and Sage had already informed their parents they supported a White House run as long as they left the sisters off the campaign trail, ads, and debates. They detested everything associated with politics.

Now, Poppy had a better reason than ever to avoid the political scene. Her friend, Logan, with the deep voice and attitude. Poppy's mouth curved. Quiet, sometimes cranky, always bossy, and handsome-as-sin Logan Fletcher. Former Texas cop turned deadly operative for Fortress Security. He worked in the shadows. No political high life for him. Poppy shrugged. Suited her. She didn't like the high life anyway.

Not that it mattered. They were friends. Good friends, but still only friends. She sighed.

Poppy set her laptop on the couch and walked to the kitchen to brew a pot a coffee and clear out the last of the odious memories of her short time in Mexican captivity.

Scanning her coffee options, Poppy chose a bold Sumatran blend and brewed a full pot of twelve cups. If that didn't clear the fog in her brain, nothing would. Whether coffee strong enough to wake the most sleep deprived cop or soldier on the planet also cured writer's block was anyone's guess. If it worked, she'd sell the cure to desperate writers and make a fortune. Padding her bank account was always welcome, especially in these days when her creativity meter registered near zero.

Moments later, Poppy took her first sip of the black elixir. Bold, beautiful, hot enough to scald her mouth. Perfect. Coffee would make her feel better. Not perfect, but better. If the caffeine buzz cured her writer's block, she'd file a patent and watch the money roll into her account. No need to write another thing for the rest of her life.

Poppy snorted. Right. Like the voices in her head would stay silent. They never shut up. As she continued to sip her coffee, she perused the shelves of her pantry and refrigerator for a snack to take with her to the living room.

When nothing appealed, she closed the pantry door and blew out a breath, recognizing the tactic from experience. Delay, delay, delay until it was too late to write or until a spark generated enough excitement to send her running to her laptop.

Sure. Poppy shook her head. Just the thought of opening her writing program and staring at another blank screen made her stomach twist into a knot. Again.

She rolled her eyes. Suck it up, Reynolds. Bad writing is better than no writing. You can't fix a blank page. Refill your million-dollar cure for writer's block, sit on the couch, and write a bad article or book proposal. By the time the editor sees it, the paragraphs will practically sing and dance.

Poppy smiled. Oh, boy. Whatever words ended up in her document were bound to be terrible if the drivel she just spouted was an example of words to come. But, hey, no one should expect Nobel Prize winning prose at this ungodly hour of the morning. If so, they would be disappointed.

She refilled her mug, peered into the pantry again, and selected a box of her favorite blueberry-flavored protein bars. If she snacked while writing, and she *was* going to write, Poppy assured herself, a protein bar was a healthier snack than the container of chocolate-chip cookies calling her name. She mentally patted herself on the back for leaving the cookies on the shelf. Her stomach, however, thought little of her food choice.

She set the box on the kitchen counter and opened it. After pulling one of the wrapped bars free, Poppy returned the box to the pantry. Time to grab her coffee, go to the living room, and fill a blank page with bad writing.

She turned to retrieve her coffee and came face-to-face with a man dressed in black from head to toe, holding a gun pointed at her chest.

Poppy stared first at the weapon, a Sig Sauer, a favorite weapon of Logan and his Fortress Security teammates. Since her security alarm wasn't blaring, she had to assume this guy had either bypassed or cut the alarm. Either way, Fortress had been notified of a security breach.

Calm. She had to be calm and breathe so she could think.

"Looks like I'm paying too much for my alarm system," Poppy said as she slid the protein bar into the pocket of her yoga pants. "What do you want?"

"You're coming with us."

Her eyebrow winged up. "Unless you have a mouse in your pocket, I only see you waving a gun in my face." She'd been training hard enough with Logan and company to escape and evade this one guy until help arrived.

A noise to her right caught Poppy's attention. She glanced toward the living room.

Her heart sank as another man walked into her line of vision, dressed the same as the first gunman.

"We're running out of time," the second man said.

Great. Just great. Thing One and Thing Two. Some help she would be in describing these turkeys. If she survived, the only description she could offer the authorities was the first man's voice was in the bass range. The second man's voice was in the tenor range. Nice to know she had put her high school choir knowledge to good use. Unfortunately, her musical knowledge wouldn't help law enforcement or Fortress Security operatives identify the men who broke into her home.

Assuming Poppy survived to share her musical knowledge, that is. No guarantees on that score. She didn't like the setup here.

She turned back to the first gunman. "What do you gentlemen want?"

Thing Two's head tilted slightly to the side, as though puzzled. "You're not screaming."

"You sound disappointed."

He shrugged. "Surprised."

"I'm not much of a screamer." Except in Mexico.

"Saves us headaches," Thing One said. He motioned toward the back door with his Sig. "Time to go."

Poppy's stomach knotted. Not good. Her phone was on the couch beside her laptop. She knew better. Logan had drilled into her head to always carry her phone wherever she went, even in the house. Letting down her guard might cost Poppy more than she wanted to pay.

She took a half step back to give herself maneuvering room. Although she didn't have a good chance of escaping the two men, she must try. "Regrettably, I'll have to pass on your kind invitation."

Thing One surged forward and shoved Poppy against the counter, the cold steel of his Sig pressed against the underside of her chin forcing her head up so her gaze locked with his. The thug's eyes glittered. "You have two choices. Option one is to come with us nice and quiet, and you won't get hurt."

"Nice to know. What's option two?"

"We knock you out and tie you up, kidnap your sister, and continue on with the plan." His mouth curved. "Either of you will serve the purpose. So, which one will it be? You or Sage?"

No. She couldn't let these men anywhere near Sage. "Leave my sister alone."

Thing Two grabbed Poppy's wrists and bound them behind her back with zip ties. At the last second, she remembered to fist her hands. "Move," he said and pushed her toward Thing One, who took hold of her upper arm and steered her toward the back door.

As soon as Poppy cleared the threshold, she ripped her arm from the hold of Thing One and sprinted across her yard and toward the safety of the darkened woods behind her home. Before she'd covered over fifteen yards, a heavy weight slammed into her back, taking her to the ground and forcing air from her lungs.

Seconds later, Thing Two flipped Poppy to her back, and punched her.

Lights out.

#

Chapter Two

When his phone vibrated in his pocket, Logan Fletcher woke from a light sleep and slid the phone from his pocket. He glanced at the message on his screen and frowned at the few cryptic words.

"What's wrong?" Brody Weaver, his team leader and best friend, asked.

Conversation around the jet's cabin immediately stopped, and the rest of Logan's Fortress teammates turned toward him, alert for trouble.

"Don't know. Zane sent a message to call him immediately." Although none of the worry churning inside him showed on his face, Logan's gut knotted. Zane Murphy, the team's tech and communication guru, wouldn't send him a message like this unless something serious was happening with Poppy. No other explanation made sense. Logan had no family who mattered. His closest friends were on the jet with him. That left Poppy.

Logan debated calling Z without placing the phone on speaker to give himself a chance to process the blow before telling his teammates the news. Based on the tension in Brody's body, that wouldn't fly. End of story.

Brody was Poppy's brother-in-law, and he had a soft spot for her. Although Brody knew Logan and Poppy were sort of involved, if something had happened to Poppy, he'd want to know as soon as possible for his own sake and his wife's. To refuse Brody the information would lead to a fist in Logan's face and the phone call on speaker anyway.

Might as well spare himself a black eye. Brody packed quite a punch. Logan placed the call to Zane and tapped the speaker button.

Z answered on the first ring. "Yeah, Murphy."

"It's Logan. You're on speaker with the Texas Team. What's wrong, Z?"

"Received an alert two minutes ago. Security breach at Poppy's house."

Logan stilled. Her alarm system was the best Fortress sold. He'd chosen the system himself. The best of everything. Top of the line. Even a few things not yet sold to the public. He'd wanted Poppy safe. She was the vice president's daughter, after all. Wouldn't do to have her kidnapped again. And yet here they were.

Logan's jaw clenched. He needed to be at Poppy's place. Right now. When had he last felt this helpless? His lips curled. Oh, yeah. When Poppy had been kidnapped and flown to Mexico.

Beside Logan, Brody leaned closer to the phone. "It's Brody. What about my place?"

"Secure. I dispatched two response teams. Both will be on site in ten minutes or less. In the meantime, two Fortress agents in the area are heading to Poppy's house, and two agents are thirty seconds from Weaver's place."

Logan growled. "We're two hours from Nashville, Z. I need to be on the ground. Now."

"I can make that happen. However, you'll reach Poppy faster if you stay in the air."

No one spoke the truth, a truth Logan couldn't bear to voice himself. Poppy could already lay dead in her house at this moment, forever gone from his reach. Pain ripped through Logan, stealing his breath.

No. That couldn't be true. Poppy couldn't be gone. He clamped down on the satellite phone with an iron grip. If he lost her tonight, he would tear the world apart to find the people responsible and destroy them in the most painful way possible, one inch at a time. They would regret taking Poppy from him. "Are you patched in to the comms of the men headed to Poppy's?"

"Working on it."

"Loop me in when you're connected." Waiting for secondhand news might kill him.

Z didn't argue with him. "Copy that."

"Z," Brody said. "Same."

"Yep. Hold." Seconds later, Zane said, "Brody, Mateo is the comm coordinator for the second team. He'll contact you when Team Two reaches your home."

"Copy." Brody stood, walked to the round conference table where the team held discussions, and sat with a phone in his hand and his comm device in his ear.

In less than a minute, Zane said, "Team One is three hundred yards from Poppy's house. Looping you in now, Logan."

After hearing two clicks, Z said, "Rafe, Jackson, I looped the Texas team into your comm link."

"Copy," Rafe Torres murmured. "Everything appears quiet. Low-level lights are on all over the house."

"Standard," Logan said.

"Poppy isn't responding," Zane said. "Proceed with caution. Jackson, you carrying your mike bag?"

"Yes, sir," Jackson Conner said. "Never leave home without it."

The medic sounded as grim as Logan felt with each additional piece of bad news. He swallowed the bile pooling in his mouth. Man, he hated this. Logan wanted to be on the ground to see firsthand for himself what had happened to Poppy, not waiting on the sideline for someone to dole out the information in droplets. He never was one to sit back and wait, especially when it mattered.

Poppy mattered.

He stared hard at the screen, silently willing the response team to approach her home faster. Logan needed to know Poppy's status, whether it was good or bad.

The operatives closing in on Poppy's home, Rafe and Jackson, were fierce and well trained. If the threat was still ongoing, the operatives would neutralize it, extricate Poppy, and provide any help she needed.

He wished Jackson and Rafe wore body cameras so he could see what was happening as well as hear it over the phone. Not happening, though. This middle-of-the-night rollout was an emergency rescue, not a sanctioned, planned mission. The operatives wouldn't have taken time to add a camera to their gear. For them to reach Poppy's side faster, he'd suck it up and deal.

"Jackson, check the front," Rafe whispered. "I'll take the back."

"Copy."

"Logan, is there a dog in the house?"

"Negative."

The minutes ticked by with agonizing slowness for Logan and the rest of the team. While he waited for a report from the team at Poppy's house, Logan monitored his team leader and saw the moment relief swept over his friend. Excellent. Everything must be secure at Sage and Brody's home.

The only better news would be to hear the same about Poppy. Deep in his gut, though, Logan knew differently. Something was wrong.

"Windows on the right side of the house are secure," Rafe whispered. "Proceeding to the back."

"Windows on the left side secure. Proceeding to the front," said Jackson.

"So far, things sound good," Max Norton said from his seat across the aisle.

Logan glanced at him.

Jesse Phelps, their team medic, shook his head. "Poppy is paranoid about keeping her phone charged, and she wouldn't ignore a call from Fortress. Even if he didn't care about Logan, she'd worry about Brody's safety while he was deployed."

"Accurate statement," Sawyer Chapman said. "She's also a true crime writer, always after the next story. She's never out of touch with the world news just in case another story breaks or in case something happens involving her parents. Can't blame her."

"Front windows and door locked. No signs of tampering," Jackson reported.

That left Rafe to check the back of Poppy's house before he and his teammate breached the home and searched for Poppy.

Seconds ticked by. What was taking Rafe so long?

"New scratches on the back door lock," Rafe whispered.

Logan scowled. Someone had picked the lock. "Security alarm?"

"Wires cut at the box and rerouted."

Idiots. He snorted as Brody returned to the seat beside him. The people who broke in either didn't research the alarm system well enough or didn't care whether the system had a failsafe that signaled a security breach the second the wires were cut.

Logan swallowed hard. That didn't mean good things for Poppy. "Find Poppy, Rafe. Now."

"Copy that," Rafe murmured.

Brody glanced at Logan.

"Don't." The team leader was wasting his breath if he thought to corral Logan's impatience. Wasn't happening. "Sage is safe?"

"She's fine. I talked to her, told her we were two hours out of Nashville and wanted to hear her voice."

Logan's lip curled. "She bought that excuse?"

"Not really, but she let me get by with it for the moment. Team Two reports no attempts to breach the house."

He gave a slight nod in acknowledgment of the information. So, Poppy was targeted. If this was a simple burglary, the thief may still be in the house, but more than likely was already gone. Burglars, however, preferred not to carry weapons or confront homeowners.

Poppy's continued silence worried Logan. Had a burglar encountered Poppy by accident and panicked, hurting her without intending to? He frowned. Wouldn't prevent Logan from tracking down anyone responsible for this debacle.

"Jackson." Rafe whispered. "On three." He counted down.

The two men entered Poppy's residence at the same time.

Inside the jet's cabin, they could hear only the noise of the engines as the Texas team waited in silence for the response team in Poppy's house to search for her.

Room by room, Rafe and Jackson cleared Poppy's house. Ten minutes after entering the house, Rafe said, "The house is clear. No sign of Poppy."

"Anything out of place?" Logan asked. He needed to see the house for himself to recognize subtle signs of items moved if Poppy had the chance to leave him a clue to who had taken her. No doubt in Logan's mind now that this wasn't a burglary.

Someone had kidnapped her. Why did he take her? He dismissed the idea of a woman. Poppy was fast enough and strong enough to take down a woman by herself and escape, even if the woman had a weapon.

The same might be true of one man. He couldn't say the same about two men who carried weapons. He'd been drumming into her head to cooperate so she could survive and escape. Whether she remembered his instructions during her middle-of-the-night encounter was the wild card in the equation.

The more he thought about it, the more sense it made for two men to come after Poppy. One to control her with a weapon while the other either bound her or knocked her out. Logan's jaw clenched. If the men who entered the house thought they'd cow Poppy Reynolds into cooperation and submission through fear, they learned differently within the first five minutes. Of that, Logan was positive.

"Her computer and sat phone are on the sofa in the living room, along with two books," Jackson said.

Logan growled. "I told Poppy to keep her phone on her at all times, even in the house."

Brody signaled him to dial it down. "She must have been up and working and stopped for a quick break."

"Maybe," Logan said. "Who wrote the books she left on the sofa, Jackson?"

"Does it matter?"

"I'll let you know when I get the information," he snapped.

"Hold." Jackson's voice came over the speaker seconds later. "Sara Donati and Jean Auel. Ring a bell?"

He closed his eyes briefly as disappointment swirled in his gut. "Yeah. The books aren't important." At least not to her disappearance. "Sorry I jumped down your throat."

"No problem. I understand your concern."

Concern. Mild word for the icy dread threatening to paralyze him.

"Logan."

Something in Rafe's voice warned Logan he wouldn't like the next words he heard and braced himself for the next blow. "Tell me."

"Three things. One, Team One just arrived on site. They're checking the perimeter. Two, I found flex cuffs on the kitchen floor."

He scowled. Confirmation this night's work wasn't a simple burglary. If these men kidnapped Poppy, they needed her for something. Ransom? Leverage? Over who? Him? Brody? Both? Poppy's father? "You said three things. What's the third?"

"Her coffee pot is on and hot. Almost a full twelve cups in the pot. We didn't miss them by much."

Just long enough for her to disappear into thin air.

Brody massaged the back of his neck. "Poppy doesn't have her phone, and I know for a fact she doesn't put on the jewelry with the trackers in it unless she's leaving the house. How will we find her? We don't have a clue where to start since she pitched a fit about having cameras inside the house. She and Sage had enough of that when they lived with their parents. They refuse to do it now that they live on their own. Sage won't have them in our home either."

"Too many enemies to zero in on," Sawyer added. "Ours, Vice President Reynolds's enemies, and her own."

"Too many ways to spirit Poppy away from the area," Max added. "No nosy neighbors to describe a vehicle that doesn't belong or describe a man or men coming out of Poppy's place with her in the middle of the night."

"We've got zip," Jesse said.

"Hold," Rafe interrupted.

Texas team fell silent again.

Two minutes later, Rafe said, "Found signs of a scuffle in the backyard. The way I read it, Poppy broke away from these guys, but one of them chased her down and tackled her. From that point on, there are only two sets of footprints instead of three."

Ice water flowed through Logan's veins.

Chapter Three

Logan dragged a hand down his face as he stared at the phone cradled in the palm of his other hand. This was the one phone call he had promised himself he would never have to make, that he would protect Poppy so well the call would never be necessary. Looks like the laugh was on him. Again. How would Logan explain this when he didn't know what "this" was?

"Want me to make the call?" Brody squeezed Logan's shoulder.

"No. She's my responsibility."

A slight hesitation from his friend. "Technically, you're not family. You don't have to do this."

He stared at Brody. Logan refused to justify his decision. Reynolds would expect him to call and explain his failure to protect Poppy and the circumstances of her disappearance. More important, Logan never shied away from hard tasks and situations to spare himself discomfort. He owed it to himself and Poppy to stand up for her.

Brody raised both hands in silent surrender. "When the vice president is tearing a strip off your hide, remember I volunteered to throw myself on the sword for you."

Without replying, he strode to the back of the jet and shut himself into the bedroom. Zane was keeping him and the rest of his team informed. After Logan finished this call, he'd regroup, create a plan, and find Poppy.

Unable to sit when speaking to Poppy's father on such an important matter, he remained standing and pressed the speed dial number for Ivan Reynolds. The vice president picked up on the first ring. "One minute. Go."

"Poppy's missing." In rapid-fire fashion, he reported what he knew, which was only enough to be sure Poppy was in serious trouble. Whether the problem originated with Poppy's world, her father's, or Logan's and Brody's, remained to be seen.

"You said this wouldn't happen," Reynolds snapped.

"Yes, sir."

The vice president's voice dropped lower. "Find her. Now."

"That's the plan, sir."

"I'm putting my detail on it."

"Don't."

"Why not? We're short on time."

"Once the news leaks, we lose every advantage we have. They'll know people are searching for Poppy. They'll either move her or kill her."

More silence, then, "Considering the circumstances, you're asking a lot."

"I know."

"Do you?" Reynolds whispered. "I already trusted you once, and you failed. Why should I take the risk?"

"I won't fail again."

Several more seconds of silence went by. Finally, Poppy's father said, "See that you don't. Bring her to Beverly when you get her back. If you don't, you and your company won't see another penny of government money." The call ended.

A weird mix of fury and guilt swirled in Logan's gut. Great. Not enough to endanger his relationship with Poppy's father, such as it was. Now, his screwup might affect his employer.

He sighed. *Good job, Fletch. Way to alienate the second most powerful man in the country and the man who signs your paycheck.* If Poppy was smart, she'd kicked him to the curb as soon as she saw his ugly mug. He wouldn't blame her.

With the mission clock ticking in his head, Logan called his boss despite the early hour. His situation was precarious enough without adding to his boss's ire by allowing him to be blindsided by the one of the most powerful men in the world before the sun rose. No, Logan would rather take Brent Maddox's dressing down now rather than later.

Logan straightened to attention as the Navy SEAL who was now his boss greeted him with, "Do you know what time it is, Fletcher? This better be important."

"Poppy Reynolds is missing."

"Sit rep."

Maddox's voice sounded as grim as Logan felt. Too much time had passed. Why hadn't he or Poppy's father received a ransom demand? He recounted what little the operatives at the scene knew as well as Zane.

"Ivan knows?"

"Yes, sir."

"And yet you still live."

"Because I informed him by phone instead of in person."

A slight pause. "What did you leave out?"

He scowled. "Do you have a camera in the jet?"

A snort. "Nope. Don't need one. I know my people. What's the rest of the story?"

"If I don't find Poppy and bring her to Beverly unharmed, Fortress won't see another dime of government money. The company might skate by unscathed if you fire me, but I won't find work for any company receiving government funds. Reynolds will see that my career is toast."

Maddox growled. "If Reynolds thinks threatening me or one of my employees will get Poppy back faster, he and the president are in for an expensive surprise next time the government needs our off-the-books services. Our fees just doubled for any future contracts."

Logan froze. "Sir?"

"No one threatens me or my people, no matter how dire the circumstances. They need us to do their off-the-books work more than we need their jobs. Our income base depends less on government work these days than in the beginning, and President Martin knows that to be true. We're turning away jobs, and we're recruiting and training operatives as fast as possible. We still can't keep up with demand for our services. Suddenly, I'm not feeling the desire to offer Martin our services."

His throat tightened. "Don't burn bridges on my account, sir."

"Shut up, Fletcher."

"Yes, sir."

"Find Poppy, no matter what it takes. Any resource we have is yours. Just say the word. Do the job quickly and quietly."

Logan froze. Had he heard Brent correctly? "Boundaries?"

"I didn't hear that question. Report in every six hours." The call ended.

Still gripping his sat phone, Logan slowly lowered his hand. Holy smoke. His boss had removed all restraints on the mission to find and retrieve Poppy.

He would do anything necessary to rescue her, with or without Maddox's permission. Still, the weight of Fortress's help and permission carried more influence than his alone. He'd burned too many bridges of his own and walked away. Most of the time, Logan didn't care. With Poppy's life on the line, he did.

After returning the phone to his pocket, Logan retraced his steps to the cabin. His teammates fell silent as he approached.

Brody's gaze scanned him from head to toe. "Well, you look like you're still intact. I thought Ivan might crawl through the phone and tear a strip or two from your hide. What happened?"

"He's not happy."

Sawyer snorted. "Understatement of the year."

Logan inclined his head in agreement. "If I don't deliver Poppy unharmed to Beverly, my career is toast and Fortress will be blackballed by the government."

Silence fell.

Max whistled. "Takes guts to threaten the boss."

"I don't think Reynolds looks at it that way."

"I guarantee Brent will." Brody rubbed his jaw. "Family meals will be awkward if he goes through with it."

"Sorry," Logan muttered. He wasn't. Not really. Well, okay, he was sorry to cause his friend a few awkward moments with the new in-laws. Ticking off Ivan and Beverly Reynolds didn't bother Logan. He had other priorities.

At the top of the list was rescuing their daughter and bringing the kidnappers to justice. Whether the people who took Poppy ended up behind bars or six feet under was up to them. Logan didn't have a preference as long as the men who had her now weren't able to touch her again.

Jesse tossed him a bottle of water. "Don't lie."

He shot the medic a narrow-eyed stare.

His teammate, who should have been intimidated, rolled his eyes. "Let's clarify. The only thing you're sorry about is causing Brody trouble with Sage's parents."

How did his teammates know him so well? For a man who thrived on a rep of intimidating everyone around him, he'd lost his edge with Texas Team. They treated him like a pet with a poor attitude and worked around him. It was embarrassing. "Maybe," he muttered.

His former friends chuckled.

"Don't sweat it," Brody said. "I routinely tick off Ivan. The habit is a family tradition now. If you decide to join the party, you'll fit right in."

The others glanced at each other, then turned faces with curious expressions toward him. "Have something to share with the class, Logan?" Sawyer asked.

"Nope. Ready to get back to business instead of sitting around gossiping like that bunch of busybodies at headquarters?"

That brought a round of laughter from the men.

Brody gave a rolling motion with his finger, signaling Logan to go on with his report.

"I called the boss. You were right, Brody. Brent didn't like Reynolds's threat. The government's bill for Fortress's fees will double from now on."

Another whistle, this one from Jesse. "Ouch. You don't cross Maddox and come out the winner. He hits where it hurts the worst."

Brody stared at Logan. "What else?"

"The boss took off the gloves."

Max straightened. "No rules?"

"Only one. Get Poppy back and take care of the people who took her." The corners of Logan's mouth tugged upward. "While I'm glad the boss approves, that was my plan anyway."

"Nice," Sawyer said. "Resources?"

"Everything Fortress has." Logan glanced at his phone again, hoping for an update from Zane but the screen was still blank.

"Where do we start?" Jesse asked. "We have nothing to go on unless Rafe and Jackson found something to show where the kidnappers might have taken Poppy."

Logan's phone rang. Zane's name scrolled across the screen. Finally. Maybe now he and the rest of the team could create a plan to find and rescue Poppy. He hated sitting on the sidelines, doing nothing. He wanted to be in the middle of the action.

He swiped his thumb across the glass and tapped the speaker button. "It's Logan. You're on speaker with Texas Team. Do you have her signal?"

"For now."

"What does that mean?"

"I'm tracking the GPS signal, but I think the kidnappers are driving to an airfield."

#

Chapter Four

Logan frowned. "You should be able to track the GPS in the air."

"As long as the battery holds out. That's not the problem."

"What is?" Brody asked.

"I talked to the pilot. The jet doesn't have enough fuel to fly more than another hour. You must refuel and restock the jet. The best place to do it is Nashville."

Logan clenched his jaw. "How long will that take?"

"About an hour. They'll move as fast as they can. The crew knows what's at stake. Before you ask, we don't have another jet available. I checked."

Zane knew him well.

"Our ground crew will be ready to go as soon as the jet lands. Brent is at headquarters collecting supplies you might need. He'll have them at the airport when you land."

"Anything else?"

"Unfortunately, no."

Logan and his teammates looked at each other, various expressions of dismay on their faces. "No plates, no traffic cam shots, no security cam footage?" Brody sounded skeptical. "The kidnappers couldn't have avoided every camera from Poppy's home to the nearest airstrip."

"The way their van is tricked out, they didn't have to avoid the cameras."

"Explain."

"Windows are too dark to see inside the vehicle, and the van has stolen plates. Although not enough to catch the attention of the police, the front windshield is also darkened. I pulled still photos from a traffic cam near Poppy's home. I'm working on cleaning up the images as we speak. However, we won't get much. The two men wore masks."

"Get me everything," Logan said. "As soon as you have it. Z, is it possible for you to connect Poppy's GPS tracker signal into the tracking program on the computer on board the jet?"

"Give me a minute."

Sawyer walked to the conference area at the front of the Lear and booted up the computer system. "We have the signal, Zane," Sawyer said. He tapped two keys in succession on the keyboard, and the wall screen came to life. A flashing red dot moved along a map of Hartman, Tennessee, showing the route the kidnappers were taking with Poppy.

"Zane, did you see Poppy?" Logan asked.

Silence.

He stiffened. Logan's hand tightened around his phone. "Spill it."

"Look, what I saw might not be accurate."

"Z," he snapped.

"I enhanced the images of the front of the van and ran the pictures through some specialized programs still in the development stage."

"And?" If the tech guru didn't get on with his report, Logan might lose his temper with one of the best friends he had, aside from Brody and the rest of his teammates.

"When I send you the still photos of the van, you'll see the vehicle is a soccer-mom van with upgrades, not a cargo van."

His heart skipped a beat and surged into a faster rhythm. "You saw her."

"Her leg and foot, I think."

"Send me the picture. I might be able to confirm."

Brody glared at him.

Tough if his team leader didn't like Logan's interest in Poppy. He'd have to deal. Logan wasn't going away.

"Sending the photo to the jet's computer now."

Logan joined Sawyer and the rest of his teammates in the conference area and studied the photo on the screen. He pointed to the section of the picture showing a woman's leg and foot shod in a running shoe.

After Sawyer blew up that portion of the image, Logan moved closer to the screen. While he hated Poppy was in the hands of these men, and, yeah, he could tell the jerks who took her were men, at least he had something to work from rather than nothing. "It's Poppy, Zane."

"How do you know?" Brody demanded. "All I see is a leg and a running shoe."

"I recognize her sock and the design on her shoe." And the shape of her leg, but he wouldn't share that with Brody. To do so was asking for a beat down.

The other man narrowed his eyes. "You're kidding."

"Nope."

"More than that, I'll bet."

He shrugged. "Think what you want."

Zane growled. "Focus. Fight later. Do you see where these guys are headed?"

Logan refocused on the screen and scowled. The airport in Hartman was just big enough to handle a Lear jet. He and his team would be at least three hours behind these guys. No telling where they would take Poppy or what she would face before he found her.

His fist clenched. He'd find her, no matter how long it took or how many obstacles he had to go through. "Airport. Probably a private plane. The Hartman airport can handle planes up to the size of a Lear. Do not lose her signal, Z. I don't care what you have to do to boost it, but don't lose her. I want the fastest ground crew we have on the ground at John C. Tune Airport, ready to service our jet."

"Already on it, Logan. Does Brody know you're taking over the team?" Amusement filled Zane's voice.

Logan's teammates chuckled. Logan didn't. This was too important. *She* was too important. "Just get it done. Fletcher out." He ended the call and stared at the screen.

Where were these men going? What did they want with Poppy? Questions circled in his mind, driving him crazy. He and his team were trapped in the jet for the next two hours, unless the pilot caught a great tailwind. Might as well put the time to good use. He straightened. "I have work to do."

Brody caught Logan's shoulder as he turned. "*We* have work to do. This isn't a one-man show, buddy. We're a team. The more work we split up, the more ground we'll cover."

He resisted breaking the other man's hold. Barely. He understood the value of teamwork. If they covered as much territory as possible, they eliminated blind alleys. He gave a curt nod.

"Get your computers. We'll work at the conference table," Brody said. "We need to work fast. As soon as the jet's serviced, we're wheels up."

They returned with their laptops, sat around the table, and divided the assignments. As he worked, Logan kept checking the wall screen. The red dot representing his only connection to Poppy was moving much faster now than it had earlier. Poppy and her kidnappers were in the air. The question of the night was, where were they taking her?

"Hey," Jesse said, breaking the silence. "How is Zane tracking Poppy? Does she wear her tracking jewelry to bed?"

"I doubt she was sleeping."

Brody's fists clenched. "That better not be firsthand knowledge talking."

Logan flicked his friend a glare, then returned his attention to Jesse. "She doesn't sleep well since she was taken to Mexico. The only part of the jewelry she wears to bed is her watch. Since it's waterproof, she refuses to take it off, especially if we're deployed. She doesn't want to miss a call or text from one of us."

A snort from Max. "From you. She doesn't care about missing calls from the rest of us."

The corners of his mouth tugged upward. "Maybe."

"Get back to work," Brody snapped. "Clock's ticking." In the cabin, silence fell again as the men settled back into their Internet searches.

When Logan finished his search with no results, he studied the wall screen again to check the kidnappers' progress. Huh. Where were the men taking Poppy? Instead of heading south like he'd half expected, the jet had turned north. Canada?

A lot of trouble dealing with immigration unless you know the right people and had the right amount of money to grease a palm for an official to look the other way. Not a problem if you have enough power. Someone who dispatched a two-man team with a private plane to kidnap the Vice President's daughter and fly her to an unknown location had plenty of money and power.

So, was this kidnapping political or personal? Didn't matter. Poppy's kidnapping was personal to Logan, a point he planned to make to the men who took her.

He searched his memory for a terrorist or one of his enemies who might use Poppy as leverage against him and came up with too many to narrow down the possibilities. According to the deep Internet search, no one had shown any interest in him for several months, but that didn't mean someone better than he was on the computer hadn't poked into Logan's whereabouts. Finding a computer geek just took some cash, and Logan's tech skills were good, but nowhere in Zane's league.

Logan's phone rang. He glanced at the screen, swept his thumb across the glass, and tapped the speaker button. "What do you have for me, Z?"

"License plate of the van and jet information."

"Send it to our email and the jet's computer. Thanks, Zane."

"Don't thank me yet, buddy. What I sent isn't worth much."

"It's more than what we have, which is nothing."

"No line to tug from the Internet searches into your backgrounds?"

"Nothing."

"Huh. That's interesting. I thought you, Brody, or your team would have some sign of where the threat to Poppy was coming from."

"No such luck, my friend."

"We'll find them." Zane ended the call.

Yeah, they would. But would they find these creeps fast enough to free Poppy before she ended up injured or, God forbid, dead?

"I have the plate," Max said.

"I'm on the jet," Sawyer said.

A moment later, Max said, "Although the license plate was attached to a black van, it's assigned to a late-model Mazda four-door sedan. The car is registered to a Ken Roberts of Maple Valley, Tennessee."

Brody nodded. "Good. I'll call David Montgomery. If we're lucky, we'll find the location where the car came from and score an image of the perp for Zane to clean up."

Excellent. Logan stretched in his seat while he waited for Brody's call to Montgomery to connect. Unless M Team was deployed and in a hot zone, or he was in a dangerous situation as sheriff of his county, David would answer Brody's call. He and his brothers were part of the sheriff's department of Morgan County, Tennessee, and worked part time for Fortress. Over the past several months, they had deployed frequently with Logan's team. As a result, the two teams formed tight bonds of friendship.

The call connected, and a deep male voice said, "Yeah, Montgomery. Do you know what time it is, Brody?"

"Yeah. Sorry, man. This is important."

"Hold."

A murmured conversation could barely be heard in the background, then the soft click of a closing door. "Go."

"I need everything you have on Ken Roberts's car theft."

A short pause. "You woke me at two in the morning over a stolen car? This better be good, my friend."

"Someone kidnapped Poppy Reynolds at midnight. The crew that took her used a van with Ken Roberts's plates."

A soft whistle came over the speaker. "I hope you don't think Ken was involved in her kidnapping. Ken is a thousand years old and weighs one hundred pounds soaking wet. I assure you, he's not your guy."

"He'd have to be as dumb as a box of rocks to use his own plates on a stolen vehicle to commit a crime law enforcement and the Secret Service will be all over like white on rice."

A snort from the other man. "That's the truth. Ken might be old as dirt, but he's not stupid. Looking for anything in particular?"

"A photo or a print. Something we can use to get a bead on these guys."

"No contact from the kidnappers yet?" He sounded surprised.

Logan answered the question. "No ransom demand. No phone call, email, or text. Nothing."

"So, no one has any idea what these people want."

"None."

"Huh. Want help?"

Some knots in Logan's gut loosened. Those words right there represented the best reason why he loved working for Fortress Security. They had each other's backs, no matter what. If he said he needed help and Logan's teammates weren't available, all he had to do was ask, and M Team would come to his aid.

He glanced at Brody, received permission to answer the question, and said, "Not yet. Mind if we hold that option in reserve?"

"Any time. You know that. We owe you." The team heard another door shut over the phone's speaker. "Give me a second to boot up the computer." Seconds later, David said, "I'm in. You'll want everything, so I'll send the files. What are you looking for specifically besides the fingerprints and photos?"

"Background on any sketchy relatives of Roberts."

"Doesn't have any relatives. He's the last of the line, and he was an only child of only children."

"That simplifies things." Brody rubbed his jaw. "Send the files to my email and Logan's. We'll take it from there."

"You got it."

"Thanks, David. Sorry to wake you."

"No problem. Will I hear about Poppy's kidnapping on the news later today?"

"Not if we can keep a lid on it."

"These guys didn't come up with the kidnapping scheme on their own," Logan said, his voice soft. "They're flunkies. If the White House doesn't leak the news to the media for another few hours, Poppy will be out of their hands and back where she belongs."

Even if it was the last thing he ever did.

"Keep me updated. We're available to help if you need us. Montgomery out." The call ended.

Logan glanced at the wall screen. The jet carrying Poppy was still in the air. He hoped that meant she was still safe.

Brody pointed at Jesse. "I just sent you a copy of the file David sent."

A second later, the medic nodded. "Got it. Give me a couple of minutes to look it over."

"Fast," Logan said.

Jesse held up one hand, keeping his eyes on the screen. "I know what's at stake, buddy."

"Sorry."

A snort.

Yeah, he really wasn't.

"Sawyer," Brody said. "What do you have on the jet?"

"Same as the vehicle. Nothing. The tail numbers exist, but they belong on another jet. Someone did a creative paint job."

"So, we do no know who owns the jet." Logan rubbed his knotted neck muscles.

"Sorry, man," Sawyer said. "I don't make the news, just report it."

He turned to the medic. "Well? Anything?"

"No prints except the old man's and lots of smudges. The kidnappers wore gloves. They hot-wired the van, did minimal damage. Professional job. These guys knew what they were doing."

Logan narrowed his eyes. "Nice for the insurance company. I don't care about them. What about photos of the perps?"

"Hold your horses. I was getting to it."

He rolled his finger in a signal to move along. If Jesse didn't speed up the information flow, Logan might leap over the table and shake the knowledge from his friend.

"The men didn't miss a trick, Logan. Masks the whole time. Gloves. Dressed in black from head to toe. The only details you can make out in the pictures are dark eyes and a small area of white skin showing around the eyes."

Nice. Professionals dressed in black who knew how to jack a car. He rolled his eyes. A description sure to help him find Poppy in an enormous world filled with men who had cultivated such skills. "Weapons, shoes, tech gear?"

"Working on it."

"We have to work faster. The jet will land in Nashville soon." Didn't matter that the kidnapper's jet hadn't landed yet. It would. The Fortress jet would take off as soon as the ground crew finished servicing it, and Logan and the others would go wheels up to follow the other jet. They didn't have time to waste.

Brody said, "Jesse, you and Max isolate photos from security and traffic cams around the area where the kidnappers stole the van. Maybe one of the Montgomery brothers missed something."

Max shook his head. "Not likely."

A shrug from the team leader. "Worth a shot. Sawyer, focus on the kidnappers' shoes and locating a video. Watching their movements for a few seconds will tell us a lot. Logan and I will focus on their weapons and awareness. We need to know about their backgrounds. Until we have faces and names, this will have to do."

Thirty minutes later, the pilot banked to the left and slowly descended. Over the intercom, he requested for the team to return to their seats.

Logan complied and resumed watching the plane flying Poppy farther away from him by the minute. So far, the trajectory hadn't changed.

He frowned. Were the men who took Poppy so arrogant that they didn't consider the possibility someone might track her? What would happen if they discovered the truth and the spunky writer was still in their hands?

Within ten minutes, the jet was wheels down on the tarmac at John C. Tune Airport. Dawn had yet to lighten the sky and wouldn't for a few more hours. As the jet stopped, the Fortress ground crew scrambled to service the aircraft.

Through the window, Logan noted the approach of an unmarked black van toward the jet's cargo area. A cargo loader followed in the van's wake.

Excellent. As the mission clock ticked away in his head, sounding more like the rumble of an oncoming train than the ticking of a grandfather clock, Logan rose and headed toward the back of the plane. "Supplies are here."

His teammates followed him down the aisle to assist the crew in loading supplies for their unexpected mission. Soon, Brent Maddox joined them at the conference table on the jet.

"Sit rep."

Brody reported what they'd learned so far. Precious little information, Logan thought as his team leader finished summarizing for their boss.

Brent waited a beat, then said, "That's it?"

"We're working on it," Max said.

The Fortress CEO stared at him, eyebrow raised.

Max sighed and held up a hand. "I know, sir. You don't have to say it. Work faster."

"Your mind-reading skills are rusty, Max."

"Yeah?"

"Did you check for threats to M Team or Ivan and Beverly Reynolds?"

Silence.

"Get on it," Brent snapped. "I doubt Poppy's disappearance has anything to do with the Montgomery brothers, despite the stolen van from Maple Valley. That's just pure bad luck for the kidnappers. Ivan and Beverly are a different story."

"Secret Service won't like us treading into their territory," Sawyer said.

"You planning to get caught?"

"No, sir."

"So, what's the problem?"

A quick grin. "Shutting up now, sir."

Brent slid his phone from his pocket and glanced at the screen. "Ground crew is finished. The jet is refueled and the food, beverages, and medical supplies have been restocked." He focused on the wall screen and studied it a moment. "They've stopped moving."

Logan's gaze shifted to the screen. "Poppy's in Montana."

Chapter Five

Poppy opened her eyes to slits and hissed as the dim light burning in the corner seemed to make her head explode. Holy smoke. She hoped someone caught the license plate of the truck that slammed into her.

Had she come down with the flu or something? What terrible timing since Texas Team was due back from deployment any time. Logan was gone so often, Poppy hated to miss time with him when he was home.

Not that she told him. Nope, the big, tough black ops soldier had a big enough ego. He didn't need her to feed that monster.

A wave of nausea twisted Poppy's gut. She moaned. Oh, man. Not that, too. She hated to barf. Slow breathing. That might be the ticket.

While she argued with her misbehaving stomach, Poppy opened her eyes to slits again and kept them open. Barely. The lone light burning in a low-wattage night light wasn't familiar.

Heart pounding in her chest at the speed of a thoroughbred racehorse, Poppy studied her surroundings. When she clenched her jaw, she finally noticed the pain on one side of her face. Great. Appeared someone had nailed her in the jaw as well as drugged her with something. Not only that, she wasn't in her home.

No panicking, Poppy told herself firmly. Go into problem-solving mode now. Panic later when the consequences won't matter and the enemy wasn't at the door, watching the performance.

Were they watching? She scanned what she could make out of the room, which was precious little.

Where was she? This didn't smell like any hospital she'd ever been in, nor did the scent remind her of home, so she definitely wasn't in Washington, D.C. with her parents.

Another glance around confirmed this place didn't look or feel like Sage's and Brody's house or Logan's place. This room felt chilly, sterile, and almost unused. She thought about that for a moment.

Nope, definitely not at home. So where was she? Although her mind was fuzzy, she remembered Thing One and Thing Two confronting her in the kitchen. What happened after that was anyone's guess. Based on the sore jaw, one creep had punched her in the face.

Poppy tugged again on her hands. The restraints flexed easily. Outstanding. Her mouth curved a little. Thanks to what she'd thought was Logan's unnecessary training, she knew how to escape from flexible ties. When she was positive she wasn't being observed, Poppy would break the ties and get out of this room.

She again turned her attention to the room itself. Although the amount of light emanating from the small lamp limited her sight, the room temperature was cold enough for Poppy to be uncomfortable. Deliberate or a result of disuse? Maybe the latter because the room also smelled of mustiness.

Slowly, Poppy sat up. Disoriented at first, the room spun as though she rode a carousel. Her stomach lurched. Oh, man. Not good.

She shut her eyes for a few seconds, hoping her stomach would fall back into place. If Poppy had to vomit, she hoped to find a bathroom nearby. If not, she'd be in a real bind. Not only that, she had to break the zip ties, too. Otherwise, her hair would be a problem as well.

As her stomach finally settled, Poppy heard footsteps outside the room. Didn't need to ask if it was friend or foe. Was this an interrogation or something more heinous?

She shuddered as memories of her prior kidnapping experience flooded her mind. No. She'd deal with that garbage later. She had to stay focused on the here and now if she was to survive and escape.

Floorboards creaked. Someone shoved a key in the old lock and twisted the knob. A metallic screech filled the air, assaulting Poppy's ear.

Bright light from the hallway blinded Poppy for a moment. When her eyes adjusted, she recognized Thing Two, the jerk who punched her in the face. Oh, yeah, she remembered now who had taken great pleasure in knocking her out. "Well, well," she drawled. "Look what the wind blew in. Punch any other women lately?"

Thing Two grinned. "Only mouthy ones who deserve it."

"Aww. I feel special." And sick, although she didn't intend to let on about that minor problem. The members of Texas Team stressed the need to hide your weaknesses from the enemy. No need to hand Things One and Two an advantage to press while they interrogated her. Poppy refused to think about anything they might do to her. One minute, one hour at a time, she'd survive. She wanted to see her family again. She wanted to see Logan. That meant surviving.

The thug rolled his eyes. Yeah, she impressed him with her sense of humor. "Whatever. Let's go." He motioned to the door.

"Where?" Poppy rose to her feet, shocked at how weak she felt. She needed to cooperate for now and give her body a chance to recover before escaping and getting back home.

When the two men broke into her home and kidnapped her, Poppy didn't have her phone on her, much less her identification or any way to pay for a plane or bus ticket out of here. She didn't even know where they'd taken her. For an ace crime reporter and true crime writer, Poppy was in a bind of the highest order.

As much as Poppy hated to contact law enforcement because of the leaks sure to follow, she didn't have many options. She had to arrange for a Fortress pick up.

First step was to gather her strength. Second step was to ditch these two guys and find the nearest police station to call Fortress for a ride out of wherever she'd been taken. She wasn't in Hartman anymore. Her town wasn't this cold. So, where had Things One and Two taken her?

Poppy stiffened her knees and stumbled toward the door. "Hey, do a girl a favor, would you?"

"What's that?"

"Remove the zip ties. They're hurting my wrists."

A snort. "Sorry, lady. No can do. The boss wouldn't like it."

Ah ha. Now they were getting somewhere. "The boss? Who's the boss?"

"None of your business. Turn right in the hall and walk straight ahead. We'll talk in the kitchen."

"Look, this won't work long term. You know that, right?"

"Huh?"

"Depending on how long you intend to keep me here in Wonderland, I'll eventually have to use the facilities."

He stared, his expression puzzled.

Poppy sighed. "The bathroom."

Thing Two blinked. "Oh, yeah."

"The task requires two free hands, buddy. You'll have to cut me loose."

A shadow appeared at the end of the long hall. "Do it," a deep voice said.

Well, well. Thing One was still around. "Nice of you to join the party."

"Good to see you're no worse for the journey. The boss will be pleased."

"Does the boss have a name?"

"Of course. You don't need to know what it is. Being nosy isn't in your best interest, Ms. Reynolds." Although his voice came out silky, the implied threat was apparent enough that even in her muddled state, Poppy didn't miss the danger she faced.

"Right. First things first." Much as she hated to turn her back on these men, Poppy needed her hands free. She turned and wiggled her fingers. "Cut me loose. It's not like I'm going to overpower the two of you." She might have a chance against one of them once she felt better.

A slow smile from Thing One. "You wouldn't have a chance against either of us. We're good at our jobs."

She knew at least five men who were better. "Yeah, yeah. Come on. Cut me loose. Where am I going to go? I don't even know where I am, and I'm well known for not being able to find my way out of a paper bag, much less find my way home without GPS. You have nothing to worry about."

GPS. Poppy stilled. While she didn't have a phone, Fortress Security had placed a GPS tracker inside her watch. The watch also gave her the ability to communicate directly with someone monitoring the activated tracker at Fortress.

Poppy heard movement behind her, felt the cold slide of steel between her wrists, and a sharp tug, and then her wrists were free. Thank goodness.

Pain shot through her shoulders, followed quickly by fierce heat as the joints moved freely for the first time in a long while. She breathed through the pain of blood flowing through swollen joints. When she could talk, she said, "Where's the nearest bathroom?"

Thing One pointed to the partially closed door down the hall and to the left.

"Thanks," she murmured. No need to antagonize the jerks more than necessary. Shaking her hands to encourage more blood flow, Poppy walked to the bathroom and locked herself in.

She glanced around the small rustic room. Not seeing cameras mounted anywhere, she pressed the emergency button on her watch. A second later, a text appeared on the screen. "*Safe to talk?*"

Poppy tapped in a simple, "*No.*"

"*Copy*," was the response. "*Help coming*." All the messages disappeared. Once again, the screen showed the time.

After making use of the rudimentary facilities which actually worked, Poppy searched the small space, starting with easing aside the dirty, ragged curtains to find a locked window with bars outside the glass.

Dismayed, she stared at the gleaming iron bars. Oh, man. If all the windows in this place had bars, Poppy would have to find another way to escape. She trusted Fortress to send help. She trusted herself to get out of immediate danger and let Fortress do the cleanup.

The door knob rattled. One thug pounded on the door. "Hey, hurry up in there."

Thing Two. Of course. Of the two men, he was the most impatient.

"Almost finished," she called out and turned on the faucet. While she waited for the water to warm up, Poppy quietly searched for anything she could use as a weapon and found nothing but a few dead cockroaches.

Shuddering, she used the pitiful excuse for a bar of soap to wash her hands and dried them on a paper towel.

She opened the door to find Thing Two standing near the doorway with his booted foot raised and scowls on the faces of both men.

Her eyebrow rose. "Planning to kick me in the gut?"

"Don't tempt me, lady," he spat out. Two grabbed Poppy's arm and tugged her into the hall.

A moment later, they emerged in what passed for a kitchen. Barely. The appliances had to be at least 20 years old, perhaps more. If she was stuck here for a while, she hoped the coffee pot worked at least. Otherwise, the situation was likely to turn ugly.

Two shoved Poppy into the nearest chair. He sat a bottle of beer in front of her with a loud thunk. "Want a drink?"

"Don't think my stomach will tolerate alcohol. How about a bottle of water?"

The broad-shouldered man grunted and turned away while One watched Poppy with his arms crossed, an inscrutable expression on his face.

So, would she score water or not? Poppy needed water and, from the looks of this place, trusted nothing coming out of the pipes.

Two returned with two bottles of water. He set both in front of her and broke the seal on one, then pushed the bottle toward her with his ham-size fist. "Here."

Gambling that he hadn't drugged her drink, Poppy guzzled a third of the bottle before moving both bottles closer. "Thanks."

After a brief nod, Two took a position in front of the only door in sight and settled back to watch the show.

Poppy shifted her attention to One. He must be the ringleader of the two men. Instead of holding her here, why weren't they taking her to the boss as fast as possible?

Time to find out what these guys wanted with her. In the back of her mind, she heard Logan's low-voiced growl warning her to wait Things One and Two out, to not give them an advantage. She didn't mind admitting she was afraid. The situation she found herself in reminded her a little too much of her other kidnapping. At least this one didn't involve a sadist who was into his work as a human trafficker.

"All right, boys. You went to a lot of trouble and expense to have a conversation with me, but, hey, it's your boss's dime, right? So, what do you want to talk about? World peace? I'm all for it. Politics? I leave that to people familiar with power players on the world stage. Me? I'm not interested in anything to do with politics on any level. If you want to talk books, I'll be happy to tell you about the fifteen books I read in the past month plus over three hundred books on my to-be-read list. That's not counting my wish list, which now tops one thousand titles."

"What do you know about animals?"

Poppy blinked. Okay. That topic wasn't one she'd expected to cover tonight. "Animals?" This had to be the strangest conversation she'd ever had. "If you mean dogs, my family always had at least one when I was growing up. What do you want to know about them?" And why did he care? One could have gone to the Internet or the pet store for information. What was really behind all the cloak-and-dagger stuff?

One placed both hands on the scarred wooden table and leaned closer. He appeared even larger and harder up close.

Despite Poppy raising an eyebrow in a show of defiance, the man scared her. A lot. "What? You don't want to talk about dogs? We can try talking about cats. I've never had one as a pet. Mom's allergic to them."

"We don't want to talk about dogs or cats. We're interested in discussing a lynx."

Her eyebrows knitted. A lynx? "I can't help you."

"Can't or won't?"

"I know nothing about wild cats, buddy. Check the Internet or, better yet, the library, for information on lynxes. So, if that's all you wanted with me, point me to the nearest phone so I can call a friend to come pick me up."

"You're a real riot, Ms. Reynolds. But that's not how this is going to work."

Yeah, Poppy didn't think her problem would be resolved that easily. "You're wasting your time."

He smiled.

Goosebumps swept over Poppy's body. That smile meant bad things for her soon.

"While I'm not happy with your smart-aleck answers, you should be more concerned about the boss's response to your lack of information."

Two sneered. "If you want to live, you won't hold back."

Hold back? Under cover of the table, Poppy gripped the edges of her chair. How could she hold back when she didn't know to what he was referring?

One glanced at his companion. "Take Ms. Reynolds to the room we prepared, and lock her in."

Two straightened from the door. "Want me to tie her up again?"

"That won't be necessary. She's not going anywhere. Just make sure the door is secure."

After a nod, Two gripped Poppy's arm. She barely had time to grab the bottles of water and take them with her.

Instead of returning to the room she'd been in before, Two propelled her up two flights of rickety stairs and then along a narrow hall to the last room on the right. He shoved her across the threshold. "Better rest while you can." The thug slammed the door, locked it, and strode down the hall, laughing and leaving her in the dark.

Having spotted the light switch just before Two locked her in, Poppy rushed to the wall and flipped up the switch.

Nothing happened.

Her throat tightened.

No, no, no. Panicking wasn't allowed yet. Poppy still wasn't in a safe place where she could let down. *Get a grip, Reynolds. No wimping out.*

She closed her eyes and concentrated on box breathing for a minute. After all, what else did she have to do?

Her watch vibrated once.

Poppy's eyelids flew up, and she stared at the dark screen. Had she imagined it? Seconds later, her watch vibrated again.

Glad for a distraction from the panic slowly building inside, Poppy focused on the curious puzzle. Why didn't the screen light up? A tech from Fortress must want to talk. Why didn't he or she just say something? "I'm alone," she murmured.

"You okay?"

Relief swept through her. Zane Murphy, Logan's friend. Thank God. "A few bumps and bruises."

"Can you escape on your own?"

"Don't know." She sucked in a wheezy breath. "No light." Ugh. Not now.

"Problems with darkness?"

"Yeah, thanks to my stay in Mexico."

"Understood. Close your eyes. What did you see when you entered the room?"

"Not much. I only saw the room for a split second."

"Every detail will help," he prompted.

Focus, she reminded herself. "A single bed, nightstand, two windows, and two doors besides the one to the hall."

"Windows locked?"

"Unknown. The window to the bathroom downstairs had bars on the outside."

"Check now."

Poppy felt along the wall toward the first window and eased aside the curtains. She sneezed. "I don't think anyone lives here," she muttered. "If so, they're worse at housekeeping than I am."

She followed the window frame with her fingers until she reached the lock and checked to see if the mechanism was engaged. "It's locked."

"Unlock it if you can."

Poppy wrestled with the lock for a moment until it finally gave way and shifted with a soft metallic creak. "Got it."

"Bars?"

Her eyes widened. "I don't see any."

"Huh. Wonder why not?"

"This room is on the third floor, and the only door out is locked from the outside. They probably figure they have nothing to worry about."

"How many men are involved?"

"I've only seen two."

"Any guards outside?"

She froze. Poppy hadn't considered guards outside this place. If she had escaped on her own, she might have fled right into the arms of a guard roaming the perimeter.

She shuddered. Now, Poppy would be on the lookout for men on patrol. "I don't know. When I regained consciousness, I was inside this place."

A slight pause. "You sure you're all right, Poppy?"

"I don't know." She knew what Zane wanted to know. Poppy couldn't think about what might have happened while she was unconscious. Not if she wanted to maintain control.

"All right. Watch outside for movement while I check to see if the satellite is in the right position."

Her eyebrows soared. Satellite? Sweet. The black ops and security business must pay very well.

"We're in luck," Zane said a moment later. "No outside roaming guards. This is either a low-rent operation or they've seriously underestimated you."

Poppy preferred to believe the latter. She studied the window frame, then ran her fingers lightly along the wood. Didn't seem too swollen. If she was lucky, the window wouldn't squeal like a greased pig when she raised it. "Any advice, Zane?"

"The closest team is still over an hour out. Based on what I see, we have a little time to work with, but not long. The sooner you escape, the better."

A particular note in Zane's voice warned her something was up. "What's wrong?"

"More men will arrive at your location in a few minutes."

Poppy's best chance for escape was now. Otherwise, she'd have to outsmart and outrun more men.

She blew out a breath. "No time like the present," she murmured. "This is an old building, Zane, and the window will probably squeal like a pig when I raise it."

"Have a plan before you raise the window. You have two choices, Reynolds. Go up or down. Look out the window and decide."

Sounded easy when he said it. Then again, Zane Murphy was a Navy SEAL. Escaping from a third-floor window would have been a piece of cake during active military duty. Even riding a wheelchair these days, the job might have been a little more challenging, but she knew he'd have gotten the job done. "I hear you."

Poppy stepped close to the window again and peered out. No convenient tree close by to leap onto and shimmy to the ground. No balcony railing to hang from and shorten her jump by one story. Since a broken leg or ankle would short-circuit her escape, she either needed to create a ladder or come up with another avenue of escape. "I don't suppose you have a convenient helicopter handy, do you?"

"Sorry, sugar. They're all in use. What's your decision?"

"Down isn't an option."

"Hope you're not afraid of heights, Reynolds. Get moving."

Fear bloomed in her gut at the warning. Her only option was to climb up to the roof and find a way down to the ground from there. "Good thing I enjoyed gymnastics as a kid," she muttered. The only problem was she hadn't practiced in years.

Poppy hoped the drug was out of her system. Otherwise, her balance and strength would be compromised.

She gripped the edge of the window and gathered her strength as her stomach knotted. This could be terrible if she couldn't raise the window fast enough. Things One and Two would come running as soon as they heard any odd noises from this room. "Watch my back, Z."

"You got it, sugar. Move fast, but be careful."

"Yep." Poppy breathed a quick silent prayer and shoved at the window with all her might.

Chapter Six

Like Poppy had expected, the window to her small prison gave way with a loud pop and tortured groans that were sure to carry throughout the structure.

Without listening to find out if the two jerks downstairs overheard her opening the window, she straddled the ledge and peered to the left and right. No secure downspouts to slide down. That left the roof.

Poppy looked up. Doable. Too bad the building wasn't a two-story structure, but you dealt with what you had.

A decorative trim ran along the roofline. The only way for her to grip the trim was to stand on the ledge. She swallowed hard, hoping termites hadn't been busy along the roofline.

Holding onto the window frame, she balanced on the ledge and reached up to grip the trim along the roof. When a hard tug proved that the trim remained solid, Poppy maneuvered onto the roof and moved back from the edge.

Just in time, too. As soon as she'd made her way at an angle toward the other side of the house where a tree limb hung close to the roof, Poppy heard shouts and curses from the kidnappers. Not daring to delay, she leaped for the tree limb, caught hold of the thick branch with her hands, and pulled herself into the tree.

Praying she wasn't making a huge mistake, Poppy balanced on the branch and reached up for a higher limb. Thankful the tree was a large, mature pine, she continued to climb higher under she heard the gruesome twosome on the ground, arguing over who was at fault for her escape and would therefore tell the boss about the loss of their hostage.

Poppy froze. Most people didn't look up. If the men broke with tradition, was Poppy high enough in the tree to prevent them from seeing her hiding in the branches?

"If you want to confess your failure, be my guest," Thing One snapped. "I'm not taking responsibility for your goof up. I've done that one too many times since they hired you. Not doing it again. This is your fault."

"I locked her in," Two insisted. "Just like your said."

"Then how did she get out of that room? This ain't no Agatha Christie locked-room murder mystery with a secret passageway."

"How should I know?"

Silence. "No way she could have climbed down from the window. I made sure of that myself before we put her in there."

More cursing. "That leaves the roof," Two said. "This pine looks pretty close to the roof. Bet she climbed down the tree and ran off."

"We have to find her. The boss will arrive in minutes."

"It's dark out here. Where do we start?"

"We split up. You go that way. I'll go this way. She's probably still weak from the drug and might have a concussion, too. She won't get far. Besides, where will she go? We're in the middle of nowhere. Even if she goes farther than I think she might, there aren't any people out here for miles. She'll have to come back here to find shelter."

"What if we can't find her, and she doesn't come back?"

"She'll freeze to death, and we'll grab the other sister. Come on. Let's go. Meet you back here in fifteen minutes. Keep your phone handy. Text me if you find her. I'll do the same."

Poppy remained in place, afraid to move for a full minute. Finally, she whispered, "Zane?"

"You're clear for the moment. Can you see at all?"

"Not much." Clouds scuttled across the sky, and the wind had grown stronger in the last few minutes, hinting at a storm. She shivered. "I think a storm is brewing." Poppy heard the clicking of keys on a keyboard.

A growl of frustration from the tech guy. "You're right. Get out of the tree, Poppy. Hurry. The satellite will be out of position soon, and I won't have eyes in the sky until the next one moves into place, provided the storm moves on. I'll use the satellite to help you as much as I can, then we'll have to wing it."

She needed every advantage possible. Losing the satellite was bad news. Poppy shimmied down the tree. "I'm on the ground. Which way?"

"Straight ahead. You'll travel parallel to the road. The two men will expect you to go to the road and try to follow it to the nearest town or hitch a ride with a passing motorist."

Poppy started off at a jog, but soon had to drop to a fast walk. "Terrain's rough," she murmured when she stumbled over another rock hidden in deep shadow.

"Tough. Be as quiet as you can, but pick up the pace."

Oh, boy. That didn't sound good. She obeyed his order. Poppy shivered again, clenching her jaw to prevent her teeth from chattering and giving away her position if One or Two was close. The ache from her bruised face intensified.

"One man is closing in on you from the right," Zane murmured. "Six hundred yards."

She stopped and glanced around for shelter. Trees and more trees. None of them were close together or particularly fat, so they were out.

Rocks and more rocks. They were tall enough to make her stumble and twist an ankle. None were useful for her purposes. That left one place.

The ravine. Man, Poppy did not want to go into a dark ravine at night. What if she lost her grip on the way down, fell, and couldn't climb back out on her own? The prospect of hanging out with snakes and spiders the size of dinner plates was not appealing, not to mention the prospect of a broken bone.

So, she had a sissy streak with creatures that slithered and spun webs. Who wouldn't be a sissy, especially at night when you couldn't see to defend yourself against attack from critters? Also, she'd never broken a bone and didn't want to shatter her clean record now at this inopportune moment.

Poppy sighed at her inevitable choice. With no other option in sight and Thing One or Two fast approaching, the ravine looked more and more appealing.

She hurried to the edge of the ravine and peered over. Pitch black. She shuddered, sucked in a deep breath, and eased over the side.

Feeling for a foothold, Poppy found a ledge a few inches wide with the toes of her sneakers. She gathered her courage and let go of the ravine's edge.

She breathed a sigh of relief when the ledge held. Thank goodness. Much as she wanted to cling to the side of the ravine and wait for Logan and his buddies to arrive toting their weapons, Poppy was out in the open. All the kidnapper had to do was look over the edge and he'd see her.

Cursing and twigs snapping heralded the approach of an angry man. Time to get moving, regardless of whether she was ready.

"Bogey is 200 yards and closing fast," Zane murmured. "Are you safe?"

"Not even close. I'm in a ravine. No other options available. Where is the Fortress team?"

"Still 20 minutes out." The tech guru sounded grim. "Do what you have to do to protect yourself, Poppy."

"Yes, sir."

More cursing sounded nearby.

Poppy flinched. Thing Two. Not the guy she'd hoped to confront if she faced fighting for her life. Two liked to hurt people. She could see it in his eyes when he had punched her. *Don't think about it,* she told herself. *Act now. React later.*

Having Logan's voice in her head could be annoying. Not tonight, though. Tonight, she appreciated the comfort of his snapped orders telling her what to do, even if the orders were only remembered from earlier drills. His growling voice in her head spurred her to action.

Poppy felt her way across the ledge to a darker part of the ravine, praying she didn't run out of real estate before she reached the relative safety of the dark patch ahead.

Pebbles and dirt cascaded down the steep slope some distance behind her. Afraid to turn and look back over her shoulder for fear of attracting Two's attention, Poppy continued to press forward at slightly faster than a snail's pace. It was hard to speed up when the darkness was so dense and one misstep would send her careening into the bottom of the ravine.

She inched closer to her goal, an area in deep shadow with large rocks and young pines nestled against a shallow alcove near the middle of the ravine wall. Her problem? To reach safety, Poppy had to descend one hundred feet deeper into the ravine, much of the journey in the open. Thing Two needed to search another area. Otherwise, Poppy would be exposed the next time a gap in the clouds allowed the moon to shine on her doing her Spider Woman impression.

The ledge dropped off to nothing. Poppy stopped, dismayed. Now what? Stay or start the climb down with Two peering into the ravine?

Once again, she remembered Logan reminding her repeatedly that movement drew the eye. Guess that answered her question. She stilled against the side of the ravine and waited to see if someone discovered her clinging to the dirt, scrub, and rocks.

Although she didn't dare look, Poppy heard Two cursing and grousing nearby. More small stones and dirt fell to the bottom of the ravine. Seconds later, a beam of light pierced the darkness.

She swallowed hard. Not good. Pressing herself closer to the earth wall, Poppy prayed hard that she would remain unseen.

From the corner of her eye, she watched the beam of light move closer and closer to her location as Two searched the ravine and its steep walls. Seconds before the kidnapper would have spotted her, a faint sound broke the stillness.

Another growl. "Did you find her?" Silence. "How can she just disappear into thin air? Did she slip by you?" A muttered curse. "Yeah, yeah. I'll be there in a few minutes. But I'm not taking responsibility. This screw up is on you. Your plan. Your missing hostage. I just followed your orders to the letter." He sounded smug.

A gust of wind swirled through the ravine, buffeting Poppy while she gripped a scrub bush and a scraggly pine tree for support. She shivered, scowling as she listened to one side of the conversation. Taunting your coworker who sported weapons and worked for a criminal wasn't wise. Talk about slapping a target on your back.

A snort of laughter from Two. "Whatever." The thug muttered a string of curses that was followed by silence.

More frequent shivers tempted Poppy to continue her journey toward safety. Instinct convinced her to stay still. When Thing Two walked close to her precarious hiding place in the ravine, he'd sounded like a herd of elephants stomping around. How could he suddenly develop the skill of moving silently, like Logan and Brody?

He couldn't. Either Two had been deliberately pushing her to run from her hiding place earlier, or he was waiting to see if the end of his conversation and sudden silence coaxed her from safety.

Her body trembled from fear and cold. If Two was playing a game of cat and mouse with her, Poppy didn't intend to lose.

Five minutes passed, and still Poppy waited. After another five minutes of listening for movement above her, she finally heard Two spin and walk off with heavy footsteps.

Shaking continuously now, she remained in place for another few minutes. Centimeter by centimeter, she shifted her right hand closer to her mouth. Praying her voice wouldn't carry above the wind, Poppy whispered, "Zane?"

"Wait."

Wait until another satellite moved into position, or until Thing Two really walked back to the house? Either way, she didn't dare continue toward her goal until Zane told her she was safe.

Pebbles, small rocks, and dirt rolled down the side of the ravine and onto her head. Poppy kept her head down and pressed hard against the side. She didn't dare raise her arms to cover her head for fear of attracting Two's attention to the movement.

The thug's phone chirped, signaling an incoming call. "Yeah? I'm coming. It's pitch black out here and the wind is blowing in a storm, so get off my back. I'll see you in five minutes." Two's ugly cursing preceded more rocks and dirt falling on Poppy's head.

A larger rock struck her shoulder and bounced off Poppy. Nice. She'd have a football-size bruise to treat after the Fortress team plucked her from this ravine. One thing Fortress medics carried in plentiful supply was chemically activated cold packs and mild pain medicine, including her preferred over-the-counter brand.

Only a few more minutes, and she'd have a warm blanket wrapped around her and a large cup of hot coffee in her hands. Poppy remained still, waiting. More waiting.

Finally, Zane said, "Go."

Thank God. She didn't know how much longer she could hang out on the side of this ravine without shivering so much she'd slide right off this tiny ledge beginning to crumble under her feet.

With slow movements, Poppy crouched, gripped an older pine tree, eased her right foot off the tiny strip of dirt, and felt for a toehold somewhere below.

She found a rock that seemed solid enough to hold her and shifted her weight to her foot. Poppy breathed a relieved sigh when the rock didn't budge. Inch by inch, she made her way down the steep incline until she came even with her goal. Excellent. Only fifteen feet to go before she'd be hidden from hostile eyes and partially protected from the whipping cold wind.

"Fortress team is ten minutes out," Zane murmured.

She shuddered hard as her body's temperature continued to drop in the damp night air. "Tell them to hurry. I'm freezing." Poppy wished she could have a redo and take advantage of the opportunity to dress in warmer clothes before she'd encountered the two men in her kitchen.

A soft chuckle. "Yes, ma'am."

She wanted to ask which team to expect, but it didn't matter. As long as the good guys were close, Poppy didn't care who the team members were. "T-t-tell the medic I need an infusion of c-c-coffee."

"Get moving, Poppy."

"Maybe I should just hang out here." She shuddered again, almost losing her grip on the rock she was inching around. "I'm tired." If she could just stop and rest for a few minutes, she'd be fine.

"Reynolds," Zane snapped. "Listen to me. The team ran into resistance."

She frowned, confused. Resistance? "Huh?" Oh, listen to that. Her vocabulary was dropping faster than the temperature. She would laugh at her own joke, but who had the energy to waste?

Several loud popping noises sounded near her location. Poppy's breath caught in her throat. "Oh, man. That's not good." Her words came out a little slurred. That wasn't good, either. Was it? "Gunshots?"

"The Fortress team ran into a group of heavily armed men. The men have scattered, and the Fortress team is running them to ground."

"Why?"

A pause. "Poppy, go to a safe place. Movement will raise your body temperature."

"You sure?" What she wouldn't give to curl up somewhere and sleep.

"Yeah, sugar, I'm positive. Go to your safe space right now."

Poppy sighed and concentrated hard on convincing her body to move. Gunshots continued to pepper the night while she made slow progress toward safety. Who knew fifteen feet could take what felt like a lifetime to span?

"Second satellite has moved out of position," Logan's friend warned.

She froze. "You can't watch my back?"

"I'm sorry."

"Advice?"

"Get to safety and make yourself as small a target as possible. The next satellite won't be in position for another 20 minutes."

She gave a soft huff of laughter. "I'd rather not be out here that long."

More gunshots peppered the night. The shots sounded closer this time.

Poppy glanced around. "Are you hearing that?"

"Yeah." Zane's voice sounded grim. "Sounds like the fighting is moving in your direction."

Another pistol shot spurred Poppy into motion. Since she literally had nothing but rocks and dirt to defend herself if caught, she kept her focus on reaching safety. One problem at a time. First, safety. Second, gather ammunition to slow down an attacker if the bad guys located her before the Fortress team did.

The rain-filled clouds formed a heavy gray blanket across the sky and obscured the sporadic moonlight she'd been using to inch her way across the expanse of ravine wall to her destination. "Perfect timing," she muttered.

"You okay?"

"Sure." If you didn't count her light disappearing behind storm clouds rolling in. "Clouds are blocking the moonlight. I'm finding hand and footholds by feel."

After a few keystrokes, Zane said, "Watch yourself. Rain will fall soon."

She groaned. "Wonderful. Can this night get any worse?"

"You'd be surprised."

More pebbles and dirt rolled down the steep incline and onto Poppy's head. She went stock still. Which side had found her? Fortress or the other side?

A deep laugh sent a curl of dread through Poppy. Slowly, she raised her gaze to scan the top of the ravine.

Thing Two stood near the edge with a pistol pointed at her. He grinned. "I knew you were hiding around here somewhere. Figured if I waited, you'd come out of hiding."

Wind whipped his hair, and his smiled faded. "Get up here."

"I don't think so. I'm too afraid to climb in the dark. Why do you think I'm holding on for dear life to this pitiful pine tree? I don't want to fall."

Two cursed. "Climb or you'll be eating the next bullet."

"Do what he says," Zane murmured. "Don't antagonize him further."

Easy for him to say. Zane didn't see the expression on Two's face. The thug enjoyed hurting people, and Poppy didn't want to be on the receiving end of his fist strikes again.

Two adjusted his aim.

"All right," Poppy snapped. "I'm coming up."

"Move!" He fired off a shot. The bullet struck near Poppy's hand.

She yelped and jerked her hand toward her body on instinct. Poppy lost her grip with her other hand.

She clawed at the rock and scraggly pine tree, but could not grip either.

A scream ripped from her throat as she plunged into the darkness.

Chapter Seven

Logan's hand gripped his weapon tighter, and he put on a burst of speed. He tapped the comm device in his ear. "Zane?"

"One kidnapper found Poppy in a ravine and insisted she climb out. He fired one shot."

His gut clenched into a knot. "He shot her?"

"Unknown. She's not responding."

"Satellite?"

"Not for several minutes. Her location is the same, Logan. She hasn't moved."

Couldn't move because someone injured her or the kidnapper wouldn't bother because she was dead?

He ran faster. Not dead. He couldn't live with that kind of failure searing his conscience.

Despite his pace, Logan still ran through the woods without making a sound. Nothing and no one would stop him from getting to Poppy. Anyone who tried wouldn't survive the encounter. Seconds counted with battlefield injuries. He didn't intend to waste any of the time he had to aid Poppy.

He slowed as he approached the edge of the woods and paused behind a tree with his weapon up and aimed while he quartered the area.

To his left, a large man stood with a weapon in his hand, peering down into the darkness. Vicious curses filled the air despite the whipping wind. Without warning, the man fired multiple rounds into the ravine.

Logan raced for the man. "Drop your weapon and put your hands up. Now," he shouted. Had to draw the man's attention away from Poppy.

The man spun, eyes narrowed. "Get out of here. This ain't your business." He aimed his weapon.

Logan fired one shot.

The other man remained motionless for a moment, his expression blank. Then he glanced down at his shoulder and sank to his knees, weapon falling from his hand. After clutching his shoulder, he toppled face down on the ground. He didn't move.

Huh. Guess the guy didn't have a high pain tolerance. Logan would deal with the kidnapper after finding Poppy. She was his top priority. The thug could wait.

Logan's stride lengthened as he raced closer and closer to the ravine edge. He skidded to a stop a bare inch from the precipice and crouched. Logan scanned the ravine, looking for movement. He saw nothing except an ocean of black ink. Where was she? "Poppy!"

No response. No movement.

Logan shoved his weapon into his holster and made his way down the side of the steep incline, skidding and sliding on the loose pebbles and dirt. He tapped his comm device. "Z, do you know where Poppy's safe place was? I can't see anything out here, and I don't want to shine a light and give away our position in case one bogey is still in the area."

"Behind a formation of rocks, she spotted a shallow alcove. Poppy saw nothing better for shelter."

Logan looked toward his left and finally pinpointed the alcove. If Poppy fell, she must have rolled deeper into the ravine near there.

He corrected his course and angled toward the alcove. Didn't take long to see where Poppy had first fallen and the reason she fell. A bullet had gouged a crease along a rock that made an excellent hand hold.

Following the signs of her passage down into the ravine, Logan maintained a parallel path in case he missed her and had to retrace his steps.

Rocks and dirt rolled down the side of the ravine ahead of him. "Poppy!" The only thing he heard was the wind.

He pressed on, fear gnawing at his belly like a starved rat. Skidding on a patch of pebbles, Logan slowed his uncontrolled descent by grabbing scrub brush and large rocks. Still, the terrain was tough to traverse, and he was prepared for almost anything with his tactical boots. Poppy didn't own boots like his, an error he'd correct as soon as possible.

What was she wearing? Concern for her pushed Logan to move faster than was prudent. He didn't care. He was desperate to reach her and didn't mind admitting the truth to himself. Zane told the team Poppy had complained about being cold. The kidnappers had banked on using the cold Montana night to keep her contained. Mistake on their part. Stubborn determination was Poppy Reynolds's middle name.

Near the bottom of the ravine, Logan skidded to a stop and quartered the area. Poppy must be close.

Something white caught his attention. He headed toward the object, heart speeding up when he recognized the running shoe. Seconds later, he dropped to his knees beside the motionless form of the only woman who mattered to him.

He touched his fingertips to her pulse, praying he'd find one. Good thing he was already on his knees because finding that pulse left him weak. Thank God.

Logan activated his comm device again. "I found her at the bottom of a ravine." He rattled off the coordinates. "She's unconscious. I don't see a bullet wound."

Jesse's voice came through the earpiece. "Don't move her. I'm on my way."

"Copy that." He paused, then added, "Hurry, Jesse."

"Three minutes," the medic promised.

"Be careful. I shot one man hunting Poppy in the shoulder and left him near the ravine's edge."

"Copy."

Logan gently ran his hands over Poppy's arms and legs, feeling for a broken bone. When he didn't feel a break, he shrugged out of his jacket and laid the garment over Poppy before wrapping his hand around hers. "Poppy, can you hear me?"

Nothing.

He rubbed her icy hand between his large palms. "Come on, baby. Wake up. You're scaring me," Logan murmured.

"Baby?" Brody's shock at the endearment came through the comm device loud and clear. "Do you have something to tell me?"

"Yeah. No comments from the peanut gallery, and mind your own business."

Despite the gunshots continuing to pepper the night along with rumbles of thunder, Logan's teammates chuckled.

"I'm 30 seconds out," Jesse said. "Any change?"

"Negative." Although Logan wanted to run his hands over Poppy's head to check for injuries, he feared causing further injury to her neck or spine.

When rocks, pebbles, and dirt rolling down the side of the ravine heralded the medic's approach, Logan hovered over Poppy to protect her from falling debris.

Jesse slid to a stop close by and dropped to his knees on the other side of Poppy. He shrugged off his mike bag and set it beside him, then with his hands retraced the path Logan had taken over Poppy's extremities. "Legs and arms are fine."

After removing Logan's jacket, Jesse shifted his examination to Poppy's torso. He paused halfway down her rib cage and frowned. "Possible fractured rib on the right side. I'll know more when I get her into better lighting."

Throughout Jesse's exam, Logan kept Poppy's hand in his. When Jesse moved on to Poppy's left side, Logan felt her fingers tighten fractionally around his. "Jesse, wait." He leaned closer to Poppy's ear. "Poppy, it's Logan. Can you hear me?"

She moaned.

"Open your eyes, and look at me," he coaxed. He needed to see her eyes, needed to know she was with him once again. "Come on, baby. You can do it."

Her fingers flexed in his, then wrapped tighter around his hand. Poppy's eyelids fluttered and slowly lifted. "I'm not dreaming, am I?" she murmured.

Relief swept through Logan. "Only if you dreamed about seeing me in the rain in Montana. How do you feel?"

"Cold and hungry." She shivered. "Need coffee."

"We'll take care of that soon." Jesse's hands hovered over Poppy's left side. "May I check your left ribs? We can't move you until we're sure we won't cause more damage than you've already suffered."

"Everything hurts."

"I bet." The medic remained motionless. "Poppy, may I continue to check for injuries?"

She gave a slight nod.

A moment later, Jesse said, "No broken ribs, although I won't be able to rule out fractures until I see X-rays." He shifted his examination to her head, asking a series of questions. Finally, the medic sat back. "No sign of skull fractures, although you have a decent goose egg on the right side. Do you have a headache?"

"Oh, definitely along with a whole-body ache. I have a feeling I'll be black and blue all over in a few hours. Can we get on with this? There's a rock digging into my hip to go along with the cold seeping into me from the ground."

"Answer a few more questions first." He asked her to move her arms and legs one at a time. When she was successful, he said, "I want to check your back and spine, Poppy. Logan, help me move Poppy to her right side." To Poppy, he said, "Don't move anything. Allow me and Logan to do all the work."

Two minutes later, he and Logan slowly raised her to a sitting position. She flinched and pressed a hand to her side. "I think I hit a rock or ten on my way down to the bottom. Ouch."

"I'll check your head more carefully on the jet," Jesse promised.

"Think you can walk?" Logan asked. He slid his arm around her back to give Poppy support.

"Of course," she said tartly.

He rolled his eyes, glad to see the snarky writer narrow her own eyes in response. "Don't be a hero, Reynolds. If you're hurt, let me help."

"We'll see."

Sheer stubbornness. That was Poppy Reynolds in a nutshell.

Jesse rose. "Come on. Let's see if you can stand up. If you can't, we carry you." He held up a hand when Poppy protested. "End of discussion, Poppy. We need to get you warmed up as soon as possible. You aren't dressed for the weather."

A scowl formed on her face. "I can decide."

Brody's growl came over the comm devices. "Tell Poppy to stop whining like a little girl and get up already. She's not the only one who's cold."

Logan's lips curved as he rose. "Brody said to stop whining. He's cold, too."

"I'll bet he said more than that," she muttered. "And he's dressed in warmer clothes than I am. I have a legitimate case."

"Take it up with Brody when you see him." He leaned down. "Wrap your arms around my neck and I'll help you stand."

When Poppy did as he directed, Logan rested his hands at her waist and lifted her from the ground. He held onto her until she was steady, then released her, although he stayed close. Not much would move him away from Poppy's side until she was safe. "You good?"

"I'll make it. Let's get out of here."

"Wait." Logan activated his comm device while Jesse quickly assessed Poppy. "She's on her feet, Brody. Jesse feels it's safe enough to move her. He plans to do a more thorough assessment when we're wheels up."

"Do you and Jesse need help to get her out of the ravine?"

"Unknown." She looked shaky to him. He wasn't born yesterday, though. He knew better than to voice that opinion out loud. If Poppy needed help, he and Jesse would handle it.

"Stay where you are. We'll arrive in two minutes and give you a hand. What about the man you shot?"

The medic glanced up. "He was gone when I arrived," Jesse said.

Logan scowled as irritation washed over him. He'd hoped to have at least one kidnapper to question. Although his priority had been Poppy, he should have checked the thug for a pulse before entering the ravine. Big mistake on his part. The guy could have just as easily shot at them rather than run off to join his comrades.

He looked at Jesse and indicated for him to exit the ravine and check the area for threats. "That's on me," Logan admitted to his team leader. "I shot him in the shoulder but didn't take time to check that he wouldn't be getting back up soon. He might have had a vest on."

"We'll talk later."

He flinched. "Yes, sir." Logan wasn't looking forward to that discussion. Brody would tear strips from his hide for a mistake that might have cost Poppy her life. Great. Not only was his best friend gunning for him, Poppy's parents were out for blood as well. "We'll start making our way out of the ravine."

"Copy that. We're one minute out."

Jesse crested the ravine and disappeared from view.

Logan wrapped his hand around Poppy's and led her toward the easiest route to the top. Although the climb still wouldn't be a piece of cake, at least she'd have help.

He paused at the foot of the ravine incline and turned to Poppy. "Ready to do this?"

"With the prospect of hot coffee and a warm blanket at the end of the journey, you bet."

"I'll go first." Logan shrugged off his pack and pulled out a rope and two harnesses. He put a harness on each of them and connected the two together with the rope. "We'll go slow. If you need to stop, tell me. If you can't make the climb, I'll carry you."

Poppy nudged him. "Go. I'll keep up."

Although not convinced her strength would hold out, Logan began the climb at an angle, carefully choosing easy hand holds and moderating his pace to accommodate Poppy.

She made it ten feet before her foot slipped on loose pebbles. Poppy fell and slid back down into the ravine. The rope and harness stopped her descent before she'd slid more than a few feet.

Logan crouched beside her. "You okay?"

Poppy nodded. "Yeah. Help me up and let's keep going."

"Poppy!" Brody's voice drifted down from the top of the ravine. "What are you doing?" He sounded incredulous.

She frowned. "What does it look like? Getting out of here. I want that coffee."

"You need to wait for us to help you. You're too weak to climb out of there without aid."

"Watch me," she snapped.

Really? Logan stared at his best friend. There was a reason he had resisted saying just those words to Poppy. He knew she'd react exactly like she did.

"Move, Logan." Poppy nudged him again.

"He's right, you know." And most likely Brody would rip into him for letting Poppy try the climb.

"Don't go there, Fletcher. I'm not helpless, and I won't let you treat me like I am."

"All right." He held up both hands. "Try not to cause more harm to yourself. Otherwise, I'll be the one to pay the price."

She glared at him. "Go."

He gave a quick nod, reduced the length of rope between them, and set off again. At the halfway point, Logan reached back and tugged Poppy against him. "Rest a minute and catch your breath."

"I'm fine," she murmured. "I don't need to stop."

Brave words from the woman trembling in his arms. "Tough. I do."

Poppy gave a soft huff. "Liar."

He tightened his hold. "Maybe." After Poppy's trembling ceased, Logan loosened his hold and stepped back far enough to see her face. "Ready?"

"I still want that coffee."

He chuckled. "Yes, ma'am." After wrapping his arm around her waist, he set off again. Ten more minutes, and Poppy would be out of energy and Brody out of patience. If he couldn't help her to the top of the ravine by that time, his team leader would step in and haul her up to level ground.

Logan tucked Poppy closer to his side and stepped up the pace, practically carrying her up the steep slope. Near the end of the climb, her legs gave out, and Logan scooped her into his arms and powered up the final few feet.

"Sorry," she whispered in his ear. "I thought I could make it on my own."

He squeezed her gently in response and turned toward his team's leader. "Let's go."

"Form a circle around Logan and Poppy," Brody said. "Max, take the lead."

"Yes, sir." Max set off toward the vehicles at a fast clip with the rest falling into formation.

Minutes later, the group reached the edge of the woods where the vehicles were hidden.

"Sawyer and I will check the vehicles. The rest of you wait here." Brody and Sawyer pulled out scanners and walked a circle around the SUVs.

Poppy watched the men. "What are they doing?"

"Making sure no one tampered with the vehicles."

Her gaze locked with Logan's. "A bomb?"

"Or trackers."

A minute later, Brody said, "We're clear. Let's get out of here. Logan, you, Poppy, and Jesse are with me. Max and Sawyer will take the second SUV."

Once they were on the road, Brody tapped his comm device. "Zane, tell the boss we have the package and are en route to the jet."

"Injuries?"

"None sustained by the team. We won't know the extent of Poppy's injuries until we're wheels up. We'll be landing in Nashville in six hours."

"Copy that. We'll be ready."

Brody glanced in the rearview mirror and frowned. "Max?"

"I see them."

Logan twisted in his seat and stared out the back window. Two pairs of headlights trailed behind them. "Could be locals."

"Maybe. Want to risk it?"

He snorted. "Not a chance." Logan glanced at Poppy. "How much pain are you in?"

"Enough to make me grumpy."

"Too much to get on the floor? It's the safest place for you."

"I'll try. What are you going to do?"

"Whatever is necessary to keep you safe. Brody?"

"Go. Jesse, get into the back with Poppy."

"Yes, sir."

"Max, if they pursue, keep them off our tail as long as possible."

"Copy that."

Brody pulled out his satellite phone and tapped a button. "It's Brody. We have the package and are coming in hot. Have the jet ready."

"They followed us, didn't they?" Poppy scowled. "I don't understand why they want me. It makes little sense."

"Did they tell you why they kidnapped you?" Brody asked.

"Not really."

Logan maneuvered into the cargo area of the SUV. "What does that mean?"

"They didn't tell me why they wanted me, only that if I didn't cooperate, they'd go after Sage."

"What?" Brody's gaze shifted toward Poppy.

"Watch the road," Logan snapped as he pressed a button to lower the back window. "Poppy, get on the floor. The people trailing us are catching up." He grabbed his rifle, then activated his comm device. "Sawyer?"

"I'll take the one on the left."

That left Logan the vehicle on the right to stop. Suited him fine. He shifted to the right side of the cargo area, lined up his target vehicle, and settled in to wait.

Didn't take long for the pursuit to become obvious and for more gunshots to add to the rolling thunder of the storm bearing down on them. "Go, go, go, Brody. We can't afford to delay the flight."

"Who's in charge of this op?" his friend snapped.

"Does it matter?" Logan retorted.

Despite the attitude, Brody stomped on the accelerator, and the large SUV leaped ahead.

More shots peppered the night, and the left SUV swerved to the right side of the road, straightened, and continued the pursuit.

"Vehicle is retrofitted with armor plating and bullet-resistant glass," Sawyer said.

"At least slow them down," Brody said. "We need enough time to get off the ground."

"Yes, sir."

Logan readjusted his aim. "Hold it steady, Brody."

"What's going on?" Poppy asked. "I hate not being able to see what's happening."

Jesse chuckled. "Spoken like a true journalist."

"Answer my question," she demanded.

"Aggressive pursuers are trying to stop us, and Sawyer and Logan are going to take them out if possible."

"W-w-what happens if they can't?"

Logan glanced over his shoulder, frowning. "Poppy, are you still cold?"

"I feel like I'm in the North P-p-pole." Her teeth chattered between words.

"Here." Jesse snagged a Mylar blanket from his pack and tucked it around her, then dug into his mike bag and brought out a couple of packets.

Excellent. Logan breathed easier. Jesse would increase Poppy's temperature with hand warmers. Coffee on the jet would help. If that wasn't enough, he'd encourage Poppy to take a hot shower in the bedroom at the back of the plane.

He refocused on his target. First things first. He had to take care of their pursuers so his team could get her to the jet safely. Everything else was of secondary importance. "Ready," he murmured.

"Cover your ears," Jesse said to Poppy. "Go, Logan."

Logan zeroed in on the front tire of the vehicle, drew in a breath, let it out halfway, and squeezed the trigger. The sound of his shot reverberated in the cabin of their SUV.

Behind them, the targeted SUV swerved to the right, skidded off the road, and slammed into the side of the mountain.

"One down," Logan said. The second vehicle trailing behind them backed off and followed at a distance. "Brody, we might have trouble ahead."

"Yeah, I think you're right. Max, pull ahead of us."

"Yes, sir."

A moment later, the rest of the Texas team passed them and zoomed ahead to provide protection in case of an ambush.

"Logan, can you take the second vehicle out?" Brody asked as he guided the big vehicle around a curve.

"Nope. Too far back."

"Jesse, take his place and monitor them. Get up here with me, Logan. I have a feeling we're heading into trouble."

Logan climbed into the backseat and waited for Jesse to slide into the cargo area before shifting to the shotgun seat with his rifle in hand. "How far are we from the airfield?"

"Fifteen minutes."

He frowned. "Too long." Too many places between here and the jet for an ambush. Not only that, he wasn't sure how long Poppy would last on the floor. Although she hadn't complained, she must hurt being curled up on the floor of the SUV.

"I know." Brody sounded grim. "Do you know details?" he asked softly.

"No." If he did, Logan wouldn't share the information without Poppy's permission. Just the idea of what Poppy might have gone through made him sick to his stomach and even more furious at himself for not protecting her better, a fact her parents would be sure to throw in his face from now on. He'd never live this down, no matter how well he protected her from this point forward.

Five miles from the airfield, Max's voice came through the comm system. "Two bogeys ahead, coming in fast."

#

Chapter Eight

Logan lowered the window and maneuvered the upper half of his body outside the vehicle. He sat on the edge of the frame and wedged himself in. Two vehicles raced toward the Fortress team while the vehicle trailing them sped up to join the party.

Wonderful. A Pincer move. "Front or back, Brody?"

"Right front. Sawyer, take the left."

"Copy."

Lightning lit up the night sky, and thunder rolled across the heavens. Seconds later, the clouds opened up and dumped buckets of rain on them.

Fabulous. Instead of going for the riskier shot, Logan fired several rounds at the windshield of his target SUV.

The driver jerked the wheel, and the vehicle went into a spin, ending up nose down in a deep ditch. As the Fortress vehicles barreled past the disabled SUV, the driver and passengers opened fire.

Logan hissed at the burning sensation streaking across his shoulder, twisted and returned fire. One passenger dropped to the ground.

"Inside," Brody snapped.

He eased his body back inside in time to see the second SUV ahead of them spin out of control, hit a tree, and burst into flame. The Fortress vehicles sped past the wreck as two men staggered from the ruin of metal.

"How bad?" Jesse asked.

"A scratch. I'm fine."

The medic snorted. "You'd say that if you were bleeding to death."

"Logan's hurt? Get off me, you oaf. I have to see." Poppy's voice sounded panicked.

"Knock it off, Poppy." Brody scowled into the rearview mirror. "It's pitch black in here. You can slap a Band-Aid on his boo boo when we're airborne."

Logan reached over the seat and rested his hand on the top of Poppy's head. "I'm fine. A bullet grazed my shoulder. Jesse will probably just use butterfly tape or glue it."

"If I find out you lied to me...."

"No lie, baby. You'll see for yourself soon." He eyed the vehicle inching up on them from behind. "Jesse, can you make the shot?"

"Nope. They're staying just out of range." Jesse fired a few warning shots, and the vehicle backed off again but remained in their line of sight.

"Max, go," Brody ordered.

The other Fortress vehicle surged ahead, leading the way around a sharp right turn onto a straightaway that led to the airfield.

Logan shrugged into his pack. "Poppy, get ready to bail. Jesse will cover you."

"What about you?"

"I'll be right behind both of you." Providing protection.

"You better be," she muttered.

Max skidded to a stop near the jet, then he and Sawyer threw open their doors, grabbed their gear and circled to the side nearest the plane with their weapons drawn.

Brody parked closer to the jet. "Go fast, Poppy." He joined Max and Sawyer while Logan helped Poppy from the vehicle.

"Up the stairs," Jesse ordered.

Poppy didn't argue. She sprinted the few feet to the stairs and raced up them. She stumbled on the top stair and went down hard.

Jesse scooped her up and carried her into the cabin of the jet.

"She's clear. Go, go, go." Logan fired round after round at the approaching vehicle's windshield, and continued to fire as his teammates surged up the stairs.

"Logan, go," Brody ordered as he and the others opened fire to give him cover.

He sprinted up the stairs and raced past his team. They continued to fire off rounds until Brody ordered the pilot to take off, then they secured the door and hurried to their seats.

The jet taxied down the runway, rolling faster and faster until it lifted into the air, hitting pockets of turbulence and shuddering from the impact of the wind. By the time the aircraft leveled out, the pilot had taken them above the storm.

Logan unhooked his seatbelt, slid his pack off, and headed for the back bedroom. At the door, he knocked. "It's Logan."

"Come join the party," Jesse called out.

Right. Some party. He hated being poked and prodded but wanted to see Poppy bad enough to put up with Jesse's version of tender loving care.

Logan walked into the bedroom. Seconds later, Poppy was in his arms. He held her close. "She's okay, Jesse? No fresh injuries?"

"She wouldn't let me touch her."

Poppy buried her face against Logan's neck and inched closer.

He signaled the medic to give them a minute. Dread curled in his gut as his friend left the room without a word. "Only the two of us are here now," Logan murmured. "Talk to me. Why won't you let Jesse check you for injuries?"

She shook her head.

"Hey." He inched back enough to cup her face between his palms. "Tell me what's going on so I can help."

"I was unconscious for several hours, Logan. After Thing Two slugged me, I think one of them drugged me to keep me knocked out. I haven't been conscious that long."

"All the more reason for Jesse to check you along with your fall in the ravine."

"What if he finds evidence of something I don't want to know?" Tears pooled in her eyes.

Ice flowed through his veins as the implication of what she meant sank in. "He's only going to check you for fractures, cuts, and scrapes. You'll see a Fortress doctor after we land in Nashville."

She shuddered and sagged against him. "Are you sure?"

"Yes." He'd also be sticking around to make sure Jesse only did as much as Poppy was comfortable with.

"What if...."

"We'll deal with it together. I have your back in everything, Poppy. Always."

After a moment, she nodded. "I don't want Sage to know. Please."

"One hurdle at a time. Let Jesse check you first. After you see the Fortress doctor, decide what you want to tell to family. I'll support you, whatever you decide."

"Even if my decision puts you at odds with Brody?"

"No one is more important to me than you." He trailed his thumb gently over her bruised jaw. "Are you ready for Jesse now?"

"He needs to work on you, too." She stepped out of his embrace and wrapped her arms around her middle. "Bring him in."

Logan opened the door and signaled Jesse. When the medic returned to the room, Logan said, "She's ready. I'm staying with her."

Jesse looked at Poppy. "Do you want him to stay?"

"Yes."

"Why don't you lay on the bed? You'll be more comfortable, and Logan can sit beside you until it's his turn for treatment."

Following a glance at Logan, Poppy stretched out on the bed on her back.

Logan eased onto the bed beside her and propped his back against the wall. "Still want that coffee, or would you prefer hot chocolate?" he asked Poppy as Jesse started his exam.

"Hot chocolate sounds even better. Do you have some on board?"

"We do. I'll make you some as soon Jesse finishes with us."

"I thought operatives only drank high-octane coffee."

"Most of them do. Some, however, prefer hot chocolate and don't mind admitting it. We also transport families and kidnapping victims who might need a soothing drink instead of our version of coffee."

"I'll take either." Poppy shivered and drew Logan's jacket tighter around herself. "I can't seem to get warm."

"Part of the cold is shock. Part is your body temperature hasn't returned to normal," Jesse said. He straightened and walked to a nearby cabinet to grab a thick blanket. When he returned to the bedside, he draped the cover over Poppy. "I'll uncover one limb at a time to help you retain heat."

Logan scooted close so his side pressed against Poppy's and arranged the blanket to cover them both. Perhaps his body heat would help her warm up faster.

Poppy sighed and inched even closer.

"Better?"

"Much. Thanks."

He captured her hand with his and threaded their fingers together, grateful she hadn't shied away from him or his touch.

Jesse eased back after he finished checking for fractures. "You have some scrapes and bruises, but nothing serious. You said your head hurts. Where?"

Poppy indicated the back of her head on the right side. "I remember feeling a sharp pain before I blacked out."

"Sit up for me, and I'll look."

Logan released Poppy's hand and helped her to a sitting position. His gaze locked on the tangle of red-stained hair near her right ear. He winced. No wonder her head hurt.

The medic parted Poppy's hair and examined the injury. He whistled softly. "Ouch."

Poppy smiled. "Is that your official medical diagnosis?"

"No, ma'am. It's the hint that more treatment will be necessary."

Her smile faded. "How much more treatment?"

"A few stitches. You have a nice-size gash back here."

"That I didn't want to hear."

"Sorry, sugar. I can take care of it for you or put a bandage on it and let the Fortress doctor do the work when we land."

"Do it now."

After numbing her scalp, Jesse cleaned the cut and closed the wound with five stitches. He covered the injury with a bandage. "I know you want to shower off the dirt and blood. It's best if you don't until after a doctor has examined you. I need to take a blood sample, Poppy. Some drugs disappear from the bloodstream in a short time. We're already pushing the limit now."

"Go ahead."

He didn't waste any time getting the sample. "We have a small lab up front. I'll get the samples started, then come back. Logan, I'll check you next."

"Yes, sir."

When the door closed behind Jesse, Poppy turned to Logan. "Take off your shirt."

His eyebrow rose. "You sure?"

"You said your injury was a scratch. Did you lie?"

"Bullet wounds are never pretty."

She tugged at his shirt. "Off."

Logan stripped off his shirt and tossed it aside. Blood resumed trickling down his back.

Poppy scooted back to examine his wound. She caught her breath. "That's more than a scratch, Logan. I think you need stitches."

He shrugged. He'd had worse injuries. "I heal fast."

She grabbed a pair of gloves and a handful of wipes from Jesse's mike bag. "Turn your back toward me so I can clean the blood from your skin."

Logan started to tell her not to bother, that it wouldn't help since the furrow was still oozing blood, then thought better of it. If aiding him gave Poppy a sense of control, he'd gladly sit still for her ministrations.

She tugged on gloves, ripped open a packet and wiped the blood from his back. When she finished, Poppy took a pad of gauze and held it against his injury. "Thank you," she whispered.

"For what?"

"Rescuing me."

He covered her hand with his. "I will always come for you if you need me."

Logan would give anything to turn around and kiss Poppy like he'd dreamed of doing for months. This wasn't the time. Jesse would return any second, and the fact Brody hadn't burst into the room yet, demanding an update, was a miracle. Soon, though.

Guilt assailed him. He shouldn't be thinking about kissing her. In fact, if he did what was best for Poppy, Logan would devise a plan to put distance between them for her protection.

Too late, though, he realized. Whether they'd admitted as much to each other, whether it was formal, he and Poppy were involved. They had been since the night his team rescued her and Sage in Mexico.

He should regret the connection. He didn't. Now, his life's mission was to keep her safe and happy.

Jesse returned with Brody on his heels. "Mind if Brody comes in, too?" the medic asked Poppy.

Her brother-in-law scowled. "Hey, we're family. Of course she doesn't mind."

"You don't get a vote. Poppy?"

"It's fine."

"You sure?" Logan eyed her.

"Yeah. He'll find out every detail anyway. Makes no difference if he learns the information now or later."

Although he didn't question her further, Logan knew she didn't want Brody in the room. Did she remember more than she was saying, or was she worried that her brother-in-law would assume the worst and treat her like a victim?

He flashed Brody a warning glance and received a glare in return. His friend better not push Poppy too hard.

"Go easy," Jesse murmured to Brody, then motioned for Logan to turn around.

"Nice gash. I think you win the prize for the most stitches on this mission."

"Yeah, yeah. Just fix me up so I can help Poppy with her hair."

"You opening a salon, Fletcher?" Brody folded his arms across his chest and leaned against the door like he was stationing himself to prevent an escape.

"I'm going to help Poppy wash the blood from her hair."

He straightened. "You said she was fine, Jesse."

"She needed a few stitches. No big deal."

"What about her jaw?"

The medic plunged a hand into his bag and pulled out a chemically activated cold pack, which he shook, then handed to Poppy. "Should help the swelling and pain. I don't want to give you any pain killers on top of whatever drug the kidnappers gave you. Once I determine what you were given, I'll feel easier about giving you pain meds if you need them."

"I understand."

"Move to sit in front of Logan." Jesse winked at Poppy. "He needs someone to hold his hand while I work on him. He's a wimp with stitches."

She smiled. "Can't have him looking weak in front of his team leader."

Jesse waited for Poppy to move before he tugged on a fresh pair of gloves and scrutinized the furrow the bullet left behind. "Part of this gash is pretty deep. I'll need to numb your shoulder before I repair the damage."

"Go ahead."

After giving him a shot of Lidocaine, Jesse eased back. "Now we wait for the medicine to work."

"While we wait, we need to know what happened, Poppy." Brody crossed the bedroom and grabbed a chair. He sat near Poppy. "Start at the beginning, and give us as many details as possible so we can catch these guys."

"I remember little," she warned. "Don't nag me."

"Anything you remember will put us one step closer to nailing them."

She told them about waking up and being unable to go back to sleep. "I went downstairs to make coffee and work. The coffeemaker had just completed the brewing cycle when I heard something behind me. Thing One and Thing Two were standing there with guns pointed at me."

Brody snorted. "Things One and Two, huh?"

She shrugged. "They didn't introduce themselves. I had to call them something. Anyway, they bound my hands with a zip tie and marched me outside. I broke free and ran, but didn't get far. Thing Two tackled me and punched me. I woke up in a rundown three-story cabin."

Poppy told of her escape out the third-story window and fleeing over the darkened countryside and hiding in the ravine. "Thing Two lost sight of me in the darkness, but he fired his gun at me a few times. When a bullet got too close, I lost my grip and fell. The rest, you know."

Jesse worked on Logan's shoulder. Thankfully, all Logan felt was the cold liquid from the antiseptic wipe and the tug of the thread pulling the edges of his wound together. Later, when the meds wore off, he'd feel every stitch. Again, it was nothing he hadn't experienced before and survived. This time, though, he wouldn't be able to take heavy pain meds. Couldn't afford to have slow reaction times. To be slow might mean injury or death for Poppy or for him.

"Did the kidnappers ever say why they'd grabbed you?" Brody leaned his forearms on his knees, his gaze locked on Poppy.

"Not really."

He blinked. "Come on, Poppy. They must have mentioned something. Did they indicate they would contact your father, or that this was related to me or Logan?"

She shook her head. "What they asked me made little sense."

Logan wrapped his hand around hers. "What did they want to know?"

"What I knew about cats."

His eyebrows winged up. "Cats?"

"I know, right? I told you it made little sense."

"Explain," Brody demanded.

"I just did," she snapped. "They asked if I knew about a specific cat and told me I needed to come up with an answer or I wouldn't like the consequences when the boss arrived. And, no, before you ask, they never mentioned a name. I don't even know if the boss is a man or woman."

"What kind of cat?" Logan asked.

"A lynx."

"Does that mean anything to you?" Brody asked.

She was silent a moment. "No."

Logan and Brody exchanged glances, then refocused on Poppy. "Are you sure?"

Poppy frowned at her brother-in-law. "You think I'm lying to you?"

"I'm asking if you're sure you don't remember hearing the name Lynx."

"If I did, I would have told you as much."

"You don't seem positive," Jesse murmured.

"Let's drop it, okay?"

Hmm. Something was up with Poppy and the cat thing. But what? Time to get attention off Poppy. He'd revisit the topic with her later. "Are you finished, Jesse? I'm starving, and Poppy needs something hot to drink."

After one last tug, the medic pulled off his gloves. "Done. Congratulations, Logan. You're the proud owner of 23 stitches." He dropped two packets of pills beside Logan. "Two antibiotic capsules a day. One pain capsule every four hours." He held up a hand. "Yes, the pain meds are mild. No problem with sluggish reaction times. I want to check your shoulder tomorrow."

"Sure. If we're finished here, everybody else clear out."

Brody gave him a hard stare, which Logan returned. Finally, his team leader glanced at Jesse and inclined his head toward the door. "Poppy, I'll check on you in a few minutes."

"I can handle washing my hands, face, and hair, Dad."

He tilted his head. "You don't want to shower?"

Jesse cleared his throat. "Brody." When the other man turned, Jesse motioned him from the room and closed the door behind them.

Poppy sighed. "This is awkward."

"Want me to talk to him?"

"I have a feeling Jesse is telling him the bare minimum right now." She stood. "Come on. I want the blood out of my hair. After that, I want to wrap up in a blanket and sip hot chocolate."

Unless he missed his guess, Logan figured Poppy might have half an hour before the adrenaline dump faded and she looked for the closest pillow and blanket. "Let's go." He nudged her toward the bathroom.

After locating a towel, he turned on the shower to warm the water and located a bottle of shampoo. "Ready?"

She eyed him, then the running water. "How are we going to do this?"

Logan handed her the shampoo bottle. "You handle the soap. I'll deal with the water. If you can bend at the waist for about a minute, we'll have your hair clean and shiny."

"Sounds good." She bent enough to rest her hands on her knees.

"Perfect." He quickly got her hair wet, lathered the shampoo in her tresses, and rinsed the suds from her hair. Turning off the shower, he draped the cloth over her head and toweled most of the water from her hair. "Better?"

"Much. Thanks, Logan. Although I probably should have left my hair alone in case the doctor wanted to check for forensic evidence, I just couldn't stand the thought of blood drying on my scalp."

"Maddox will send a forensic team in to sweep through the cabin."

"How do you know?"

He shrugged. "It's what I would do. We want the guys who kidnapped you, Poppy. We need evidence in case we hand them over to law enforcement."

She blinked. "In case?"

"Depends on them, doesn't it? Ready for that hot chocolate now?"

"Yes."

Her heartfelt answer made him laugh. "Do you want to drink it in the cabin with the team, or would you prefer to stay back here?"

"The cabin. The last thing I want is to be alone with my own thoughts. Your teammates can be annoying, but they're entertaining."

He escorted her to the jet's cabin, led Poppy to a seat, and walked to the galley to make hot chocolate for her. Brody joined him a moment later.

"Why didn't you tell me? I wouldn't have pushed her so hard if I'd known."

Logan flicked his friend a glance, then poured water into a coffee mug and slid the mug into the microwave. "Nothing to tell. We're taking precautions since she was unconscious for several hours, something you should have expected."

A wince. "Yeah, I should have. I guess I didn't want to consider something so painful could happen to her a second time." Brody sighed. "I should apologize."

"Leave it. Poppy understands." At the end of the heating cycle, Logan opened a packet of chocolate mix and poured the contents into steaming water. "Did you catch her hesitation about the reference to the lynx?"

"Yep. She knows more than she admitted. I don't understand why she's keeping information from us. We need every bit of information to secure her safety."

Whatever the reason, Logan intended to discover the truth because Poppy's life might depend on it.

Chapter Nine

Poppy frowned and batted at the hand shaking her to wakefulness. She was too tired to wake up and face the world yet. A deep, masculine chuckle coaxed her to open her eyes. "Go away," she mumbled.

"Nope," Logan said. "Time to wake up, Sleeping Beauty. We're wheels down in Nashville."

She blinked. "We are? I can't believe I slept for six hours."

"You needed the rest." He stood and held out his hand to her. "Come on. The team is waiting for us on the tarmac."

"Why? They should go home and get some sleep."

"Not happening. You're our top priority, Poppy."

She preceded him to the exit. "I don't need a team of bodyguards. You and Brody are bad enough. Five is definitely overkill."

"Willing to bet your life on that?"

Poppy glared at him over her shoulder. "The kidnappers didn't hurt me."

"This time."

She stopped and spun to face Logan. "This time? You think they'll try again?"

"Don't you?"

"Do you have to answer every question with a question?"

"Maybe."

"It's annoying, Fletcher. Knock it off."

"Hey," Brody said as he peered up the aisle. "What's the hold up? The doc is waiting to see you at headquarters, Poppy. Get a move on."

After staring at Logan a few more seconds, Poppy turned toward her sister's husband. "Let's go. The sooner we get this over with, the sooner I'll be able to go home."

"Yeah, about that."

She growled. "Don't say it."

"Sorry, kid. You're barred from entering your house until further notice."

"Oh, come on. I'm willing to put up with a bodyguard or two, but I don't want to give up my house."

"No choice. It's a crime scene."

Dismay knotted her stomach. She needed the sanctuary of her home to process the kidnapping. A hotel room would do, but that location presented problems, too, including the logistical issue of housing five operatives loaded to their eyebrows with weapons that would make most people run for the hills in a blind panic. Not an ideal way to hide without drawing attention to herself. "For how long?"

"As long as it takes to process the house and find out what's going on."

As they walked down the stairs to the SUV waiting on the tarmac, Brody remained squarely in front of her. Poppy swallowed hard. This was so wrong. What if a sniper shot him by mistake? She didn't want to be responsible for the injury or death of Sage's husband. Although he annoyed her like a big brother would, she loved him.

Losing any member of the Texas Team on her account would gut her. Poppy glanced at Logan as he hustled her to the backseat of the SUV. Losing him would devastate her. She couldn't let that happen.

The operative opened the back door, helped her into the vehicle, and followed her inside. "Go, Brody," he said as soon as he closed the door.

Brody put the SUV in gear and drove away from the airport with one Fortress SUV in front of them and one behind. When he drove onto the interstate, Brody called Fortress headquarters. "It's Brody. You're on speaker with Logan and Poppy. We should arrive in 30 minutes."

"We're ready," Brent Maddox said. "Any trouble?"

"Not so far."

"Good. Poppy, expect problems when you arrive."

She pressed a hand to her stomach. Oh, no. "My parents flew in?"

"No. They're demanding that Logan and Brody bring you to D.C. immediately."

"Not a good idea, boss," Logan said. "We have too many unanswered questions."

"I said as much to the vice president. He wasn't impressed with my reasoning."

"He won't like it any better when I tell him the same thing, but it's true. Until we know what's going on, the last place Poppy needs to be is a fishbowl like Washington, D.C. The news media will be sure to report her appearance in town, blowing any chance we have at keeping her in secure surroundings."

"Good luck presenting your case to Dad," Poppy said. "He has faith in his security detail and believes they're better qualified to keep his daughters safe than anyone else."

"He's wrong," the Fortress CEO said.

"I realize that. You'll waste your breath trying to convince him, though."

"Security at headquarters is heightened?" Brody asked.

"Barriers are up, and we've doubled the security force. Since when don't you trust my preparations?"

"Since the threat is to family," he countered.

"We've been ready for anything since Poppy was taken, so dial back the mistrust. You're ticking me off."

"Sorry," Brody muttered.

A snort. "Don't lie. Contact us if you run into trouble." Maddox ended the call.

Logan whistled softly. "You better duck and run when you see the boss."

"Thanks for the breaking news announcement. I got the message before you chimed in. Just monitor the traffic."

Logan gave Brody a snappy salute. "Yes, sir."

Although Poppy expected an attack every minute of the journey, they arrived at Fortress Security headquarters without incident. As soon as they cleared the gate, the iron barriers swung closed and security personnel armed to the teeth returned to their positions, alert and ready.

After the caravan of SUVs parked in the garage, Logan opened the door and reached back to help Poppy from the backseat. Hand wrapped around hers, he walked with her to the elevator and rode to the second floor where the medical clinic was located.

Brody got off the elevator with Poppy and Logan and turned to the rest of the team. "While Logan and Poppy are being checked by the doctor, the rest of you restock supplies, then head to the conference room. We'll join you as soon as possible."

Halfway down the long corridor, Brody opened the door leading to the medical clinic and stepped inside. He greeted a woman wearing a white coat. "Dr. Whitmeyer, this is Poppy Reynolds, my sister-in-law."

The doctor's honey-colored hair gleamed in the sunlight streaming through the windows as she stepped toward Poppy. "Ms. Reynolds, I'm so pleased to put a face with the name. I've heard many wonderful things about you from the members of the Texas Team."

"Thank you."

Whitmeyer looked at Brody. "Anyone else need medical attention?"

He pointed at Logan. "Shoulder wound. Jesse treated him on the jet."

"Good. I'll just have a look at the injury when Ms. Reynolds and I are finished, but Jesse never leaves me any work to do." She smiled. "You're lucky to have him on your team."

"Agreed." Brody edged toward the corridor door. "I'll wait in the hall."

The doctor laughed. "Tell Sage I said hello."

"Yes, ma'am."

When he left, Whitmeyer said to Poppy, "Come with me, and we'll talk."

Logan squeezed Poppy's hand. "I'll be here if you need me." To the doctor, he said, "Take good care of her, Doc."

"You know I will."

Poppy followed the doctor into an exam room and jerked when the door closed behind her. Man, she dreaded going through this exam again.

Instead of motioning her toward the table, Whitmeyer indicated the two chairs set against the wall. "Let's talk for a few minutes, all right?" When they were seated, she said, "Tell me what's brought you here, Ms. Reynolds."

"Please, call me Poppy." She explained about the kidnapping and the gap in her memory. "I think the kidnappers drugged me."

"What gives you that impression?"

"I lost several hours, more than can be accounted for by a clip to the jaw." She motioned toward the colorful bruise.

"And you're worried about what happened while you were unconscious."

"Do you blame me?"

Whitmeyer patted Poppy's hand. "I don't. Let's get started, shall we?" She handed Poppy a gown. "Change into this while I step into the other room and check Logan's shoulder." She paused. "Unless you want to sit in on his exam."

"I do if he doesn't mind." Her face burned.

The doctor smiled. "Something tells me the handsome operative will want you close by."

An hour later, Whitmeyer opened the door to the exam room and motioned for Logan to join them.

Logan walked to Poppy's side. "You doing okay?" he asked softly after taking her hand in his.

She nodded.

He squeezed her hand and turned to the doctor. "What can you tell me, Dr. Whitmeyer?"

"First, under normal circumstances, I would tell you nothing. However, Poppy gave me permission to tell you everything. Based on my examination, I don't believe Poppy was sexually assaulted. I'll run the samples I collected to be sure, though. Also, I found a puncture wound which supports her belief that she was drugged. I should know in a few hours what drug the kidnappers injected Poppy with to keep her unconscious."

"Jesse ran a test on the jet. He said it was ketamine. What about the cut on her head?"

"Your medic did a great job stitching the injury. I don't expect any problems but I've given her antibiotics to prevent infection. I also gave her mild pain medicine if her headache requires something stronger than over-the-counter meds. No concussion."

Whitmeyer grabbed a pair of gloves. "Now, it's your turn, Logan. Take off your shirt so I can see your injury."

"Jesse took care of it for me."

She pointed to the exam table. "Quit stalling or I'll have to get mean."

He sighed. "Yes, ma'am." Logan reached behind his neck, tugged off his shirt, and climbed on the table.

Poppy flinched as she examined Logan's shoulder. The injury must be painful, yet he hadn't acted as though it didn't bother him in the least. His stoicism made her feel like a wuss. Her head and her jaw were pounding in sync, and all she wanted to do was crawl into the nearest bed, pull a blanket over her head, and sleep.

Following a thorough exam, Whitmeyer declared Logan fit to leave the clinic. "I know better than to tell you to take the pain meds until you're healed. However, I will insist you take all the antibiotics Jesse gave you. Otherwise, I'll bench you from duty until your shoulder is healed. I'd prefer you take a few days off before returning to full duty. Since you're in the middle of an operation, I won't make an issue of it. If you have problems with the injury and your medic feels you should see me, I expect you to cooperate with his recommendation. Am I clear, Mr. Fletcher?"

"I got the message. Take all my antibiotics and don't give Jesse grief."

"Good. I expect you have a meeting with Brent. You should go. Poppy, if you need me, call me. Don't forget to call your counselor. This experience will resurrect terrible memories from last year."

"I will. Thank you, Dr. Whitmeyer."

Logan escorted Poppy from the clinic.

Brody straightened from the corridor wall. "How'd it go, Poppy?"

"She gave me antibiotics and pain meds if I need them for a headache." Her cheeks burned. "No signs of assault, though."

The tense lines of his shoulders relaxed. "Thank God. Look, I know you're tired, but we have a meeting with Brent. Although I can make your excuses to him, I won't be able to do the same with your parents. You know it won't fly."

She froze. "They're here?"

Logan rested his hand against her lower back, offering silent support.

Brody shook his head. "They've agreed to a video chat for now. If you don't show up to answer a few questions, they will be down here within hours or they'll send a plane along with a security detail to bring you to them."

"A threat?"

"Nope, a promise. They're worried, Poppy. Answering questions will buy you more time. An in-person appearance will have to be on your agenda soon. No way to get around it."

"You've talked to them, haven't you?"

He lifted one shoulder in a shrug. "I tried to put them off with limited success." Brody grimaced. "Your father insisted."

She sighed. Not surprising. Her father was tough and well known for standing his ground unless it came to making her mother happy. This had Beverly Reynolds's fingerprints all over it. "Thanks for trying."

"Sure. Am I forgiven for keeping you from going home?"

"Ha. Nice try. No way." She patted his upper arm. "Based on your view of your own abilities, you should be able to pull off a minor miracle, like getting me back into my home in a few hours. Sorry, buddy. You'll have to do better than that to earn a pass."

He chuckled. "Didn't think it would be that easy. All right, Flower Child. Let's go. The boss is waiting."

Poppy's dread grew with every step. Dealing with Brent Maddox and fending off her parents wouldn't be a pleasant experience.

When she followed Brody into the conference room, the remaining members of the Texas team and Brent stood. A man in a wheelchair stationed behind a computer smiled at her.

Brent pulled out a chair for her. "Please, take a seat, Poppy." He glanced at the other man. "Zane, contact Ivan and tell him we're ready."

Poppy wanted to protest. She wasn't ready to face an inquisition from her parents. Didn't matter. She was an adult. If she didn't want to answer a question or two, she could decline.

Right. The only way to avoid answering her mother's questions in the next few minutes was to walk out and turn off her phone. Hated to admit it but Poppy wasn't above doing just that if she had to.

The large screen on the wall flickered to life, and her father and mother's concerned, larger-than-life faces appeared.

Relief flooded Beverly's face. "Poppy, are you all right, baby?"

"I'm fine, Mom."

Her father scowled. "You don't look fine. You look like someone punched you in the face." Ivan's glare shifted to Logan. "You promised you would keep her safe. Look at her face. That is not keeping my daughter safe. I thought I could trust you, Fletcher. Was I mistaken?"

"Dad," Poppy warned. "That's enough. Logan was out of town when I was kidnapped. You can't lay this on him."

"Want to bet? He's supposed to be an expert in threat assessment. Seems to me he didn't do a good job."

Under cover of the table, Logan's hand covered Poppy's fist. "Your father's right," he murmured. "I should have asked a team of operatives to watch over you while I was deployed."

"Do you have a team on the other operatives' families when you're deployed?" she countered.

"Not the same thing and you know it," Ivan snapped. "You're the daughter of the Vice President of the United States, Poppy. You're a high value target. People with an agenda would love to get their hands on you. Anyone who knows me at all understands that the most effective leverage to use against me is my family."

"I'm just a writer, Dad. I've also deliberately made myself uninteresting to the press by staying out of controversy and politics. No one cares about me." Poppy could almost feel a glass cage forming around her, and panic made her heart rate increase.

"You know that's not true, sweetheart. You need a protection detail," Beverly said. "I insist you accept the added security or Brent will bring you personally to our home, where you will stay until this matter is resolved and you're safe again."

"I refuse to come to D.C. I can't live in a glass cage anymore. Don't bother sending a Secret Service detail. I won't put up with their high-handed tactics. If you send them against my wishes, I'll slip the leash like I've always done and disappear."

"Don't be foolish, Poppy." Her father slammed a fist on his office desk. "You can't play hide-and-seek with these people, and you can't reason with them. No matter how much you claim to be uninteresting, it's not true. Don't act like you don't have the common sense God gave a flea."

"Enough," Logan snapped. "Poppy made her preferences clear. You will respect her decision. She'll have Fortress bodyguards with her 24/7."

"You're risking her life."

"I know my teammates, and I trust them with my life and hers. We will protect her from anyone who comes at her. No one will touch her again on our watch."

"Admirable sentiments," Beverly said. "The execution hasn't been up to your claim of being the best in the private security business." She looked at her husband. "Perhaps we should request a Special Forces team be assigned. Call in one of those many favors you're owed, and protect our daughter, Ivan."

"No." Why weren't they listening? "Mom, I'll accept a security detail from Fortress. No one else. No military or federal law enforcement team. I trust the Texas Team. I know them and, as many times as you've hosted them in your home, so do you. You know what they can do, the skill and training they have. They will keep me safe."

Ivan waved that off. "We'll come back to this discussion before we end our call. We never received a ransom demand, Poppy. What did these people want?"

"I don't know."

Beverly and Ivan exchanged glances before he asked, "They didn't tell you anything?"

"No."

"Did they ask for information?"

"Not really."

Beverly leaned closer, her gaze sharp and locked on Poppy. "What does that mean?" she demanded. "They either wanted information or they didn't."

"Things One and Two asked about something that made zero sense to me. They weren't happy with my answers."

"Is that how you were bruised?"

She shook her head. "That happened before they asked the weird questions. One kidnapper took exception to me trying to escape. He tackled me and followed it up with a right cross to the jaw."

"What did they want to know, baby? Something about your father, information that would damage national security, what?"

"Nothing like that."

"So, what was it, then?" she asked, impatience obvious in her tone.

"They asked me about cats."

Her parents stared. "Cats?" Her mother's expression went blank. "That's ridiculous."

"See? I told you it made little sense." Something was up with this interrogation. That's exactly what it felt like, too. Not a parent inquiring after a child who'd been in danger. An interrogation.

"What did you tell them?" Ivan asked, his tone sharp.

"That I was a dog person."

"What was their response?"

"That I needed to come up with a better answer before their boss arrived. Otherwise, I wouldn't like the consequences."

"Cats," her mother murmured. "Did the men say anything more about the cats?"

"Well, they asked about one specific type of cat," Poppy corrected. "A lynx. When I couldn't tell them anything, they got angry, threatened me with the boss, then locked me in a third-story bedroom."

"How did you get away?"

She smiled at the man behind the computer, who winked at her before she refocused on the giant wall screen. "Zane helped me create a plan to escape out the window and go up to the roof. From there, I climbed down a tree and ran. Logan and his teammates found me." A watered-down version of events, but the truth as far as it went. No need to add more fuel to her parents' argument for more security.

"Are you sure you're all right?" Ivan demanded. "They didn't hurt you?"

Poppy stiffened. She knew what her father was asking and didn't blame him. Talking about the subject with her father was uncomfortable enough. Discussing it in a room full of men was impossible. She just couldn't do it.

Logan squeezed her hand again and said, "One of the Fortress physicians confirmed Poppy wasn't assaulted. We're waiting on the results of the tox screen run by the doctor to see what the kidnappers used to knock her out. Our medic says the drug was a sedative. Other than that, the doc assured us that Poppy would recover with no repercussions from the bruises, cuts, and scrapes."

Beverly gasped. "You were drugged, too, Poppy?"

"I'm fine, Mom. If I wasn't, I would tell you."

"I don't like this, Ivan. We need to send the jet."

Poppy stood. "You can send an entire fleet of jets. I won't get on any of them."

"Be reasonable," her father snapped. "This is a serious threat to your safety and to ours. You can't run around the countryside without protection. They will hunt you down."

"How do you know these men weren't hired by some person with a weird agenda?" she countered. She could do stubborn just as well as her father. "We've seen more than our share of those threats, and they came to nothing."

"Not this time."

Wait. What? She stared as suspicion twined with disbelief inside her. What did her father mean by that? Just how much did Ivan Reynolds know about her kidnapping?

Logan stood, forming a united front with Poppy. "How do you know that, sir?" His stance conveyed his own concern.

Ivan blinked, his face losing all expression. "I don't. Pure supposition. No one goes to the trouble of snatching the daughter of the second in command of the United States unless they're serious. You might be willing to risk her life, but we aren't."

"Ivan." Maddox's eyes narrowed. "Don't go there. You know that's not true. None of us want anything to happen to Poppy."

Beverly frowned. "If anything happens to my daughter, you and your company will pay the price. I'll see to it myself."

Poppy gasped. "Mom, you don't mean that."

"Want to bet?"

Ivan leaned closer to the screen, his eyes snapping with anger. "We want Poppy here within 24 hours, Fletcher. Make it happen." The screen went blank.

The occupants of the conference room looked at each other in silence. Finally, Brent said, "What was that?"

Poppy straightened. "I don't know what got into them." She turned to Logan. "I know one thing, though."

"What's that?"

"My parents just lied to me."

Chapter Ten

Logan unlocked his door, disarmed his alarm system, and opened the door wide. "Make yourself at home."

Poppy walked into the living room followed by Jesse who carried his Go bag and a Duffel bag for Poppy.

"Which room will Poppy be in?" Jesse asked.

"Upstairs in the last room on the right."

"I'll take the Duffel up." Poppy held out her hand for the bag.

Jesse's eyebrow raised. "You sure? I don't mind carrying the bag to your room."

"I appreciate the offer but I can handle it."

The medic glanced at Logan.

He gave a slight nod to his friend. As Poppy made her way upstairs, Logan clapped Jesse on the shoulder. "Coffee?"

"Thought you'd never ask."

He led the medic to the kitchen and prepped the coffeemaker, then turned and leaned his back against the counter while they waited for the aromatic brew to finish.

"I didn't think Sage would let Poppy leave," Jesse said.

"She did everything possible to delay us," Logan agreed.

"Wonder if she knows why their parents lied."

"Maybe." He heard the doubt in his voice. If Poppy had known the reason, she would have told him, wouldn't she? "If she does, Brody will find out the truth and tell the rest of us."

Jesse watched him a moment. "Poppy held something back."

Stomach knotting, Logan inclined his head. "I know." And the knowledge ate at him. Why hadn't she told him everything? Possibly because she didn't remember it all, maybe just a niggling at the back of her mind? "I'll talk to her in a few minutes. At the moment, I think Poppy needs some time to herself."

"She's certainly earned it." Jesse accepted a mug of steaming coffee with a nod of thanks. "Your woman isn't the only one holding back."

"What do you mean?"

A snort. "For a man who spent a lot of time undercover as a cop, you can't lie worth anything."

"The question stands."

"You and Brody know more than you admitted. So, what was it? Do you know why Ivan and Beverly lied or was it something about the lynx you two didn't want to discuss?"

Huh. Maybe Logan had lost his finesse in prevarication. More likely, Jesse and the rest of the team knew him and Brody better than their own families did, and they had no reason to lie to their friends. If they were right, the information would be shared with the others anyway.

The question was, were they right? Logan's fingers tightened around the handle of his mug, praying he and Brody were wrong. If not, the team was in for a world of trouble in keeping Poppy and Sage safe.

Ivan Reynolds was right about one thing. His daughters were the perfect tool to use as leverage against him and his wife. They must keep Sage and Poppy from the enemy's hands at all costs. Why would the vice president and his wife want Poppy in Washington where the person who commissioned the kidnapping expected to see her?

A sound of fabric brushing against a wall forewarned them Poppy was approaching. She walked into the kitchen seconds later. When she breathed deep, her face brightened. "You made coffee. Please tell me it's strong enough to peel paint."

Logan chuckled and poured steaming liquid into a mug and handed it to her. "See for yourself."

She sipped, closed her eyes, and sighed. "Perfect. You're hired as my favorite barista for life."

"Deal." Did she realize what she'd said? He didn't want to ask in case Poppy hadn't meant her statement the way it sounded.

"The water's getting deep in here," Jesse muttered. "I'm going outside to familiarize myself with the perimeter." He was gone a minute later.

Poppy frowned. "What got into him?"

"Trouble in paradise."

"He's dating someone?" She set her mug on the counter, eyes dancing with mischief. "You're kidding. Why didn't I know this? What's her name? Why haven't we been introduced to her? Why haven't you or one of the others mentioned this woman in casual conversation? What are you hiding?"

He held up a hand. "Hold on. Jesse is very closemouthed about his private life. He's also protective of the women in his life. You, Sage, and Willow should know." Willow was Max's wife. "And this woman may be out of his life now."

"Oh, come on. Dish, Fletcher. This is something I can hold over his head when he annoys me as much as Brody does."

Logan shook his head. "Nope. If you want to know about her, weasel the information from Jesse for yourself. If I tell you the information, I'll still have to work with him and listen to him complain about my big mouth while he's stitching up my next injury. You're a reporter, Reynolds. Work your magic on him."

"Yeah, yeah. You think I can't do it. Just watch me."

His lips curved. Good. The task would give her a challenge to occupy her mind instead of worrying over the secrets her parents were keeping from their daughters and wondering at the outcome of the medical tests. "Care to make a wager on the outcome of your interrogation attempts?"

Poppy grinned. "A bet? Bring it on, Logan. What are the details?"

"If you win, you can ask me for a favor."

"What kind of favor?"

"Maybe a honey-do list, driving you to a location for your research, or information." He paused after saying the last word. That one needed a qualification. "Within reason, okay? If you ask for information, I'll try to tell you what I know. However, I'll have to refuse if the information is classified."

"If you refuse, I reserve the right to ask for something else."

"Deal."

"What if I lose?"

He caged Poppy in by placing his hands on the counter on both sides of her body. Time to put himself out there. She might say no but at least she'd understand without a doubt that he wanted to change the nature of their relationship.

Logan looked into her eyes, hoping he wasn't making a huge mistake that would cost him Poppy's friendship. That would gut him. "If I win, you go on a date with me."

He waited long, agonizing seconds for her response.

Finally, her brow wrinkled. "We go out all the time, Logan."

"As friends. I'm asking for an actual date."

Poppy tilted her head. "A date date?"

Amused, the corner of his lips curved upward. "Is there any other kind?"

Color flooded her cheeks. "Are you sure you want a date with me?"

He blinked. Not what he'd expected. "Why wouldn't I be?" She dropped her gaze, placed her hands on his chest, and attempted to push him away, to no avail. He wasn't letting her slip past him without answering his question.

Logan stepped closer, keeping her pinned against the counter. "If you don't want to go on a proper date, say so. I don't want to cross boundaries if you hate the idea." Might kill him if she turned him down.

"It's not that."

Thank God. Not a ringing endorsement, but he could work with a neutral response and stoke her interest in dating him. Hopefully.

What bothered him more than her weak response was Poppy's demeanor. He liked her sass and powerful personality. Looking everywhere but in his eyes wasn't like his Poppy.

Logan cupped her chin with the palm of his hand and tilted her face up to his. "Look at me, Poppy," he murmured. When she lifted her gaze to his eyes, he said, "Talk to me. If something's wrong, tell me so I can fix it."

To his horror, tears pooled in her eyes. "You can't fix this." Her voice sounded hoarse.

Oh, man. His heart ached. Had he done or said something to cause her pain? Worse, had he scared her? Perhaps he should have waited longer. What if he'd moved too soon and ruined everything between them? "If I hurt or scared you...."

"No. You did nothing wrong." She laid her hand over his heart. "I apologize if I gave you that impression."

Poppy swallowed hard. "What I meant to ask was, are you sure you want to be with someone who carries an entire trunk full of baggage around with her?"

That's what was bothering her? "Sweetheart, I have my own baggage. Your suitcases don't scare me."

A tear streaked down her cheek, followed by another and another. "You know what happened to me in Mexico."

Logan threaded his fingers into her hair. "I do. I also remember the strong, defiant woman who beat the odds and survived hours of torture and conditioning at the hands of human traffickers, and came out the other side stronger than ever. But, baby, when I look at you, I see a woman I care for a great deal, not a victim. We all have scars. We don't get through life without them. Some scars you see. Some you don't."

"The invisible ones are the hardest to get past."

"I know. I have several of my own. Whatever you need to work through, we can deal with it together if you'll allow me to walk through the valley with you."

She wiped the tears from her cheeks. "I don't know why you'd want to go to all that trouble."

"Easy. You're worth it. So, what do you say? Will you agree to go on a date with me if you cannot wheedle information from the medic?"

Poppy watched him. "What if I want to change the conditions of the wager?"

Logan froze. Was she getting ready to kick him to the curb after all? "Name the change."

"If I win the wager, we go on my choice of date."

His heart sped up. This change wasn't a rejection. "And if you lose?"

"The date is your choice." She held up a hand. "One qualification on that one."

"What is it?"

"No jumping out of planes. I refuse to leap from a perfectly good airplane."

A smile curved his lips. "Afraid of heights, Reynolds?"

"You bet, Fletcher. So, what do you say? Do you agree to the new terms?"

He drew her closer. "Absolutely. I can't lose."

"You don't know what my choice of date might be."

"Don't care. All that matters is spending time with you." A pause, then, "Just to be clear, I want more than just one date with you, Poppy. I want to build a relationship to see where this might go. Are you willing to give us a shot?"

"You aren't afraid of my father?"

"Are you kidding? He's a tame house cat compared to your mother. I'm more afraid of Beverly than I am of Ivan."

She laughed. "You are one smart man, Logan."

"Do I get an answer to my question now?"

Poppy smiled. "I'm willing to see where this goes as long as you promise we'll always be friends, no matter how it turns out."

Thank God. At least he had a chance. As long as he didn't screw up, life would be outstanding. "You have my word." No matter the cost to himself, Logan refused to let her down.

"All right, then. Shake to seal the deal?"

"Nope." His gaze dropped to her mouth. "A kiss to seal the bargain, unless you feel it's too soon."

"I thought you'd never ask."

Logan's gaze flicked up to her eyes. She was serious. Better than that, her eyes sparkled with anticipation instead of fear. Excellent.

Taking his time, Logan lowered his head and captured her mouth with his. Sparks flew the second their lips touched. Their chemistry blew off the top of the heat meter. He'd known it would be this way. This was half the reason he'd avoided moving their relationship forward before now. The other half was because he'd been too chicken to put himself at risk. So much time he'd lost with her because of his own cowardice.

Now that Logan knew he was right about their chemistry, dating another woman was out of the question. For him, it was Poppy or no one. If she didn't feel the same, Logan was toast.

By degrees, he changed the angle of the kiss until it was perfect. Keeping his hands lightly on her waist, Logan deepened the kiss. One kiss led to another and another until he had to raise his head and drag in a needed breath. He was gratified to note she was also sucking in air.

When Poppy glanced up at him, her unfocused gaze made him smile. "Are you okay?"

"I don't know." She blinked. "Ask me again in a few minutes. Maybe by then I'll be able to feel my feet touching the ground."

He chuckled.

"Good grief, Logan." Poppy shook her head. "I had no idea you were so skilled in the art of kissing."

"You approve of my technique?"

"I'd be crazy not to approve."

The back door opened, and Jesse stepped inside the kitchen. He closed the door and, spotting them so close to each other, froze. "Should I do another circuit around the perimeter?"

When Poppy laughed and turned to face the medic while still in the circle of Logan's arms, he breathed a sigh of relief and counted her move as a huge step forward in their relationship. She didn't appear hesitant to stay near him. Logan took a chance and rested his hand against her waist. To his surprise, Poppy leaned against him instead of away.

"Unnecessary," Poppy said to Jesse. "See anything interesting out there?"

"Only if you count a curious fox and a rabbit racing for safety."

"Ah, so you met Red," Logan said.

"Red?" Poppy looked up at him. "You made a pet out of a fox?"

"Not really. We're nodding acquaintances who offer each other respect. When we cross paths, I don't bother Red, and he doesn't bother me. Red's not worried about me being a threat to his safety."

"Well, Red doesn't trust me." Jesse walked to a cabinet and grabbed a glass that he filled with water from a pitcher in the refrigerator. "He took off as soon as he saw me."

"Maybe he doesn't like your cologne."

"Ha ha." Jesse downed the water and set his glass on the counter. "Want me to keep watch while you catch up on your sleep?"

Logan looked at Poppy. "Your choice." He winked. "This time."

She watched him a few seconds, then said, "I hope you mean that because I've been thinking about my next move."

"*Our* next move. We stay together, remember? Where you go, I go, too. So, what's your conclusion about what we're doing next?" Research, studying the still photos Zane had sent to Logan's email, possibly consulting an artist Fortress employed to create a sketch of the two men who kidnapped Poppy?

"Contact Brent and ask him if Fortress has a jet available or if I need to charter one."

He stilled. "Why?"

"I want to fly to Washington, D.C. Today."

Chapter Eleven

After her announcement, Poppy waited for Logan's reaction. She suspected he wouldn't like with her decision. She wasn't wrong.

Logan paced away from her and back again, his hair mussed from running his fingers through the dark, silky strands. "You fought with your father over this decision, and you were right to defy his order. What induced you to change your mind now?"

"The kidnappers weren't in the same class as the Texas Team, but they were professional enough to get the job done with a minimum of fuss. If they'd known Fortress had installed an automatic silent secondary alarm, Things One and Two would have bypassed that system as well. They were good enough or lucky enough to abduct me with no one except Zane noticing. If it hadn't been for the GPS tracker in my watch, you wouldn't have known where I was."

"I would have combed the globe to find you, Poppy. No matter how long it took, I would have found you and brought you home."

"I don't doubt that for a minute." She wrapped her fingers around his wrist. "But if you and your team had been a few minutes slower, the kidnappers' boss would have arrived where I was held, and I couldn't tell him what he wanted to know. I don't know what would have happened to me."

"You would have survived."

Such faith Logan had in her. "How do you know?" She wasn't so sure. What extremes would the kidnappers' boss have gone to in discovering the secret of the lynx?

"Because I know you. Your best weapon is your brain, Poppy. You would devise a way to keep yourself alive until we found you." Logan folded his arms across his chest. "So, back to D.C. What happened to not putting yourself in a glass box again?"

"This is the right move, and you know it." He had to support her in this decision. If he refused to go along with it, Brody and the others would back him rather than her. The plan might not be the best one, but it was the only option to draw out the kidnappers and their boss.

Poppy had to do this. If she didn't, the next kidnapping victim would be Sage. She refused to hide away like a coward while her sister was in the line of fire.

Jesse sighed and dropped onto the nearest breakfast barstool. "We won't like your plan, will we?"

She kept her attention focused on Logan as she shook her head. "I don't see another way."

"Bait?" His hands wrapped around her upper arms and drew her toward him. "You're planning to use yourself as bait?"

"Can you think of a better way to draw them out and keep my sister safe?"

"Let Zane work his magic for 48 hours. We'll do our part to dig into the research, too, and find the answers we need without putting your life at risk."

She shook her head. "That's too long. I can't take the chance they'll go after Sage."

"Do you believe Brody and the rest of us would allow Sage to be harmed in any way? Baby, Brody would kill anyone who even looked at his wife intending to harm her. He knows she's at risk. By this time, he's heightened security so much he'll know every breath she takes. No one will touch your sister."

"Brody can't remain vigilant every minute. He has to sleep sometime. Not only that, Texas Team is still on the mission rotation schedule for two more weeks. Brent could send your team back into the field." Fortress was shorthanded, and Logan's boss constantly recruited and trained new teams to take on missions and jobs offered to Fortress for a premium price tag.

"Take Sage out of the equation for a moment. Do you honestly think I would leave you unprotected when you have an unknown enemy stalking you?"

"If your team is deployed, you have to go with them. They need you."

"We always have a choice. I can choose to go with my team, or I can ask Brent to assign another operative to cover for me."

"But...."

Logan cut her off. "Brent won't send us on a mission when we already have one. You and Sage are our mission. Texas Team won't accept another assignment until you and your sister are safe."

"A nice sentiment, but your stance can't go on indefinitely. Brent needs you."

"I need you to be safe, Poppy. I'll do whatever it takes to bring that to pass, including taking time off from work or quitting if he refuses my leave. Nothing matters more to me than you."

"The boss won't fire us," Jesse said. "He's the first one to tell recruits that family comes first with Fortress. We protect our own."

Stunned, she remained speechless for long seconds. "But I'm not family."

"Aren't you?" Logan bent his head and kissed her lightly. "Have you forgotten our agreement already?"

"Agreement?" Jesse straightened. "What did I miss?"

"Poppy and I are dating. We sealed the bargain with a kiss."

She smiled. "More than one." Excellent kisses that she would dream about for a long time.

"Even better. You're not weaseling out of our deal."

"Please," Jesse muttered. "Spare me."

Poppy seized the opening he'd given her. "What's wrong?"

"Nothing except you lovebirds are causing me to cringe. Too much sap flowing in this kitchen."

"Aww, come on, Jesse. That's not like you. I expected snarky remarks, not a grumpy attitude."

He snorted. "You're a fine one to talk. You corner the market on attitude."

"True statement. However, in this case, I'm concerned. Tell us what's going on. We're good listeners."

"Pass."

Hmm. Looked like the medic would be a harder man to coerce into talking than she'd supposed. One glance at Logan revealed the amusement glinting in his eyes.

Poppy turned back to Jesse. "I'm available if you want to vent, and I'm a vault with information."

"I'll keep it in mind."

Right. She wouldn't hold her breath, but didn't have time to press the matter. Besides, they still needed to come to an agreement on her desire to return to Washington. "Logan, I'm serious about contacting Brent. It's important to go back to D.C."

"Why? We've already established your need to protect Sage by offering yourself as bait isn't a viable reason to beard the lions in the glass den." He frowned. "I know you're holding something back, Poppy. Time to come clean."

Dismay filled her. He knew? How? "Am I that transparent?"

"Not to most people. Brody and I noticed during the video call with your parents."

"You said they lied." Jesse rested his folded arms on the breakfast bar, watching Poppy. "What did they lie about?"

Her face burned. "I'm not sure they did."

Logan's eyebrow rose.

"No proof," she reminded him. Just a mountain of suspicions and vague memories of whispers about a lynx.

"Poppy."

"I need to check it out. I can't do that unless I'm in D.C. This isn't the kind of investigation I can do from afar. Too many ways for information to end up in the wrong hands."

"The person aiming to use you as leverage will discover you're looking into this lynx connection?"

"Why not? Zane seems to be a miracle worker on the Internet. I'm beginning to believe no information is truly safe."

"Z is in a class all his own. However, exceptional tech people are available for hire, and Things One and Two work for a person willing to go to great expense to find any information about this lynx."

"Wonder what all the interest is in a wild cat," Jesse said.

Poppy bit her lip and remained mute. What if she was wrong? Worse, what if she was right and her parents had lied to her and Sage their whole lives?

"Tell us what you know." Logan wrapped his hand around hers and squeezed gently. "No more delays. Your life is on the line."

"I don't have proof, just suspicions, and those are nebulous. I could be chasing the wrong lead." She tugged her hand free of Logan's and paced. She always thought better when she moved.

"Talk. We'll help you think it through."

Poppy thrust her fingers into her hair and winced when she encountered her stitches. She paced back toward the two men. "Last night wasn't the first time I've heard the word lynx."

"When was the first time?" Jesse asked.

"I was in middle school, maybe in eighth grade. Dad was out of the military and already into politics by that time. I was home sick from school on the day I first overheard my father use the term. I went to the kitchen for a drink, and Dad was saying to Mom that if he ran for a higher office, they would have to bury the cat. We never had a cat."

"Did he say anything else?" Logan asked.

She shook her head. "I sneezed and messed up any chance of hearing more. They changed the subject. That snippet of conversation made little sense to me then or now."

"Except you connected it to the lynx question. Why?"

"The next time I overheard a mention of a cat, Mom actually said lynx. I was a senior then and making plans to attend college. Mom asked Dad if he thought I would be safe when I left home."

"How did he respond?"

"He played down her concern, said something about not having inquiries for years. Why was she worried? Mom replied that someone could find the lynx if he dug deep enough."

"I can't imagine you letting something unusual drop without poking it with a stick. Did you ask them about it?"

"Of course. Dad grew angry. Mom laughed and claimed I'd misunderstood, that she'd said the word link, not lynx. Then she told me eavesdropping was rude, and I was raised better than that."

"Huh." Logan's brow furrowed. "Did they reference a lynx after that?"

"Not in my hearing."

"Did you and Sage talk about it?"

"After I left for college, we didn't speak of it again."

"We should ask Sage if she overheard references to a lynx or cat after you left home." Jesse pulled out his phone. "Want me to text Brody and arrange a time to meet?"

"Do it." Logan refreshed Poppy's coffee. "You sure I can't talk you into waiting two days before we head to Washington?"

"I don't want to wait. I have a gut feeling that Things One and Two will be back on the job before long."

"Perhaps."

"You think I'm wrong?"

He refilled his own mug. "That remains to be seen."

"What does that mean?"

"If their boss is angry enough at their failure to keep you under wraps, your kidnappers might be taking a dirt nap now." Jesse stood. "Brody said to give them an hour. He also wanted to know if he and Sage should bring lunch."

"Oh, yes." Poppy pressed a hand to her stomach as it growled. "Food."

Logan laughed. "Tell Brody that's a definite yes on lunch. The sooner, the better."

Forty-five minutes later, Poppy descended the stairs at a fast clip and hurried to the kitchen where her sister and brother-in-law unloaded bags of takeout with Logan and Jesse's helping hands.

She breathed deep and moaned. "You brought lasagna from Luigi's, didn't you?"

Sage laughed. "Luigi put a rush on the order. We thought you would appreciate the treat."

"Did you bring Teresa's famous chocolate cake for dessert?"

"Please." Her sister pressed a hand to her heart. "Would I forget the best item on Luigi's fine menu?" She pointed to the remaining bag on the counter. "Five large slices of cake with Teresa's compliments."

"As soon as my headache goes away, I'll have to resume jogging again." More than worth the extra miles she'd have to pound out, though. Teresa's cakes were legendary in Hartman.

Jesse glanced at her. "How bad is the pain?"

"Tolerable." She waved his concern aside. "I'm fine."

"Uh huh. How long ago did you take pain meds?"

Poppy shrugged without saying a word. How much trouble would she be in if she admitted to not taking any pain medicine?

Unfortunately, the medic wasn't fooled for one minute. Jesse rolled his eyes. "You're as bad as my teammates. You took nothing."

She refused to admit the truth. What was the point? Poppy had been found out.

"Oh, Poppy," Sage said. "You should have taken the medicine your doctor prescribed. You need to stay on top of pain or it's harder to control."

"She's right," Brody chimed in. "We've all been in your shoes. Now is not the time to suffer through pain. We need you in top form, especially that sharp mind of yours. You won't be at your best if you're hurting so much you can't think or sleep."

"I didn't want to take pain meds on top of whatever the kidnappers gave me. We don't even know what it is yet."

"Yeah, we do. Remember, I checked the results from the tests on your blood. They gave you ketamine," Jesse said. "Easy to purchase on the street. I have mild pain medicine in my mike bag that won't interact with the drug. We use it to control pain when we need to stay alert in the field. Will you take it if I give you a few doses to try?"

Although Poppy hated to give in, her headache was growing unwieldy. Perhaps they were right.

Logan cupped her chin and turned Poppy's face up to his. "Take the meds, sweetheart," he murmured. He ignored Sage's gasp of surprise. "Please."

Poppy's heart melted at the sweet name. How could she resist him? "All right."

He bent and brushed his mouth over hers, the touch light as the kiss from a butterfly's wings.

She shivered, wishing they were alone so she could enjoy more kisses from this man.

Brody whistled. "I guess Ivan doesn't know about this or we would have heard the explosion all the way from Washington."

Logan looked at him. "No, he doesn't, and you won't tell him. I'll take care of it."

"Fine with me. I've already faced an inquisition from the vice president. I have no interest in repeating the experience. Ivan Reynolds is an intimidating man."

"Oh, please," Sage scoffed. "Dad isn't that bad."

Logan and Brody faced her. Brody said, "Baby, you've forgotten the closed-door meetings I had with your father before he allowed me to place my ring on your finger. Your father is ten levels worse than bad."

Poppy and Sage exchanged glances, then burst into laughter.

"Listen to them," he groused to his teammates. "We'll gain no sympathy from that corner."

"A pure crime," Logan agreed.

Jesse headed for the food. "The crime is letting our food get cold. Let's eat. I'm starving."

"Nothing new about that." Poppy brushed past him to help Sage hand out the takeout containers along with the plastic utensils.

Logan gave each person a bottle of water. "I don't have iced tea. Haven't been home long enough to make it."

"Water is fine." Sage took her food to the dining table and sat down. The others joined her. "So, why are we having a lunch meeting, Logan?"

"We wanted to ask you a few questions and make travel plans."

She glanced at Poppy. "You're going into hiding?"

"No way. The kidnappers aren't scaring me off."

"You must be afraid, Sis. I am."

"Same, but I refuse to run to a remote location and cower under a blanket while the Texas Team actively pursues every lead to run these guys down."

Sage dropped her fork onto her plate and sat back. "If you aren't going into hiding, where are you going?"

Brody narrowed his eyes and pointed at Poppy with his fork. "No, Poppy. You're not doing it."

"Have a better idea?"

"What idea?" Sage demanded, looking from her husband to her sister. "Tell me what I missed."

"I'm going to D.C."

"No, you're not." Brody scooped a bite of lasagna onto his fork. "I'm surprised you even considered the idea, Logan."

Before Logan could defend himself, Poppy jumped in. "He doesn't have a choice. Either he goes with me or I'll go alone."

"That's not how this bodyguard gig works, Reynolds." Her brother-in-law's jaw hardened. "We call the shots, not you. While we're responsible for your safety, you will do exactly what we tell you to do."

She rolled her eyes, then asked Sage, "Does he pull this He-Man routine with you all the time?"

"Only every other day."

"Does it work?"

Her sister grinned. "What do you think?"

"That's what I thought." She turned back to Brody. "Let's review, Brody. First, you are my brother-in-law, not my jailer. Second, while you're part of my protection detail, I'm the principal, and my choice is to go to D.C. Your job is to set up protection while I do my job, but not interfere. Third, I'll do anything to keep Sage safe."

"Explain that," he demanded.

"Watch the tone," Logan warned.

"Zip it, Fletcher. What's this about Sage being in danger, Poppy?"

"The kidnappers said their boss didn't care which of us they used for leverage. I think they grabbed me because they thought I was an easier target."

"They were wrong," Logan said. "You delayed them, then escaped."

Yes, she had slipped out of captivity with help from Zane. Poppy raised her chin. "They said if I didn't give them the information they wanted, they'd come back for Sage."

Brody scowled. "They won't touch her."

"Things One and Two will try."

"If they're still alive. Whether or not they try, the kidnappers will fail."

"You need one of them so you can question them, right?"

"It would help," Brody admitted.

"Then let's draw them out. The most visible place I can go is to see Mom and Dad."

"I'm going with you," Sage said. "You're not doing this alone."

"She won't be alone." Logan pushed his empty plate aside. "I'm not letting Poppy out of my sight."

"It's not the same. I should go, too. What better way to draw them out than for both of us to be in the limelight? How can they resist?"

"That's exactly the reason you shouldn't be out in the open," Brody snapped. "The last thing we want is for them to get their hands on both of you."

"He's right." Poppy hated to admit it since she usually argued with Brody on principle. "We're better off letting me be the bait since they already came after me once."

"They have to know you'll be ready for them," Sage said. "Why would they try again?"

"Same logic applies to you," Poppy pointed out. "The kidnappers have to be dense not to suspect Brody will tighten your security."

"Short of locking me in a room, Brody can't keep me from going along or finding my way to Washington."

"This is a lame plan," Jesse muttered. "We should shuttle both of you off to a tropical island for a long vacation with another team to keep you out of trouble while we track down the thugs and their boss."

Brody gave a brief nod. "I like it."

"Jesse doesn't get a vote," Sage said. "Right, Poppy?"

"Exactly. Now that we have the matter of our next stop decided, we need to ask Sage a few questions."

"Nothing's been decided," Jesse protested. "You're bulldozing right over our objections."

"Tough," Sage and Poppy said at the same time.

"You're worried about our safety?" Poppy folded her arms across her chest. "Fine. Make whatever plans are necessary to ensure our safety, and let us help you put these guys behind bars."

Sage smiled, her expression a little smug. "Ditto. So, Poppy, what did you want to ask me?"

"Do you remember overhearing Mom or Dad talking about a lynx after I went to college?"

Her sister was quiet a moment, then said, "I heard Mom mention that word once."

"What did she say?"

"That I misunderstood and to never mention that word again to anyone." Sage looked at Poppy, her expression grim. "For the first time that I remember, Mom lied to me."

Chapter Twelve

Logan threaded his fingers through Poppy's and squeezed gently as the sadness in Sage's eyes deepened. "Did you confront your mom about the lie, Sage?"

She flinched. "Confront is too strong a term. I'm not Poppy. However, I called Mom on it. She said some things should never see the light of day or there could be dangerous consequences. This subject was one of them."

Sage drained the rest of her water and set the empty bottle aside. "Mom changed the subject, acting like we'd never had that conversation. It was as though someone had flipped a switch inside her, and she had become a different person, then settled back into being Mom, the sweet woman who loves entertaining and adores Dad."

Jesse's eyebrows shot up. "That's an interesting observation."

Poppy gestured to her sister with her half-empty bottle. "Sage is right. I didn't think of it in those terms, but she's right. Mom acted the same way with me."

"Why would she lie?" Brody asked. "Why not tell you the cat was a national security matter and to drop the subject?"

"Good question." Logan frowned. "Why make a big deal out of it when you were exposed to other high-stakes security matters at other times during your father's political career? You and Sage were trained from childhood to keep information you might learn a secret from anyone outside your immediate family."

"Exactly," Poppy said. "We would have shrugged and moved on to the next item on our busy agendas. Based on her reaction, I knew this was very different."

"Dad had to know," Sage added. "He and Mom never keep secrets from each other."

"They're protecting this lynx." Brody wrapped an arm around his wife's shoulders. "We need to find out what the lynx is and who wants it bad enough to come after the second most powerful man in the world to get it."

"Could be anything. Leaders of trading partners have gifted our parents with works of arts and books of all kinds."

"Paintings and other handmade items, too," Poppy said. "Several state governors did the same. I can't count the number of presents that feature wildlife because preservation is a passion of our parents."

"We can't forget the gifts from wildlife charities that they contribute to each year," Sage added. "Narrowing down the right item with a lynx on it or in it will be a humongous task."

Logan looked at Brody, who wore an unreadable expression. Dismay grew in his gut. The sisters' thoughts automatically turned to gifts from outsiders. Perhaps he and Brody were on the wrong trail. Wouldn't be the first time. However, to ignore the lynx connection to a mission or an operative was foolish.

"What is it?" Poppy asked.

Jesse rose from the table and headed for the coffeemaker. "Why do you assume the lynx is a gift?"

"You don't?"

"Nope." He retrieved his coffee mug from the counter and poured more steaming liquid into the cup. "Your father has been in politics for years."

"And?"

"People at the upper echelons of politics will have knowledge of missions and names of people who work those missions."

Sage groaned and covered her face with her hands. "Do you know how many possibilities this opens up?"

"Too many to name."

"You know more than you're saying," Poppy said to Logan. "You and Brody. Spill, Fletcher. Let's hear this secret."

Sage nudged her husband with her elbow as Jesse returned to his seat. "Same goes for you, sweetheart. Tell us what you know. Maybe your knowledge will help solve this puzzle. I want my sister safe, and knowledge is the best way to steer clear of danger."

Brody gave a chin lift to Logan.

Guess the ball was in his court. "We work with several groups when we're on missions. Some teams are employed by Fortress. Some aren't."

Poppy leaned toward Logan. "You heard someone mention a lynx while deployed?"

He nodded. "Look, we can't tell you a lot because we heard a rumor without basis in fact."

"The rumor stuck out, though, didn't it?"

Definitely.

"What did you hear, Logan?" Sage asked. "Was it enough to tell us where to look for this cat?" She glanced at Poppy. "I'm still saying the lynx has to be a work of art or a statue."

"Why do you say that?"

"I overheard Mom say they needed to bury the lynx deeper."

Poppy frowned. "Bury the lynx," she murmured. "It sounds like a pet, but who would want a lynx for a house pet? Logan, are you able to say where you were when you heard the rumor?"

"South America." The information was vague enough that the ladies wouldn't have a clue what mission the team had been sent to complete or the time frame.

"What did you hear about the lynx?" Sage asked. "Are we right? Is this art or perhaps a sculpture?"

He glanced at Brody, who said, "Neither. The team we were working with on the mission was a retired Special Forces group from another black ops company. The team had been working primarily in Europe, and their CEO asked Brent to send in a team familiar with that part of the world to help with intelligence and serve as backup. We were available, so the boss sent us."

Logan picked up the story. "On the flight home, the other team mentioned someone known as Lynx, who had been active in Europe until about ten years ago."

"An operative, an assassin, an agent?" Poppy asked.

"Agent."

Sage's mouth gaped. "FBI?"

"Most likely CIA. The agent had quite a reputation for stealing the most securely held files and documents without tipping off anyone to his or her presence. Lynx was known for clean kills when given the order."

"Had to be CIA," Poppy murmured. "Did the operatives know the identity of Lynx?"

"I'm afraid not. No one ever captured an image of him or her."

"That's some accomplishment." Jesse stretched his legs out under the table. "Was Lynx just that lucky?"

"I don't think so," Brody said. "You can't walk down the street without cameras and cell phones capturing your image, much less pull off crimes without someone noticing."

"Lynx waltzing in and out of secured areas and making off with the goods without being seen is a scary thought," Sage said. "Lynx's moniker should have been Ghost."

Logan huffed out a laugh. "Couldn't use that name. A rogue operative in The Company used the name Ghost."

"Do you know this Ghost person?"

"Fortress caught him and eventually handed him off to the government."

Poppy's eyebrow rose. "Eventually?"

"One of our black ops teams needed information from him. Ghost wasn't inclined to cooperate."

"I guess the interrogators were persuasive."

"They're well trained." Understatement of the century. "No one withstands our interrogators for long."

"Remind me not to cross one of them. Something tells me I wouldn't win the skirmish."

"You've already met two."

"Who?"

"Nate Armstrong and Alex Morgan."

"But they seem so nice," Sage said.

All three men chuckled. "They are," Jesse said. "But when they're working, they're all business."

"Especially when one of our own is at risk." Logan threaded his fingers through Poppy's. He studied her expression a moment, then said, "What are you thinking?"

"I hope the lynx is a work of art or a sculpture, but I'm afraid the reference is to that agent the operatives mentioned."

"Probably." Did Poppy realize the trouble he and his team would cause when they continued to dig for information?

Poppy sighed and dragged a hand down her face, grimacing when she brushed against the bruise on her jaw. "This will cause big trouble."

"How?" Sage asked.

"In order to protect you and Poppy, we have to dig deep for information about Lynx," Logan answered. "Although we'll do our best to stay under the radar, word will leak."

"Unless we move fast enough to uncover the information we need and warn Lynx of the danger coming before it lands on the agent's doorstep," Brody said.

"Maybe Mom and Dad can help." Sage's expression was hopeful. "If they know who Lynx is, they can warn the agent to be ready for trouble."

"Nice thought."

"You don't think they'll cooperate?"

"They've been denying the existence of this agent for years, including today in the video conference with Poppy. I don't see a reason for them to change their behavior."

"Your parents will see it as a way to protect this agent." Jesse stood. "Time for me to take another walk about the perimeter. I'll be back soon."

As the door closed behind the medic, Sage said, "I don't know what to do if Mom and Dad won't help us or this agent."

"I don't think either of those conclusions is true," Brody said, his voice gentle. "Your parents want to put you and Poppy under lock and key to protect you."

"No." Her eyes flashed with anger. "I won't leave you."

He winked at her. "Good to know."

"What about the agent? Will they leave the agent out in the cold with no warning?"

"Agents are careful and more than a little paranoid. They spend too much time dealing with the worst of humanity not to be. Lynx has plenty of skills to protect himself."

Sage turned to Poppy. "What's next?"

"D.C."

"Why?"

"Two reasons. One, I want to draw these creeps out so Logan, Brody, and the others can take them down and end this threat."

She scowled. "Poor plan. In case you wanted to know my opinion."

"I told her the same thing." Did no good, though. He wouldn't have any more luck than her father at controlling Poppy's movements. She was a force unto herself, with a mind of her own, and she was as stubborn as the proverbial mule. Once she had decided, nothing short of dynamite would change it.

"Still not convinced," Brody said, scowling. "What's the second reason for setting yourself up for another kidnapping attempt?"

Jesse returned to sit at the table with the others. "Did I miss anything?"

"A discussion of why Poppy feels the need to put herself out there as bait by returning to Washington." He motioned to Poppy to continue her explanation.

"I need someone with an insider's knowledge of D.C."

"Who has more insider knowledge than you and Sage?" Jesse asked.

"Simone Kent. She's a historian who works for a think tank outside of the nation's capital."

"What makes her your go-to resource?"

Poppy grinned. "She is the best computer hacker I know. If you want a piece of information tracked down, Simone is the one to contact."

"We shouldn't involve anyone from outside in this search." Logan knew all too well how quickly rumors spread and information leaked to the wrong people. He had the scars to prove it. "Too dangerous, and too great a risk that our search for Lynx will leak."

"I don't want to involve Simone." Sage stood with a grimace and grabbed another bottle of water, which Brody opened for her.

Logan noted the concern in his friend's eyes. Sage's rheumatoid arthritis must be flaring up today.

"Why not?" Poppy asked. "She's in a perfect position to give us a hand."

"You heard what Logan said. We can't drag Simone into a dangerous situation."

"I can almost guarantee she already knows or has an inkling of what's going on."

"Zane can handle any hacking you need," Brody pointed out. "Fortress also has a host of other hackers who are almost as good as he is. You don't need to involve your friend in this."

She shook her head. "This investigation could blow up in our faces. Zane helped me. I'd rather not drag him any deeper into this debacle."

Jesse's brows knitted. "But you don't mind putting your friend in harm's way?"

"She knows how to disappear and reinvent herself, and she likes nothing better than thumbing her nose at the government."

Logan looked at Brody and saw the same reluctance in his friend's eyes that he felt. When his team leader gave a slight nod, Logan said, "I'll call Brent to find out if a jet is available." No way would he take the Reynolds sisters to Washington on a commercial flight. "If not, we wait until a company jet is free and work from here in the meantime. Agreed?"

"Thanks." Poppy leaned close and brushed his mouth with hers.

When Logan opened his eyes, he noticed that everyone else at the table had their attention glued to him and Poppy with varying expression of amusement. "Get used to it. That won't be the last kiss you see between us." He hoped.

"Takes getting used to after months of denials," Jesse said. "When are you going to tell Ivan and Beverly?"

"The first chance I get."

"Best of luck, buddy. I don't think the vice president will be happy with the news."

Brody gave a wry laugh. "He's not the one Logan should worry about."

The medic stared. "Beverly is the sweetest woman I've ever met."

Sage and Poppy exchanged glances and burst into laughter. "If anyone tells you Mom's bark is worse than her bite, they're lying," Sage said. "If she thinks you're a threat to one of us, she'll act like a lioness protecting her cubs. You don't want to cross her or threaten us or Dad. She'll take you out with a smile on her face before you see her coming."

#

Chapter Thirteen

Logan stepped outside onto the deck to make the call to his boss. Even though Brent wouldn't like the change in plans, he wouldn't be surprised. After so many months of interacting with Poppy, her tenacity was legendary around Fortress. This time, however, her life was at stake.

Wasn't it?

He leaned against the wooden railing and pondered what he'd learned in the past few hours. The moment Logan learned Poppy was missing, his world stopped while he focused on locating and rescuing the woman who meant so much to him. Now that she was safe for the moment, Logan had time to consider her kidnapping.

No actual harm had been done, although Logan planned to plant his fist in the face of Thing Two in the exact spot where the thug had nailed Poppy with his punch.

Poppy's kidnapping didn't make sense. Nab the vice president's daughter, and you had serious leverage. But for what reason? To draw out Lynx, a probable agent. What Logan didn't understand was why the men had taken Poppy. What connection did she have to Lynx? In order for her to be used as a pawn, she had to know the mysterious agent.

Who could it be? No question in his mind the vice president and his wife knew the identity of this person and were determined to protect him or her. Was it a relative, a friend, a person from their past? Whoever it was, this person was connected enough to Poppy and Sage for the kidnappers to be sure Lynx would come out of hiding to save them.

Logan tightened his jaw. He didn't like this at all. While Lynx had been silent enough to protect his identity, someone had leaked enough information that the mastermind behind the kidnapping had pieces of the puzzle of the agent's identity. Knowing the feds as he did, Logan didn't count on their cooperation in this investigation. In fact, they'd impede his team and spirit the agent out of reach.

If that happened, Poppy and Sage would remain in danger, along with their parents. The kidnappers must suspect Ivan and Beverly knew the Lynx's identity. Otherwise, they wouldn't have threatened the daughters.

His reasoning didn't make him feel any better. Any way you sliced it, this was bad news. The only way to keep Poppy and her sister safe was to hide them in an inaccessible place with another team of operatives to keep watch over them while Logan's team went after the kidnappers.

He grimaced. Not going to happen. The Reynolds sisters wouldn't go along with any plan that included running from trouble and leaving their parents out in the open.

No other choice, he realized. The best way to protect the women? Take them to Washington and surround them with security so tight the kidnappers had no chance of getting to them. That plan would bring its own set of problems to handle.

Logan slid his phone from his pocket and called his boss. Brent answered on the first ring.

"Yeah, Maddox. What do you need, Logan?"

"A jet."

Silence. "You're going to Washington."

"Yes, sir."

"You're sure this is a good plan?"

"No, sir. It's terrible."

"And you're going through with it. Why?"

"Have you tried to say no to a strong, stubborn, and beautiful woman?"

Brent laughed. "All the time, my friend. You just described my wife."

"So, you understand why I couldn't say no."

"Sure. Poppy would smile at you and do what she wanted without you by her side."

"Yes, sir. Exactly."

"What's her plan, then?"

"Using herself as bait."

A groan. "I was afraid of that. How are you going to handle security?"

"We're working on a plan."

"If you need a safe house, we have three available within an hour of D.C."

Amusement flashed through Logan. "You already expected we'd go to the capital."

"That's what I get paid to do. Zane volunteered to take on the role of your tech support. I believe he has a soft spot for Poppy."

"She feels the same about him. I owe him a debt, Brent."

"We all do. Good thing he's not keeping score. Do you want us to stock one of the safe houses?"

"We'd appreciate it."

"Done. Sage is going, too?"

"Unless Brody convinces her to stay home."

A snort. "Not likely. We'll have the safe house ready soon. How quickly do you want to leave?"

He knew what Poppy would say. Right now. Not going to happen, though. Logan didn't want to arrive in the Washington area during daylight hours. The chances of someone cracking Fortress cybersecurity to track Poppy's movements were slim to none. No need to allow the enemy to get a look at them before they were ready to appear on the scene to draw attention. "I'd prefer to leave around 7 o'clock tonight. Gives us time to nail down a security plan and purchase clothes for Poppy before we leave."

Logan also wanted Poppy to rest before they left. That he left unsaid.

"Anything else you need to tell me?"

He froze. Had Brody or one of his other teammates spilled the news about him and Poppy starting a dating relationship? "Sir?"

"Logan."

Fine. Might as well tell his boss the truth. He'd find out soon through the company grapevine, anyway. Besides, Brent didn't appreciate being blindsided by news about his operatives. "Poppy and I are dating."

The silence was long and seemed heavy. Not good. Logan tightened his grip around the phone. "I know the timing is terrible."

"You think?" Sarcasm came through loud and clear.

He flinched. Whew. Definitely not good. "I had to wait until now. Poppy wasn't ready, not after what she went through in Mexico. When she was kidnapped this time, I realized if I waited any longer, I might lose her. I can't take that chance, sir."

"Like that, is it?"

"Yes, sir."

"I need you to be brutally honest with yourself and with me. How objective are you?"

"Enough."

"Try again."

"Boss...."

"As her bodyguard, you're responsible for her safety."

"I know that, sir."

"I hope you're right, Fletcher. One wrong move, and you'll lose everything. A second of distraction could end her life and yours or one of your teammates. Think about that long and hard before you blithely tell me you're objective enough to do the job. I'll leave the logistics of the situation to you and your teammates to work out. Cooperate with their decision or I'll replace you on this mission."

His face burned. Really? After all the training and time he'd spent on missions with his team, he would just be replaced because his heart was involved? Yeah, Logan understood his objectivity was lower than normal. That didn't mean he couldn't function in the field. Of all people, he would do absolutely anything necessary to protect the woman who had etched her name on his heart. None of his teammates cared as much for Poppy as he did. To his way of thinking, that made him the perfect person to protect her.

"Yes, sir," he bit out. As much as he disagreed with Brent's assessment, no one disrespected the boss without serious consequences.

"The jet will be on the tarmac and ready to go wheels up at 7:00 p.m. Don't be late. I have another team who needs the jet. The rest of the jets are already assigned."

"We'll be there. Thanks." He ended the call before he did something stupid, like smart off to the man who was giving him great latitude at the moment.

Logan shoved the phone into one of his cargo pockets and gripped the rail. Waves of fury washed through him. He hated for anyone to question his integrity. After spending two years undercover, Logan spoke the truth unless forced to lie on an op to protect himself, his teammates, or their principals. To be questioned like this by a man he respected so highly stung.

Behind him, the door opened. When the air felt charged, he knew without turning around that Poppy had joined him on the deck. He held out his hand to her.

Seconds later, her small, soft hand slipped into his. "How did it go?"

"Give me a couple of minutes before we talk."

Poppy studied his expression for a moment. She stepped close and wrapped her arms around his middle. For several minutes, Poppy held him, comfortable with the silence.

Little by little, the fury gnawing at his gut melted away, leaving an ache. He shoved the pain behind a mental steel door to deal with later. Since when had he become so sappy? He shouldn't care that Brent didn't trust his judgment.

But he did. A lot. Brent Maddox was one of the finest men he knew. Was he right?

Logan tightened his hold on Poppy. This was not the time to question himself. The stakes were too high. If he hesitated at the wrong time to second guess himself, Poppy or one of the guys might pay the price.

"Ready to talk now?"

"Brent will have a jet ready for us."

She waited.

Smart lady. "He wasn't happy that we're dating."

Poppy stiffened. "What business is it of his? We're adults. We can date who we want."

"He's not disputing our right to starting a relationship. His problem is the timing. Brent is concerned you'll be at risk because I'm distracted."

"Won't be a problem."

Logan freed one arm and lifted her chin with his hand. He captured her mouth with his and indulged in the long and possessive kiss he'd been aching to share with her. Only her. The longer he kissed Poppy, the hotter the flames leaped between them until he had to pull back before they both burned to ash.

He lifted his head. "That's why dating now is a problem, baby. You're a distraction in the best way possible. But under these circumstances, the distraction is dangerous."

"We'll figure it out. I meant what I told my father. My protection will be you and your team, or no one. I don't trust anyone else."

"Fortress has other teams. You know and like the Wolf Pack. They're available for an assignment."

"No."

Logan couldn't deny the satisfaction he felt over her steadfast trust in him and his teammates. That satisfaction went a long way in soothing his disappointment with Brent's response. "If you change your mind...."

"I won't."

"If you do, tell me. I'll have Eli and his team assigned."

"What else did Brent say?"

"He'll have a jet ready to fly us to Washington at 7:00 tonight."

She tilted her head up to look at him, frowning. "Why can't we leave sooner?"

"We need a plan in place before we leave Nashville." Logan handed Poppy his phone. "Text your friend. Tell her you'll call from a blocked number in five minutes."

She did as he'd said. "Now what?"

He walked with Poppy toward the house. "We'll go inside and talk to her so the others can hear what's said. Saves time since they'll want to know what's said, anyway."

Brody and Sage glanced up when Logan and Poppy walked into the kitchen. "We're set?" Brody asked.

"Jet will be ready at 7:00 tonight."

"Excellent. We should have enough time to come up with a plan by then. Hotel or safe house?"

"Safe house." He seated Poppy at the table across from her sister, then said, "As much as I want to be in charge of this operation, I can't."

Brody straightened, his eyes narrowing. "Brent's decision?"

"Mine." Didn't pay to throw his boss under the bus. "He pointed out that I would be distracted on this mission. He's right. For operational safety, I'll step back and maintain my role as Poppy's bodyguard."

His team leader stood and pulled out his phone. "I'll talk to the boss."

"No, Brody. He left the decision up to the team. This is what's best for everyone's safety."

"Although I know you can handle the lead, I'll respect your wishes."

"Call Sawyer and Max to the house, and let's put our heads together. It's time to form a plan to keep Poppy and Sage safe."

"We should call Simone," Poppy said.

Logan sat in the chair next to hers. "Go ahead."

She called her friend's number and tapped the speaker button. When Simone answered after the first ring, Poppy said, "It's me. Can you talk?"

"I'm alone in a secure location. Are you safe?"

"For the moment."

"How can I help?"

"Ever heard of Lynx?"

"Rumors only, and not in a while. Why?"

"A couple of beefy guys kidnapped me to use me as leverage. They want Lynx."

"Where are you?" Simone said, her voice sharp. "I'll send help and schedule a flight to come to you."

"Don't bother. Told you, Simone. I'm safe for the moment. In fact, I have a group of first-class black ops guys as my bodyguards. Besides, we're coming to Washington soon."

"How soon?"

Poppy turned to Logan, her eyebrow raised.

He shook his head. He didn't want Simone Kent, an unknown friend, to have too many details about their travel plans, at least not until his team had a chance to do background checks on her. Of course, if she was as good as Poppy said, Simone could have buried or erased any questionable items in her background.

"I'm not sure of the specifics. The timing depends on several factors. I'll call you when we arrive in the area."

Simone was silent for a beat. "Are you sure you're safe?" She sounded uneasy. The distinctive tapping of computer keys came through the speaker.

Logan's lips curved. The lady hacker was trying to pinpoint Poppy's location. Wouldn't work. The program blocking a trace of their location had been written by Zane. No matter how good Simone was at computer work, Z was better. "Don't waste your time, Ms. Kent."

Total silence for several seconds. "Who are you?"

"My name is Logan."

She sucked in a breath. "The man you call in the middle of the night, Poppy?"

"We're dating, Simone." Poppy slid a glance Logan's way. Thankfully, his girl appeared amused rather than annoyed.

"He's your security?"

"Logan is more than capable of protecting me."

"Look, I'm sure he's nice."

Nice? Logan flinched. Why that description? Nice was a painful way to describe a guy. Why didn't Simone characterize him as tough, capable, or smart? Nice was almost an insult.

He glared at Brody, whose shoulders shook with silent laughter. The jerk.

"But you need more than just a nice man to fight off trouble. I know you won't like what I'm about to say."

"Then don't waste your breath," Poppy said.

"Hear me out," Simone countered. "At least consider calling the members of your Secret Service protection detail and ask them to do their jobs for a few days. They should earn their salaries for once."

"That's not fair."

"You're too kind, Poppy. Your detail hasn't had to work all that hard in the past year."

"Not true, and you know it. The Secret Service doesn't pay their people to sit around under a shade tree, sip sweet tea, and watch the clouds roll by. I'm sure my team was reassigned to someone more important when I refused their protection."

Simone laughed.

Jesse's eyebrows rose.

"What planet do you live on, my friend? Although you didn't see them, I assure you, your detail wasn't far from you during the past year."

Logan stilled, his gaze flicking to Brody. His team leader grabbed his phone and shot off a text, probably to Zane. If anyone could confirm the information quickly, it was Z.

How did Simone know Poppy's detail was still watching over her? What disturbed Logan more was that he hadn't spotted them. What else had he missed in the past year while obsessing over Poppy Reynolds?

He dragged his hand down his face. Great. What a time to discover his boss was right, that he was too involved with Poppy to remain objective enough to protect her.

"How do you know about the detail?" Poppy demanded.

Wait. What did that mean? Did Poppy know or suspect her Secret Service protection had been around, still on the job? Logan scowled. If so, why hadn't they prevented the kidnapping in the first place?

"Oh, come on. How do you think?"

"You hacked their computer system?"

"If I did, that would make me a lawbreaker and a rebel."

Oh, Simone was brilliant indeed. No admission of guilt, but what other explanation fit, especially given her skill at hacking?

Brody glanced down at his phone, read the message, then looked at Logan and nodded.

"Time to stop talking in vagaries, Ms. Kent." Logan pressed his thigh against Poppy's as he leaned closer to the phone. What he wouldn't give to see this woman's face while she spoke. Better yet would be to see her in person. Soon, he'd have the chance to judge for himself just how honest she was and how much of a friend Simone Kent was to Poppy. "We've confirmed your information about the Secret Service detail."

Poppy's head whipped toward Logan. "That fast?"

"Told you he was good."

"Who are you talking about?" Simone demanded. "Who is this hacker, and why haven't you mentioned him before now, Poppy?"

"He's a friend of Logan's. Why didn't you tell me about the detail hanging around?"

"You needed the protection whether or not you wanted it."

"You should have told me," she insisted.

"So you could complain to your father until he called them off? No. Way."

"The detail doesn't matter now. Logan and his team will keep me safe. I don't need the Secret Service."

More silence. "Logan has a team? Is he a cop?"

"Former cop, and don't hang up," Logan said. "We're all former law enforcement."

"What's your job now?"

"We're employed by Fortress Security."

"Wait. You're Brody's friend. You're part of his black ops team?"

"That's right."

Simone sighed. "I suppose you really can protect Poppy from another kidnapping attempt."

Brody frowned. "Ms. Kent, this is Brody. Do you have information we should know?"

"Maybe."

"Specifics, Simone," Poppy snapped.

"Not over a cell phone."

"Sat phone," Logan corrected. "The same man who confirmed your information designed the security on our phones. No one will break his encryption program."

"I can hack anything," she said flatly.

He opened his mouth to refute her statement and realized she was right. Given enough time, even Z's program could be breached. "Not today," he amended. "Look, it's obvious you care about Poppy. I need every bit of information you have to protect her."

"I don't have specifics."

"Give me what you have."

"Rumors about another kidnapping attempt."

When Poppy jerked, Logan covered her hand with his and squeezed. Although he'd expected the news, he had hoped for more time. Looked as though they would not get it. "When?"

"Soon. No time table. And before you ask, I haven't been able to track down the source." She sounded grim.

A soft whistle from Brody. "That says something about this group's ability to hide in plain sight."

"Yeah, nothing good." Logan sent a text of his own to Zane, asking his friend for help in tracking down the source of this rumor. "Where did you hear about it, Ms. Kent?"

"Ms. Kent is my mother. Call me Simone. The rumor came to light in a dark web chat room."

"Which one?"

"Doesn't matter. The rumor that sent me searching for confirmation has disappeared now. It's as though someone caught me tracking."

Jesse grinned at the offended tone coming through the speaker.

"Simone." Logan waited her out.

Finally, she spat out the name of the chat room. "I'm still hunting."

"Good. Do that. You'll have help soon."

"Who?" she demanded.

"The friend who created our encryption program. If he's inclined, he'll introduce himself." Logan sent Z the name of the chat room and received an immediate acknowledgment.

"How will I know it's your friend?" A soft gasp. "Never mind. Holy cow, Poppy. You didn't tell me you were friends with Zane Murphy."

"You know him?"

"By reputation only. He's a legend in the gaming community."

Logan glanced at Poppy. Would she be angry? If so, he'd apologize later for upsetting her. No matter how she felt, Logan needed the information. "How long have you been friends with Poppy?"

"Since college."

"You're good friends?"

"Very."

A muscle in his jaw twitched. "You have a strange way of showing loyalty, Simone."

"Why do you say that?"

"You troll the Net routinely. You have bots set up to alert you when things or people who matter to you are mentioned."

"So?"

"A close friend would have warned Poppy she was in danger before she was kidnapped, especially given her recent trauma. So, Simone, if you really cared about Poppy, why didn't you give her a heads up?"

"You're a jerk, Logan. For your information, I did contact Poppy to warn her."

Logan's head whipped toward Poppy. One glance was all it took for him to realize Simone Kent had spoken the truth.

Chapter Fourteen

Poppy winced. Busted. She waited for the explosive response sure to come. Didn't take long.

Logan shoved back from the table, surged to his feet, and tugged Poppy to hers. He thrust the sat phone into Brody's hand. "Excuse us."

"Logan, wait." Sage stood. Her husband held her in place by laying a hand on her shoulder.

"Hey, what's going on?" Simone's voice rose. "Poppy, are you okay?"

After a glance at the expression on Logan's face, Poppy remained silent. Oh, man. This wasn't good. Logan had never been this angry with her. Irritated, sure. Never furious. Well, he'd have to get over his anger, wouldn't he?

She lifted her chin, opened the door, and would have sailed outside on a perfect note of defiance in her exit, except Jesse stepped in front of her to walk out first.

Poppy frowned. She didn't want an audience for her dressing down. No doubt in her mind that's what was coming. She started to follow the medic when Logan stopped her.

"No," he said, voice curt. "Wait."

Simone continued to protest over Logan's abrupt end to the conversation.

Poppy ignored her. "Why?" she asked the man at her side.

"Security first, no matter what else is happening."

Jesse returned a minute later. "Clear. Where?"

"Gazebo."

A nod. "Security cam?"

"Of course. Turn off the sound." A firm order. "I don't want an audience. Got me?"

"Understood. I'll watch your six until you're safely inside, then pull back."

"Appreciate it." Logan propelled Poppy through the door, off the deck, and onto an almost non-existent path toward the back of his property. Despite his heightened emotions, he remained alert to their surroundings and careful with Poppy.

While she had to appreciate his caution, Logan's actions caused waves of guilt to assail her. Poppy opted to remain silent until they were inside the safety of his gazebo.

Logan guided her toward the woods at the back of his property, then nudged her toward the left. In the distance, a gazebo sat on a hill, windows gleaming in the sunlight.

"Oh, it's beautiful. How did I not know this was back here?"

He flicked her a glance before returning to his continuous vigilance. "My teammates helped me finish it the night before we deployed."

Helped him finish the gazebo? Logan had been constructing this building in secret. "Why didn't you tell me you were doing this? I could have helped." Especially considering her writing life was almost nonexistent at the moment. Who knew trauma could put her career on hold?

"I wanted to surprise you."

Stunned, she turned her head toward him. "You built it for me?"

He lifted one shoulder in a slight shrug. "You said you always wanted a gazebo. I wanted to give you one."

"Logan, the work must have taken you a long time. You didn't have to do this."

"Hold that thought until we're inside."

Minutes later, he tapped in a security code at the gazebo's door and ushered Poppy into the pretty building.

Her breath caught, and she stopped a few feet into the gazebo to absorb her surroundings. Books, a fireplace, comfy couches, lamps, end tables, a desk with a cushioned chair, and a laptop were the only decorations. She'd bet her last dollar the windows were bullet resistant and Logan had another exit from the large gazebo.

Her gaze locked onto the second door on the other side of the building. If that was the second exit, the door was an odd size, more like a closet. A bathroom, perhaps?

After securing the entrance door, Logan inclined his head toward the second door. "A small bathroom, so you can stay out here as long as you like when you're writing."

So, Poppy had been right about the second door. "The gazebo is amazing. I can't believe you did this for me."

"You matter to me. You have since the first moment I saw you."

Her eyes stung. "Logan."

He led her to a couch and motioned for her to sit. He folded his arms, his expression forbidding. "Explain, Poppy."

Right. Back to the business at hand. "Simone contacted me two days before the kidnapping. She told me about the rumor."

"Two days." His voice was flat. "You knew there was a real possibility that someone wanted to kidnap you, and you sat on the knowledge for 48 hours?"

Sheesh. Her actions sounded so much worse when he put it in those words. "Yes."

"Why didn't you tell me?"

"You were on a mission. The last thing I wanted to do was distract you."

"Not buying what you're selling. Try again."

Poppy scowled. "Oh, get over yourself, Fletcher. I didn't want you to come home in a body bag. You satisfied now?"

"Not even close." His voice rose with every word. "I can take care of myself. The law enforcement academy and Fortress Security poured millions of dollars into my training so I can protect myself, my team, and your stubborn self. Since when do you ignore an imminent threat to your own safety to protect me?"

Her temper spiked. "Since I fell in love with you, you big oaf." Uh oh. That's not what she'd meant to say at all.

Where Poppy had been hot, she was now ice cold. Since when did her mouth spew out whatever it wanted without her permission? Right now was not the time to tell the man she was crazy about that she was in love with him. Maybe he didn't notice.

Fat chance. Logan Fletcher noticed everything in his orbit, and he was as focused as a laser on her at that moment. Nothing short of a bomb going off or a direct attack would shift his attention.

"What did you say?"

Oh, seriously? He was going to make her repeat her blurted out confession? Fine. If he wanted repetition before he totally humiliated her, Poppy would provide the impetus for his entertainment. But, oh, he'd pay big if he hurt her. She'd had enough of that, thank you very much. "I. Love. You."

Logan's hands wrapped around Poppy's upper arms, and he lifted her to her feet. "Say it again," he demanded.

Her heart rate jumped. Wait. He wasn't setting her up for humiliation? "I love you, Logan."

His grip tightened. "You can't take it back. I won't let you."

"Lucky for you I didn't plan to withdraw the statement."

He drew her to him and slid his arms around her waist. "Again. Say it again."

"I love you." Wow, look at that? Each time she said the words, they came out easier, especially since he hadn't rejected her declaration outright in favor of laughing at her and telling her to take a hike.

He hadn't returned the statement, though. Did he love her? Did she dare ask? Poppy decided her store of courage was now officially depleted. She would prefer to live in ignorance a while longer.

His mouth came down on hers and just took possession. No other words described his actions. Where his kisses before were face-fanning hot, these kisses shot her body temperature into the scalding range. Never before had Poppy felt like this over a simple kiss.

Simple? This was anything but simple. This kiss stamped Poppy as his.

Long minutes later when Logan broke the last kiss, his eyes glittered and his mouth looked as swollen as hers felt. "You're mine, Poppy, and I love you to the moon and back. No one will ever love you as much as I do."

Her eyes widened as his words sank into her bones. Logan loved her.

"You better mean what you said, baby, because I won't let you go, and I'll kill anyone who tries to take you from me."

Joy exploded inside her. "Make a note in that fascinating brain of yours. I meant every word each time I told you I love you. I love you more than anything in this world, Logan. I adore every cranky inch of you, and I'm not going anywhere. More important, I don't want to leave your side. The only thing I want to do is walk down the church aisle one day to become your wife and have a family with you."

Triumph and humor sparked in his eyes. "Deal. I accept your proposal to be your husband and have a family. Is tomorrow too soon?"

She laughed. How could she not? Then she noticed his humor had morphed into fierce determination. Wait a second. He was serious? "Logan. You can't mean that. Tomorrow? Really?"

"I know what I want, Reynolds. Do you? Yes or no to a wedding tomorrow?"

Her answer had to be a marriage between them tomorrow was too soon. Of course it did. Who got married on one day's notice? She opened her mouth to speak her mind, and said, "Yes."

That sparked another round of kisses so hot Poppy almost combusted on the spot. When she needed a breath or feared passing out, she broke the kiss and stared up at him. "You said I was a distraction. Won't being newlyweds make me more of a detriment to your concentration?"

"You're not backing out. I want to marry you tomorrow."

Her happiness popped like a soap bubble. Trouble was her middle name these days. Did he know what he was letting himself in for? Poppy was all about the scorching-hot kisses. More than that? She just didn't know if she was ready for more. "Remember the baggage, Logan? I still have it in spades."

"Told you I'd help you unpack it and toss the suitcases. I meant it. I want you as my wife, and I want to make that happen tomorrow. We'll obtain the marriage license and get married immediately afterward. I'll have Z make an appointment for us with the justice of the peace."

"But I don't have a wedding dress." This was crazy. Who did this?

"We'll do a church wedding with all the trimmings after you're safe, if that's what you want. I'll even pose in an ungodly amount of pictures without complaining much if you insist on them. You still with me?"

"Dad will kill you if we do this." Her, too. Worse, her mother would have their hides.

A slow smile curved his mouth. "He can try. He'll fail. The only thing that matters to me is what you want. If you're on board, you'll be my wife by this time tomorrow night. I'll be by your side day and night, and no one will separate us."

"You're marrying me to protect me?"

Logan shook his head. "I'm marrying you because I love you more than life itself and have since the first moment I saw you. I can protect you, married or not. I don't care what anyone else thinks, Poppy. If I feel the need to stay in your room and sleep on the floor in front of the door to keep you safe, I'll do it. Doesn't matter to me if your dad or your intimidating mom protest that I'm in room with you as a single man. Hear me well, Poppy Reynolds. I want you to be my wife. The sooner, the better."

She watched him for a minute, two. Finally, she whispered, "All right. Tomorrow."

Satisfaction gleamed in his eyes.

"I hope you don't look back on this and regret your decision to marry me."

"Never."

Time would tell. "Are you still angry with me?"

"Yes." He captured Poppy's hand and kissed her palm. "No more secrets, baby. They're too dangerous for both of us."

"I wanted to keep you safe, Logan. I would have told you when you returned stateside."

"I'm trusting you to tell me the truth so I can protect both of us. If I can't do that, I'll turn in my resignation to Fortress immediately."

She stared. "Logan, you love your job."

"I love you more than my work. I won't be able to focus on my job if you're not brutally honest with me. We have other teams and bodyguards I would have at my back any time. If I can't be with you as your shield and protector, I have a short list of people I trust to be that for you until I have my boots on the ground."

Poppy shook her head. "You aren't resigning from Fortress." She wouldn't take away his career. It wasn't fair to him.

"I want your promise to never keep something like this from me again."

"Done."

Logan pulled out his phone and made a call. He tapped the speaker button.

"Yeah, Murphy."

"It's Logan. I need a favor."

"Ask."

"Schedule back-to-back appointments with the county clerk and a judge or justice of the peace wherever the safe house is located."

Silence. "I need a name."

"Mine only. I don't want Poppy's name mentioned anywhere on paper until we're finished."

A soft whistle from the tech guru. "You don't waste any time, do you, Fletcher?"

"Why should I? I know what I want."

"Uh huh. Does the vice president know?"

Logan said nothing.

Zane chuckled. "Guess that tells me what I need to know. Let me know what hospital to send your flowers to after Ivan Reynolds is through with you. Just a reminder that you don't want to make an enemy of the second most powerful man in the world."

"Can't be helped."

"Am I on speaker?"

"Yeah, sorry. I'm with Poppy."

"Are you on board with this, Poppy?"

"Yes." However insane this was, Poppy was all the way in.

"He's not pressuring you?"

Logan stiffened. "Zane."

"Shut up, Fletcher. It's a legitimate question given the supercharged speed of this relationship. Poppy, answer my question, sugar."

She rested her hand on his forearm while she answered Zane. "Of course he's pushing. I'd think an alien had taken over his body if Logan was a gentleman about it."

Zane laughed. "True statement. Logan, have you told Brent?"

"No. You're the only one besides Poppy who knows. Aside from my teammates and Sage, that's the way it will stay until my wedding band is on Poppy's finger."

More silence. "Has the threat level increased?"

"What do you think?"

"That I'd wring your neck if you were standing in the same room with me. Answer the question."

"The information from Simone confirmed what I suspected anyway."

"Which is?"

"Poppy's kidnapping is much more involved than just a couple of guys trying to make a big score off a political powerhouse's daughter. This is all about Lynx. Poppy was just a means to an end."

"What does that tell you?"

Logan turned toward Poppy. "She knows Lynx."

Chapter Fifteen

As soon as the jet leveled out, Logan rose from his seat and turned to face his teammates and Sage. "Poppy and I have an announcement."

"If you're going to spill the news that you're dating, it's too late. The cat's out of the bag already." Sawyer drawled.

Texas Team and Sage laughed. Even Poppy smiled at Sawyer's remark.

When the laughter petered out, Logan said, "Poppy and I are inviting you to our wedding tomorrow morning at 11:00."

Brody stalked toward Logan. "What did you say?"

"Poppy asked me to marry her, and I agreed." He glanced at his watch. "Our wedding is in exactly twelve hours. I'd like you to be my best man, and Poppy wants Sage to be her matron of honor. The rest of you can serve as witnesses. Maybe Poppy's friend Simone, too, if she wants to invite her."

"You are going to tell Ivan and Beverly, right?"

Logan shook his head. "Their appearance at the courthouse will bring a media circus in their wake. Too much of a security risk to Poppy and Sage."

"You're asking for major in-law trouble. That's not a smart move, Logan."

"I love Poppy. She loves me. If I'm with her day and night, no one will get to her. It's logical and reasonable. Why should we wait?"

"Oh, I don't know," Jesse said. "Perhaps because Poppy is expected to get married in the glare of media lights, not in secret."

"Wasting your breath, guys," Max said. "Look at Logan's face. His mind is made up. He's doing this whether or not we agree with him, so we should enjoy the event and the fireworks to follow when Ivan and Beverly find out."

Brody shook his head. "You're an idiot, buddy. Just saying. Ivan and Beverly will never forgive you for leaving them out of one of the most important days of Poppy's life."

"They'll be part of the church wedding to follow after Poppy is safe."

"What did the boss say about the wedding?" Sawyer asked.

"Before or after he yelled at me for five minutes?"

More laughter from his teammates.

Temper rising again at the remembered dressing down by his boss, Logan said, "He said my role in this op has transitioned to bodyguard duty." The words had ripped his heart out and stomped on it with cleats.

Silence followed his second announcement.

"You should have told me before now." Brody scowled at him. "I'll talk to Brent." He grabbed his phone and started toward the back of jet.

"Wait a second, Brody," Max said. "What exactly did Brent say to you, Logan?"

He thought a moment, then repeated his boss's statement. "Stepping back as lead was safest because my objectivity was suspect."

Sawyer snorted. "That's rich coming from a man who refused to allow anyone else to lead the mission to save his wife and daughter."

Brody slipped his phone back into his pocket. "It's a team decision. He'll have to live with what we decide to do."

Spoken like a genuine leader. Logan's lips twitched. "So, does that mean you're still in charge?"

"I never ceded leadership to you. You just thought you were in charge."

More laughter.

Brody turned to the rest of the Texas Team. "What's your vote?"

"Business as usual," Sawyer said.

Max and Jesse nodded in agreement.

"Done." Brody glanced at Logan. "Sorry, buddy. If you expected a cushy assignment on this op, you're out of luck. We need a plan for the next phase of this mission. Parading Poppy around Washington is off the table."

"Agreed. Too risky."

"I have to see Mom and Dad," Poppy protested. "They always have a media presence camped out across the street from their place. Plus, no one is keeping me cooped up like a prisoner again, not even someone I like. The whole point for this risk is to flush Things One and Two or their replacements out into the open."

"What if it's for your safety, Poppy?" Brody asked.

Her hands fisted. "No."

Why did no one see the panic flaring in her eyes? "Enough, Brody. She's decided. Our job is to protect, not smother."

"I'll go along with it. For now."

Logan inclined his head. That was the best concession he'd get.

"Team meeting at the conference table. Logan, take the lead. I'll join you in fifteen. Poppy, with me."

Logan narrowed his eyes. His friend better not pressure Poppy into changing her mind about marrying Logan or leaving the safe house. "Don't," he murmured.

Brody flicked him a glance that conveyed an order to shut up clearly, then held out his hand to Poppy. "Come with me. We need to talk."

"You all right with this?" Logan asked Poppy as she accepted Brody's help.

"It's fine. If you hear Brody groaning in pain, you'll know I put him in his place for annoying me."

He watched as the pair made their way to the bedroom at the back of the jet. Although he didn't like being shut out, he'd deal. If Brody upset her, though, his friend might go into this mission with a shiner. He'd allow no one to upset her. Poppy had been through enough already without a friend adding to her stress level.

And, yeah, she would not be happy with him if she knew how he felt about protecting her. Tough. She could be upset all she wanted as long as Poppy understood he loved her. His job, above all others, was to protect her when he could. This was one of those times.

With one last look at Poppy and Brody, Logan motioned for the others to join him at the conference table. He pulled up the email Zane had sent with the schematics for the house in the countryside outside of D.C. as well as the generous acreage surrounding the two-story abode. Once the information popped up on the wall screen, Logan began the planning meeting. As he and his teammates debated ideas for security and protection, Logan monitored the bedroom door.

Fifteen minutes. If Brody and Poppy didn't come out by that time, Logan would join the discussion in the bedroom, whether or not his friend and team leader liked it.

At the fourteen-minute mark, the door opened and Brody came out and strode down the aisle of the jet. He stopped to check on Sage, who was sleeping, then continued to make his way to the front.

No Poppy. Logan stopped mid-sentence and stood. "Sawyer, take over."

Seamlessly, his teammate did as ordered. "Let's look at the perimeter security. Looks like Z included the perimeters, too."

"Nice," Max said. "Fortress doesn't mess around when they set up a safe house."

Logan shoulder checked Brody in the aisle and continued toward the bedroom without speaking to his friend. Not yet, anyway. That discussion would come when they had time and the privacy to address Brody's impromptu meeting.

He opened the door and peered inside. Poppy stood with her back to the door, arms wrapped around her middle, head bowed.

"Poppy?" Her body language said Brody had upset her. The question was, had he upset Poppy enough to convince her to change her mind about marrying Logan tomorrow.

She stiffened. "Have you changed your mind, after all?"

He blinked. "About?"

"Accepting my proposal."

"No."

Poppy swung around. "Just no?"

"What else am I supposed to say? I want to marry you, baby. Brody upset you. What did he say?"

"Getting married tomorrow isn't fair to you."

He stared. "How did he come up with that?"

"I have....hangups, Logan."

"Baggage."

She nodded.

"Who doesn't? We already talked about this. I'll help you with the baggage and burn the suitcases. We can burn mine while we're at it."

"He has a point." Poppy approached, her faced flushed. "It's not fair to you. I don't want you to think I'm using you to escape a dangerous situation and as a fortress for safety."

He laughed. "You can't be serious. Poppy, I want to be your shelter in storms. If I could wrap you up in cotton and bubble wrap to keep you safe, I'd do it in a heartbeat. If you let me. If you needed me to do that. But you don't. You're strong enough to stand on your own two feet. I don't have to be your shelter, baby, but I want to be the person you turn to when things are rough."

Logan studied her red cheeks and tear-streaked face. "That's not what's bothering you, is it?" When she didn't respond, he cupped her chin with his palm and lifted her head to his. "Talk to me, Poppy. I can't help if you don't tell me what's troubling you."

She drew in a deep breath and said, "I love you more than anyone on this planet, Logan. But what if I can't handle the physical side of marriage?"

He gathered Poppy into his arms and held her against his body. "That's all you're worried about?"

She frowned. "Well, since we're getting married in less than twelve hours, it's uppermost in my mind."

"If you can't, we'll seek counseling together and wait until you can."

"What if it's a long time?"

"Then it's a long time. Look, sweetheart, the only thing that matters is putting my ring on your finger and knowing you're mine for the rest of our lives. The rest will work itself out in time."

She smiled. "You're incredible."

"You might change your mind about that when you hear my one stipulation."

"What's that?"

"You sleep in our bed and in my arms every night."

Blood drained from her face. "Logan."

"I know it's asking for a great deal of trust on your part. I won't abuse your trust, baby. You have to get used to me touching you, especially at night when we're alone. Will you do that for me?"

She nodded.

Triumph roared through Logan. If he could help Poppy get used to his touch, the rest would come in time. He knew it would.

"It's not fair to you," she murmured.

"I'll have you for a lifetime, Poppy. However long it takes for that side of our marriage to develop will be worth the delay."

Logan bent his head and kissed her for long minutes until he finally had to break the kiss or lose his almost nonexistent control. He threaded his fingers through hers. "Come on. I left my team hashing out the details of a security plan. I need to get back to the work. We don't have a long flight and must have a plan by the time we land."

He escorted her from the bedroom and left her at their seats with a brush of his mouth over hers. "Sleep if you can." After another kiss, this one longer than was wise, Logan made himself rejoin his teammates.

For the next hour, he and his team came up with plans to tighten security while still giving Poppy the freedom she craved.

"What about Simone Kent?" Jesse asked, voice low. "She's an unknown ingredient in the mix."

"Poppy trusts her," Brody said.

"Doesn't mean she should."

"We'll ask Zane to dig into her background. If she's clear, we'll use her as a resource. Z has more than enough on his plate at the moment. He could use a hand." His lips curved. "If she's as good as Poppy says, Brent will recruit her."

Perhaps. Simone didn't seem like a joiner, though. She was more of a rebel. When the pilot announced they were approaching the airport, Logan and his teammates rose from the conference table and returned to their seats.

As he wrapped his hand around Poppy's, she stirred, stretched, and turned her head toward him. "Have a nice nap?"

"Too short. Well?"

"It's a go."

"Yes!"

"After these clowns are behind bars or six feet under the ground, we'll take off on our honeymoon." He squeezed her fingers. "No deadlines, no annoying in-laws, no interruptions. Just time with you." Another squeeze. "No pressure, baby," he murmured. "If all we do is act like tourists and catch up on our sleep, that's fine. Anything else is a bonus and a blessing. Okay?"

Tears sparkled in her eyes in contrast to her bright smile. "All right."

Minutes later, the jet was wheels down on the tarmac at the private airstrip of a billionaire who owed Brent a personal favor. Bright lights lit up the strip like a major-league ball field. Nearby, four men spread out, guarding two large SUVs parked near the tarmac. Despite the jet taxiing into position, the guards remained watchful, their backs to the slowing aircraft.

As soon as the jet came to a stop, Brody strode up the aisle, tapping Logan on the shoulder as he passed.

He unlatched his seatbelt and stood. "Wait here until Brody and I make sure everything is secure," he told Poppy.

Logan followed his team leader to the exit, and together, they lowered the steps. Weapons in hand and held by their thighs, both men scanned the area, searching for threats.

One of the four guards pivoted after a last visual sweep around the area and approached the jet. The blond-haired, blue-eyed giant of a man appraised Brody and Logan with a glance. Seeming satisfied with his assessment, he held out his hand. "Tom Moreland."

Brody clasped Moreland's hand briefly. "Brody. Thanks for meeting the jet."

A slight nod. "The boss provided two vehicles for your use. Both are retrofitted for safety." He handed Brody and Logan business cards. "If you need a hand, call me. We have men and women we'll reassign to you temporarily as backup. We're all Special Forces soldiers." He handed them four key fobs. "When you're ready to leave the strip, press the blue button to turn off the landing lights."

Logan couldn't help but be impressed. Moreland's boss must owe Brent big for him to offer this much cooperation.

Moreland turned, stopped. He looked at Logan for a moment, flicked a glance toward the jet, then Moreland's gaze settled once more on him. "I recognize you. You're Logan Fletcher, the man involved with the VP's daughter."

He inclined his head. No use denying it. The media blitz would hit soon enough when word leaked that he'd married the vice president's daughter right under his nose. His picture would be plastered all over the media. Too bad, that. At least he and his team usually worked at night under cover of darkness. Minimal chance of recognition in the dead of night. He'd take precautions, though, as would his team.

A soft whistle. "HVT?"

He stared without responding.

"Got it. Call if you need a hand." With that, he returned to the other guards and motioned for them to move out. Soon, the four of them climbed into a third SUV parked some distance away and drove off into the night.

When the taillights disappeared from view, Brody and Logan returned to the jet. "Clear," Brody said. He handed a key fob to Max, Sawyer, and Logan, keeping the fourth one for himself. "Jesse, you're with Logan, Poppy, and Max. Sawyer, you're with me and Sage." He sent the location of the safe house to the team's phones. "Baby, you and Poppy stay on board for another minute until we load our gear into the vehicles. Then we'll escort you ladies to the SUVs. We have about an hour's drive."

Adding in minutes to be certain they weren't followed to the safe house was an excellent precaution under the circumstances. "I'll check the SUVs for trackers and bugs before we load up."

"Go," Brody said. "The rest of us will gather the gear."

Logan returned to the tarmac, grabbed an electronic signal detector from his pocket, and went to work. Ten minutes later, he entered the jet's cabin. "Both vehicles are clean."

"Excellent." Sawyer rubbed his hands together. "Let's get out of here. I'm starved."

Max snorted. "So, what's new about that? You're always hungry."

"I'm a growing boy, Max. You have a sweet wife to keep you fed. I'm all alone in the world and reduced to mooching meals wherever I can."

While the others teased Max, Logan grabbed his gear and Poppy's, and returned to the second SUV. Jesse followed him out with more bags of equipment.

"How's she doing?" the medic asked.

"Holding her own. She's battling nightmares from her experience in Mexico every time she sleeps now."

"Understandable."

"Yeah, but it makes her angry and frustrated. Poppy sees the nightmares as a weakness." Logan understood. He saw them that way as well when nightmares came after him in the dead of night.

"Set up a session with one of the Fortress counselors. Might help."

"I'll think about it." He'd talk to her first. Blindsiding Poppy wasn't smart. He'd prefer not to start a marriage with his new wife royally ticked off at him. Enough time for that as their marriage progressed. Logan was bound to upset his wife before too much time had passed.

Once the equipment had been loaded, Logan and Brody escorted Poppy and Sage to the vehicles, with the rest of the team providing a circle of safety.

After helping Poppy into the backseat of their SUV, Logan climbed in beside her as Jesse got in behind the wheel and Max dropped into the shotgun seat. While he didn't expect trouble, if trouble found them, Logan wanted to be by Poppy's side. "A smooth ride, my friend," he told Jesse.

"Wonder if Sawyer will remember that I'm hungry, too," Max muttered.

"How can he forget?" Jesse guided the SUV onto a road leading from the airstrip in the first SUV's wake. "You never let us forget."

The bantering between the two operatives continued as the entourage drove through the dark night toward the safe house.

Ninety minutes from the time the jet landed, the SUVs circled around to park behind a large, two-story home. Jesse and Max exited the vehicle and met Sawyer and Brody. Following a brief conversation, the four men separated. Brody entered the house, weapon drawn. The others merged with the shadows as they searched the grounds and perimeter of the house for signs of a breach in security.

"Stay inside." Logan opened the door and stepped outside the vehicle. He drew his weapon and held it by his thigh as he quartered the area, committing the surroundings to memory.

Soon, Brody returned, along with the rest of the team. "Clear. Let's get the women inside."

After escorting Poppy and Sage into the house, Logan and the others carried their gear inside and reset the alarm.

"I call first watch in the security room," Max said and headed out of the kitchen.

"I have the perimeter watch." Sawyer grabbed his Go bag and Max's. "I'll take another look outside after I drop these in our room. Where are Max and I bunking, Brody?"

"First room on the right at the top of the stairs."

Brody and Logan picked up their Go bags and the bags of the women. "After you," Brody said to Sage. "We're upstairs in the last room on the left, baby. Poppy, you're in the last room on the right. Logan's room is next to yours."

For tonight. The thought almost brought Logan to his knees. In less than twelve hours, Poppy Reynolds would be his wife. Satisfaction swelled inside him. He couldn't wait until his ring told the world that Poppy was his to love and protect.

He tightened his hold on Poppy's hand. He had to get a grip on his emotions. No pressure on his lady, he reminded himself. They had the rest of their lives together. That's all that mattered.

Logan walked with Poppy to her room and turned on the light. He glanced around, impressed with what he saw. A nice quilt lay on the bed with another one on some kind of stand in the corner. Pictures of the Great Smoky Mountains in all their glory graced the walls. Rustic furniture, including a lamp hefty enough to take out a linebacker if Poppy swung for the stands with it. A walk-in closet door stood open. Another door on the side where his room was located turned out to be a bathroom. A large dresser occupied the exterior wall.

After setting Poppy's bag at the foot of the bed and checking both windows to make sure they were locked, Logan turned back to her. "Need anything before I go?"

She shook her head. "Thank you."

"For?"

"Bringing me to Washington, even though you objected."

Logan tugged her into his arms. "I hope we don't regret it."

"Everything will be fine. You'll see."

Famous last words.

Chapter Sixteen

The next morning, Poppy stared at herself in the mirror and smoothed her hand over the aquamarine dress Sage had given her a few minutes earlier. The matching pumps completed the outfit. Poppy felt like a princess about to marry her prince.

She smiled. Well, perhaps not the prince. More like the black-garbed knight sweeping in from the plain on his black steed or, in this case, in his black SUV. No one would mistake Logan Fletcher for a prince. He resembled a street thug more than royalty, but he was about to be hers.

What would her parents say? Poppy flinched. Plenty, she imagined. None of it fit for gentle ears. They liked Logan just fine as part of the black ops group. Bringing him into the bosom of their family as a new son was something else altogether.

She tilted her chin up. Too bad. Logan was her choice. He'd been her choice since she saw him the first time. He'd only grown more important to her over the months since they met. And now, she was the blessed woman who had his love.

Poppy laughed, joy and excitement bubbling over inside her. No matter how her parents reacted, this marriage was exactly what she wanted. Logan was the man she needed with every breath she took. And look at her? Who knew she could be so sappy?

A light knock sounded on the door. "Poppy, it's me."

"Door's unlocked, Sage."

Her sister slipped into the room and caught her breath. "Oh, Poppy! You look stunning in the dress."

"It's beautiful. Thank you for the gift."

"I don't care if this wedding is in front of a judge. You aren't getting married in jeans and a t-shirt. We'll plan the whole state affair wedding when things are back to normal, but you should at least feel that this day is special and woven with dreams." She studied Poppy. "You do, don't you? You're sure this is what you want?"

"Yes, and yes. Nothing is more important to me than marrying Logan."

Sage captured her hands. "You love him, don't you?"

"So much, and I like him most of the time, too. He has his moments of aggravation. I can live with them because he loves me and looks at me as though I'm the only person in his world."

Her sister squeezed her hands a moment before releasing her. "You deserve the same happiness I found with Brody. But promise me you'll let me or Brody know if Logan ever hurts you."

"He would sooner cut his own throat, sis."

"Promise me."

She shrugged, knowing in her heart she'd never have to fulfill the promise. "I promise."

Relief flooded her sister's face. "Good. Now, your almost husband has sent word that it's time to leave. He and Brody arranged for a guard at the courthouse to open the door to a side entrance to the County Clerk's office so you can pick up your paperwork and go directly to the judge's chambers."

With one last glance in the mirror, Poppy turned to face her sister. "Let's go. We don't want to keep the team waiting."

Logan waited at the foot of the stairs, dressed in a black suit, white shirt, and a tie that matched her dress.

Oh, wow. Poppy paused at the top of the staircase. She'd only seen Logan in a suit once, and that was at Sage and Brody's wedding.

Logan slowly climbed the stairs and held his hand out to her. "You take my breath away, Poppy," he murmured. "Ready to do this?"

"Yes."

He drew her hand through his crooked arm and escorted Poppy downstairs to Brody and the rest of the team. Sage descended the stairs behind them. Logan nodded at Brody.

Soon, the vehicles sped down the long, winding driveway to the road.

Twenty minutes later, they parked at the back of the county courthouse and exited the vehicles. After a short walk to the courthouse, a side entrance door opened and a security guard motioned for them to enter the building.

"This way. The clerk is waiting, and so is the judge."

"Appreciate this, Chris," Brody said. "We owe you."

The guard waved that aside. "Doesn't come close to what you did for my family last year, man. The scales will never be balanced in my books." He led them to an elevator with limited access via swipe card and indicated for them to precede him.

Within minutes, the marriage paperwork was signed, and Logan, Poppy, and the rest of their entourage were standing in the judge's chambers.

"Ready?" Logan asked Poppy, voice soft.

Poppy smiled, her eyes sparkling. "That's my question for you, Fletcher. After all, I'm the one who started this adventure. So, what do you say? Are you ready?"

"Oh, yeah, baby. I'm ready." Logan planted a hard kiss on her mouth, then straightened and turned to the judge. "Any time you're ready, sir."

Judge Harcourt Johansen chuckled. "No time like the present. Dearly beloved...."

Soon, Logan slid the Celtic wedding band with an embedded diamond onto Poppy's fourth finger and followed up with a kiss to the top of her hand. His teammates chuckled.

He pulled a matching dark version of the wedding band minus the diamond from his pocket and watched as she slid the large black ring over his knuckle.

When Judge Johansen pronounced them husband and wife, Logan gathered Poppy against him and captured her mouth for a long, deep kiss that ended only because Brody cleared his throat, and said, "Time."

Logan broke the kiss and stared deep into Poppy's eyes.

She couldn't believe it. She was his wife. Man, that sounded good.

Her husband smiled. "Hello, Mrs. Fletcher."

Poppy laughed. "Hello, Mr. Fletcher. What do you say about getting out of here?"

"Excellent idea." He and Poppy accepted the congratulations of their friends, signed the paperwork, duly notarized, and took their leave of the courthouse.

As Jesse turned onto the main street behind the courthouse, Poppy rubbed a thumb over her wedding band.

"Like it?"

"It's beautiful, and the fit is perfect. Elegant without being fussy or a show stopper. The ring is exactly what I dreamed of as I grew up. How did you know the right size?"

"Sage said you and she wear the same size ring. I borrowed hers and told the jewelry store owner what I wanted." Logan shifted, as though suddenly aware he might have made a mistake in choosing her ring, that although she said the ring was perfect, Poppy might have preferred to select her own ring. "If you want something different, we'll go together to select something else."

Poppy fisted her ring hand. Fat chance of that. No one was taking her ring from her. "No way. You're not getting this ring back. I'll be wearing this one when we're great-grandparents and rocking on the front porch, watching the sunrise and the wildlife. I love my ring, Logan. I'm glad your ring matches mine."

"I had to buy a black one."

She shrugged. "Less chance of reflection giving away your position on the job. Sage told me why Brody's ring is black."

Max turned in his seat to look at Logan. "Are we sticking to the plan?"

He nodded. "As much as I would like a ride to the airstrip to hop on a company jet to anywhere with sun, sand, and surf where Poppy and I can spend a month together on a honeymoon away from danger, I need to be sure my wife's family is safe while we're out of touch with the world. Poppy wouldn't be able to enjoy time away if she believed her sister and parents were still targets of the kidnappers who took her for leverage."

Almost an hour later, they parked in back of a chalet in the woods. The closest neighbor had been at least a mile away, maybe more.

The men climbed from the vehicles and scanned the area.

Poppy noted the locations of five security cameras, including a clever one almost hidden by a bird's nest high in the tree at the edge of the yard. Perfect angle, too. Most of the front yard would be visible with the camera. If it was motion activated and able to rotate, all the better. Simone didn't take chances.

Sawyer glanced at Poppy. "She paranoid much?"

"Do you blame her? Simone's sideline is dangerous. If the wrong people find out she's hacking into secure databases, she'll wind up in prison or the morgue."

"She should work for the boss."

"If he's smart, he'll investigate her and make an offer," Logan said. "From what I can see of her security, Simone could use the protections Fortress offered."

He held out his hand to Poppy. "Text Simone and tell her we're here. I don't want to approach the back door without her being aware of who we are."

Her eyebrows shot up. "She's not violent."

"As far as you know. I'd rather not find out you were wrong." He handed her his phone.

Poppy made a face at him but sent a message. Seconds later, her phone lit up with a response. She laughed. "Simone said you sound grumpy."

He snorted.

"She said I should throw you back in the dating pool and fish for someone better."

Logan tossed a glare at the closest camera. "So, the paranoid tech nerd has sound capability as well. Don't shoot us, Simone. We shoot back."

Poppy rolled her eyes. "Really? Not the best way to convince her you and your team are the good guys."

"Probably not. Made the point, though. I want Simone to know I'm more dangerous than she is." Logan cupped Poppy's arm and escorted her toward the back door of the chalet, with the rest of their group following.

The door opened before they reached the deck. A woman eyed each of them unsmiling until she got to Poppy. Her frown morphed into a grin. "Great to see you, Poppy, Sage. Both of you look good."

Simone stepped back from the doorway and motioned everyone inside. When the last person cleared the threshold, she relocked her door and reset the alarm.

The subtle tension in her shoulder disappeared. "Come into the living room and have a seat. I'll be back in a minute with coffee for everyone."

"I'll give you a hand," Jesse said. "I'm Jesse."

"I'm Simone." She motioned the others through the arched doorway into the well-lit room beyond. "Make yourselves comfortable."

Poppy and Sage headed into the living room and sat on the sofa while Logan and the others glanced around.

Brody stood to the side of the large picture window and pushed aside the curtain just enough to see outside. "Opinion?" he asked quietly.

"Undetermined."

A nod.

"Zane sent word. The first security pass is clear."

"Good. Hopefully, the other passes will be the same. But I'm not banking on it. Someone who goes to this much trouble to hide from the world has more reason to hide than she simply likes privacy."

Simone and Jesse returned with two large trays. Jesse's tray held two large carafes and mugs while Simone's tray had a large assortment of cookies and small plates.

They placed the trays on a stone and wood coffee table. Simone poured coffee in mugs and handed one to each person except Sage. She poured steaming liquid from the second carafe into a mug and handed it to Sage. "Herbal tea."

Sage beamed. "You remembered. Thank you."

"You were the only tea drinker. Hard to forget that." She sat beside Poppy. "So, tell me everything. I want to help, Poppy. Frankly, you'll need every ally you have to get out of this mess in one piece. Your friends, too."

Poppy glanced at Logan.

He nodded. "If I'm wrong in my judgment call, we'll deal with the fallout. For the moment, we have to start somewhere. Simone knows something she hasn't yet told us. We need every piece of information we can get. While I have full confidence in Zane and the tech team at Fortress, time is short. My gut says the kidnappers and their boss were desperate to grab one of the vice president's daughters, wrongly assuming she had less security than the parents."

Simone rolled her eyes. "Thanks for the vote of confidence, Grumpy Logan."

Time to intervene before her friend and her husband got into an argument. Poppy started her story at the beginning, giving all the details she could remember. When she finished, she said, "You have something, don't you?"

"Why do you say that?"

She pointed. "You just confirmed it. You always answer a question with a question when you don't want to own up to something. Just spill it, Simone. Logan and the others need everything you have to find these guys before they hurt someone or come after Sage."

Simone sipped her coffee. "You're too smart for your own good, Poppy."

"What does that mean?"

"You should drop this investigation."

"I can't."

She sighed. "I figured you'd say that."

"Why did you say Poppy should quit?" Logan asked.

"It's too dangerous." Simone glared at him. "You ought to know that more than anyone."

He stilled. "You're a hacker," he said drawled. "Have you sneaked through Zane's safeguards?

She smiled.

Logan gave her a small salute. "I'll let Zane know he needs to update them."

Poppy stared at her friend. "You hacked into secure records?"

Simone shrugged.

"Why?"

"I wanted to know everything I could find about the man you were involved with." She flicked a glance at Logan before refocusing on Poppy.

"Were you satisfied?"

"Yeah." Simone gave Logan her grudging approval. "He's tough as nails and loyal to a fault."

"You have a problem with him?" Poppy challenged.

"Nope. If what I dug up is true, you'll need Logan or someone like him to stand up for you."

Logan folded his arms across his chest. "Since I have your approval, how about you answer our questions now? What did you learn that has you running scared, Simone?"

Her chin tipped up. "I'm not afraid for myself. I'm terrified for Poppy. The people who are after her aren't playing around. People who refuse to give them what they want have a nasty habit of disappearing or ending up dead."

Jesse straightened from the wall, his gaze locked on the computer hacker.

"Who are they?" Poppy asked.

"I don't know. They're as slippery as eels on the dark web, diving into deep holes when I come too close." Anger simmered through her words. "I hear rumors online, track them as fast as I can, and when I get there? Poof. They've disappeared as though they'd never been in the vicinity."

"Why do these people want Poppy?" Logan asked. "Makes little sense. Why not go after the target instead of Poppy?"

Simone frowned. "Don't you get it?"

His eyebrow rose. "Enlighten me before I strangle you for drawing this out to irritating lengths."

"Poppy knows Lynx."

"How?" Poppy demanded.

"He is in your inner circle, close enough that you will draw Lynx out of hiding."

Poppy's face turned white. "To sacrifice himself to save me." She groaned. "What have I done by coming here?"

"Set events in motion that can't be stopped." Simone looked grim. "They know you're coming to Washington, Poppy. I don't know how they found out, but they know and they're ready."

Logan and his teammates exchanged glances. "This is the exact scenario we've been afraid would happen," Logan said. He looked at Simone. "Where's the leak?"

Chapter Seventeen

Shock jolted through Poppy. She should have realized the truth. The only people who knew she was headed for Washington soon were her parents, Logan's team, and his friends Brent and Zane.

The leak must be with her parents or someone they trusted because she knew beyond a doubt that Logan's team and his Fortress coworkers were trustworthy.

She thrust her hands through her hair, wincing when her fingers brushed the stitches. The pain, however, helped her push aside disbelief and straight into a decision. "I need to talk to Mom and Dad."

"Especially Mom," Sage added.

She wouldn't lie to herself. Knowing her mother had lied to her and Sage hurt. They had no choice but to confront her. Would she tell the truth or continue to lie to them?

Poppy turned to Logan. "We need to go. I'll call Mom's social secretary to find out where she's going to be today."

"Don't bother." Simone pulled a piece of paper from her jeans pocket and handed it to Poppy. "I figured you'd want to confront your mom, so I printed a copy of her schedule for the next five days."

"Do I want to know where you got this?"

"Nope." Her friend sounded positively cheerful. Then her gaze dropped to Poppy's left hand. She gasped. "Poppy!"

"What?"

"You're engaged?"

Oh, that. She smiled. "Married."

Simone stared. "You're kidding."

"Problem?" Logan asked softly.

Poppy's friend scowled at him. "Oh, get your feelings off your shoulder, Fletcher. Someone is bound to knock them off, eventually.

I was just surprised because Poppy never mentioned she was engaged."

"We didn't want a long engagement," Poppy said, cutting off a bad-tempered response from Logan. "We didn't see any point in waiting to get married."

"Wait a minute. Why didn't I see news of your wedding in the media? The marriage of the vice president's daughter is a major news story. How did you pull off a media blackout?"

"Easy. We eloped."

Simone's jaw dropped. "When?"

Poppy glanced at her watch. "An hour ago."

More silence, then amusement glittered in her friend's eyes. "You didn't tell your parents, did you?" She laughed. "Oh, to be a fly on the wall when you spill the news to Ivan and Beverly. Logan, you're either very brave or a total idiot. Either way, good luck to you."

Max said, "Incoming."

The rest of the team scattered to different windows to peer outside. At the front window, Brody growled. "Looks like two vehicles, at least four men in each one. They're coming in fast. Sawyer, check the back."

"Yes, sir." Sawyer headed toward the back part of the house at a fast clip.

"I don't understand," Simone muttered. "Why didn't the security system alert me when these guys crossed the perimeter?"

"Probably used jamming equipment," Jesse said from a window at the side of the living room. "No one approaching from this side," he said to Brody.

"Sawyer?" Brody called out.

"All clear so far," he replied.

Brody glanced at Logan and inclined his head toward the other side of the house.

After a slight nod, Logan brushed his mouth over Poppy's and murmured, "Stay away from the windows, and do what Brody tells you."

"I'll be fine. Go. Be careful, Logan."

"Always." He turned to look at Brody, received a slight nod from his best friend, then jogged to the other side of the house.

Poppy frowned. What was that about? She'd seen Brody give Logan the same stare before when he had to leave Sage alone. When she and her sister were by themselves, she'd ask Sage for an explanation.

"Poppy, Sage, sit on the floor against the wall near the stairs. You, too, Simone."

Her friend scowled. "Hey, this is my house. I'm not letting these clowns invade my territory without a protest."

"Do you have a weapon?" Jesse asked, without turning away from his post.

"Are you kidding? My weapon of choice is a computer."

"All right," he said. "You take your computer up against the eight thugs armed to the teeth surrounding your house as we speak. Take your weapon into a gunfight and see who wins the showdown coming in the next five minutes."

"They're armed?"

Jesse risked a quick glance over his shoulder. "Did you think they were here for a social call? My guess is you've done everything possible to stay off the grid. Yet these guys seem to know exactly where to go and who they're after. They have more tricks up their sleeves than simply weapons tucked in every pocket. Unless you're going to join the gun fight, join Poppy and Sage on the floor so you're not hit by bullets flying through windows and doors."

"Come on," Sage said, patting the floor beside her. "Join the party."

Simone dropped beside her. "How did they find me? I was careful when I trolled the Net." She sounded worried.

Poppy reached over and squeezed her hand. "Don't worry about that now. You'll figure it out."

"Did they follow you and your friends? That's the only explanation that makes sense."

"You're good, but you're not infallible. They didn't follow us, Simone. Logan and his team would have spotted them."

"They probably have a hacker as talented as you," Sage said. "Someone uncovered your friendship with Poppy and guessed she would come to you for help."

Simone blew out a breath. "If you're right and they already knew about me, all they had to do was wait for you to come to me."

"And I walked us right into a trap," Poppy said, guilt roiling in her gut. Something else to add to her mountain of regret.

When would she learn to pay attention to the advice of her personal security detail, especially the advice of her husband? Yes, she understood that a confrontation with these men was inevitable. However, she and Logan weren't at their best. Would that affect the outcome of this skirmish?

Gunshots rang out from the front of the house. Glass shattered.

"Flat on the ground, ladies," Brody snapped. "Don't raise your heads until I tell you it's safe."

Sage and Simone obeyed immediately. Poppy was slower to respond. Dratted ribs. Lying on the floor would be torture. Getting up again without help might be beyond her ability.

"Poppy!" Brody glared at her.

"Working on it. Keep your pants on."

"Work faster."

"Yeah, yeah." She finally stretched out flat, groaning as pain wracked her ribs.

"Brody, I need fifteen seconds," Jesse said.

"Go."

The medic spun and raced in a crouch to the sofa. He grabbed a seat cushion and tossed it toward Poppy, then sped back to his original watch position. "Use the cushion, Poppy. You'll still be flat, but your ribs will appreciate the soft surface."

"Thanks." Instead of standing and making herself even more of a target, Poppy scooted onto the cushion and almost cried with relief. Who knew a sofa cushion could make such an enormous difference? At least now she could breathe.

Brody and Max returned fire from the front windows.

Poppy's ears rang from the deafening noise in such a small space. Simone's home was beautiful, but the hardwood floors made the sound of gunshots echo even more inside the place. The noise grew louder when Jesse joined the fight from his position.

"One down," Brody called.

"Two down," Max said.

"Three down." This from Jesse.

Five more to go. Poppy prayed Texas Team ended the conflict soon. Even though Simone lived away from her neighbors, sound carried in the countryside. Someone would call the police to report the continuous gunfire coming from this direction.

Brody signaled Max, who nodded, then the team leader sprinted down the hall toward Logan.

Was something wrong? Poppy's heart skipped a beat. Should she be concerned? Yeah, see, this was the reason she wasn't allowed to go along on one of their missions. She would be constantly afraid something had happened to Logan or the others. Not good.

Unable to move without help, Poppy watched down the hallway, wishing she could get up and go see for herself what was going on. That insatiable curiosity of hers had her contemplating a way to go about it until she realized she might well end up in the crossfire if Logan and Brody didn't know where she was.

Didn't take her long to realize no gunfire came from Logan's side of the house. She frowned. No way would Logan just sit back and wait for orders from Brody. Why wasn't Brody firing off a single shot?

One answer popped into her mind. The more she thought about it, the more Poppy realized she'd hit on the solution to her question. Logan and Brody weren't inside the house. They'd gone outside to hunt down and take out the attackers.

She wanted to hop up and go after them. Stupid impulse. This was what they did. Logan and the others were trained to handle just such scenarios. No matter how much she wanted to be in the thick of things to see it all firsthand, she'd be in the way. Not only that, Logan would be more worried about her safety than his own. If anyone was in more danger, it would be the man she'd married less than two hours ago. To keep him safe, she'd have to curtail her curiosity and deal with the situation as it was. Essentially, she was blind and deaf.

"What's going on?" Sage asked. "Where's Brody?"

Max and Jesse ignored her.

Simone started to get up.

Jesse snapped, "Down."

She glared at him. He returned the scowl.

"Sawyer," Max called. "Sit rep."

"One man down. Three more changed position. They're waiting."

For what? More men? The boss? Poppy shuddered and immediately wished she hadn't as pain shot through her body. Guess her pain meds had worn off. Nice timing.

Max and Jesse continued to fire their weapons. Soon, Max hissed.

"Problem?" Jesse asked.

"Oh, yeah. Simone, do you have another way out of here?"

"Windows and the back door. Why?"

"Safe room?"

"No. Again, why?"

"These guys just pulled a rocket-propelled grenade from their SUV. Sawyer," Max yelled. "RPG at the front."

"Back isn't clear."

"West side. Now. Go, go, go!" Max and Jesse raced toward the hall as Sage and Simone scrambled to their feet.

Sage turned to help Poppy.

"Run," Jesse ordered. "I've got her." The medic bent and scooped Poppy from the cushion and ran with her in his arms.

She wrapped her arms around his neck and held on for dear life. Good grief! The medic could move.

Jesse was two steps into the bedroom at the west side of the house when a blinding flash of light and a deafening boom rocked the entire house.

Max checked out the window, then motioned for Simone and Sage to follow Sawyer outside. "As soon as you're out, run as fast as you can to the woods to the left. Stay in line with the house so you aren't spotted until you reach the woods. Go into the forest and wait for us. We'll be right behind you. Don't wander around out there. You might run into the other teams. Got it?"

"Got it," Sage said.

Sawyer slid through the open window to the ground, then turned to reach for Sage. He plucked her from the ledge and turned back for Simone, who was sliding through the window, then he motioned for both of them to run.

Max turned to Jesse. "How do we handle Poppy?"

"The same," she answered tartly. "I can run."

"No," Jesse said. "You can't. Not with those ribs. Sawyer, I'll hand her to you. Run for safety with her. I'll cover you."

Poppy frowned. She wasn't an invalid.

"Don't argue, kid," Max snapped. "If you balk, you and the man covering you will die."

She closed her mouth.

The hand off was smooth, as though these men had done something like this a million times before today. And perhaps they had. Part of their missions were to rescue hostages. Terrorists weren't kind to those they held against their will.

In seconds, Sawyer sprinted for the woods with her in his arms. As soon as they crossed the tree line, the black ops soldier set Poppy on her feet and pushed her behind a large tree. "Stay here. Can you shoot?"

"Logan's been training me to handle and shoot weapons."

He reached down to his ankle holster and pulled a weapon, which he handed to Poppy.

She checked the chamber and the magazine. Fully loaded. Excellent.

"You good?"

"Yep. What about Sage and Simone?"

"We're here," Sage whispered. She and their friend hurried to her side. "What now, Sawyer?"

"We wait for the others to take care of business."

"You should go help them."

A snort. "Logan and Brody would tear strips off my hide if I left you. The other teams aren't playing. They mean to take you or kill you. Right now, I'm all that stands between you and them. I'm not budging. No offense, but I'm more afraid of Logan and Brody than you three."

Another explosion ripped through the air. Simone flinched. "My house is gone, isn't it?"

"Better your house than you," Sage said. She squeezed Simone's hand briefly. "You can rebuild." She paused, then said, "Although I can't figure out how you'll explain to the insurance company that an RPG blew up your house."

"Pictures are worth a thousand words," Poppy murmured.

"Quiet." Sawyer motioned for them to sit on the ground at the base of the tree. "Poppy, keep watch to the right. I'll take the left. Sage, Simone, watch our six."

"Where's Jesse?" Simone whispered.

"Tracking down the men who blew up your house."

They fell silent, each one keeping watch in their assigned locations. Didn't take Poppy long to figure out that Sawyer constantly scanned all around them, not just his assigned area. Probably for the best. She hated to admit it, but she was terrified.

Two shots rang out, followed by more silence. Tension built by the minute until Poppy thought she would have to go hunting herself or go insane. Who were these guys, and why did they want Lynx to come out of hiding? What had the agent done to set off this vendetta?

A man's scream was cut off abruptly.

Near Poppy, a branch broke a split second before Thing One burst from the underbrush. He sneered and raised his gun, pointed the barrel straight at Poppy.

"Well, well. Look who I found? You've led us on a merry chase. Drop the gun like a good little girl and come with me." He glanced at Sage. "You, too. The boss will be very glad to see both of you."

He smiled at Poppy, triumph gleaming in his eyes. "Tell your friend with the gun if he doesn't drop it now and lay flat on the ground, I'll kill you right here and take your sister to the boss. You know I'm not joking, sweetheart."

"All right. Don't hurt her," Sawyer said.

"Drop the gun."

The operative did as instructed.

"Get on the ground, face down. One wrong move, and I'll shoot your principal." He snorted. "Some bodyguard you turned out to be."

Poppy glanced at Sawyer, whose face remained expressionless as he went to his knees, hands out to the side. He was too close to Thing One. The thug couldn't miss him. She had to protect Sawyer.

The operative stared at her as he went to the ground. He gave a slight nod before he flattened himself on the ground.

"Now, you're next, Poppy. You shouldn't have run. My buddy got shot because of you." He glared at her. "You'll pay for that. Once the boss finishes with you, I'll teach you a lesson you won't ever forget. You'll never disrespect me that way again. I know how to discipline women who don't obey."

Her blood ran cold. The creep meant what he said. The determination was written all over his face. He planned to hurt her and Sage.

Thing One laughed and took one step toward Poppy.

She pulled the trigger.

#

Chapter Eighteen

Logan's head whipped toward the shot. That was the area where Poppy and the others had gone. Had Sawyer shot one of the enemy? Please, God, that was what happened. If one thug had shot him or one of the women....

Brody scowled at him and signaled him to focus.

Though every instinct he possessed screamed at Logan to run to Poppy, he pushed the distraction aside and focused on placing every step on the path leading to their targets.

His jaw clenched. If he wanted to go to his wife, he'd have to take care of business first, then go find her.

The mission clock ticked in his head. Not only was he concerned about Poppy and the others, the team needed to vacate the area before the first responders arrived en masse to check out the scene and search for survivors. Local law enforcement wouldn't appreciate all the bodies Logan and the others were leaving behind. Unless they wanted a long, drawn out session at the police station, they needed to be gone before the authorities found them on the scene.

Besides that, the news media would have a field day with the fact that the vice president's daughters were targets of another attack, especially since they didn't know about Poppy's kidnapping. That would come out as well.

Furious murmurs sounded a few yards ahead. Logan held up his fist, signaling Brody to wait. He eased closer, hugging shadows and thick cover, until he saw two men. Both were heavily armed and dressed in black. The men hadn't bothered to cover their faces.

His lips curled. Guess they didn't plan to leave witnesses behind to identify them.

The two men, one with red hair, one with blond, were involved in a heated argument. "You're an idiot," Red hissed. "Those women aren't the ones shooting at us. The gunmen have to be the target's boyfriend and his friends."

"Do you know them?" Blond demanded. "Otherwise, you shouldn't assume anything."

"Did you see the target's boyfriend? He's a big bruiser with cop eyes."

Blond's eyes widened. "Nobody said anything about him being a cop."

"What difference does it make? We got a job to do. If he stands in our way, he's a dead man."

"I'm not killing no cop."

"How about you shut up so we can find the Reynolds sisters and get out of here before the real cops arrive?"

"How are we supposed to find them in these woods?" Blond looked around him, gaze darting in one direction, then another. "The women might have gone for help by now."

Logan glanced at Brody and inclined his head toward his right. His team leader melted into the shadows, only to emerge a short distance away on the right.

Excellent. He and Brody would flank the men and take them down. That left three more to handle.

Red clouted his buddy on the back of the head. "Use your noggin for once. No way the target will leave without her boyfriend." He pointed toward where Poppy and the others had taken refuge. "You heard the gunshot. Trey's taking care of business. We need to go. The bodyguard or his friends will follow the sound of that shot."

He took off toward Poppy's location at a jog, only to skid to a halt when Logan and Brody stepped out from cover with their weapons drawn and aimed.

"Stop right there," Brody ordered. "Drop your weapons. Now."

Red's eyes narrowed. Blond watched his buddy.

"Don't do it," Logan warned. "We will shoot, and we don't miss."

Still, the other men hesitated.

"Drop your weapons." Brody glared at them. "You and your friends kidnapped his wife. My buddy isn't in the mood to talk. He'd rather drop you where you stand and be done with the hassle of dealing with you."

Logan's finger tightened on the trigger.

Red growled. "All right," he snapped, dropping his gun on the ground.

"Kick it away."

He complied and motioned for his friend to do the same.

"The boss will kill us," Blond groused as he dropped his gun and kicked it away.

"He has to catch us first. These guys are serious. I'm not planning to eat lead today. Are you?"

"Get rid of the rest of your weapons," Logan ordered.

Red and Blond exchanged glances before removing the obvious weapons.

"Keep going," Brody snapped when they paused. "Backup pieces and the knives in your boots. Hurry. We don't have all day."

When the men had removed the rest of their weapons, Brody secured their hands behind their backs with zip ties.

"What do we do with them?" Logan asked. "My vote is to kill them both."

"Hey," Red protested. "We did what you asked."

"You hurt my wife. I haven't forgotten."

"Not me, man. I didn't take her."

"I was only a perimeter guard," Blond said. "I didn't know Trey and Van were kidnapping your wife. I swear."

Unfortunately for his burning need to avenge his wife's injuries, Logan believed the two men. "Let's go."

"Where are you taking us?" Red demanded.

"You wanted to find my wife. That's what we're going to do."

Brody took the lead. Red and Blond followed behind him, with Logan bringing up the rear.

Five minutes later, Brody held up his fist, signaling the others to stop. "Sawyer."

"Clear, except we have a slight problem."

Logan's heart skipped a beat. What did that mean?

"Yeah, so I see. We brought two prisoners with us. Logan, take a look." Brody stepped to the side and motioned for Red and Blond to stand still. He trained his weapon on them.

Logan jogged past them and came to a stop at the sight of Poppy holding a weapon aimed at a fallen man. She was trembling from head to foot. The man on the ground had a gunshot wound in his right shoulder and moaned in pain in between cursing her.

"Lower the weapon, baby." Logan walked to her.

She blinked.

"Poppy."

She didn't respond.

"Look at me, sweetheart. I need to see your beautiful face."

A long minute later, Poppy turned her head. Her face was the color of white marble. "Logan?"

"Right here. Give me the weapon, love." He held out his hand.

She blinked again, frowned slightly, and dropped her gaze to her right hand. Her lips trembled. "I can't let go." Poppy looked back at him. "Help me."

Logan closed the remaining distance between them and wrapped his arm around her waist, drawing her against him. "We've got this now. Stand down."

"He was going to kill Sawyer."

Poppy had shot the man to save Logan's teammate? "You stopped him. It's time to let us take over now."

"My hand won't let go."

"I'll help you. Ready?" Logan slowly raised his hand until he reached for the weapon. After shifting her aim toward the ground, he said, "Move your finger away from the trigger." When she did, he said, "Good girl. Do you trust me, Poppy?"

"With my life. I love you."

He smiled. He'd never tire of hearing those words. "I love you, too." Logan wrapped his hand around the weapon. "I have the Glock, babe. You can let go. Let me take care of you now. Please."

Her trembling increased. "Logan."

"Trust me," he whispered. "Let go for me, baby. I've got this."

Finally, her grip on the gun loosened, and Logan removed the Glock from her hand.

The second he took the gun from her hand, Poppy sagged against Logan. "I've got you, Poppy." He handed the weapon to Sawyer and gathered his amazing wife into his arms.

"I'm sorry," she whispered.

"Don't be. You protected Sawyer, Sage, and Simone. No one could ask more." He kissed her temple. "You were amazing."

"I froze."

"After getting the job done."

Jesse walked up. "Anybody hurt?"

"Just this guy," Brody said, motioning to the man on the ground still cursing a blue streak.

"That's Thing One," Poppy said.

Logan tightened his hold on her. "Is he the one who hit you?"

She shook her head. "His friend punched me."

Still, this man kidnapped Poppy. He wasn't getting a pass on this. Logan looked at Brody. "We're taking him, too."

"He needs medical care."

"Tough."

"I need a doctor," Thing One demanded. "Your stupid girlfriend shot me."

Logan glanced at Poppy. "Can you stand on your own for a minute?"

"What are you going to do?"

"Don't ask."

She flicked a glance at Thing One, then stepped out of the circle of Logan's arms.

He covered the distance between himself and Thing One in a few strides, and placed his booted foot on the thug. Without a twinge of guilt, Logan pressed on the wound.

When the screams died down to moans, Logan said, "Do I look like I care about your injury? You kidnapped my wife. You're lucky I'm letting you live."

"I didn't know she was your wife. I just followed orders. I swear, it wasn't nothing personal."

"You know what?" Logan stared down at the man now sweating heavily. "I believe you." He increased the pressure. "But it doesn't matter. You still put my woman through hours of terror, and I found her with injuries."

"Please, man. I need a doctor."

"Sure. You'll get medical care." He paused. "As soon as you tell me the name of your boss and why he wants my wife so much that he sent you after her a second time. I want a name. Now."

"I can't. He'll kill me."

Ah. So, the boss was a man. "He's not your biggest problem, buddy. I am."

"Logan," Jesse said. "Ease up. I need to bandage his wound if we're taking him with us."

He wanted to demand time with this creep, but Logan didn't want this man to know where they were staying or have him under the same roof as Poppy. She was having enough trouble sleeping as it was. She wouldn't sleep at all if Thing One was close.

He looked at Brody. "Black site?" Fortress had several black sites around the country to hold terrorists and other dangerous criminals while they were being interrogated. Once Fortress got the information they needed, the prisoners were released to the proper authorities. Since Thing One had kidnapped Poppy, the feds would have a field day charging and prosecuting him. If they didn't take care of business, Logan would do it himself. Thing One wouldn't be a threat to Poppy any more.

"I'll take care of the arrangements," Brody said.

Max arrived. "We're clear. The rest are dead."

"First responders?"

"Five minutes out."

"Jesse, go with Sawyer and Max. Do what you can for our friend here." Brody turned to the other two prisoners. "Logan, what do you want to do with these two?"

"Same as Thing One." As far as he was concerned, they were all terrorists and deserved to rot in a federal prison for what they'd done.

A nod. "Let's move out. Take care of your wife. We'll handle the rest."

"What about Simone?" Sage asked. "We can't just leave her here. She's a target now, too."

"She comes with us," Jesse said. "We'll smooth the way with the authorities after we're sure she's safe."

"Do I get a say in this?" Simone asked.

"Nope." Jesse helped Max haul Thing One to his feet. "Stay behind us and out of touching distance from the three prisoners."

"What are you going to do with them?" she asked as she followed the men through the trees.

"Do you really want to know?"

She was quiet a moment, then said, "You know what? They blew up my house. I don't care where they end up."

Logan returned to Poppy's side, scooped her into his arms, and set off after the others.

"I can walk," she protested.

"I know." He kept walking.

"And you won't put me down?"

"Nope. Deal with it."

She laughed and wrapped her arms around his neck. "I adore you."

"Right back at you, beautiful."

Logan carried her to their SUV and set her in the middle seat, then climbed in after her.

"What about Simone?" Sage asked as she climbed into the shotgun seat.

"She stayed with Jesse." Brody started the engine and drove down the driveway toward the street. He turned right and drove away from Simone's burning home.

"How did the SUVs survive without being blown up by the RPGs?"

"We parked far enough away from the house to escape serious damage. The boss will have to spring for a new paint job, though. The heat from the fire caused some damage."

Logan wrapped his hand around Poppy's. "You okay?"

She nodded and leaned her head against his shoulder. "Where to now?"

"Back to the safe house. Jesse and the others will blindfold the prisoners until we're inside. Then, we'll wait until Fortress sends a team to transport them to the black site. Once the prisoners are gone, we'll go see Ivan and Beverly." If she was up to it.

"I hope the transport team shows up soon."

"Why?" Was Poppy worried about having the prisoners inside the house?

"Our deadline from Dad is approaching soon. He wasn't kidding about sending law enforcement or a Special Forces team after you if I don't make an appearance."

"Sweetheart, I'm a black ops soldier. Your father doesn't intimidate me. Your mother is a different story. She makes me nervous."

Brody chuckled. "Smart man. Don't worry, Poppy. We'll get you to your parents before the deadline. We might have to split the team to do it, but we'll take care of it."

Logan hoped he survived the encounter.

Chapter Nineteen

At the safe house, Logan escorted Poppy upstairs to her room. Their room, now. Satisfaction bloomed in his gut at the thought that Poppy was his to protect night and day. No more late night phone calls when he was in the country. He'd be able to hold her against him all night and know she was safe. If she woke with a nightmare, Logan could comfort her in person.

He closed the door behind them and took Poppy in his arms. He held her against him, trailing a hand up and down her back. "Are you sure you're all right? The didn't hurt you?"

She tightened her hold around his waist. "I need more pain medicine. Otherwise, I'm fine. No fresh injuries."

Tilting her chin up, Logan captured her mouth with his. Man, the taste of her was fire and honey, a perfect combination for him. He took his time, enjoying the silk and heat of her mouth and reveling because he had the right to kiss her.

When his control frayed, he broke the kiss and rested his forehead against hers. "You're a menace, Mrs. Fletcher."

"Why?"

"You unravel my control with your touch and taste. We have to stop, baby, or I won't be able to keep my promise."

"What if I don't want you to keep your promise?" she whispered.

Logan froze. Once the roar in his head died down to a whimper, he said, "There are too many people in this house. I want you all to myself before we go down that path, and only when you're ready. I meant what I said. We wait until you are with me one hundred percent on making this marriage real in every sense of the word. No rushing things. We do it right." If they didn't, Logan worried he'd damage her trust in him. That wasn't happening.

He dropped a gentle kiss on her lips and stepped back. "Take the meds and some time for yourself. I'll let you know when the prisoners are gone."

Logan paused at the door and looked back over his shoulder. "I love you." He left while he still could make the choice to leave her and shut the door. Took every ounce of discipline he had to keep going down the hallway and descend the staircase, but he did it. He was hooked but good on his wife.

Entering the kitchen, he saw the three prisoners seated in the middle of the room.

Jesse glanced up from his work patching up Thing One. "Poppy's okay?"

"Needs pain meds."

Sage stood and motioned to Simone. "Come on. Let's keep her company while the medicine works." The two women left the room.

"Transport is twenty minutes out," Brody said. "Simone's house blowing up has already made the news cycle. If Poppy talked to her folks about Simone, we'll be receiving a phone call soon."

Brody's phone signaled an incoming call. He palmed his phone and glanced at the screen. Brody turned it around so Logan could see the name on the screen. Ivan.

"Want me to take it?"

A head shake. "I've got it. Monitor these three." He walked toward the living room. Seconds later, he answered the call in a low-voiced murmur.

"How is he, Jesse?" Logan asked, staring at the injured man.

"He'll live. The wound is a through-and-through, but he needs a doctor to check him. Needs X-rays to check for fragments as well. The site has doctors on staff, so he'll be well taken care of."

He grunted. Too bad Poppy hadn't done a little more damage to the creep. Whatever. "What's your name?"

Silence.

"I guess he wants to be known as Thing One in prison," Sawyer said. "They can stitch that on his jumpsuit."

The man glared at Sawyer.

"Might as well tell us your name," Max said. "We'll get it anyway when we run your prints. I'm betting you have a nice, long rap sheet."

Thing One glared at Max.

"Guess that's a no on story time." He turned to the other prisoners. "What about you two? Want to do yourselves a favor and tell us your names before we run your prints?"

"What good would that do? We're still going to jail," Red said.

"We'll pass the word to the feds that you cooperated in protecting the vice president's daughters. They'll share the information with the judge. If you tell us more than your name, it's possible the prosecuting attorney could recommend a more lenient sentence to the judge."

Blond snorted.

"If you want to survive your prison sentence, you'll keep your mouths shut," Thing One snapped.

Red and Blond flinched and fell silent. No amount of cajoling or threats convinced them to cooperate.

Brody's phone signaled an incoming text. He glanced at the screen. "Transport team is here."

"You better be taking me to a doctor," Thing One growled. "I'll sue you for every penny you have and make sure you're in the cell right next to me in prison."

"You'll see a doctor," Logan said. Thing One, better known as Trey, would also get up close and personal with the interrogation team at the nearest black site. As tough as old Trey thought he was, the interrogators were one hundred times tougher. Their skills gave Logan nightmares. He didn't know how Fortress trained them, but these men and women got results every time. "I'll let the team inside."

"I demand to see a lawyer," Trey said. "I know my rights."

As far as Logan was concerned, Trey gave up his rights the minute he put his hands on Poppy. "Tell it to someone who cares."

He walked out of the house as the team drove up to the back door in two large SUVs. He recognized one man who exited the lead vehicle. Logan shook Parker Denton's hand. "Long time, buddy."

"Five years, right?"

"At least. Didn't know Maddox had tapped you for this side of Fortress."

A wry smile curved Parker's mouth. "That's what happens when the CIA trains you in illegal skill sets that can't be used anywhere else in civilian life. You end up in black ops. At least I can stay home with my family."

Logan frowned. "You were an agent for The Company when I met you?"

"Yeah. Sorry, man. Couldn't tell you the truth. National security, you know?"

Right. Plenty of secrets to go around these days.

Parker motioned toward the safe house. "What do we have inside?"

"Three men, one of whom kidnapped my wife. My team and I found her before too much damage was done, but I need to stop the ongoing threat to her."

His friend stared. "You're married?"

"That's right."

"Congratulations, Logan. Who's the lucky lady?"

"Poppy Reynolds."

Silence. "The vice president's daughter?"

"The same."

A soft whistle. "You must have a spine of steel, my friend. I wouldn't want to marry into that family."

"Poppy is worth everything."

Parker chuckled. "Spoken like a man in love."

His friend had been in the CIA. Would he have heard about Lynx? If he hadn't, Parker might make an inquiry with someone he trusted. "Send your team inside. I want to ask you about something."

The other man called to his teammates and sent them into the house. He turned back to Logan. "What's this about?"

"I need information about a former agent."

Parker's brows knitted. "Former means retired. Why should I give you any information that might endanger a colleague?"

"The people who want Poppy will not stop until they bring the agent out of the shadows."

"Your wife knows the agent?"

"I'm not sure. However, the kidnappers are convinced she does, and they're using Poppy to draw out your former colleague."

"Does she know who it is?"

"Nope. That's why I wanted to talk to you. We need to warn the agent that he or she is in danger."

"I need something to go on, Logan. You have a name?"

"Lynx."

Parker's face went blank. "You're kidding."

"Afraid not. Do you know who Lynx is?"

"Heard of him. No one at the agency will admit to knowing who this person is. The junior agents think Lynx is a myth, a story the older agents tell to newbies."

"Look, we can't call The Company and tell whoever answers the phone to warn Lynx of the danger. We have to warn the agent. Have any ideas?"

"I might." Parker pulled out his phone. "Give me a minute."

Logan returned to the deck and sat on the stairs, watching his friend and listening to Trey's cursing inside the house.

Two minutes later, Parker slid his phone into his pocket and crossed the yard. "Before you ask, I still don't know Lynx's identity. I called in a favor and learned the name of someone who might know who Lynx is. No guarantees, Logan. This person might not tell you Lynx's identity. He might insist on being the go between. If that's his decision, respect it. He can't be bought or pressured to spill the name if he doesn't believe your story."

"Good enough. How do I contact this agent?"

"Retired agent, and he'll contact you. I gave him your number."

"How did you get my number, Parker?" Logan's voice was soft.

His friend's gaze sharpened. "Take it down a notch or ten, my friend. Zane sent it to me after I told him why I needed it. You're the one asking for help. Do you trust me to provide the assist or not?"

The back door opened. Brody stepped out. "Ready to get these guys out of here?"

Logan gave a small nod. "I want their names, Parker, and anything you can get out of them about their boss. We need to know who sent these men after my wife. I have a feeling Lynx and the boss of these men have history between them, and the boss has a long memory. I won't share the agent's identity, but I won't allow Poppy to pay the price for protecting the agent. You get what I'm saying?"

"Yeah, I understand. I'd do the same if my family's lives were on the line. A piece of advice? Don't cross Lynx. That agent will cut your heart out and feed it to you if you cross him."

"So noted." He held out his hand to Parker. "I owe you."

"We do whatever is necessary to protect our families. One day perhaps you can return the favor."

"Any time, anywhere." His lips curved. "You have my number."

He laughed. "So I do. I'll send you mine in a few minutes."

"Get what I need, my friend. The sooner, the better."

Parker sobered. "My word on that. We'll get the job done."

His team exited the house with the three prisoners and escorted them to the SUVs. Within two minutes, they were gone, leaving a cloud of dust in their wake.

Brody came to stand beside Logan. "We should hear something in the next few hours."

"Will it be soon enough to protect Lynx, Poppy, and Sage?"

"Lynx will have safeguards in place. If not, the agent would have been taken out long ago."

No question. So why was Logan's gut in a knot? "We need to see Ivan and Beverly before they send a team to track us down and drag us back to their place."

"Or drag us to a dungeon somewhere and conveniently forget about us while they take off with our wives for their own protection."

"No one is taking Poppy from me again."

"Then don't make the parents angry." Brody smirked. "Oh, wait. You already did. They just don't know it yet."

"Not funny."

Brody laughed and led the way into the house.

Two hours later, the SUVs carrying the Texas Team and the women parked behind the Reynolds's home.

The leader of Ivan's Secret Service detail met them at the back door. Gavin stared at Simone. "Security has not cleared her. No one may see the vice president or his wife without proper clearance."

"Back off," Brody said. "Fortress cleared her."

"I haven't," countered Gavin.

"I'm not leaving her out here unprotected. Simone is in as much danger as Poppy and Sage. Either you move out of the way, Gavin, or we'll move you."

"It's all right, Gavin." Ivan Reynolds came up behind his security chief. "Let them pass."

"But, sir...."

"We know Simone. She and Poppy were good friends in college. Simone's been here several times over the years." He tapped Gavin on the shoulder. When the agent moved aside, Ivan motioned all of them into the house.

"Good to see you again, Brody." Ivan shook his hand, then hugged Sage. "Welcome home, sweetheart."

"Thanks, Dad. Where's Mom?"

"In the sitting room, reading a book. She'll be surprised to see you." His gaze shifted to Logan. Anger blazed in their depths. "We only expected to see Logan and Poppy. Took you long enough to follow my orders, Fletcher."

"Dad," Poppy said. "Don't start. We have a lot to discuss, and we won't get to any of it if you and Logan start in on each other the minute we walk into the house. Come on, Sage, Simone. Let's go see Mom."

Amused at Poppy's tactic, he followed his wife. Ivan had no choice but to trail the group to the sitting room.

Ahead, he heard Beverly exclaim, "Sage! Oh, baby, it's so good to see you. What a wonderful surprise. And Simone, too. How delightful. Poppy, let me look at you, honey."

Logan entered the room in time to see Beverly cup Poppy's face.

"You're bruised. Are you injured anywhere else?"

"Just the ribs, Mom, plus a few stitches in my scalp. Nothing new since we talked to you from Brent's conference room."

"You look tired, baby."

"A common side effect when I'm not sleeping well. I'll be fine. Don't worry about me."

Beverly clasped Poppy's hand, then frowned as she looked down. "A ring? What's this, Poppy? Who gave this to you?"

"Logan." Poppy smiled at him. "I love it."

"Yes," her mother murmured. "It's beautiful. What does the ring mean, sweetheart? Are you engaged to Logan now?"

"More than that. Logan has a matching ring, Mom."

Silence fell in the room until Ivan grabbed Logan and shoved him against the wall. "What's the meaning of this? What have you done?"

"Dad," Poppy cried. "No."

Logan held up his hand in a signal to let him handle this. "I married your daughter at 11:00 o'clock this morning."

Beverly stared. "You married Poppy without at least inviting us to the wedding? How could you? I thought we could trust you with our precious daughter."

"We wanted a private wedding today. We'll do the big, splashy society wedding after she's safe if that's what Poppy wants. If she doesn't, we'll throw a huge bash to celebrate our wedding with family and friends."

"Are you insane?" Ivan snapped. "She's not ready for marriage. After what she went through in Mexico, I thought you understood how fragile she is."

Logan's eyebrows soared. "Fragile? Are you kidding? Sir, Poppy is the strongest woman I've ever met. She is a warrior from the top of her head to the soles of her feet."

"That doesn't change the facts, Fletcher. Poppy isn't ready to be any man's wife, especially the wife of a hard-nosed man who kills for a living without remorse."

"Take your hands off me, Mr. Vice President." Logan's voice was flat. He was seconds away from punching his father-in-law. Not a smart move, considering he would end up behind bars within minutes. Smart men did not belt the second most powerful man in the nation. Besides, Logan was looking forward to going on his honeymoon with Poppy. He'd prefer to take that honeymoon in this decade.

Ivan frowned, uncertainty flickering in his eyes.

Gavin started toward them.

Brody intercepted him and shook his head. "Family business. Back off."

"My job is to protect him. Your friend is an obvious threat to my principal."

"Ivan doesn't have a mark on him and won't when we leave. This doesn't concern you."

"I'll decide if it concerns me or not. I'm leaning toward the former. The vice president's welfare is my top priority."

"See, we have a meeting of the minds." Brody grinned. "Sage has an interest in her father's wellbeing as well. I'll do anything to make my wife happy. You don't have to worry about Ivan. If you want to stay and watch the fireworks, be my guest, but don't interfere."

"Oh, for heaven's sake, Gavin. Back off," Beverly said. "Logan can't afford to make us angry, either. He won't hurt Ivan, will you, Logan?"

"That's up to your husband, ma'am."

After a long stare, the vice president released Logan and stepped away to stand by Beverly's side. "Explain. Now."

"I love your daughter."

"You just decided that in the past two days?"

"I fell in love with her the moment I first saw her. I've been waiting until Poppy was ready before I pursued more than a friendship with her."

"And you thought now was the time to do that? Give me a break, Fletcher. This is the worst time in her life, and you compounded the issue by forcing her to marry you."

He narrowed his eyes, fury boiling in his blood. "What did you say?"

"You heard me. You forced my daughter to marry you, probably in some misguided attempt to keep her safe."

"Dad," Poppy said. "Look at me." When he did, she said, "Logan didn't force me to do anything. I'm the one who asked him to marry me."

Beverly gasped. "What? Oh, Poppy, how could you be so foolish?"

"I thought you liked Logan."

"We do, sweetheart, as a friend, not family."

"I'm ready to go, Logan," Poppy said. She started toward the door. "You deserve better than to be treated like an outsider."

He shook his head. "We have questions to ask before we go."

"Go where?" Beverly demanded. "You're staying here, all of you." She glanced at Logan. "You're supposed to have our daughter's best interests at heart. Staying here is the safest option for everyone. We can protect you as well, Logan, since you're a target now as well."

"Not a chance."

Ivan took a step toward him again, hands clenched. "What does that mean?"

"This isn't a safe place for Poppy. Your address isn't a secret. This is the most obvious place for Poppy to be when she feels threatened. The men who kidnapped Poppy will have this house under surveillance. They know she's here."

"Surveillance is one thing. Gaining access to this home would require getting through all of our security, plus our details. That won't happen."

"Don't be too sure. No security is foolproof."

"Something else to keep in mind," Brody said. "If Poppy stays here, she'll draw Lynx out of hiding."

#

Chapter Twenty

"That again?" Beverly glared at Logan and Brody. "We told you to drop it. There is no Lynx. If you persist, you'll place a target on an innocent agent's back. Is that what you want?"

Poppy's heart sank. So, her mother was standing by her lie despite Poppy being the target of a kidnapping plot. On the good news front, Beverly had just confirmed the existence of the agent and that she knew the person. Chances were excellent Ivan did as well.

But where did that leave her? In continuous danger from a group of men determined to separate her from Logan, expose Lynx, and kill the agent. "You know Lynx's identity." It was a statement, not a question. Her mother knew the truth. Why wouldn't she just admit the agent was a real person, at least? "We want to warn the agent, not expose him to danger."

"The Company kills to keep their agents' identities a secret, Poppy," her father said. "You can't expect a name or for an agent to walk up and introduce himself. You're wasting your time. Move on."

"You know who Lynx is, don't you?"

Ivan remained mute.

"I'll take that as a confirmation that I'm right."

"Leave it alone, Poppy. We're dropping the subject now." Her father glared at every person in the room. "No one is to speak of this matter outside this room. If you do, you'll suffer the consequences and risk the safety of us all."

Poppy held out her hand to Logan. "I'm ready."

He squeezed her hand and turned toward the sitting-room door.

"Wait a minute." Beverly grasped Poppy's arm. "What are you doing? You mustn't leave this house, Poppy. Logan and Brody are right about one thing. You could be shot the moment you walk outside these walls of safety. Talk to her, Logan. Tell her to stay until we can put together a protection team."

"I have a team," Poppy insisted. "I'm not trading it in for strangers whose loyalty might have been bought by the man who ordered my kidnapping. I have a job to do, and I'll do it with your help or without. Either way, the job will be finished." Even if it was the last thing she did. Poppy refused to be responsible for the death of Lynx.

Besides Lynx's identity, the question that plagued her the most was why these people wanted the agent. The agent had retired more than a decade ago. What could have happened between Lynx and Thing One's boss to cause such a long-term vendetta?

Worse, Poppy knew Lynx. She must. Otherwise, using her as bait made no sense.

Fine. If her parents wouldn't help, Poppy would put her research skills to use. With a little help from Simone, they would track down this agent and warn the former operative of the impending danger.

She kissed her mother's cheeks, then her father's, and left the room with Logan despite her mother's protests. The others followed. Sage and Brody were the last to return to the SUV. Her sister was crying.

"You okay, sis?" Poppy asked.

"I will be." She sniffed. "I've never seen Mom and Dad so angry. They tried to pressure Brody into ordering Logan to stand down and threatened to have Fortress blackballed."

Logan released Poppy's hand and gripped the door handle.

"No," Brody said, voice sharp. "I handled it. Leave it alone for now, Logan."

"Are you telling me that as my team leader or as my best friend?"

"Both. We have other things to do and not much time to finish the job. Hash this out with Ivan after a family dinner."

A snort. "I'd be afraid to eat or drink anything in that house. The way things stand, I wouldn't put it past Beverly to poison me to rid herself of my presence."

When Logan removed his hand from the handle, Poppy relaxed against him and reclaimed his hand. "Thanks," she whispered.

"Where to?" Brody asked as he cranked the engine.

"Safe house," Logan said. "We need to regroup and come up with a plan. If Ivan and Beverly won't help, we'll find Lynx ourselves. I refuse to allow a patriot to die if I can prevent the death."

Brody sent a text, then drove from the Reynolds estate. "Sit back and relax, ladies. We're taking the scenic route."

Twenty minutes into the drive, Logan's phone rang. He checked the screen and swiped his thumb across the glass. "Parker, you're on speaker with Brody and his wife, Sage, and Poppy."

"Copy that. I have permission to share my contact's name and a secure location to meet."

He frowned. "I appreciate the name. Not going to meet anyone at a place I haven't vetted personally."

"I told him that would be your response. Glad I haven't forgotten how you operate."

"Name?"

"I'll send it in a text. Same with the meeting site. He agreed to meet in three hours so, you'll have adequate time to scout the area."

"You sure your contact is trustworthy?"

"Positive. He was my partner for several missions. We keep in close contact, Logan. I'd know if he was dirty."

"I trust you. I don't trust him. If I don't like what I see, I'll text you an alternative location to pass along to your friend."

"He may not agree."

"His choice. My priority is Poppy's safety."

"Let me know as soon as you can." Parker ended the call.

"I don't like it," Brody said. "Too many things can go wrong."

Logan's lips curved. "That's supposed to be my line." His phone signaled. Once again, he checked the screen. "Meeting site is Hazel Grove Lakeside Log Cabins. Cabin 15." He pulled up a map of the area and studied it for a moment. "Looks like the cabin is relatively secluded."

"Is that good?" Sage asked.

"Could be. Might be a perfect spot for an ambush, too."

"We'll check the security. If it looks dicey, we'll find another place to meet. There's another safe house near there. We could use that as a last resort."

Another safe house? Wouldn't that be a better spot than a public campground? "Why don't we tell Parker that we prefer to meet there for security reasons and skip the assessment of the cabin?" Poppy asked.

"Compromises the safe house. Fortress won't be able to use that site anymore."

"Why not? Parker's friend is a former CIA agent. He has as much to lose from being exposed to danger as the rest of us."

"Safe houses are supposed to be off-the-grid locations for the safety of our principals," Brody said. "If the agent isn't as trustworthy as Parker believes, he could leak the location."

"We don't want anyone connected to the CIA knowing the safe house location. The Company is well known for using every piece of information they learn. If we use the safe house, Fortress will need to sell it and buy another place."

Sage sighed. "That would be a hassle."

"Brent will do it in a heartbeat to protect one of our own. Poppy is his to protect as much as she is Logan's, mine, and our team's. Logan, call Max and tell him the change in plans."

After a brief conversation with the other half of the team, they chose a route with enough twists and turns to spot a tail but quick enough to get them on site to assess the security risks before accepting or changing the meeting location.

Once the route had been sent to Max, Jesse, and Simone, Poppy asked, "Who are we meeting?"

"Jamie Greeley."

Sage twisted in her seat to look at Poppy. "That has to be a coincidence."

"What is, baby?" Brody asked.

"We've met a man named Jamie Greeley."

"When was the last time you saw him?" Logan asked. "How well do you know him?"

Poppy considered his questions for a minute. "Must have been about twelve years ago. What do you think, Sage?"

She looked thoughtful. "Sounds right. We were still in high school the last time he stopped by to see Mom and Dad when we lived at home."

"Do you know what he wanted?"

"Not really. He was an infrequent visitor, Logan. I only remember him stopping by to see our parents a handful of times before we left home."

"How was he connected to Beverly and Ivan?" Brody asked.

Poppy and Sage exchanged glances. "We don't know. He was in and out of our lives infrequently during our school years," Poppy said. "Jamie never stayed more than an hour or two."

"I got the impression that he and Mom were friends in their school days," Sage said. "I might be wrong, though. When Jamie was in the house, we were encouraged to go do something somewhere else while the grownups talked. As we grew older, Poppy and I were involved in so many school activities and advanced classes, Mom and Dad didn't have to tell us to do schoolwork or go to the library. We were already headed there, anyway."

Brody looked skeptical. "You're telling me you and Poppy curbed your curiosity enough to get out of earshot without protest every time Greeley showed up?"

Poppy laughed. "You know us too well."

"What stopped you?"

"Mom and Dad always talked to Jamie in Dad's office."

Brody frowned. "That room was soundproof."

"Which is why we never knew the reason Jamie stopped by to visit." Sage smiled. "He always brought us small gifts from various countries."

"The gifts made him one of our favorite visitors." Poppy shifted, flinching at the pain in her ribs. She wished her ribs would heal already. The bruises were painful and annoying. Worse, they had slowed her down when they ran from the second kidnapping team. "Any word from the interrogators?"

"Not yet," Logan said. "They haven't been at the site for long. The priority is to treat wounds. After that, they'll start the interrogation process. Parker knows what we need and why. He'll get the job done as soon as he can."

Ugh. She needed to back off. Of all people, Poppy knew the process took time. Rushing might mean missing an important piece of information.

If she had anything to go on, Poppy knew she and Simone could run with it. Between them, they might piece together enough information to identify Lynx.

The easiest way to get the information would be for her and Sage to persuade Jamie to tell them Lynx's name. Perhaps with his history in their lives, he would be more inclined to tell them the name or, if nothing else, pass the warning on to Lynx himself, so the retired agent was ready.

Brody used the SUV's Bluetooth to call Brent and update him on the latest information and their plans.

"Watch your back," Brent warned. "Any time the CIA is involved, even peripherally, you can expect trouble. I'm looking at a map of the campsite. Too many places for a sniper to create a nest and wait."

"How would the sniper know?" Brody said. "We didn't know where we were headed until fifteen minutes ago."

"Hackers are everywhere. I ought to know. I'm constantly looking for another one for the Fortress tech teams."

"You should talk to Simone Kent," Sage said. "She's almost as good as Zane."

"I'll look at her background. Thanks for the recommendation."

"Jesse will appreciate it," Poppy said.

He groaned. "You're kidding."

"Afraid not. Simone seems to have captured his interest."

"Oh, brother," Brent muttered. "If this develops into something, Fortress will gain the reputation of being a matchmaking agency instead of a security company."

"Doesn't fit with the macho image, does it?" she teased.

"No, ma'am. It doesn't. So, Poppy, I understand you married Logan this morning."

"I did."

"Congratulations. He's a good man when he's not being pigheaded or prickly."

She laughed. "I'll remember that when Logan makes me angry."

"Logan."

"Yes, sir?"

"When you're ready to go on your honeymoon, let me know. If I can, I'll fly you to your destination in one of the jets."

"Thank you, sir."

"Brody, update me in four hours." He ended the call.

"Not much for small talk, is he?" Sage said.

"Not his strong suit," Brody agreed. "So, Logan, have you made plans for your honeymoon?"

A frown. "Of course. I've already made tentative reservations for us. The hotel is holding a rental for us."

"Where are you going?"

"Nope, not going there."

"Aww, come on. Why not?"

"Forget it. You and the rest of Texas Team would show up. I want Poppy to myself. Pranksters and babysitters are not required. I can handle it on my own."

"I don't know, man. You're not the best at wooing the ladies."

"I got the only woman that matters without your help. I think I'll be fine without your advice."

The bantering continued until they drove onto the grounds of the Hazel Grove Lakeside Cabins. Following the signs, Brody located Cabin 15 and parked. "Stay inside, ladies. You're protected in here."

"If you determine it's safe, I need to get out and walk," Sage said.

"Hurting?"

She nodded. "Sorry."

"Don't be. I should have realized. If I don't think this is safe enough, we'll go someplace that is for you to walk."

"Thanks, sweetheart."

Brody and Logan exited the SUV and met Max and Jesse at the front. After a short debate, Jesse and Max stationed themselves with the vehicles while Brody, Logan, and Sawyer started their assessment of security.

Ten minutes later, they returned and opened the doors for Poppy and Sage. Jesse helped Simone from the vehicle, too.

"It's safe?" Poppy asked.

"Enough. Come on. Jamie is waiting for us."

Sage gasped. "He's inside?"

"He knew we'd come early to evaluate the security setup and figured his best protection for himself was to show up at the site ahead of time."

"In case someone caught wind of what he was doing and tried to stop him?"

"A leak," Poppy said, tone grim. That was all they needed. A traitor in the ranks of the CIA.

Logan inclined his head. "Can't take anything for granted."

"Does he know how many of us are going to come into the cabin?" Poppy asked. "From what I remember, he wasn't a fan of crowds."

"He knows and agreed to the group. Jamie is eager to reconnect with you and Sage."

"We were just acquaintances." Why did he want to reconnect now? She hadn't seen him since she graduated from college.

"He probably wants an update on Mom and Dad," Sage said.

Logical. "He should contact them. They'd love to talk to him."

"Maybe he's distancing himself from them for a reason," Logan murmured. "His sudden appearance at the estate puts a target on his back and creates a bigger risk for Ivan and Beverly. He was an agent which means he created enemies who carry a grudge."

Poppy started toward the cabin. "How would they find him?"

"We're not the only ones with hackers in our arsenal of weapons," Brody said. He scanned the area as he escorted Sage toward the cabin. "We need to get you and Poppy inside."

"I don't like the setup." Sawyer passed the couples and moved into point position.

"Even though we passed vacationers coming onto the grounds, the tree cover, bushes, and landscaping keep you from seeing anyone," Simone said. "If I didn't know better, I'd say we were out here all alone. For a city girl like me, this is downright creepy."

"At least you're not required to stay in a tent and sleep on the ground like we had to do one July weekend as kids," Poppy said.

Sage laughed. "What a nightmare."

"Sounds like a good story." Logan wrapped his arm around Poppy's shoulders and drew her up against his side as they approached the back of the cabin. His free hand held a gun near his thigh.

"Oh, it is," Sage said. "You'll particularly appreciate Poppy's close encounter with a raccoon."

Poppy groaned. "You'll never let me live that down."

"Oh, no. It's too good a story to let it die."

Sawyer held up his fist, signaling everyone behind him to wait. He eased around the corner of the cabin with his gun in hand, returning less than a minute later. "Clear."

Brody eased Sage behind him and took the lead. Standing to the side, he knocked on the door, then turned the knob. "It's Brody. My team and I are entering with the women."

"Come."

Poppy's heart beat faster. She recognized that voice. This man was their Jamie Greeley. Couldn't be a coincidence that he was involved. Was Jamie the former agent known as Lynx? If so, this part of their mission was finished, which left identifying the person determined to capture Lynx by using Poppy.

Logan nudged Poppy behind him and followed Brody and Sage into the cabin, keeping his free hand wrapped around hers. He didn't holster his gun.

Poppy walked into the cabin and glanced around. Nice. Very nice. The beautiful wood gleamed in the fading light. The kitchen, though rustic, looked as though making family dinners in there would be a breeze.

The team spread out around the dining/kitchen area, forming a loose circle around Sage, Poppy, and Simone. "Is there coffee in the kitchen?" Brody asked Jamie. "I think we can all use some."

A slight rustling came from the front room of the cabin. "Yeah. I'll fix it. Could use a cup myself."

Jamie Greeley stepped into the kitchen, his gaze sweeping the group until he saw Sage and Poppy. A smile tugged at his mouth. "Wow," he said. "Look at you two."

He glanced at Brody and Logan, then gestured toward Poppy and her sister. "May I approach?"

Brody inclined his head.

Keeping his hands away from his body, the former agent breached the circle and hugged Sage. "You look beautiful, Sage. Your husband is one lucky man."

She laughed. "I tell him that all the time."

Jamie turned to Poppy, and after receiving a slight nod from Logan, embraced her. "Poppy, I heard about the kidnapping. You're all right?"

Poppy hugged him back, memories of other brief hugs from him swirling in the back of her mind. "I'll heal. A few bruises and a handful of stitches."

"I'm glad." He set her away from him and looked at her. "I've read your books. You're a talented writer."

"Thanks."

"When's the next book coming out?"

If she had a dollar for every time someone asked her that question, she'd be a wealthy woman. "I haven't decided on my next project yet. Life has been hectic lately." For months.

Jamie said nothing for a moment. "PTSD can do strange things to you. You'll get your writing mojo back. You're a writer, Poppy. You can't help but write. When your mind finally accepts that you're safe, you'll be back in front of the keyboard with words flowing onto the screen at a record pace. I'm looking forward to reading the next Poppy Reynolds book."

"It may not be what I've written in the past," she warned.

"I read many genres." He crossed the kitchen to the coffeemaker. Once he prepped the machine, Jamie turned to the others as the brew cycle began. "Let's sit down."

Once everyone took a seat, he said, "Parker called in a favor, Logan. So, here I am. How can I help?"

"Do you know why Poppy was kidnapped?"

"We didn't get into details." A wry smile curved his mouth. "He was a little busy when he called."

"The men who took Poppy wanted to use her as leverage to draw Lynx out of the shadows. Their boss wants the former agent, and he's willing to do anything to get what he wants."

The agent's eyes darkened. "The threat is still active?"

"They tried to take Poppy a second time earlier today."

"Obviously, they failed."

"They blew up my house with us in it," Simone muttered.

"A bomb?"

"RPG," Jesse said.

Jamie whistled. "Heavy firepower."

"Will you help us, Jamie?" Sage asked. "We don't want to endanger Lynx, but we want to warn him to be alert."

"This isn't something we wanted to go through proper channels at The Company," Poppy added. "We're afraid of a leak."

He sighed. "You're wise to be concerned. Trust me, sweetheart. Lynx already knows about the danger and is taking proper precautions."

"You've talked to the agent?"

Jamie shook his head. "Nope. Haven't talked to her in several months."

Lynx was a woman? Woohoo, Poppy thought. Half of the agents from the CIA had been eliminated from the pool of possibilities.

"If you haven't talked to her, how do you know she's aware of the danger? The news media doesn't know about the kidnapping although they must know about Simone's house. Lynx couldn't possibly know I was kidnapped unless she's still working for the CIA or has informants who keep her informed of things that pertain to her." Poppy folded her arms on the tabletop and leaned closer to Jamie. "You knew, though. Are you the leak, Jamie?"

"No." He pushed back from the table and walked to the coffeemaker. He pulled several to-go cups from the cabinet and poured coffee into each of them. After a quick glance at Sage, he nuked a cup of water in the microwave and added a bag of herbal tea to the steaming water. Jamie set Sage's tea in front of her and seated himself again. "The rest of you can grab your own."

Brody, Logan, and the other men rose to retrieve the other cups of coffee. Logan and Jesse carried two cups to the table and handed them to Poppy and Simone.

Once the group returned to their seats, Logan resumed their conversation with Jamie. "Just no? You're not the leak, but you won't offer proof?"

"Come on, Logan. How do you prove a negative?"

"Give us the name of the person feeding information to the man after Poppy and Lynx."

"Trust me. If I knew who was leaking information, that person wouldn't be among the living. I'll do anything to protect Lynx. Anything."

"We need to talk to her," Brody said. "Even if she's aware of the danger and is in hiding, that still leaves Poppy and Sage in the crosshairs of the man who wants her."

"And now that Simone's connection to Poppy has been discovered, she's in danger as well," Jesse added. "We need information from her that only she can give us, and we need it yesterday."

Jamie shook his head. "I can't help you. I'm sorry."

"You mean you won't." Sage scowled at him. "These men hurt my sister, Jamie. They're not playing around. If the attacks continue, one of them will take us and injure or kill our husbands and their teammates."

The agent frowned. "Husbands?" His gaze shifted from Sage to Poppy. "You're married, too?"

She held up her hand with her wedding ring. "As of this morning."

"Congratulations. I'm sure your parents were glad to add another fine man to the family."

"You'd be wrong," Logan said. "I need to get Poppy out of here. Either put us in contact with Lynx or give us her name."

Jamie chuckled. "I don't have to tell you a thing. You've already talked to her."

Poppy froze. No. It couldn't be true. Could it? She looked at Sage and saw the same shock on her sister's face that she felt.

But what if Jamie was right? All her trips away when she and Sage were kids weren't to visit friends but were instead work-related absences?

Was it possible?

"Poppy." Logan's hand wrapped around hers and squeezed. "What is it, baby?"

"It's Mom. She is Lynx."

#

Chapter Twenty-One

Brody dragged a hand down his face. "Oh, man. I never would have guessed Beverly was Lynx. It sure explains a few things, though."

"Like what?" Logan asked. The only thing Beverly's alternate identity explained to him was the open hostility when he and Brody pushed Beverly and Ivan to tell them Lynx's identity so they could warn her of the danger she was in. The joke was on them, it seemed. Beverly didn't need the warning.

"Her extensive travel schedule when Sage and Poppy were kids, her confidence and awareness of her surroundings."

"No wonder she was so security conscious when we lived at home," Sage said. "She's always armed, and she is well known for ordering around the security details when she's not happy with the arrangements. How did we not figure this out on our own, Poppy?"

"Who expects your mother, the perfect politician's wife, to be some super spy?" She looked thoughtful. "You know, now that I think about it, Mom might be part of Dad's security team."

"Really?"

"For the past ten years, Mom hasn't traveled without Dad. Anywhere he's sent by President Martin, Mom goes with him. If you watch the media coverage, she's always beside him, alert and scanning the area just like Logan and Brody." Poppy looked at Jamie. "Am I right?"

He smiled. "Clever woman, just like your mother."

"I feel stupid. I noticed none of that. I should have."

Brody wrapped his arm around her shoulders. "She's your mother, Sage. You saw what you expected to see. A woman who loved you and worked hard to make the world a safer place for you and your sister."

"Why didn't she just tell us in the first place? We're not gossips, especially when family safety is at stake."

"She couldn't." Jamie swallowed another sip of coffee. "Company rules. It's for the safety of the families, Sage, another protection measure. You can't tell what you don't know."

"Lot of good that did me," Poppy said. "My kidnappers didn't believe me when I said I didn't know who Lynx was. They hinted that a lot of pain was in my near future if I didn't tell them what they wanted to know because they believed I was lying."

Jamie frowned. "I'm sorry. Did they carry through on their threat?"

She shook her head. "Logan and his team rescued me before they could."

Logan squeezed Poppy's hand. "You rescued yourself. We just mopped up." Knowing the fear she'd gone through gutted him, and he vowed that would never happen again. His life's mission from now on was to keep his wife safe.

She brushed her lips over his, then turned back to Jamie. "We have one question answered, thanks to you. Will you answer a second one?"

"If I can. I'm still bound to protect national security, sweetheart."

"Fair enough."

"What's your question?"

"Who wants Mom dead?"

He chuckled. "That's a long list, and I don't know most of them. I only know about the missions we worked on together."

"Beverly and Ivan trust you," Logan said. "Otherwise, they wouldn't have invited you into their home and introduced you to their daughters. Who has Beverly been concerned would come after her for revenge if they learned her identity?"

Jamie hesitated. "None of her targets lived to exact revenge."

"Understood. That leaves family and friends with enough hate to fuel the fire for a decade. Give us names."

A head shake. "National security risk. I can't."

"You'd rather I go trolling through Lynx's file at the CIA to get the information we need?" Simone demanded. "Because that's my next step, and I won't regret breaking a million laws to keep Poppy and Sage safe. You say you're friends with Lynx. Hopefully, you're a good enough friend so that you'll want to protect the Reynolds sisters as well."

The agent leaned closer, anger flickering in the depths of his eyes. "Those files are classified. How would you gain access to them?"

"Nothing is classified if you're good enough."

"And you are?"

She smiled.

Jamie blew out a breath. "I could turn you in and have you tossed in prison."

"But you won't. So, what's it going to be? You or me?"

He stared at her for a long moment before shifting his gaze to Logan. "Ask Beverly."

"We did. She blew us off, refusing to acknowledge that Lynx actually exists. Help us protect Lynx's daughters."

"Three names that you didn't hear from me."

Logan gave a slight nod. He understood the seriousness of this breach in security. Jamie was risking his freedom and his life by giving them the information. If The Company found out, they would take steps to punish Jamie for passing along classified information.

"Ashley Holden, Amir Al-Abad, and Raul Fontaine."

Brody grimaced and grabbed his phone to send a text.

Logan froze, recognizing the names of all three high-profile assassinations. "Were you her partner for those missions?"

Jamie nodded. "Lynx did the work. I was her backup if she got into trouble. Those were Lynx's last missions. Look into all of them, but your most likely suspects will be the Holden family and the Fontaine family. I've monitored all three of the families from a distance, but no one in Al-Abad's family misses him in the slightest. The prince was a sadist and his family is glad to be rid of him."

"Anyone else?"

He snorted. "Plenty. These three are the most likely. Everyone else would be further down the list. Listen, Beverly was a world-class assassin and an excellent tactician. I wouldn't want her on my trail. She didn't make mistakes."

"No one's perfect," Brody said.

"She was as close to it as I've ever seen. I've heard no rumors about someone looking for her by her given name, just by her nickname. For a few years after she retired, I heard of a few families turning over every rock they could find to locate the assassin who murdered their loved ones. Nothing ever came of the inquiries. After a while, they gave up and moved on. The only families that have been consistent in looking for Lynx are Holden and Fontaine. Zip from Al-Abad's family."

"Thanks for the information."

"You're out of this," Logan said. "Whatever plan you have in place to disappear with a new identity, implement it now. No contact with Beverly, Ivan, Poppy, or Sage until this is over. You'll know when it's finished. Stay gone until it is."

He didn't want Jamie Greeley caught up in the fallout over this. Another problem was protecting Lynx's identity from the media. If she was identified in the media as a former agent, the danger to her and Ivan would escalate. Talk about a high profile CIA operative.

Jamie handed Logan a slip of paper. "My phone number. It's a burner phone. No way to trace it. If I can help from the shadows, I will."

He put the number in his contact list and handed the paper back to Jamie. "When are you leaving?"

"Right now. My bags and new identification are in the SUV." The agent hugged Poppy and Sage. "Be safe, both of you. Leave the hero business to your husbands." He shook hands with the rest of the group and left.

"We need to clean the coffeepot and get out of here." Brody stood. "My skin is crawling."

"Same," Sawyer said as he pushed back from the table. "We've been here too long."

A deafening explosion rocked the cabin and rattled the windows. Logan and his teammates leaped to their feet. Bomb. That was the last thing they wanted to hear.

Sage's face went sheet white. "What was that?"

Brody and Logan raced for the back door, weapons in their hands. "Stay here," Brody said. "Max, you're with us. The rest of you get ready to move."

The three of them slipped from the cabin and quickly located the source of the explosion. Back in the trees, an SUV had burst into flame. Behind the wheel, the driver slumped in his seat. Jamie Greeley had had no chance to survive. Someone had planted a bomb that detonated the moment he turned on the ignition which meant the person responsible had either planted the device after Jamie was in the cabin or planted it earlier with a cell phone attached and triggered the explosion when the agent was ready to leave. With either scenario, the bomber had been too close to Poppy, Sage, and Simone.

"Let's go," Brody said. "We can't help Jamie, and he wouldn't thank us for sacrificing the women's safety to watch the fire."

"First responders will be here soon," Max said.

"Check the SUVs." Logan didn't like this scenario at all. He needed to get Poppy to safety, but rushing to climb into compromised vehicles would kill them all.

"I'll take care of it."

The three of them ran back to Cabin 15. Max headed toward the front of the structure to check the vehicles. Logan and Brody returned to the cabin.

Logan stepped inside. "Sawyer, help Max with the SUVs."

The women stood, watching him and Brody.

"What happened?" Poppy asked. "Is Jamie all right?"

Man, he hated to tell her the news. She and Sage would be devastated. Worse, Poppy would blame herself.

He drew her into his arms and saw Brody embrace Sage. "I'm sorry, baby. He's gone."

"What?" Poppy peered up at him.

"Someone planted a bomb in his SUV. That was the explosion we heard. As soon as Max and Sawyer check our vehicles for bombs, we're out of here. We don't want the first responders to see or question us. The delay isn't safe."

"No," Sage whispered. "We can't just leave Jamie. It's wrong. We have to do something."

"We can't help him, sweetheart," Brody said. "He'd want us to protect you, and that's what we're going to do."

Tears streaked down her face. "How will we tell Mom? This is horrible. Jamie was her friend. She'll be heartbroken."

"I know. I'm sorry."

Poppy buried her face in Logan's neck, and soon he felt the wetness of her tears against his skin. Her silent crying broke him apart inside, as nothing had ever done in his life. He ached for her pain at the loss. Once again, he'd been too late to spare her from yet another blow. "I'm so sorry," he whispered in her ear.

She pressed closer to him. "Get me out of here. Please."

"As soon as we're clear," he promised.

Two minutes later, Max entered the cabin. "We're clear." His expression was grim. "Sawyer and I deactivated one bomb on each vehicle. The devices were set to go off when we turned on the engines."

Fury filled Logan. Whoever was doing this was dead. "Let's go." He released Poppy and threaded his fingers through hers, leading her from the cabin. The sound of sirens and screams of women drifted in the air. They had little time before first responders descended on them, and the questions would begin. Time to escape without detection was almost gone.

Scanning the area, Logan hustled Poppy to the SUV, helped her into the backseat, and climbed in beside her. Brody buckled his weeping wife into the shotgun seat and circled to climb behind the wheel.

Behind them, Jesse tucked Simone into the backseat of the second SUV and climbed in beside her as Max and Sawyer claimed the front seats, with Max once again behind the wheel.

Brody drove away from the cabin with the other part of the team close behind. Beside him, Sage continued to cry.

Logan wrapped his arm around Poppy's shoulders and drew her against his side. The person who had murdered Jamie Greeley would pay, he vowed.

Silence filled the SUV for long minutes until Poppy drew in a deep, hitching breath. "I should call Mom."

"I'll take care of it."

She glanced up at him. "I ought to take care of this myself."

"This one is on me."

"His death isn't your fault."

"I should have insisted on a different location. Based on Jamie's actions, he was comfortable in that cabin."

"I don't know if he'd been hiding out in the facility or if he visited often enough to be familiar with the cabins," Brody said. "Either way, he wasn't careful enough. Someone found out his location and set up surveillance on him. The bomber knew where he'd be and was prepared to take out all of us to ensure he killed Jamie. That he could kill you and Sage was just a bonus."

Poppy scowled. "I don't see how that's a bonus. You and Logan called me leverage. Sage, too. We can't be used as leverage if Mom loses us both."

"Your deaths would make the news cycle for a long time, and the events surrounding the funerals wouldn't be secured. Your mother and father would attend. What better way to make an even larger splash than by assassinating the Vice President and his wife?"

"You're assuming the man who orchestrated my kidnapping knows Lynx's identity. I don't think he does. Otherwise, why take me in the first place? Why not just go for her directly?"

"You're an easier target," Logan said. "The security at the Reynolds estate is impressive. You had an alarm system that didn't do the job." He'd be overseeing upgrades himself. His wife wouldn't be at risk like that again. Later, if they were blessed with children, Logan planned to step up security measures even more. No one would touch his family and live.

He cupped her cheek with his palm. "Let me take care of contacting your mother. She won't be happy when she hears the news about Jamie."

Understatement of the year on that one. He wondered if his marriage to Poppy would be the shortest on record. Lynx would chew him up and spit him out. Worse, she was a trained assassin, the best in the business. He'd be lucky to survive to reach his one-month anniversary, much less his one year benchmark.

"Want me to make a detour?" Brody asked him.

"No. We need to take Poppy, Sage, and Simone to secure surroundings as fast as possible. I'll deal with Beverly then."

While they continued to drive through the countryside toward their safe house, Logan cobbled together a plan to inform Lynx that her occasional CIA partner was gone. He just hoped he'd be able to keep himself out of the hands of the feds and Beverly Reynolds until Poppy was safe. After that, he'd fight to keep her by his side. Whether he'd succeed was anyone's guess.

First, though, he and the others must survive the coming confrontation with the people responsible for Poppy's kidnapping and Jamie's murder.

Chapter Twenty-Two

In the safe house library, Logan slid his phone into his pocket and dragged a hand down his face. He didn't want to make a call like that again soon. Death notifications had been part of the job as a law enforcement officer, a part every cop dreaded. This notification, though, had been filled with blame, recrimination, and a demand to bring Beverly's daughters back to her immediately or he'd face serious repercussions.

Although he believed the threats, Logan would not leave Poppy's security in the hands of the Secret Service and Beverly. Barricading themselves in at the Reynolds estate was a disaster in the making. The enemy had RPGs and wasn't afraid to use them. Having all of them together in one place made wiping out the family easy. He refused to hand the enemy a victory because this was a war Logan intended to win. The price of the loss was too high.

A soft knock sounded on the door. When the knob turned, Poppy poked her head into the room and smiled. "Is it safe?"

He chuckled. "For now." He held out his hand.

She walked inside and closed the door. Poppy glanced around as she made her way to his side and took his hand. "This room is amazing. I could spend days in here."

"Do I hear book envy in your voice?"

"Depends on the books on the shelves." She breathed in. "I love the scent of books. There's nothing in the world like that scent even though ebooks are wonderful for instant delivery and gratification."

She turned into his open embrace and wrapped her arms around him. "Was the call a bad one?"

"What do you think?"

"Knowing Mom, she threatened to track you down on your next mission and kill you in the most painful way possible."

"Bingo. Beverly said she'd wait until I was dead asleep, then gut me before I woke and watch me bleed out."

Poppy flinched. "Ouch."

"That's not the worst part."

"I hate to ask, but what was that?"

"She planned to slip a tasteless and odorless slow-acting poison into my drink first, one that causes the victim excruciating pain for hours before killing them. Beverly gleefully told me there's no antidote to this poison."

"She must have been joking."

"Oh, no, baby. She was dead serious." Logan squeezed her tighter. "You know as well as anyone your mother doesn't joke about matters of life and death."

"I'll talk to her."

"Not tonight."

"We can't let her put this plan into motion."

"Part of what she said came from a well of deep grief. She'll calm down in a few days after the shock wears off." He hoped. Otherwise, Poppy would be a widow soon.

"I hope you're right. So, what's next?" She yawned. "Sorry. Sleepless nights are catching up with me."

He pressed a soft kiss to her lips. "Ready to go to bed?"

Poppy's face flushed, but she nodded.

"No pressure, baby," he murmured. "As long as your face is the last I see at night and the first I see in the morning, and I can hold you all night, I'll be happy."

"Promise?"

"Absolutely."

She relaxed and held out her hand to him. "Let's go upstairs."

Inside the bedroom they would share, Logan threaded his fingers through Poppy's hair. He nodded toward the bathroom. "While you get ready for bed, I'll grab my gear from the other room. Take your time, Poppy. There's no rush."

"Okay," she whispered.

"Do you need anything from downstairs?"

"Water, please."

"You got it." He brushed his mouth over hers and left the room, closing the door behind him.

Logan walked into the room next door and closed himself in. He sighed, surprised at how much his hands shook as he gathered his gear into the Go bag. He didn't know if Beverly would kill him first or if the wait for Poppy to come to him on her own terms would do him in.

And he was known for his self-control? What a laugh. His control felt as strong as a puff of smoke. He'd deal. No way would Logan chance losing Poppy because he didn't wait for her. If waiting was best for his wife, that's what he'd do. In the meantime, Logan planned to win Poppy's trust one kiss, hug, and caress at a time. Soon, she'd become his in every way.

He zipped his Go bag and carried it to their bedroom, opening the door just enough to place the bag on the floor beside the door.

In the kitchen, Logan grabbed two bottles of water and turned to retrace his steps when he came face to face with Brody. "Hey."

"How is Poppy?"

"Upset about Jamie and nervous about sharing a bed with me."

His team leader nodded. "Figured. Is there anything I can do to help?"

"Yeah, convince Beverly not to kill me."

Brody grunted. "The call went that well, huh?"

"She threatened to poison me and watch me suffer for hours before she gutted me, then sat back to watch me bleed out."

His friend whistled. "I wouldn't want her after me. Guess I'll be the favorite son-in-law again after you're dead."

"Ha ha. She wants us to bring Poppy and Sage back to the estate and promised we'd regret it if we didn't."

"I was afraid of that. Not happening."

"That's what I told Poppy. We'd paint a target on the estate and lose all four of them at once."

"Want me to talk to Beverly?"

"Not tonight. Let's give her time for the shock to ease off. Then we'll tackle Lynx. Who's on watch tonight?"

"Not you. You have a wife to comfort. Max, Jesse, and Sawyer are splitting the shifts."

"Is Simone okay?" He hadn't seen the computer hacker since they finished a simple dinner of sandwiches and chips.

"She's ticked off and vowing revenge on the people who destroyed her house."

"Don't blame her. What's her plan for the night?"

"Research on the Holden and Fontaine families. Zane also sent me a text. Simone cleared the security checks. She's been given limited access to Fortress database information on the two families. I was also instructed to give her the extra laptop we keep ready for use here. She's working in the security room now alongside Jesse while he's on shift." Brody gave him a pointed look. "Our medic wanted to be available in case Poppy or Sage needed him overnight."

"He won't have to intervene."

Brody watched him a moment, then gave a curt nod. "If you need me, I'll be across the hall. Try to get some rest."

"Same to you."

"I plan on it."

The two men climbed the stairs together and headed to their respective bedrooms.

Logan waited until his friend went inside his room before turning his door knob. He breathed a silent prayer for his own self-control and stepped inside the room. Poppy was nowhere to be seen. Good or bad? He couldn't decide, since he didn't know how long her bedtime routine normally took.

After setting a bottle of water on each of their nightstands and considering the problem of Poppy's continued absence, he grabbed his toothbrush, toothpaste, lightweight sweats, and a t-shirt and returned to the bathroom down the hall. After finishing his night routine in five minutes, Logan traipsed down the hall again and entered the bedroom.

Poppy huddled under the covers, her eyes wide and her face pale as she watched him close the door.

"Ready for me to turn out the light?"

She nodded. "Do you mind leaving the bathroom light on?"

"Of course not, sweetheart." He flipped the wall switch, and the room plunged into darkness except for a dim light shining in the bathroom. "Will this work, or do you want the overhead light on?"

Silence. "You'd do that for me?"

"Don't you know by now that I would do anything for you, including taking a bullet? Leaving on the light to sleep is nothing."

More silence. "We'll leave the room as it is for now."

He moved with quiet steps to the opposite side of the bed. "If you wake in the night and the darkness bothers you, tell me. I'll turn the light on."

"Will you be able to sleep?"

"I can sleep anywhere. Do you mind if I hold you, Poppy?"

"I'd like that."

He hated to hear her voice shake as though she feared him. The thought that she might be terrified made his stomach knot. He wasn't a mind reader, though. Logan had to take her word as truth.

Lifting the quilt and sheet, he eased into bed and slid in behind Poppy. Logan rested his hand on her waist and slowly wrapped his arm around her. "Okay?"

"Yes. I love you, Logan."

"I love you, too, Poppy. Sleep now. I've got you."

By degrees, she relaxed against him, and minutes later slid into sleep.

Thank God. At least he hadn't traumatized her or raised terrible memories. Maybe now he would rest, too. He'd been short on sleep the night he received word from Zane that Poppy had been kidnapped, and he had slept little since.

He let himself drift into a light sleep in case Poppy woke in the night and needed him, praying she wouldn't wake up terrified she was in the hands of her kidnappers.

Logan's internal body clock woke him at 4:00 a.m. Old habits died hard. He was used to waking this early to go for runs before his shifts as a cop in Texas.

His early wake up didn't surprise him. What caught him off guard was during the night, Poppy had turned in his arms and snuggled as close as she could get to him, throwing one leg over his and lying half on and half off his chest.

He smiled. This he could get used to.

Minutes later, Poppy flinched and moaned.

Logan glanced at her. Was she in pain? Did her head and ribs hurt? Something else? Since she still slept, he hesitated to wake her.

He wrapped both arms around her to surround her with his warmth. When she sighed and snuggled closer, Logan kissed her temple and settled back to savor the pleasure of having Poppy in his arms in the wee hours of the morning.

"Logan?" she whispered.

He tightened his grip. "You okay?"

Poppy shook her head.

"What's wrong?"

"Nightmares."

"How can I help?"

She pressed a kiss to the side of his neck. "You're already doing it."

"Think you sleep more?"

A sigh. "No."

"Do you want to get up or stay in bed a while longer?"

Poppy raised her head. "I want to know what Simone discovered overnight."

His lips twitched. "You're sure she worked?"

She flashed a quick smile. "She's a night owl and prefers working at night. Not only that, she's madder than a wet cat about her house. Simone is out for revenge on the people responsible."

He chuckled. "Brody told me she planned to work while Jesse was on shift last night. Why don't you shower and get ready. I'll shower in the bathroom in the hall. Come to the kitchen when you're finished. I'll be waiting for you."

Logan brushed her lips with his and climbed out of bed. Grabbing his Go bag, he trudged down the hall to the bathroom.

When he emerged minutes later, he set his bag just inside the door of their bedroom again and went downstairs.

As he'd expected, the coffee pot was full. Bless whoever was on the last night watch. Poppy would appreciate a cup and so would he.

Logan located a to-go cup, poured the hot steaming liquid into it, and pressed on the lid. Climbing the stairs two at a time, he tapped on the door lightly. No response from inside. Good. Poppy must still be in the bathroom.

Opening the door, he set the cup on her nightstand and left again. Downstairs, he poured a second cup of coffee for himself and sipped the steaming brew. A groan rumbled in his chest. Perfect.

Didn't know if Poppy was hungry, but his stomach growled as he glanced at the refrigerator. All right, then. Time to show off his limited culinary skills. His one good meal was breakfast, aside from manning a grill, of course. Hadn't unearthed the secret to pot roast or chicken that melted in your mouth yet. He was still looking.

Jesse walked into the room. "Morning. Poppy do okay overnight?"

"Until a few minutes ago. Nightmare."

A nod. The medic poured coffee for himself.

"Everything quiet overnight?"

"Yep."

"Simone find anything for us?"

"Several things. Although she's sleeping, she should wake soon. She'll want to tell everyone what she learned without repeating herself."

Amused at his friend's knowledge of a woman he'd met one day earlier, he smiled.

"What?"

"You."

A narrowed gaze met Logan's. "What about me?"

"You're smitten with the lady."

"So?"

Ah, so he was right. Poppy and Sage would enjoy the news. Anything to coax a smile from his wife. "Will you pursue Simone?"

"Hard to do when we live in different states, and I'm deployed every other month for thirty days."

"Her security check came back clear."

Jesse paused with the cup halfway to his mouth. "You're serious?"

He nodded. "I'll be surprised if Brent doesn't bring her on board with Fortress."

"If he does, she could opt to work remotely."

"And miss out on the opportunity to live near Poppy and Sage? I don't think so. I'm betting she'll move."

"I hope so."

Poppy walked into the kitchen carrying her running shoes and her coffee cup. "Did I miss anything good?"

"Simone passed her security check."

"She's applying for a job?"

"Maddox hires by referral only," Jesse said. "The security check was necessary to approve Simone's work on one of the company laptops."

"The security check is also the first of many searches into any potential employee's background before an offer of employment may be extended," Logan said.

"Simone would love Hartman. The town is the perfect size, and if you drive fifteen minutes, you're out in the country."

"Sell her on it. If she's as good as you say she is, Fortress needs her."

"No problem. I'll get Sage in on it as well. Between the two of us, I think we can persuade Simone to change her address." She flinched. "Especially since she doesn't have a house anymore."

"Her place was a total loss?" Jesse sipped his drink.

"According to the news, the place burned to the ground, with five unidentified bodies littering the yard. The police are looking for Simone as a person of interest."

"I don't want her exposed to more danger." The medic set aside his cup, his expression grim.

"For now, we'll keep her under wraps," Logan said. "Does she have her cell phone?"

"Went up in flames with the house."

"Good. When the women are safe, you can play the attentive boyfriend who whisked her out of town for a romantic getaway at a moment's notice with no tech."

"And the first we heard of the fire is when we returned and saw the house?" Jesse nodded. "Could work."

Simone stumbled into the room, yawning. "What could work?"

"We're coming up with a plausible explanation for you not knowing your house is gone and the local police wanting to talk to you about the fire and the bodies in your yard."

She paled. "The police want to interview me?"

"You're a person of interest."

"Oh, no." She dropped into the nearest seat.

"Hey." Jesse strode to her side and knelt in front of her. "You all right?"

"I've stayed off the grid for a reason."

"Want to explain?"

"No. You'll have to be satisfied with knowing I don't want any attention in the media."

Logan and Jesse exchanged glances. Not good. If she had something to hide, Zane would find it. He missed nothing.

"I did nothing wrong," she snapped. "This time," Simone muttered.

"Which implies you did something in the past," Jesse drawled.

"I'm no angel, handsome, but the only charge anyone can lay at my feet is hacking."

His lips twitched. "So not a bad law breaker."

She pointed at him. "Exactly."

Logan chuckled as he knelt in front of Poppy and tied her shoes. "Does she know what we used to do for a living?" he asked Jesse.

Simone stiffened. "Should I be worried?"

"Not now."

"You used to be cops?"

"Got it in one, sweetheart," Jesse said.

"Terrific." She brightened. "Hey, maybe you can run interference for me with the cops when I talk to them."

He inclined his head. "Glad to help a damsel in distress."

"Please tell me the coffee is fresh," Simone said, eyeing the full pot in the coffeemaker.

"Made it myself less than half an hour ago." He poured Simone a cup, capped it, and handed the drink to her. "Get any sleep?"

"Two hours. I'll be fine for a while."

"Hungry?" Logan asked. "I'm fixing breakfast in a minute."

"Starved. Can I help?"

"Depends. Can you cook?"

"Granny taught me everything she knew."

"You're hired."

The four of them worked on breakfast. Soon, scents of the home cooked meal caused the other occupants in the house to stir.

Brody was the first to appear. He scowled. "Are you out of your minds? Do you know what time it is?"

Jesse lifted an eyebrow. "I presume you enjoyed a full night's sleep. I've been awake most of the night. Suck it up, Buttercup."

"Yeah, yeah. No respect for your leader."

Everyone but Brody laughed. Although he acted affronted, Logan caught the glint of amusement in his eyes.

The others joined them within minutes, with Sage arriving last. Brody seated Sage and brought her a cup of tea he had nuked for her.

As soon as Logan and his assistant chefs finished preparing breakfast, they set everything on the large dining table and filled their plates.

They made quick work of the meal, refilled drinks, and settled down to talk.

"All right, Simone," Poppy said. "Let's hear everything. What did you find out about the Holden and Fontaine families?"

"Lynx ticked off two powerful families."

Jesse snorted. "Tell us something we don't know. The Holdens and Fontaines are headline worthy every time they appear outside of their estates."

"Wait a minute," Sage said, frowning. "These families are US citizens. CIA operatives work outside of the country."

"Raul Fontaine's family lives in the bayou in Louisiana," Simone confirmed. "Ashley Holden's family lives in Tennessee, although they have homes and estates all over the globe."

Logan straightened. "Where?" How could he have missed that?

"Outside of Nashville."

"Doesn't answer my question," Sage said. "Why would Mom target Ashley and Raul on US soil if she's with The Company?"

"She didn't. Lynx found their travel itineraries and planned her assassinations to occur outside the US borders. Raul was meeting a contact in Venezuela to arrange for a shipment of chemical weapons. According to the CIA, his plan was to sell the weapons to terrorist groups. Most of them planned to use the weapons against each other. One group wanted to use their weapons against American troops overseas."

"What about Ashley Holden?" Poppy asked. "What was she up to?"

"Gunrunning," Logan said. "Her family is involved in the weapons trade. Knives, guns, automatic and semi-automatic weapons. They're equal opportunity buyers and sellers." He'd run across people from their organization while he worked undercover in Texas. They were ruthless operators, and their contacts were in every country around the world.

"Including RPGs?"

He nodded. "If you have the money, the Holdens will find and sell you any weapon you want. Where did Lynx assassinate Ashley, Simone?"

"Mexican resort. The authorities saw no signs of an intruder, but Ashley was murdered. They claimed it was an American assassination. Still, no proof, so they dropped the investigation and moved on."

Max shook his head. "Not like the Mexican authorities don't have enough crime to fight without focusing on an unsolvable one."

"Who wants to avenge Raul?" Sage asked.

"The entire clan is out for blood. However, most of them stick close to home." Brody wrapped his hand around Sage's clenched fist. "The one exception is Wyatt. He's now head of the family empire."

"Was Wyatt Fontaine's name mentioned in connection with threats against Beverly?" Logan asked Simone.

"Not so far, but I'll keep looking." She grimaced. "The Fontaines breed like rabbits. Each family unit has five or six kids. Some have more. The whole family numbers over 200 people and counting."

A soft whistle from Sawyer. "That's a lot of suspects to track down."

"Tell me about it."

"We'll help," Jesse said. "The work doesn't depend only on you. If you pull together information from your sources, we'll divide the work and look for the person gunning for Lynx."

"Same goes for Ashley Holden's family," Poppy said. "Dump the data on us. We'll cull through the information."

"Deal."

"In the Holden family, where do we focus first?"

"Noah Wartrace, Ashley's husband. He took over as the head of the organization when she died. He's loud and outspoken about his desire to avenge his wife's murder. There are others in both families who could pull off Poppy's kidnapping and Jamie's murder."

Brody looked at each of his team members. "Is no one going to address the other problem?"

"What's that, sweetheart?" Sage asked.

"Someone leaked Lynx's name to the families if one of them is responsible for what happened to Poppy and Jamie."

"And my house." Simone glared at him. "Don't forget that offense. I sure won't."

"My apologies. We need to know who leaked the information. Lynx will never be safe until we do, and neither will Sage and Poppy."

Anger lit his gaze. "I want the person who put my wife and sister-in-law in the crosshairs."

"Dad is also in danger," Poppy said. "Eventually, the person responsible for the kidnapping will realize the connection. Dad and Mom both are prime targets."

"Why didn't the source of the leak give Mom's name instead of throwing you and me to the wolves as bait?" Sage asked.

No one had an answer to that.

"We'll find out when we have him in an interrogation room." Logan would gladly use his skills in the most painful manner possible to get answers. By the time he finished the interrogation, the prisoner would know how angry Logan was about the kidnapping.

"What will you do with him afterward?" Sage asked.

"We can't turn him loose, baby." Brody kissed her palm. "He'll be a threat to your parents. By that time, he'll either know too much or be tempted to sell the information to the highest bidder."

"You'll kill him?"

He flicked her a glance, his eyes twinkling. "Don't have to do the deed myself. We'll turn him over to the feds. They can house the guy in a federal prison and ensure he's cut off from all communication with the outside world. Can't leak information if you can't communicate."

"Looks like we have our work cut out for us." Logan stood and gathered his dishes and Poppy's. "Simone, send your data to Jesse. Divide it into five sections. Jesse will assign them. We'll each take one section of the data. Once we figure out who's behind the events of the past few days, we'll create a plan to take him down."

Simone looked skeptical. "The five of you against an army? Poppy and Sage tell me all the time how good you guys are, but you're not super heroes. You're regular men who can bleed and die. You'll need over five men to do this."

"No problem," Brody said. "Fortress has teams on standby to assist if we need the help."

"An army?"

He smiled. "We don't need that many men. We're good at what we do, Simone. Five of us took down twenty tangos to rescue Poppy. We'll do that and more to protect you, Sage, Poppy, and Beverly and Ivan."

She shook her head. "You're probably as good as you claim, but I'm not buying that you can do this on your own. Sorry."

"Watch and learn," Jesse murmured. "We might surprise you."

Simone gazed at him, her expression somber. "I hope I am. I hate funerals."

Chapter Twenty-Three

After the group loaded the dishwasher and cleaned the kitchen counters and stove top, Poppy and Logan returned to their bedroom for his laptop. "Where do you want to set up?" Logan asked.

"If no one else has claimed it, I'd love to work in the library." The scent of paper and ink had stirred creative energy inside her last night. "I wish I had my laptop."

He glanced at her as they descended the stairs. "Feeling creative?"

"For the first time in months, I can answer yes to that question."

"Want to work on your own for about an hour?"

She blinked. "Shirking the work, Fletcher?"

"An errand to run. Since you work rings around me on a laptop, makes the most sense for you to take the first pass at the research." He tapped her nose lightly. "Don't let your curiosity send you into classified areas on my computer. Stick to Internet searches and reading the data Simone gathered."

Poppy studied him a moment, wondering about this mysterious errand. "All right."

He brushed her mouth with a light kiss, handed her the laptop at the foot of the stairs, and said, "Password is Angel820star. I'll return as soon as I can." A moment later, he left the safe house by the back door.

Poppy walked down the hall to the library and stepped inside. She breathed easier when she found the room empty. Instead of heading for the couch, which looked comfortable enough to coax her to sleep in no time flat, she opted for the desk and sat in the leather chair.

Once she was settled, Poppy booted up the laptop, entered the interesting password, and clicked on the email icon, looking for the email Jesse sent with their assigned sections of research. Once she downloaded their section, she switched to the Internet browser. She knew Zane had more security built into this computer than Simone ever dreamed of adding to hers. Not much chance of someone figuring out who was trolling the Net much less where she was located with all his protections in place.

She dove into the Net and began her search. An hour later, she came up for air when Logan opened the door with a large shopping bag in his hand. He went shopping while she worked? "Have a pleasant time?" Poppy's tone was dry.

"It was the most aggravating experience of my life," he groused. "I wouldn't do that for anyone else but you."

"Me?"

Logan set the package on the desk beside his laptop. "This is for you. A wedding gift from me."

She stood and peered into the bag. "Logan! A laptop?"

"Top of the line. All the bells and whistles, including all the encryption Zane normally downloads to our company laptops. I called him while I was at the store. He accessed your computer remotely and added programs and security measures to keep you safe while you're online." He looked uneasy. "Do you like it?"

"Are you kidding? This is the laptop I've been dreaming about getting for the past two months, but haven't been able to convince myself to hand over the money for it." She came around the front of the desk and kissed him. "Thank you."

Logan relaxed. "You're welcome. I hope this makes up for the delayed honeymoon."

She smiled. "You don't have to make up for anything. I'm going to consider this what you first labeled it. A wedding gift from my husband. Thanks for giving me a gift I needed and wanted."

"My pleasure, baby." He nodded at the new laptop. "What to try it?"

Poppy rubbed her hands together. "I'm looking forward to giving this baby a test drive."

Logan unboxed the computer, moved his aside, and set hers in front of the desk chair. "Did you find Jesse's email?"

She nodded. "I downloaded the data we're assigned and have been trolling the Internet since you left."

"Learn anything?"

"Probably the same things Simone did, but not as detailed. The Holdens and Fontaines are vicious crime lords. The only things they care about are money and family. While they'd sell someone else's mother for a buck, their own mothers are sacred."

"I heard they were family oriented while I was undercover."

She paused in her typing and glanced up. "You worked undercover? As a cop or an operative?"

"Both."

"Will you continue undercover work now that we're married?"

"I wish I could say no. Sometimes, the work requires it."

While she understood the necessity of such an assignment, Poppy didn't like the thought of Logan living and working under a false identity. She'd interviewed enough law enforcement officers and black ops operatives over the years to recognize the toll living such a life took on the undercover agent. More than one of her interviewees said those assignments took pieces of their souls. Some fell victim to their targets. Some lost themselves in the assignments and could not discern between reality and fantasy.

Poppy also didn't want a woman in a target's household to eye Logan as her next conquest. How could they help it? Her husband was a handsome man with muscles on top of muscles. Tall, dark, and mysterious, what woman could resist him?

Logan frowned slightly. "What is it?"

"Just thinking about a rival for your affections if you go undercover again."

His lips curved. "Not going to happen. I don't form attachments, fake or real, to the women in the households we target. The key to a successful assignment is to stick as close to the truth as possible so you aren't caught in a lie."

"I've heard that from agents and undercover officers."

"You're my world, Poppy. I would never betray you even under orders from Maddox, and he wouldn't ask me to do that. My heart is yours. Period. I don't want another woman's hands or mouth on me, and I won't touch any woman but you, except when it's necessary to protect a principal. That's a line I won't cross."

She covered his hand with hers. "I know you would never betray me or our wedding vows, Logan. I'm sorry if I made you feel otherwise."

"You didn't. We haven't talked about undercover assignments before now. I wanted you to know how I conduct myself on those jobs."

"Do you like them?"

He shook his head. "Usually, the longtime undercover jobs are assigned to single operatives who don't have a spouse or kids."

"Because they're dangerous."

"Very."

"What's the longest undercover assignment you have had?"

"Two years. I infiltrated a motorcycle gang who rumored to be gunrunning."

"Were they?"

"Oh, yeah."

What had he endured while he lived a life as someone else? From his expression, the experience was a bad one. "I'm glad you made it out all right."

"Me, too." He kissed her, then said, "I'll sit on the couch and start reading. Do you want to join me or keep surfing the Net for more information?"

"Surf. There's something here for me to find. I know it."

"Need anything before I start?"

"I need to stretch my legs for a minute. Want some water?"

"Sounds great. Thanks."

Poppy traipsed down the hall to the kitchen, where she opened the refrigerator and snagged two bottles of water.

"Hi."

Jesse's voice startled her. She frowned as she swung around to face him. "Texas Team needs to wear bells around their necks. The five of you move as stealthy as jungle cats. No sound to betray when you're near."

The medic chuckled. "I'll try to remember to make noise next time. Sorry for scaring you."

She waved that off. "How is the research going?"

"Simone's doing the heavy lifting. I'm actually on shift at the moment."

"She's amazing, isn't she?"

"She really is. Are you and Logan coming up with anything?"

"Logan just returned from an errand. He's searching through Simone's data now. I'm digging into a few other things that might add to the pile of data we have on both families." And might pan out to be nothing. She'd have to see. Now that she knew a little more about Logan's undercover assignment, something was nagging at her, a bit of information that she couldn't bring to the surface. Her gut said the information was important. Hopefully, she'd run across it again or something else that would spark the memory.

"Chasing something interesting?"

"I'm not sure. Might be."

"How are you?"

Poppy's brows rose. "I'm fine."

Jesse folded his arms across his chest and stared down his nose at her. "Try again."

Why did he have to be so observant? A woman couldn't keep any secrets to herself with these men around. "I will be fine. I'm still sore and have frequent headaches." She held up her hand. "I don't need to return to the hospital for further evaluation. The intensity of the headaches is lessening. I almost don't need pain medicine anymore."

"Keep taking it on schedule for another day or two. We need you mobile at a moment's notice."

She stilled. "Expecting trouble?"

"We always expect trouble. No offense, sugar, but on this mission, all we've had is trouble. The best thing to happen so far is your marriage to Logan."

A smile bloomed on her face. "I agree."

"Couldn't happen to a more deserving couple. Too bad your parents didn't see your marriage in that light."

She shrugged. "They'll accept it, or they won't see much of me or their future grandchildren."

"You don't regret marrying Logan?"

"Smartest decision I ever made. I've been in love with Logan since I met him. I will never regret becoming Mrs. Logan Fletcher."

He smiled. "Good to hear." Jesse poured coffee into two cups, capped them, and left the kitchen to return to his post.

Poppy retraced her steps to the library and found Logan engrossed in his computer. She handed him a bottle of water and slipped back into her seat at the desk. Soon, she was lost in her research.

An hour later, she stared at the screen. Not the information she had been tracking, but significant. Poppy looked at Logan. "Have a minute?"

He glanced up. "Sure. What is it?"

"You mentioned going undercover with a motorcycle gang a few years back, one who was into gunrunning."

His face went blank of all expression. "What about them?"

"What's the name of the MC?"

"Iron Outlaws."

She wrinkled her nose. "Unoriginal."

He snorted. "Don't tell them that. They'll slit your throat and laugh while you bleed out."

"Nice."

"Why did you ask the name of the MC, Poppy?"

"They're major customers of the Holden organization."

Logan stared for a long moment, then rested his head against the back of the couch with his eyes closed, disgust clear on his face. "I should have put that together myself. I knew the Holden organization supplied guns for MCs. I can't believe I missed the connection to the Outlaws."

"You were distracted."

"It's no excuse. In fact, this proves Brent was right. I am compromised because all I can see is you."

Hurt welled inside Poppy. "Then it's my turn to ask if you regret marrying me."

"No, never. I probably should have delayed the wedding." His eyes opened, and his gaze locked onto hers. "I wanted my ring on your finger, and you close to me day and night. Regret this?" he asked, pointing to the ring on his finger. "Not in any lifetime. I wanted you to be mine. I longed to rush you to the altar the day after we met. In fact, I should earn good husband points for waiting as long as I did."

Her hurt vanished in a huff of laughter. "Duly noted."

"You looked for information on the motorcycle gang?"

She nodded. "Too much of a coincidence to ignore it. You always say there's no such thing as coincidence in your business."

"Turned out you were right. Do you believe your kidnapping is connected to my time in the MC?"

"While I don't think your undercover assignment was the catalyst, it might be connected to the Holdens, and someone could take advantage of the knowledge to sell you out."

"Half of the members of the MC are in prison or dead."

"But not all, and they have long memories. No, I'm thinking about the events you attended with me in Washington. The media crawls all over them. Someone from the MC might have recognized you from news coverage or photos."

"How does that involve the Holdens?"

"I've run across several rumors on the Net, insinuating that an MC is looking for an undercover pig whose betrayal led to the deaths of several of their brothers. They want revenge."

Logan straightened. "What name did they use?"

"Leo Rainwater."

He flinched. "That's my undercover persona. What else did you learn?"

"You have a high price on your head. Doesn't Zane have bots trolling the Internet for mentions of Fortress employees?"

"He monitors it constantly."

"How did he miss this? I'm good with research, but I'm nowhere close to Zane's league. He should have caught this."

Logan set aside his laptop and slid his phone from his pocket. "Let's find out what happened." He placed the call. Seconds later, Zane answered.

"Yeah, Murphy."

"It's Logan. You're on speaker with Poppy. We have a problem."

"What do you need?"

"Poppy ran across some information. I need you to confirm and dig deeper."

"Go."

Logan explained about his undercover assignment with the Iron Outlaws and their connection to the Holden family. "Rumors on the

Net say the Outlaws are looking for my alter ego, Leo Rainwater, and have a bounty on my head."

Zane growled. "Hold." Silence for two minutes, then the tech guru returned. "I'm sorry, Logan. It's true. I didn't set the bots to troll for Rainwater's name, just yours. The screwup is on me, my friend. What can I do to help you and Poppy since I'm partially responsible for this mess?"

"I bear part of the blame myself, Z. I should have warned you to be looking for the Rainwater name as well. It's been ten years. I thought that part of my life was behind me."

"Both of us were wrong."

"If you have time, look into the Iron Outlaws. I need a current roster and their recent activities. Second, look for any connection between the Holdens and the Outlaws."

"Done. What else?"

"I need everything you can give me on Noah Wartrace, Ashley Holden's widower. His location for the past month, his employees, everything."

"You think Wartrace is responsible for Poppy's kidnapping?"

"Lynx is responsible for Ashley's death. If Noah discovered Lynx is connected to Poppy, he's ruthless enough to use her as bait to draw out the former agent."

A soft whistle came through the speaker. "Noah Wartrace is as ruthless as his wife was. If he wants someone dead, he won't stop until the job is complete. If you're right, how did Noah learn of the connection between your wife and Lynx?"

"That's another piece of the puzzle we're hoping to find," Poppy said. "We think there's a leak in the CIA."

Silence. "Please tell me you're not serious."

"Sorry, man," Logan said. "The Company lost one of their retired agents a few hours ago. A man named Jamie Greeley, Lynx's partner on several missions."

"The boss knows this?"

"Nope. He's the next call."

"I'm transferring you over. He needs to know everything. This will get ugly fast."

"Oh, yeah."

"Before I transfer you to Brent, are there other searches I can run or farm out to my minions?"

"No, thanks. Simone is taking on the other part of the research. You have enough on your plate."

"Hold."

Seconds later, Brent's voice came through the speaker. "Sit rep."

Logan and Poppy spent the next few minutes updating the Fortress CEO.

Brent sighed. "A leak in The Company. That's just great. Is Z working on uncovering the leak?"

"Simone is covering that angle."

He laughed. "Of course she is. A hacker loves to dig in where he or she isn't supposed to be."

"Are you planning to offer her a job?" Poppy asked.

"Thinking about it. Why?"

"Jesse would appreciate it."

"Jesse?" Brent groaned. "He's sweet on her?"

"Getting there."

"We'll see, all right? No promises."

"If you offer Simone a job, Sage and I would prefer that she work at your headquarters so we can see her more often."

"You would, huh? Glad I asked your opinion on the matter," he said dryly. "Any other requests from the newlyweds?"

"A month off for our honeymoon," Logan said.

"Planned on that anyway." He paused a few seconds. "I have to go. Hot zone call." He cut off the call.

Logan slid the phone into his pocket and stood. "Come on. Let's talk to the others."

In the kitchen, they found most of Texas Team working at the breakfast bar and the large dining table. Only Jesse and Simone were absent.

Brody glanced up at their entrance. "Have something?"

"Maybe." Logan seated Poppy. "I'll get Jesse and Simone. We'll talk then." He soon returned with the couple, who joined the others at the dining table.

"Let's hear it," Brody said to Logan.

"Iron Outlaws and the Holdens are in business together."

Max scowled. "You're kidding."

"I wish. Rumors are floating around the Net that the Outlaws are looking for me, or rather, my alter ego."

Sawyer shook his head, expression grim. "I thought we'd seen the last of them."

"So did I. Looks like we were wrong."

"How big is the price on your head?" Jesse asked.

"Two million dollars," Poppy said. She couldn't believe a biker gang had that much money stashed in a bank, just waiting for something like this. Then again, they probably didn't trust banks as much as they did themselves. She wondered how they laundered money in order to keep the government off their backs and where they kept cash safe if they didn't avail themselves of banks.

"Holy cow," Sage said. "They must really hate you, Logan."

He shrugged. "I did my job. Several Outlaws died in the raid because they opened fire on law enforcement officers. Club members have long memories."

"How did they learn your real name and, more important, do they know where you are?" Jesse asked.

"We're looking for the information source," Poppy said. "The most logical explanation is one of the Outlaws happened to catch sight of Logan in the media when he was escorting me to a function in Washington and recognized him. I think our leak may be to blame for the information getting out." She turned to Simone. "Have you made any progress on identifying the leak?"

"Some. I should know within an hour who the culprit is."

"Make it less," Logan said. "We need a name."

"What happens when she identifies the leak?" Sage asked.

"We pay him a visit. I want to know who he told and why. I'll get answers no matter what I have to do."

"Then what?"

"Beat him to a pulp for endangering you and Poppy and your parents."

Simone glowered. "And enabling the destruction of my house. I loved that house."

"You can rebuild," Sawyer said.

"Ha. Not on that site. Everyone knows where I live now. My security is compromised. I'll have to move."

"Come to Hartman," Sage said. "We'll be able to see each other all the time and support each other when the team is out on deployment."

"I'll think about it." Simone rose. "Since I have my marching orders, I need to go back to work." She left the room with Jesse on her heels.

Sage pushed back from the table and stood. "I'm making tea before we return to work ourselves, Brody. Want anything?"

"No, thanks, love. I need to contact Parker." He left the house by the back door.

Sage looked uncertain. "Should I go after him?"

"Give him a few minutes." Poppy walked to the coffeemaker and prepped the machine for yet another pot of coffee. These guys drank coffee like a camel consumed water. She did, too. That any of them had a stomach lining still intact was a miracle. "Telling a friend that his former partner is dead isn't easy."

"I should have called Parker myself," Logan said. "He's the one who hooked me up with Jamie."

"His death still isn't your fault, love." Poppy filled a mug with water and dropped in a chamomile mint tea bag. After nuking the drink, she set the mug on the counter for Sage to pick up for herself. She needed a handle to grip the mug more securely. "Chamomile mint."

"One of my favorites. Thanks, Poppy."

"Enjoy. I'll take my coffee over your flavored water any day."

Sage waggled a finger at her. "You don't know what you're missing."

"Ha. I do, too. I'll pass unless I'm told I have to switch to herbal tea."

"Would you do it?"

"Only under loud and long protest."

The sisters laughed as the others scattered to the various parts of the house. Only Logan remained behind, waiting for Poppy.

"Give Brody something to laugh about," Logan said. "He's hurting and assuming the blame for Jamie's death. It's not on him."

Poppy eyed him. "Jamie's death isn't on you, either," she repeated.

"I should have insisted that we meet somewhere else."

Stubborn man. She'd have her work cut out for her to convince him he had no part in Jamie's death. "No one can anticipate every scenario."

Poppy glanced at Sage. "Want to join us in the library? The couch is comfortable."

She shook her head. "I'll wait for Brody. We may join you when he returns."

Poppy and Logan returned to the library and went back to their computers. She dove back into the work, quickly losing track of time as she surfed the Net, chasing every potential lead between Iron Outlaws and anyone working in the intelligence community for the US.

For once, Poppy wished she'd taken more computer classes. Some experience in hacking would be nice about now. As it was, she was scouring websites she used in her research for books. Someone must have whispered about a traitor in the ranks.

By the time Sage and Brody entered the library, Poppy had found several references to a leak, but no name was added to the rumor. Of course not. Couldn't be that easy.

However, the rumors seemed to circulate around the CIA. Why The Company? The agents worked overseas, not inside US borders. Was this an agent with a vendetta against Lynx? If so, he smeared every hard-working and loyal agent's good name with his betrayal.

What Poppy needed were the classified files on Ashley Holden's and Raul Fontaine's deaths. She didn't have the expertise to grab the files electronically and run without the CIA tracking her down and tossing her in jail. Despite Zane's insane security on everything electronic, Poppy feared tripping some electronic alarm and missing her honeymoon and the first two decades of her married life. She grimaced. That would be a tragedy of the highest order.

Even though she couldn't retrieve the files, she knew of two phenomenal hackers who could. For either, the exercise would be child's play.

Brody sat beside Sage on one end of the couch while Logan occupied the other end.

"How did it go?" Logan asked.

"About like you'd expect. Parker was ticked off and devastated. Blames himself for persuading Jamie to help us."

"Every person on our side of the fight is taking the blame," Sage said. "No doubt the other side couldn't care less."

"That's a given." Poppy clicked on another lead. A news article touting the Second Lady's endorsement of a new literacy foundation. She remembered that event. Logan had attended the shindig with her, although he'd arrived late. The Fortress jet was late that night.

She studied one of the accompanying photos. Her mother was front and center, as was her father. Both of them were photogenic, and the press loved to include pictures of them with any article.

In the background, she and Sage were standing with Logan and Brody. Although the men had mostly turned away from the camera, they were both recognizable.

On the other side of the operatives stood another man who seemed to scowl toward her parents. A coincidence? Was he angry with them? Who was this man? She'd seen him somewhere before, but Poppy couldn't place him. Had he been at other functions with Beverly and Ivan?

She picked up her laptop and stood. "Sage, do you recognize the guy in the background mean mugging Mom and Dad?" She set the computer on her sister's lap. "He looks familiar to me, but I can't come up with a name."

Sage studied the photo. "The picture is grainy, so it's hard to tell much, but I've seen him before. Can you call in a favor and ask the newspaper editor to send you a digital copy of the original picture? Zane might help us identify this man with a better picture."

Simone and Jesse walked into the room as Sage was speaking. Simone peered at the photo. Her mouth curved. "I see you've spotted our quarry."

The others stared at her. "This is the source of the leak?" Poppy demanded.

"Meet Jonah Templeton, the rat who placed a target on your back."

Chapter Twenty-Four

Logan's hands fisted as he stared at the photo of the man whose unauthorized information sharing had led to the death of a loyal patriot and the kidnapping of the woman Logan loved with every beat of his heart. "Why did he leak information?"

"That I don't know." Simone dropped into the chair Jesse pulled over to her. "I haven't sniffed out a motive yet. I thought you'd want the name first." She grinned. "Note that I found the name in under the time I told you I would be finished."

"So noted."

"Want me to keep digging on Templeton?"

"Do you have an address for me?"

Simone pulled out a slip of paper with writing on it and handed it to him. "He lives thirty minutes from here."

"Married?"

"No. No kids, either. He's single and lives alone."

"Good." He glanced at Brody. "We need to arrange for another pick up. I don't want this guy roaming free. I want to know everything from the time he was born until now." He smiled, more a baring of teeth. "After I get a turn with him."

"We need him alive to answer questions," Brody said, tone mild.

"He can answer questions with a broken nose and bruises all over his body. I won't damage him. Much."

His leader snorted. "Right. Pardon me for doubting your control."

"Shut up."

"I want to go with you to question this creep," Poppy said. Anger glittered in her eyes.

Although Logan didn't blame her and would no doubt want the same if he was in her shoes, he couldn't allow it. "No."

"Why not? You'll be there and whoever else goes along for the ride. I'll be safe."

"I'm not taking you with us, Poppy. We don't know what we're walking into. He could be armed and dangerous. He'll definitely be desperate. No. Way."

"That's not fair. I have just as much right to question Templeton as you do. More, in fact. He's most likely the reason I was kidnapped. I have a bone to pick with him about that and deserve a chance to go one-on-one with him myself."

"If you want a chance to talk to him, I'll give you one, but not tonight. This first time is mine."

"You're having Parker and crew come get him. How will I be able to speak to him? Come on, Logan. Use your head. What better way to persuade him to talk than confront him with the woman he sold out?"

"Forget it. Not budging on this, baby."

"Why are you so stubborn?"

"Born that way. It's no surprise to you. You fell in love with my stubborn self. I'll make sure you get a crack at Templeton, but it won't be tonight. Deal with it."

Logan surged to his feet. "I'll contact Zane to arrange a pick up in about two hours. Meet you in the kitchen."

He left the library before he slipped and said something to his fuming wife he'd regret and couldn't take back. Why wouldn't Poppy listen? Yeah, he got the need to confront the enemy and demand answers. However, the methods he might have to employ to unearth the answers she wanted wouldn't be pleasant.

Allowing Poppy to see him deliberately causing someone pain wasn't on his agenda. She thought highly of him. He didn't want to mess that up this early in their marriage. Logan had hoped she would believe the best of him for a long time. Based on her expression, though, he had disappointed and disillusioned her in one go. Must be a record. One day married and already at odds.

Logan strode down the hall, through the kitchen, and outside on the back deck. Before he placed the call to Z, he took a minute to breathe in the cool, crisp air and shove his temper back under lock and key. Taking his frustration out on Zane wasn't happening. It shouldn't have happened with Poppy, either. He owed his wife of one day an apology for losing his cool.

He gripped his phone. An apology was on the docket. Changing his mind wasn't. Too many things could go wrong, and Logan would never risk Poppy's safety, even though he longed to give in to her request.

"Logan." Poppy stepped up beside him.

How had she made it outside without him being aware of it? He needed to get his head back in the game.

"I'm sorry."

Logan froze a moment, then turned to face her. "For what? Stating your opinion? I want you to do that. I would never stifle you or your nosy-parker ways."

She laughed. "I appreciate that. I'm not apologizing for being nosy. I'm sorry I put you in an awkward position in front of our friends. You didn't have a graceful way to back out of the conversation."

"Are you still angry with me?"

"Yes." She looked at him with a somber expression. "I can still adore you and be angry over your stubbornness."

His lips twitched. "I'll remind you of that when you're the one being stubborn."

"Won't take long, I'm sure."

Nope. Stubborn was in her DNA like it was in his. "We'll see."

"I have a compromise."

"Yeah? Let's hear it."

"Take me with you, but leave me in the car with one of your teammates while you find answers. Call me in when you're ready for me to come inside to confront Templeton. He might not talk to you, you know. I might convince him to pony up the information."

Amused, he cupped her nape. "I'll get answers, Poppy. My methods aren't pleasant, but they're effective."

"I know what you do for a living, Logan. I know you have to do ugly things to protect innocents. You won't shock me."

"It's one thing to know what I do as a fact. It's something else entirely when you face the screams and blood that result from reality."

"I'll be fine. Trust me."

He felt himself wavering a smidge and wondered if he'd lost his mind. "I've trusted no one more."

"Please take me with you. I'll be safe. Your teammate won't allow anything to happen to me."

"An interrogation takes a while. You're already tired and hurting." He'd seen the signs of pain on her face more than once in the past hour. "Sitting in a car for two or three hours won't help."

"I'll take pain medicine before we leave."

Logan sighed. He was an official card-carrying wuss. "All right. However, you'll stay in the SUV unless I'm positive you won't be in danger. If something feels off, you stay in the vehicle no matter what you want. Got it?"

"I'll cooperate. I promise." She planted a hard kiss on his mouth. "Thank you, sweetheart."

"Don't make me regret the concession, Poppy. I won't be able to live with myself if anything happens to you."

"It won't." She grinned. "I'll take the pain medicine and be ready to leave in five minutes." Poppy hurried across the deck and into the house.

Logan shook his head, disgusted with himself. He was pathetic. Poppy Reynolds Fletcher had him wrapped around her finger.

He called Zane. "It's Logan. I have another pick up for the black site."

"Giving those boys a lot of business lately. Who is it this time?"

"Creep named Jonah Templeton. He works for the CIA."

"He's the leak?"

"That's what Simone says." He rattled off the address on the paper Simone had given him. "I'll find out for myself soon. I'm paying Templeton a visit."

"Take someone with you."

"You don't trust me, Z?"

A snort. "I know what I'd do if this man was responsible for someone laying hands on my wife. I assume you won't do any less."

"Smart man."

"How soon do you want the pick-up team?"

"Two hours. That should give me enough time. If Templeton's the reason Poppy was targeted, I'll find out."

"What do you want done with him when you're finished?"

"Keep him on ice. When this is over and we have the proof we need, we'll hand him over to the feds with a big red bow."

"I'll take care of the arrangements. Family to be concerned about?"

"Single, no kids."

"Even better. Contact me when it's done and the perp's out of your hands. I might have some information for you by that time."

"Will do." He ended the call and returned to the house. Logan took the stairs two at a time and walked to his and Poppy's bedroom to retrieve his Go bag. He geared up, including slipping a Fortress comm device into his ear. When he and the others were outside Templeton's house, they would activate the communications device to allow Poppy and his teammate to hear everything going on inside.

Logan grimaced. He hoped Poppy was as good as her word. If his brutal methods sickened her, he'd have a lot of ground to recover.

Poppy exited their bathroom. She'd changed into dark clothes and her running shoes. "Ready."

"Let's go." He cupped her elbow and walked downstairs with her. They met Brody and Jesse in the kitchen, both dressed in similar attire. Typical Fortress uniform. Basic black, no metal gleaming in any light. Couldn't beat it for functionality on a mission.

Brody's eyebrows shot up, as did Jesse's. "What happened to your order for Poppy to stay home?" he asked.

"No comment."

His teammates chuckled.

"You are whipped," Jesse said with a smile. He winked at Poppy.

"Your turn's coming."

"Looking forward to it."

If what Logan had observed held true, the medic was well on his way to reaching that goal. The interest appeared to be two-sided. Should be entertaining to watch over the next few months if they gave their relationship a try.

"Clock's ticking." Brody pulled out a comm device from his cargo pocket and slipped it into his ear. "The pick-up team will arrive at the house in 90 minutes."

They drove from the house a minute later and headed toward Templeton's home. The clear night gave them plenty of moonlight to see their surroundings as they traveled. Taking back roads to avoid traffic cameras in case someone hacked into the system, they met little traffic. No tails that Logan saw.

Excellent. He relaxed and refocused his attention on the upcoming interrogation of Jonah Templeton. What had possessed the man to breach security protocol and leak classified information? Had he given the information to the Holdens, Fontaines, or the Iron

Outlaws? Was something more at stake for this man than simple greed?

Logan filled the remaining minutes of the drive considering the best approach to get information fast. His gut said time was running out for Poppy and Beverly.

Minutes later, Brody parked a few houses away from Templeton's place. The CIA employee owned a bungalow-style home with a decent-size yard in front and a fenced-in backyard. "Does Templeton have a dog?"

"Unknown," Logan replied. He squeezed Jesse's shoulder. "If he does, Jesse can calm the pooch."

Poppy looked horrified. "You won't drug or kill a dog, are you, Jesse?"

"If we were in the field, I'd use a non-lethal drug safe for canines. I'll work with Templeton's dog if he has one. I have a few tricks up my sleeve. Besides, unless they're trained to be vicious, most dogs love me."

"He's the dog whisperer on the team." Brody opened the door and stepped out of the vehicle.

Logan kissed Poppy. "Stay in the SUV, baby. Do everything Jesse tells you to do without an argument." He handed her a comm device. "Slip this in your ear. Tap it once and you'll be able to hear everything said. I'll let you and Jesse know when I'm ready for you."

He hesitated, then said softly, "I'm holding you to your promise."

"No worries, love. Be careful."

Logan looked at Jesse.

The medic nodded. "I've got her. She'll be safe with me. Watch your back. Something doesn't feel right here."

"Agreed." He exited the SUV and joined Brody at the front of the vehicle. "Front or back?"

"Back. We don't want to attract the attention of neighbors."

As they walked toward the target's house, Logan scanned the area. The neighborhood was quiet. No neighbors outside. No traffic on the street. Only a dog barking in the distance and the occasional car driving nearby broke the silence.

The two men scaled the fence and approached the back of the house. A dim light glowed in the room with the door. Probably the kitchen, Logan decided. Since the front rooms were dark and no other light glowed, he and Brody might catch Templeton asleep.

They found evidence of a security system and disabled it. Brody motioned for Logan to pick the lock.

He crouched and went to work. Although both of them could pick locks, Logan was faster. He'd spent hours practicing when he couldn't be with Poppy. At least he'd filled those hours with something useful. When the tumblers dropped less than 30 seconds later, a sense of satisfaction filled him. Looked like the practice paid off.

He stood and nodded at Brody. His friend counted off on his fingers, then twisted the knob and pushed open the door.

They slipped inside the kitchen, closed the door, and waited to see if anyone had noticed their entrance. When nothing stirred and Templeton didn't appear in the entrance with a weapon in his hand, Logan and Brody moved further into the house.

Room by room, they searched the bungalow with no sign of their quarry. When they reached the last room along the short hall, the door was closed. Templeton had to be in that room unless someone had picked him up and taken him to dinner or a movie because a car sat in the driveway.

When the two operatives stood on either side of the door frame, Brody grasped the knob and turned it, pushing open the door. A man lay asleep in a double bed.

Logan holstered his weapon and closed the distance between him and Templeton. When Brody stood on the other side of the bed with his weapon down by his side, Logan clamped his hand over Templeton's shoulder and shook him hard. "Wakey, wakey, Templeton."

Templeton's eyelids flew up, and he stared at Logan. "Who are you? What are you doing in my house?"

"We need to talk. Now." He ripped the covers back and jerked the man out of his bed by his pajama top. "Let's go."

"What?" Templeton's voice rose. "What do you want? I have money. Take it. It's yours."

"Now you're just ticking us off."

"Us?"

"Move." He shoved the man so hard, Templeton stumbled from the room and into the hall.

He and Brody propelled him to the kitchen and shoved him into a chair sitting in a pool of moonlight streaming from a window. The position of the chair kept their faces in shadow while allowing them to see the expression on the face of the target.

In seconds, Brody secured Templeton's hands behind his back and to the chair, then remained behind him.

Logan folded his arms across his chest. "Why did you do it, Templeton?"

"I don't know what you're talking about. Who are you?"

"Your worst nightmare. You hurt the woman I love."

"What?" Templeton stared. "I didn't. I have never hurt a woman in my life."

Brody sighed. "You'll make this worse on yourself, buddy. He's knows."

"I swear I did nothing to his woman. I would never harm a fly, much less a woman."

Logan stepped closer, keeping his back to the moonlight and his face in the darkness. "Your bank account says otherwise."

The CIA employee's eyes widened. "How did you…? I want a lawyer."

He snorted. "Do we look like cops?"

"Who are you?"

"Doesn't matter. I want two things from you."

Templeton closed his mouth.

"You don't want to tempt me," he mumbled. "I would love to break every bone in your body and toss you into the street to rot for what you did."

"You can't do that. It's against the law. I'll sue!"

"Who will you tell if you're dead?" Logan had no intention of killing the little weasel, but Templeton didn't know that.

"Don't. Please, don't kill me."

"Why shouldn't I? You endangered four women, not just mine."

"How did I do that? I swear I won't do it again if you won't hurt me. Do you want money? I'll give you all I have."

"Who paid you the money, Templeton?" Logan saw the instant the other man decided to lie.

"No one. I earned every penny. I have a good job."

He flicked a glance at Brody, who immediately clamped a hand around the other man's mouth. Logan gripped Templeton's shoulder near the neck and pinched hard.

Although Templeton's screams were muffled, Logan knew Poppy heard every scream and plea for him to stop. He eased up when tears ran down Templeton's face. "Wrong answer, Jonah. Try again. The truth this time. Who paid you?"

"I don't know what you're talking about. Please," he sobbed. "Please, don't hurt me."

Feeling like more of a monster as each second passed, Logan gripped the shoulder again and pinched a bundle of nerves as Brody covered Templeton's mouth again. More muffled screams and pleas came from Templeton.

When two minutes had passed, Brody scowled at Logan.

Yeah, he needed to let up before he did permanent damage. Logan released the prisoner and took a step back. "Last chance, Templeton."

The other man shivered. "I don't know what you want."

"Told you. I want a name. Who paid you?"

"For what?" he shouted. "There's no law against making money on the side."

"You call giving up information on an agent lawful?" Brody smacked the back of Templeton's head with his palm hard enough to hurt and intimidate, but not enough to damage. "The agent doesn't see it that way. In fact, she's furious over your betrayal."

"You don't mess with assassins, Jonah," Logan said. "They take it personally."

"Assassins? I don't know any assassins." Templeton's expression hardened. "You're lying to me. You're just digging for information I don't have."

"Jonah, Jonah." Brody sighed. "Buddy, I warned you, didn't I? You don't want to mess with my friend. He's not a happy man."

"That's not my problem."

"He's only the first of many problems. One of the four women in danger is my wife. If anything happens to her because of what you did, I'm coming for you. No one will protect you from me. Compared to me, my friend here is a pushover."

Templeton's body shook. "It's not my fault."

"What isn't your fault?" Logan laid his hand on the man's shoulder.

Templeton flinched. "Please, don't."

"Answer the question." He steadily increased the pressure until the other man begged for Logan to stop. "I'm waiting for an answer."

"I had to."

Now they were getting somewhere. The little weasel had stood up longer than Logan had hoped. "Why?"

"They threatened to kill me if I didn't tell."

"Who threatened you? Give us a name."

"They'll find out."

"Jonah, let's look at this logically. We're here now. We will keep hurting you until we get what we want. The other people who threatened you aren't here."

"Be smart, Jonah," Brody murmured in his ear. "Address the threat in front of you, not the one that isn't."

"You don't understand. These people have ears everywhere. They'll know."

Time for a little more persuasion. Logan removed his Ka-Bar from the thigh sheath and pretended to examine the razor-sharp blade. "I'm running out of patience, my friend. Start talking or I start cutting. Minor cuts at first. If you remain stubborn, I'll progress to deeper cuts. All of them will bleed and hurt. You're not a big fan of pain, are you, Jonah?"

Templeton shook his head. "No. Please, please, don't do this."

"Don't make me. The pain stops when you tell me what I want to know. After that, we'll walk away and you'll never see us again." He didn't plan on being Jonah Templeton's best friend. The sight of the man cowering in the chair sent a curl of disgust through him. "Who threatened you? Who did you tell?"

"I can't. I'm sorry."

Logan sighed. "So, you're going to be stubborn about this. What happens in the next few minutes is on you. Once I start, no amount of begging will make me stop. I enjoy the work too much."

Total lie, that one. He hated doing this. Yeah, he was good at it, and Fortress had spent a lot of money making sure he was one of the best at the job. The job made him want to barf.

He glanced at Brody, who gave a slight nod of permission to move ahead. Praying he wouldn't have to actually cut the guy, Logan went to work slicing away Templeton's pajama top.

Brody clamped a hand over his mouth in mid-scream. "Do it," he said harshly.

Templeton shook his head, screaming louder.

Logan held the tip of the wicked black blade against the center of Templeton's chest. "Have something to tell me, Jonah?"

He nodded vigorously and mumbled something behind Brody's hand.

Logan flicked his friend a glance.

Brody moved his hand away from Templeton's mouth. "Do the smart thing, Jonah. This is your last warning before we go to work doing what we do best." He leaned in close to his ear. "We're better at this than the assassins. They do a hit and run. We like to linger with our work and do it right. We're professionals."

Amidst the stress and distaste for this job, Logan wanted to laugh at Brody. However, they needed information fast before the pick-up team arrived and whisked Templeton off to the black site for more interrogation. "Talk or I start working." He pretended to scan the other man's body to select a site to begin his task. He tapped Templeton's thigh with the flat of his knife. "Right here. Hurts like crazy and bleeds like a fountain. This is where I'll start."

"Good choice," Brody said.

"No, I'll talk. Please, don't hurt me. Ask me anything."

"Who paid you? I want a name." He pressed the tip of the knife into Templeton's thigh, a pinprick and a stark warning of what was to come if he didn't give up the information Logan wanted.

"I don't know his name."

Logan pressed the blade into the skin harder.

"Please, I'm telling you the truth. I was approached by a guy dressed in black. You know, a black t-shirt and black jeans. Black biker boots. He had tattoos all over every inch of skin I could see."

Dismay filled Logan. A biker? "Where he did contact you?"

"On the street in front of my favorite coffee shop."

"Name of the shop?"

"Coffee Central. It's three blocks from here."

"Go on."

"He offered money for information." Templeton swallowed hard. "He said if I didn't give him what he wanted, he'd kill me. I believed him."

"Aside from his clothes, describe him."

"Uh, a white guy with dark hair, beard, mustache, and dark eyes. He was over six feet tall. Muscles everywhere. He looked like he ate nails for breakfast and bench pressed a city bus without a sweat."

"Was his hair long, short, shoulder length?"

"Long. Past his shoulders. Does that help?"

A ball of ice formed in Logan's stomach. Couldn't be Reaper. Could it? "What did this guy want to know?"

"The identity of an operative. I couldn't give him that. It's against the law, you know." He tried to sound justified. Didn't work.

"What did you tell him?"

"I put him off. I didn't know the information he wanted off the top of my head and couldn't get it until I returned to work the next day."

"What happened?"

"I must not have convinced the bruiser that I couldn't access the information because he hustled me around the corner to a waiting van and threw me into the back. They drove me to my house." His voice rose in remembered fear. "They know where I live."

"And yet you're still here rather than in hiding. What information did you give them?"

"Not much. The information is heavily encrypted, and I could only get surface information."

Logan pressed the knife in deeper.

Templeton hissed. "They wanted information on a retired agent named Lynx. I couldn't give them her name because they didn't list it in the file, just her working name."

Brody jerked Templeton's head back. "You gave the bruiser and his buddy something or you wouldn't still be breathing. Talk, Templeton, or I'll gut you myself."

"All right! I told them the names of people who knew Lynx. That's all. I didn't out the agent. I wouldn't."

"Who sent these clowns?"

"I heard them mention a guy named Noah. No last name. That's all I have. I swear."

Noah Wartrace, Ashley Holden's husband. Good old Noah was at least one of their targets. Now that he had more information, Logan had to consider that his old pals, the Iron Outlaws, were not only involved with the Holden group but in bed with them. Worse, they were looking for him. If they found him, Poppy's life would be at risk.

At that moment, a rumble of thunder reached his ears, growing louder as each second passed. He and Brody exchanged glances. What was that?

And then he knew.

Logan sprinted for the front door.

Chapter Twenty-Five

Poppy shifted again, hoping to find a more comfortable spot as she peered through the window toward Jonah Templeton's house. Through the earpiece, she listened to the interrogation, admiring Logan and Brody's technique.

No, she wasn't an expert. However, she had read enough books and articles on interrogation techniques as well as watched her favorite movies and television shows, which showcased the same techniques to recognize the good-cop-bad-cop routine Logan and Brody were using. Even better, Brody had played the good guy until the last minute or so when he'd switched roles. She'd have to classify the routine now as bad-cop-worse cop. Templeton was out of his league.

"How much longer do you think this will last?" she whispered to Jesse.

"A few more minutes," he murmured. "Templeton knows little."

"I wish he had more. We still have guesswork, with no proof of our suspicions."

Through the earpiece, she heard the name Noah. No definite proof but more suspicion that Ashley Holden's husband, Noah Wartrace, was the boss Things One and Two had mentioned when they threatened her with punishment for not answering their questions about Lynx.

In the distance, she heard the rumble of thunder. Poppy frowned. There wasn't a cloud in the sky. What was that noise?

Jesse turned his head, staring out the back window. He looked puzzled. "You hear that?"

"Yeah. What is it?"

"I'm not sure." His tone said he didn't like it at all.

As they listened, the noise grew louder until it was all they could hear.

"Run to the house, Poppy." Jesse jerked open his door and leaped from the vehicle. He palmed his gun and took aim down the street behind them.

She scrambled from the SUV and looked at the approaching sea of single lights. Motorcycles. Oh, no.

"Go, go, go," Jesse snapped. "I'll cover you."

"But...."

"Move!"

His order kicked her into gear. She'd promised to follow Jesse's orders while he was charged with her safety. Delaying endangered Jesse as well as herself.

She pivoted and raced toward the front door. Behind her, she heard the medic's footfalls as he raced after her.

One third of the way to her destination, the front door opened and Logan barreled toward her with his weapon in hand.

A loud bang sounded behind her, followed by a grunt and a heavy thud.

Poppy skidded to a halt and turned. Horror filled her at the sight of Jesse sprawled face first on the ground, unmoving. "Jesse!" She retraced her steps at a dead run, ignoring Logan's shouts behind her.

She dropped to her knees beside the fallen medic. "Jesse."

No response.

Poppy felt for injuries with trembling hands. She found a large hole in the back of his shirt but no blood. Frowning, she poked a finger into the opening and met stiff resistance.

Relief flooded her. Of course. He was wearing a bullet-resistant vest. Before she could tell Logan what she'd found, more motorcycles than she could count surrounded her and Jesse. Worse, they were cut off from Logan.

Afraid one bike would run over Jesse, Poppy pulled his arms close to his body, hovered over his head, and prayed.

Two more gunshots rang out. She glanced up. All she saw were bikes and leather chaps over jeans and heavy boots. Where was Logan?

Terror raced over her in a tidal wave. Even with motorcycles everywhere, she should have been able to see her husband fighting his way to her, dodging the vehicles stopping on the street and Templeton's lawn. He wasn't.

One by one, the engines turned off until the night was filled with an eerie silence.

"Is he dead?" one man shouted.

"He ain't moving." The man who seemed to be the leader walked over to something Poppy couldn't see and kicked the object hard. "I don't miss what I aim for, Leo. You should never have messed with the Iron Outlaws. We don't like traitors."

Leo? He meant Logan. He'd shot Logan. Poppy prayed these outlaws would leave Jesse alone since he was down, but she had to get to her husband. Please, God, let the leader be wrong. Poppy got to her feet and started toward the leader at a fast clip.

One Outlaw laughed. "Better look out, Reaper. The chick is coming for you."

The others joined in his laughter.

Poppy ignored them all, determined to reach Logan. Finally, she broke free of the group of bikers and ran to Logan, who was sprawled on his back, unmoving. "Logan."

The vest he wore must have done its job. If not, Reaper might finish the job by shooting Logan in the head.

She dropped to the ground beside him. "Sweetheart, talk to me," she whispered.

No response.

She reached out her hand to press her fingers against the carotid artery in his neck, praying she would find a steady rhythm.

"Well, look what we have here." Hard hands gripped her arms and jerked Poppy to her feet. Reaper peered down at her.

Man, this guy must be over six feet tall and all muscle. An ugly scar trailed down his left cheek to the corner of his mouth, giving his lips a twisted appearance. "Who are you, sweet thing?"

"Let me go."

"Hey, Reap." Another biker approached, this one even larger than Reaper. He showed the leader Poppy's image on his cell phone. "Look at this."

Reaper leered down at Poppy. "So, you're the illusive Poppy Reynolds. Noah will be thrilled we found you."

She fought to free herself. "Let me go. I have to know if he's alive."

"He ain't."

Poppy froze. No. It couldn't be true. Logan couldn't be dead.

"You're coming with me. Noah wants you. What he wants, he gets." His gaze drifted down her body. "Too bad. I could use an old lady. Maybe he'll let me have you when he gets what he wants from you."

"None of us mind used goods," the other man said, then laughed along with his biker buddies.

"Mine," Reaper declared. "No one touches her but me, and I'll be touching her plenty."

Not if she could help it.

"Let's go." He dragged her toward his bike as someone inside the house broke a window and began firing multiple shots.

Brody.

Several men dropped to the ground, writhing in agony, blood pouring from their wounds. Reaper, however, continued to drag Poppy toward his bike as his men opened fire on the house. "You ride like a good little girl or I'll knock you out and throw you over my shoulder and take you anyway, but your friend inside the house will die first. Leave with me now, and he lives. Your choice, lady."

From the size of Reaper's fists, he could break her jaw without trying. She had to protect Brody. Although he was an excellent shot, he was outnumbered, and the pick-up team wasn't due for at least half an hour. Too long to hold out on his own.

What could she do but agree? Poppy nodded. She knew Jesse was alive and believed Reaper was wrong about Logan, but this was the only way to keep all three men safe. Texas Team had found her before when she'd been kidnapped. Twice. Hopefully, they would do so again. She still had her trusty watch. She wouldn't be totally alone.

"Thought you might see it my way." He plucked her off the ground and set her on his bike. "Ever ridden a motorcycle before?"

"No."

"Wrap your arms around my waist and hold on. Lean the way I do. You try any tricks, and we'll both end up in the hospital or the morgue." Reaper climbed on and cranked his engine, ignoring the continuous shots coming from the house.

Seconds later, they roared up the street with his motley crew all around them. Everyone on the road moved out of their way.

Poppy didn't blame them. The bikers were an intimidating sight, especially given the sheer volume of riders.

With no helmet, she couldn't keep her eyes open because of the wind. Poppy rested her forehead against Reaper's leather jacket and concentrated on staying on the bike. Before long, cold seeped into her bones, causing her to shiver continuously.

When they reached their destination, she hoped coffee was part of the bargaining process. Or hot chocolate. That would be an acceptable substitute.

Her mind turned back to Logan. Was he merely unconscious, or had Reaper killed the man she loved? Tears stung her eyes.

No. She gritted her teeth, forcing aside the despair threatening to steal her will. Poppy refused to let these bikers and the Holden organization do what human traffickers in Mexico hadn't. She wouldn't give up or give in. Logan, Brody, and their friends would find her. If she was lucky, Zane might assist.

Unable to let go of Reaper long enough to push the emergency button on her watch, Poppy resolved to activate her contact button as soon as it was safe. In the meantime, Fortress could track her movements. They'd know where she was. She took comfort in that. All she had to do was keep her head and think.

On and on they rode until Poppy couldn't feel her legs or her backside. They were numb from cold and the machine's vibration. When would they stop? After they reached their destination or filled up with gas? She frowned. Motorcycles could go a long distance on one tank of gas.

After midnight, the bikers turned into a gated entrance. The gates swung wide at their approach, and the entire group rolled through one or two at a time, with Reaper and Poppy in the lead.

They parked in front of a mansion and shut off their engines. What a contrast. Bikers and mega mansions didn't go together.

Reaper dismounted his bike and plucked Poppy off the seat. When he set her on her feet, Poppy's legs buckled. She would have dropped to the asphalt if he hadn't kept his hands on her waist.

Laughing, the biker leader scooped Poppy into his arms and carried her up many stairs to the front door, which opened as soon as his booted foot stepped on the landing.

Four men exited the house, each one heavily armed. One stepped forward. "What are you doing here? Those weren't your instructions."

"Noah awake?"

"Of course not. You should have called."

"Get him up."

"Get lost, Reaper. We don't want riffraff on the property."

"I said, get him up. I brought him the prize he's been after for the past week."

The guard's gaze shifted to Poppy. His eyes flared with interest. "Poppy Reynolds?"

"Would I be carrying this lady to your boss otherwise? I'd have kept her for myself."

"You'd better come in."

"Thought you'd see it my way."

"Why are you carrying her?" The man scowled. "You didn't hurt her, did you? The boss specifically said she wasn't to be harmed by anyone but him."

Oh, that wasn't good. Things One and Two had told the truth. Noah Wartrace was open to hurting Poppy to get information. If she told the identity of Lynx, Wartrace would send his goons after her mother. If she didn't, he'd make an example out of her and make her tell. Choices, choices.

"She's not used to riding a bike. Her legs gave out."

"This way. Only you and one or two of your men. No more. The boss doesn't appreciate a crowd. He's liable to mow down a few with a hail of bullets to give himself room to breathe. Got me?"

Reaper scowled. "Yeah, I got it." He glanced over his shoulder. "Killer, Wolf, you're with me. The rest of you wait out here."

The two men, one of whom had spoken to Reaper in front of Templeton's house, followed them inside. Two of the guards stayed outside the door. The third followed the group to the back of the house and around to a large office.

Reaper set Poppy in a chair in front of the desk. "Do yourself a favor, sweet thing," he murmured. "Tell the man what he wants to know, and we'll get out of here. I don't want you in his hands for long. Noah hurts people. He likes it. Me? I only hurt someone to get a point across."

A well-built man about six feet tall strode into the room and leaned against the front of his desk, his gaze locked on Poppy. Pleasure lit his face. "At last, Ms. Reynolds. You've been a hard woman to find and catch. I congratulate you on your skill."

She shrugged, feigning nonchalance. Truthfully, she'd never been more frightened in her life. She'd known what to expect from traffickers. This man, however, was a different kettle of fish. "Dumb luck."

"Modesty. I like that in a woman, although in your case it's false."

She blinked.

"You are a worthy opponent, Ms. Reynolds. We have a lot to talk about over the next several hours." Wartrace shifted his attention to Reaper and his friends. "Thanks for bringing the prize to me. You'll be amply rewarded."

"What are you offering?" Reaper asked.

"More weapons, as we agreed. You want money, too?" Anger lit his eyes.

"Nope." He nodded at Poppy. "Her."

"Ms. Reynolds isn't part of the reward."

"Make her part of it. I want her for myself. You'll give her to me relatively undamaged."

"Or what?" Wartrace challenged. "I don't like threats, Reaper."

"Tough. If you don't give me the woman, we will cut your organization off from one of your best customers."

The boss laughed. "You've got to be kidding. Your biker club doesn't buy as many weapons as you seem to believe."

"Not just mine, Wartrace. All the biker clubs around the US. All it will take is one phone call to get the word out, and the Holden group will hold a lot of guns no one wants."

"There are always other buyers," Wartrace said. His eyes, however, showed hints of worry.

"Probably. Those buyers will be out of luck when your pals at the ATF get the locations of all your warehouses and the names of your employees."

"You wouldn't dare."

"Try me, Noah." Reaper reached out and gripped Poppy's hair at the back of her head. She hissed as pain lanced her scalp. "She's mine. I get her back or your organization is dead in the water. Pitiful way to honor Ashley's legacy."

"Shut up! Don't you dare say my beloved wife's name."

Reaper laughed. "Beloved? Come on, man. You had a mistress and a side piece Ashley didn't know about. I'll bet you still have at least two women at your beck and call. So, what's it going to be? I get the woman back or I'll take her now and you can hunt for your information somewhere else."

"You can't take her from the estate. My men will stop you."

He snorted. "Your men don't have a chance of keeping us here if we want to leave. Are we staying or going with my old lady?"

Long seconds ticked away as Wartrace debated his options. From what Poppy could see, he didn't have any. He either cooperated or he lost everything.

Finally, Wartrace said, "Fine. Come back tomorrow night at midnight. You can have her then."

"She better be in shape to travel on my bike. If I have to use a car or something to transport her to our clubhouse, I'm taking one of yours and you won't get it back. I also might take a pound of flesh from your hide for hurting what's mine. Do we understand each other?"

A slight nod. "Now, get out. I have work to do with Ms. Reynolds."

"Remember what I said. She's mine. If you kill her, I'll take you and your entire organization apart." Reaper gripped Poppy's chin in his hand, bent down, and pressed a hard kiss to her mouth. "See you soon, sweet thing." He smiled. "Dream of me."

Reaper signaled to his men and left the office, leaving Poppy alone with Noah Wartrace and his guard.

Wartrace studied Poppy in silence. Less than a minute later, motorcycles roared to life and drove away.

The second guard who had followed the men to the front door said, "They're gone, boss."

"Good. Stay alert in case our hairy friends decide to come for their prize earlier than expected."

"Yes, sir. We'll be ready."

The boss straightened and headed for the door. "Bring her to the basement. I'm eager to get started."

The two guards grabbed Poppy's arms and propelled her from the office to a steel door at the end of a long, dark hallway.

Wartrace tapped in a code Poppy couldn't see from her position and opened the door. Lights flickered on, showing a staircase leading down to a lower level.

Although she longed to fight, she wouldn't escape even if she broke free. These men didn't look as though they would mind hurting Poppy to keep her under control.

She bided her time. Something would break, some chance she could take advantage of to escape. She had to be patient and wait. Lull them into inattention.

Poppy swallowed hard. Hopefully, they'd lose interest in her before she sustained too many injuries and caved to stop the pain.

The men kept a tight grip on her arms as they forced her downstairs. They passed many rooms, all with closed doors until they reached the last one. Wartrace opened the door and strode inside. The lights flashed on, illuminating the large cavernous space.

Shudders wracked Poppy's body as she studied the concrete floor with a drain. Positioned directly over the drain were a pair of chains with manacles attached to the end. Along the walls lay metal instruments, gleaming in the light, spread out on tables. Along the opposite wall, whips lay coiled like snakes waiting to strike at the unwitting, as well as a wicked assortment of knives.

The guards dragged Poppy to stand over the drain while Wartrace lowered the manacles.

The men jerked her arms up and secured the manacles around her wrists. Once they finished, Wartrace raised the chains higher until Poppy was off the ground.

Pain wound its way through Poppy's wrists, down her arms, and into shoulders. Didn't help that the guards hadn't removed her watch, although she was glad to still have the communication device. She'd lost the earpiece in the scuffle with the Iron Outlaws who manhandled her.

Wartrace set a chair a distance away from her and sat down. "Let us begin."

#

Chapter Twenty-Six

"Logan, wake up." A hard shake accompanied the command from his team leader.

Logan groaned, took a deep breath, and regretted it. Sharp pain shot through his ribs. He grunted. He hoped someone got the license plate of the truck that hit him.

"On your feet, buddy."

He raised his eyelids a fraction. Where was he?

Relief glimmered in Brody's eyes. "There you are. How do you feel?"

He grunted again.

"That good, huh?" Brody glanced over his shoulder. "He's awake. Check him out so we can get on the road."

"Poppy?" Logan croaked. "She okay?"

His friend hesitated.

Alarm shot through him. "What happened? Where is my wife?"

"The Iron Outlaws took her. I'm sorry, Logan. I couldn't stop them even though I emptied my Sig and took out several of them. The leader left with her on his bike."

Why would she go with Reaper? Made little sense. You had to be willing to ride a motorcycle. "Why?"

"Forty Outlaws against me and Poppy. What do you think? We were outnumbered, and you and Jesse were down. Reaper told her you were dead and threatened to kill me too if she didn't go willingly. He also promised to knock her out, throw her over his shoulder anyway, and take off. He didn't give her a choice, Logan. She went to protect the three of us."

Fear for Poppy made him want to hurl. He shouldn't have brought her here despite her pleading. She wouldn't be missing and in the hands of Reaper and his buddies if he'd done what he should have. Now, his wife, the woman who owned his heart, might pay the price for his poor decision.

Jesse knelt beside Logan. "Where?"

"Ribs and center mass. Shot twice in the vest."

"Same. Good thing we geared up before we left the safe house." Jesse removed the vest and felt along Logan's ribs and chest. After a couple of minutes, the medic said, "I don't think you've done any more damage. Cracks, possibly, which I can't see without an X-ray, but definitely no broken ribs. You'll be sore for a while, though."

"Tape. I have to be functional." He clenched his hands. "I'm going after my wife. I can't leave her in Reaper's hands."

"You aren't in good shape, Logan."

"Do I look like I care? You don't know what he does to women. Rape is a sport he shares with friends. I have to find her before he hurts Poppy."

Jesse gave a brief nod. "Understood. I'll do what I can." He glanced at Brody. "Help me get him to his feet."

Between the two of them, they hoisted Logan upright and held onto him until he steadied. To save time and pain on Logan's part, Jesse cut what was left of his shirt with his Ka-Bar and tossed the scraps of material aside.

The medic dug into his mike bag, pulled out a roll of athletic tape, and quickly taped Logan's ribs to provide the most support. "Take a breath. How is it?"

"Much better. Thanks, Jesse."

"You won't say that when you have to take the tape off. You'll look like you had a wax job on your chest by the time you remove the tape."

Logan flinched. Ouch. "As long as I can maneuver, I'll live with the rest. Where's Templeton?"

"Pick-up team scooped him up about five minutes ago and left. Parker said Trey is singing like a bird. We were right. Noah Wartrace is behind Poppy's kidnapping. From what I heard over the comm device in Poppy's ear, Reaper is taking her to Wartrace, but he plans to change the terms of their deal."

That didn't sound good. "What does he want?"

"Poppy."

Logan's blood ran cold. "Oh, man."

"Yeah. You ready to roll?"

He nodded, almost bursting out of his skin to get on the road and find his wife, especially now that he knew Reaper wanted Poppy for himself. If he found out Poppy was Logan's wife, the Iron Outlaw leader would punish and rape her as often as possible for spite. "What about the cops?"

"They'll be here in a couple of minutes. We were getting ready to haul you to the SUV and treat you en route, so we wouldn't be delayed." Brody climbed behind the wheel.

"Where are the Outlaws now?"

"On Suffolk Pike, about thirty minutes ahead of us," Jesse said.

"Step on it, Brody," Logan said.

"We can't afford to get pulled over. The delay could be deadly for Poppy." His friend activated the Bluetooth and called Brent.

"Yeah, Maddox."

"It's Brody. You're on speaker with Logan and Jesse."

"What do you need?"

"The Iron Outlaws are in bed with the Holden organization, and they've kidnapped Poppy."

"How did they get their hands on your wife, Logan?" Maddox snapped.

"I screwed up."

"Sit rep."

Logan recounted what he could remember, including the information about the Outlaws looking for him and also looking for Lynx on behalf of Noah Wartrace.

"If anything happens to Poppy, it's on your head."

Bile rose in Logan's throat. "I know, sir."

"I'm to blame as well, Brent," Brody said. "I should have insisted Poppy remain at the safe house, whether or not Logan did. Nothing in our research showed Templeton was on the Outlaws' radar, much less that they would show up en masse in front of the weasel's home in the middle of the night."

"We'll talk more about this when Poppy is safe, and this case is closed."

Logan and Brody exchanged grim glances. They were in for a lecture and a half. They'd be lucky if Brent didn't suspend them from duty without pay for this debacle.

"In the meantime, what do you need from us? How can we help?"

"At least one other team," Brody said. "The Outlaws outnumbered us, boss."

"Injuries?"

"Ten dead, five wounded on their side. Jesse and Logan both have cracked ribs and bruised torsos. They took two shots each to the vest."

Over the cabin's speaker, they heard keys clicking on a keyboard. "Two teams are available and in the area. Do you know where Poppy is being held?"

"We're following the GPS signal from her watch now. At the moment, we're driving up Suffolk Pike toward the coast."

"Copy. I'll alert the teams. They'll follow your GPS signals and rendezvous with you on the road or be right behind you."

"Copy that. Thank you, sir."

"Keep me updated." Brent ended the call.

"We're in deep water." Jesse sighed. "I hate being on the outs with the boss."

"Oh, yeah," Logan said. He called Zane.

"Murphy," the other man said, voice low.

Oh, man. He'd forgotten the time, and Zane had a family. "It's Logan. Sorry to wake you."

"Not asleep, but my son is sleeping in my arms. What do you need?"

He explained briefly what had happened. "I want Poppy's GPS signal sent to my phone."

"Understood. Give me a minute." Zane's next words came out muffled, as was the feminine response. Within seconds, Z said, "Sending the signal link now. Anything else?"

"Brent is sending two teams to help. He said they're already in the area."

"Durango and Wolf Pack. They were on a joint training exercise up your way."

Relief flooded Logan. Thank God. Those teams were as tough as they came. If anyone could keep Wartrace's people busy, as well as the Iron Outlaws, if they were still on site, it was those two teams. "Have the team leaders contact us so we can fill them in on what we're probably facing."

"Copy that. Anything else?"

"Operatives to protect Sage and Simone," Brody said. "We need Sawyer and Max."

"I'll take care of it."

"Good. We'll alert the rest of our team. Tell Durango and Wolf Pack to pack heavy."

"Will do. Murphy out." He ended the call.

A moment later, a link appeared in Logan's email. When he clicked on it, he saw the blinking light showing Poppy's current position. Although Brody remained close to the legal speed limit, the Outlaws didn't bother staying close to the law. Then again, on these country roads, what county cop would attempt to stop a biker gang by himself?

As Brody drove through the night, Logan alternated between watching the blinking light on his phone screen and scanning the countryside for potential threats. He doubted the bikers suspected Logan and his friends were on their trail, but he didn't want to take chances. They couldn't afford delays.

Three hours later, Poppy's tracking signal stopped moving. He waited another minute. Still no change. "She's stopped moving."

"Coordinates?" Jesse asked.

He rattled them off.

"The Iron Outlaws took her to the Holden compound."

"Text Josh Cahill and Eli Wolfe," Brody said. "Send them the coordinates."

A minute later, Jesse said, "Done. Both teams are fifteen minutes behind us. We're to select a meeting location and send them the coordinates. They'll meet us."

They continued to drive until they were a quarter of a mile from their destination. Brody pulled off the road and maneuvered the vehicle into the woods a short distance away. "Send Josh and Eli our coordinates." He shut off the engine.

They exited the vehicle and quartered the area. To Logan's surprise, he didn't spot any security cameras or perimeter alarms. Were they that well hidden or was Wartrace so arrogant that he believed his compound couldn't be invaded?

Logan paced while they waited for the other teams. Although he wanted to go find his wife with his guns blazing and no plans, the action would be foolhardy. He wanted to go on his honeymoon with Poppy. Couldn't do that if he was dead or laid up in a hospital bed.

Ten minutes later, two pairs of headlights went out, and two black SUVs pulled off to the side of the road. As Brody had done, the drivers backed into the tree cover on either side of Logan's SUV and shut off their engines.

Two teams of heavily armed operatives exited the vehicles. A tall blond-haired man strode toward Brody. He held out his hand. "Long time, my friend. How are you, Brody?"

"Been better, Josh." He nodded at the rest of Durango and shook Eli Wolfe's hand and his partner and second-in-command Jon Smith's hand.

"What do we have?" Eli asked.

Brody gave them a brief update about the Iron Outlaws kidnapping Poppy and bringing her to Noah Wartrace's estate. He inclined his head toward the right. "The compound is a quarter of a mile that way."

Josh glanced at the sky. "We have little time before the sun rises. We need a plan, fast."

Jon grabbed a tablet from their SUV and, within a few keystrokes, had the schematics of the Holden estate on the screen. "This work?"

"Perfect." Logan and the others examined the schematics. He pointed at the screen. "Here, here, here, and here are the best entry points."

"Any way to know if the fence is electrified?" Jesse asked. "I don't fancy getting a shock on top of being shot twice in the vest tonight."

Durango's medic looked at Jesse and frowned. "You hurt?"

"I'll live. Athletic tape. Logan, too."

"We can infiltrate the compound if your team wants to take the perimeter," Josh said.

"No." Logan looked toward the compound. "My wife is in Wartrace's hands. I'm going in to get her."

Alex Morgan, Josh's second-in-command, whistled softly. "I'm sorry, Logan. Didn't know you were married."

"It's recent."

Durango's medic, Rio, chuckled. "You're a brave man to take on Ivan and Beverly Reynolds."

"No joke." If they only knew the truth about Beverly. "They're not happy with me right now." Especially when they found out Poppy had been kidnapped again. More threats from Ivan and Beverly had ensued. Yeah, that phone call to her parents had been unpleasant.

"Clock's ticking," Jon said. "Here's what I propose." He laid out a plan. "What do you think, Logan?"

He considered the plan from every angle and conceded he couldn't come up with anything better on short notice. "It's risky."

"Especially for you," Eli said. "Willing to try it?"

He glanced at Brody. "Yes or no?"

"Yes. However, we're going in together."

"No."

"Not up for debate." Brody glared at him. "You need someone in there to watch your back. You'll be outnumbered. We don't want to hand Wartrace a willing sacrifice, just dangle bait in front of him."

"Not you," he insisted. "If anything happened to you, Sage would be devastated. I can't live with that on my conscience."

Sawyer and Max arrived and were brought up to speed on the proposal. "We don't have much time," Brody said. "We need the cover of darkness to give ourselves the best advantage. Logan will go into the lion's den. I'm going with him. He's balking at the company."

Sawyer said, "You need backup, Logan."

"Not Brody."

A shrug. "He's our team leader. Suck it up, Cupcake. If you're worried about him, get the job done in a hurry, grab your wife, and get out. We won't be far behind you when you enter the estate, anyway. Your job is to distract Wartrace to keep him from hurting Poppy and give us a chance to infiltrate the compound."

Although Logan scowled at the other man, he couldn't argue with the logic. He tried one more time. "I'm trying to protect him.

Poppy let Reaper take her to protect Brody, Jesse, and me. This plan drags all of us right in the thick of things."

"It's what we do," Alex said.

"He's right," Josh said. "We face down danger for a living. Right now, your wife needs you. Let's slip inside the compound, rescue her, and leave. My wife and girls are waiting for me at home."

Eli pointed at the screen to one side of the compound. "Wolf Pack will take the east side. Josh, you and your team take the west side."

"Agreed. Brody, divide up the rest of your team. They'll enter the compound with Durango and Wolf Pack. They'll work their way to you and Logan."

"Anyone see anything we missed?" Brody asked. When no one spoke up, he said, "Let's get this done. Most of the compound is asleep. Hopefully, they'll stay that way until the fireworks begin."

"Contact Zane," Logan said. "I want him as tech support on this mission. He'll need to loop in all three teams."

"Already contacted him," Jon said. "He's waiting for our signal."

Each member of the teams slipped a comm device into his or her ear and tapped it to turn the device on.

Jon fired off another text. Within seconds, the teams had been looped together into one comm network to enable communications with each other.

Josh stood. "Stay silent unless you need help or unless you're spoken to specifically. Otherwise, communications will be chaotic. Only team leads, seconds, and Logan should be active. Understood?"

"Yes, sir."

"Let's roll. Brody, give us ten minutes to get into position."

"Copy that."

The other teams, along with Jesse, Max, and Sawyer, melted into the darkness of the woods surrounding the compound.

Logan and Brody returned to their SUV and climbed inside.

"Why?" Brody asked without looking at Logan.

"You know why."

"Spell it out."

"I don't want to lose my best friend, all right? I've had enough loss to last a lifetime. I don't want to add your name to the list."

Brody looked at him. "You're as close to me as a brother and Poppy's my sister-in-law. I care as much about you two as my family. Nothing will keep me from rescuing her and protecting you."

A slight nod. "So, we'll watch each other's backs and do what we do best. Rescue a hostage."

Throughout the next few minutes, Zane guided Josh and Eli's teams to their entry points, warning them of approaching guards when they patrolled too close to the black ops teams' positions.

Logan fidgeted, the wait seeming interminable. What was taking them so long?

"Logan." Zane's voice came through the earpiece.

"Yeah?"

"I'm monitoring what's happening with Poppy through the comm device on her watch."

He straightened. "And?"

A slight hesitation. "Wartrace is working her over while interrogating her."

Ice water ran in Logan's veins. "How bad?"

"On a scale of one to ten, a twelve."

Brody clamped a hand on Logan's shoulder to hold him in place when he reached for the door handle. "No."

"He's hurting my wife."

"If you go in guns blazing, you'll be cut down in a hail of bullets. Poppy's going to need you whole and healthy to help her heal. Think with your head, not your heart," he snapped.

"Would you sit calmly while someone tortured Sage?"

"No." He stared at Logan. "I would expect my best friend to hold me to the plan that has the best chance of saving everyone."

"Wait, Logan," Jon murmured. "Almost in position. They'll pay. Hard."

The way he felt right now, Logan would gladly mow down the lot of them without a qualm for hurting Poppy.

He drew in a deep breath, then another and another. "Z, does she know we're here?"

"I think so. I've triggered vibrations from her watch at varying intervals when the interrogation is the worst. She bucks up and endures without breaking. Your wife has a spine of steel, my friend. She'll make it until you and the teams arrive."

"If you get a chance, talk to her."

"If it's safe. Wartrace has two guards with him. They're helping him with the interrogation."

The muscles in Logan's jaw twitched. All three of the men were dead men walking. He didn't care if the feds wanted Wartrace or not. They'd have to get their information from another source. Wartrace was his.

Josh said, "Durango in position."

Seconds later, Eli chimed in. "Wolf Pack in position."

"Copy," Brody said. "We're on the move." He drove from tree cover back onto the road and headed for the front entrance of the estate.

Soon, the headlights illuminated iron gates and a guardhouse with two occupants.

Brody stopped as both men left the shelter and approached the SUV, MP5s in their hands. "Overkill," he murmured.

"Not handy in close quarters fighting." Logan scanned the fence. No wires. "Doesn't look wired."

"We'll get a better look at it inside the gates." He lowered the window at a signal from one guard.

"This is private property. You need to leave."

"Tell your boss we have the information he wants."

"What information?" the second man asked.

"Lynx's identity."

The guards exchanged glances, then Guard One said, "Wait here. I'll see if he's awake and if he wants to talk to you."

Guard Two remained where he was, fingering his weapon and staring about Brody and Logan.

Two minutes later, Guard One returned. "Names?"

"Brody and Logan."

The guards frowned. "Last names?" Guard Two snapped.

"No."

Again, the guards exchanged glances. "We don't have to let you in," Guard Two said.

"You want to explain to Wartrace why the information he's seeking slipped through his fingers because of you?"

Guard One glared at Brody. "You better pony up the goods, buddy. The boss don't like to be woken up before he's ready."

"Open the gate," Brody said softly. "Now."

Another minute of staring passed before Guard One signaled Guard Two to open the gates.

Brody drove onto the compound grounds, taking his time to give Logan a chance to scan the fence.

"Nothing. No wires."

"Good. Makes entry easier." He parked in front of the main house and climbed out from behind the wheel. "Guards roaming in pairs, heading your way," he murmured to the two teams preparing to scale the fence. "No dogs."

"Copy," Eli and Josh replied.

Logan joined Brody at the front of the SUV. "Ready."

The two operatives climbed the stairs to the landing leading to the front door. The door opened before they placed their booted feet on the top step.

Two heavily armed bruisers exited the house. "No weapons allowed."

"Tough," Logan said. "Either Wartrace sees us as we are or we leave and take our information with us."

The bruiser closest to the door murmured something into a communication device attached to his wrist. He glanced up. "Let them in, Chip. Boss's orders."

"Bad idea." The other man nodded at Brody and Logan. "Look at them. They're better armed than we are."

A shrug. "We outnumber them. They're no threat. Besides, if they so much as lift a finger toward one of those weapons, we'll kill them where they stand."

Not if he and Brody took them out first. No one would prevent him from finding Poppy.

"This way." The guard nearest the door led the way inside and along miles of winding hallways until he reached a closed door in a darkened corridor. The man knocked and opened the door. "Brody and Logan, sir." He stepped inside the office and motioned them inside the room.

Logan walked in first, determined to shield Brody's body with his own for as long as possible. He came to a halt in front of the massive cherry desk.

Noah Wartrace stood behind it, arms crossed, a scowl on his face, irritation in his eyes. "Awfully early for a social call, gentlemen. Who are you, and what do you want?"

"Doesn't matter who we are." Logan stared at him, memorizing every feature of the enemy who had dared put his hands on Logan's wife. "We have the information you want."

"How do you know what I want? I've never met you before in my life."

"Friend of mine mentioned it."

"Friend? What friend?"

"Reaper."

Wartrace's arms unfolded. "You don't look like a member of Iron Outlaws."

"I used to be. Haven't lost touch with the brothers, though."

"What information are you offering?"

"The name of an assassin, a woman known as Lynx."

"Why should I believe anything you tell me?"

"Want to take a chance on losing the information you've gone to such great lengths to get?"

"How do I know I can trust you?"

"You don't."

Wartrace tilted his head, studying Logan. "Tough man, aren't you?"

He snorted. "You think I could survive living and working with the Iron Outlaws for years unless I was as tough as nails?"

"If you're lying to me, I'll find out exactly how tough you are."

"Go for it." Logan placed his palms on the desktop and leaned closer. "I dare you."

A hard glint appeared in Wartrace's eyes. "Don't tempt me, my friend. I'm very good at my craft."

"Sadism isn't something to brag about," he said, voice soft.

"How do you know about my entertainment?"

"Rumors get around. Your little proclivities are a well-known secret in the Outlaws."

Wartrace looked thoughtful. "Your friend Reaper has a big mouth. I might have to address that with him at a later date. All right, then. You have information I want. What will it cost me?"

"One million dollars in cash."

The other man blinked. "When do you want it?"

"No money, no name."

Wartrace glanced at one guard. "Get it."

"But, sir, they're armed to the teeth."

"They're here to do business. I'm meeting the terms of their proposal. Why should they attack me? If they do, they lose the money and their lives."

"I'll call one of the other guards to get the cash. I don't want to leave you alone with these men."

Impatience crossed Wartrace's features. "Fine. But bring the money down here quickly. I'm still working, and this is interrupting the progress I was making."

"Yes, sir." The guard stepped into the hallway and activated his communication device to instruct another guard to retrieve the money.

"We apologize for interrupting your work," Brody said. "What are you working on? Perhaps we can help."

Wartrace laughed. "That's what I like to hear. Initiative and eagerness. You want a job, gentlemen? I can always use good men in my organization."

"Depends," Logan said. He would give anything to pull out his weapon and take Wartrace out. But he had to know where Poppy was located. This estate was enormous, and the GPS signal in Poppy's watch wouldn't offer a more specific location than the main house. "I have certain entertainment interests myself."

His stomach knotted at the outright lie. The thought of hurting Poppy like Wartrace had been doing made him physically ill. While undercover, he'd been able to avoid joining in when the bikers played their vicious games with women and even some men. This time, though, he'd play the role for all he was worth if it gave him access to Poppy. The sooner he was by her side, the better.

"What kind?"

"Everything is on the table if the prize is worth the effort." He straightened. "Have anything that might interest me?"

"Perhaps."

"If you do, Brody and I might be open to switching employers and loyalty."

"Scaling now," Josh murmured. "Keep him busy, Logan."

"The prize must be special, though," Logan continued. "I'm selective." His lips curved. "The more difficult the job, the more satisfied I am with the result."

Wartrace chuckled. "I know what you mean. We might do business after all, Logan. If your information is worth the price I'm paying, I'll consider adding you to my team. You're certainly more civilized than Reaper and his biker friends are."

"Civility isn't their long suit," Logan agreed. Those men and women were as crude and vicious as anyone Logan had ever met, and that included terrorists on the US hit list.

An additional guard entered the office, a large duffel bag clutched in his hand. "Here you go, sir." He set the bag on the desk.

"Thank you, Kurt. You may return to your duties now."

"Yes, sir."

When the third guard left, Logan heard sounds over the comm device, indicating the Fortress teams were quietly engaging the enemy and entering the house. So far, none of the enemy had raised an alarm. But time was running out. Logan needed to know where this sadist was holding Poppy.

"Well, gentlemen." Wartrace patted the bag. "One million in cash, as you requested."

"Open it," Brody said.

The man complied and spread the top of the bag wide.

"Fan it."

"Not a trusting sort, are you?"

"Never."

"Good. I'm not either. We'll get along famously, provided your information is worth the price." He fanned a bundle of cash, then dropped it back into the back. "Now, who is Lynx?"

Logan glanced at Brody, who gave a slight nod. They'd discussed the pros and cons of giving Beverly Reynolds's name to Wartrace. With the information Templeton had leaked to Reaper, Beverly's identity was as good as blown. Wouldn't take much investigation to put the pieces together and come up with her name, anyway.

Besides, the teams didn't plan to let Wartrace out of this compound under his own steam. He wouldn't use the information he learned. If he escaped, Logan or one of the other operatives on this mission would track Wartrace down and take him out before he became even more of a threat to Beverly and Ivan.

"Well?" Wartrace snapped. "I want the information."

"Her name is Beverly Reynolds."

Astonishment flooded the gunrunner's face. "What? The vice president's wife is an assassin?"

"That's right. She was. She's retired now."

"What proof do you have that Mrs. Reynolds is the woman I'm seeking?"

"We know about Jonah Templeton," Brody said. "He was too much of a coward to give you Beverly's name, so instead, he gave you the name of someone who knew Beverly well. Her daughter, Poppy."

"Incredible," Wartrace said. "I would never have guessed."

"Why do you want her so much?" Logan asked.

"She murdered my wife. I want her blood to cover my playroom floor." He smiled. "I can have both of them side-by-side." Wartrace sobered. "Except I made a promise to Reaper to give my current project back to him relatively unharmed."

Logan stared. "Is she unharmed?"

"How do you know my project is a woman?"

"For Reaper to show that much interest, your project must be a woman. He wouldn't insist on getting a man back into his hands. He wouldn't care what you did with a male."

Wartrace studied Logan and Brody. "How serious are you about joining my organization?"

"Very," Brody said. "I like what I've seen so far. We already know you're into the gun trade." He indicated their weapons. "We're familiar with the weapons you buy and sell. Our loyalty isn't for sale once we're on your team."

"I like what I'm hearing." Wartrace appeared to decide. "Come with me. A little test of how good you are with your hands and knives."

Was this it? Logan's heart raced as he followed the gunrunner from the office with Brody on his heels. Was Wartrace taking them to Poppy?

Through his comm device, Zane murmured, "Be prepared, Logan. Poppy's been through the wringer. You mustn't give anything away."

He didn't respond. Everything in him urged Logan to get to his wife. He'd deal with whatever Wartrace had done. Then, he'd take care of Wartrace himself.

Chapter Twenty-Seven

Poppy struggled to breathe. Man, everything hurt. Every bone and joint ached. Even her hair hurt. How many more bruises did she have now? Probably too many to count. Wartrace's guards enjoyed their work.

And the cuts? She didn't know how many times the knives had sliced into her skin or the times the guards had stabbed her in places that wouldn't kill her but would hurt. And hurt they did.

They'd used whips on her. Thankfully, her clothes protected her. The last few lashes, though, had cut through the material and into her skin. How much more she could stand without breaking, Poppy didn't know.

Once again, her watch vibrated. This time, twice. Since she was alone for the moment, Poppy said, "Zane, can you hear me?"

"I'm here."

"Do you ever sleep?"

He chuckled. "Not much, sugar. You holding up?"

"For now. I'm reaching my limit. Blood loss is making me weak. I'm afraid to lose consciousness in the hands of these people."

"Help is coming. Logan and Brody are upstairs. Two teams are infiltrating. If Wartrace brings Logan and Brody, you can't give them away. Their lives depend on it. Remember, they're playing a role. They'll have to do it well to pull this off."

She wouldn't be seeing her husband and brother-in-law, but two strangers she wouldn't want to meet in a dark alley. "Got it."

"Good girl. You'll be safe soon."

The lock in the door rattled, and the guards walked into the room ahead of Wartrace. Bringing up the rear were Logan and Brody.

At the sight of her hanging from the ceiling, Logan froze. His hands fisted.

Brody nudged him with his shoulder.

Her husband blinked, glanced at his friend, then refocused on Poppy. "This is your project?" he murmured, walking toward her. "I thought you were to return her to Reaper unharmed."

"She'll heal," he said. "The wounds are all superficial."

"You finished with her yet?"

"I don't need her now. You've given me the information she wouldn't. If you hadn't arrived, I would have locked her in a room until Reaper arrived to take her off my hands."

"I want her," Logan said. "Give her to me."

"What about your friend? He won't be happy if his prize is gone when he arrives."

"Leave Reaper to me. I'll take care of him."

Poppy swallowed hard at Logan's statement. She knew what he meant. Reaper's freedom was on a countdown. She also recognized the determination in her husband's voice. Either Reaper gave himself up or Logan would take him down permanently.

"I gave you what you wanted, Wartrace."

"For an exorbitant price."

"Is the price too high to pay for avenging your wife's murder?"

"No." Wartrace's gaze drifted over Poppy. Heat simmered in his eyes. "I find myself reluctant to let her go. I was enjoying myself. I might keep her."

"What do you want for her?" Brody asked.

Poppy tuned out Wartrace and Brody's negotiation, instead focusing on Logan's slow approach. His eyes glittered with rage as he noticed more and more injuries on her battered body. He circled around behind her and muttered something under his breath, the volume too low even for her to make out.

A second later, his hand rested against her waist. "Oh, baby," he whispered. "I'm sorry. He'll pay. They all will."

Her eyes burned with tears. "How bad?"

"Enough. You'll heal."

"What do you think of her, Logan?" Wartrace asked. "A beauty, is she not?"

"She's exquisite, a prize worth more than any other," he answered, his voice husky. "She's mine. I'm claiming her. Turn her loose and give her to me."

The other man laughed. "You willing to return the payment for Lynx to purchase this one?"

"Yes."

"Done." He paused. "One more stipulation."

"Which is?"

"You come work for me, beginning immediately after you pass your employment interview."

Logan's fingers brushed Poppy's waist, a caress of comfort that she needed. Just a few more minutes, she reminded herself. She could handle anything for a few minutes.

"Employment interview? I thought we had concluded employment negotiations."

A chuckle from Wartrace. "Perhaps a better phrase is employment test."

Logan shifted to stand in front of Poppy. "What's the test?"

The gunrunner crossed the room to the table holding his collection of whips and knives. "You and your friend said you can handle the type of weapons we supply to customers. Frequently, my people are called upon to show their skill and technique in handling the weapons."

Brody gave a bark of laughter. "You want us to shoot at targets to prove we're excellent marksmen?"

A wintry smile curved Wartrace's mouth. "If you couldn't shoot, you'd be dead considering the company you keep." He picked up a wicked-looking whip. "This is what I had in mind. How skilled are you with these, gentlemen?"

Brody's expression went blank. "Want us to demonstrate on you? Let's get the woman down and put you in the cuffs."

A scowl. "Not me. Ms. Reynolds."

"Why?" Logan asked. "You've already done a number on her. I don't damage my property or my women."

"You want to work for me, then you obey orders." Wartrace tossed the whip to Logan. "A dozen stripes. Now."

Logan removed the velcro strap keeping the whip coiled neatly. The leather tail slithered to the floor. He flicked the tail out a few times, experimenting with the grip. "Delicate balance. Where did you get it?"

Stalling, Poppy realized. He was stalling, waiting for something, some signal. But what?

"Doesn't matter." Wartrace nodded at Poppy. "Get to work, Logan. You're next, Brody. A dozen stripes from you as well on our fair maiden. Not too much damage, though. We wouldn't want your friend to be angry with me for damaging his new property."

Oh, man. Poppy shuddered. This wasn't good. Two guards, plus Wartrace, were in this room, watching every move Logan and Brody made. She knew the operatives could take the three men easily. But they wouldn't risk her life. Chained to the ceiling like a sacrifice, Poppy couldn't take refuge under a table or on the floor. The likelihood of her being shot in a confrontation was high.

The knuckles of Logan's hand turned white as his grip tightened around the handle of the whip. He turned to face her. Fury was a living thing in his eyes.

He wound the tail as he looked at Poppy. "I love you," he mouthed. "Trust me."

She risked giving him a slight nod.

Logan winked at her.

He had a plan. Good to know because she was fresh out of ideas and was in no hurry to add to the bruises and whip marks on her body.

Logan circled her again, trailing the handle of the whip lightly over one spot, then another before he stopped behind her back. Once again, his hand brushed her skin in a gentle caress.

"I'm waiting," Wartrace snapped. "If I didn't know better, Logan, I'd say you're delaying the test on purpose. Why would that be?"

"I'm an artist with a whip. You'll find that out soon enough. You didn't leave me much room to show off my technique. Sloppy work, Wartrace."

The gunrunner's face flushed. "I was getting the job done."

"I don't think so. You did a lot of damage and have nothing to show for it."

"Get on with it," he snapped. "I'm running out of patience."

And Poppy was running out of time.

"I already had one of my trusted men fail me, my friend. He's dead now. Will you and Brody be the next bodies we dump deep in the forest?"

Another brush of Logan's hand. "Trust me," he whispered behind her back.

As if she could do anything else. Poppy adored this man and trusted him with everything, including her heart and her body.

She waited for him to do whatever was necessary to get them out of this situation. Her heart melted when he brushed his fingers over her hip.

Logan walked around her body to stand in front of her again. "Get ready," he murmured.

For what?

Gunfire sounded above their heads.

That was the signal Brody and Logan were waiting for. They sprang in to action. Brody fired his weapon at the first guard, then the second. Both were down in two seconds flat.

Logan snapped the whip with a loud crack.

The tip of the tail slashed Wartrace's cheek. He dropped to the floor, screaming, hand pressed to stop the flow of blood.

Poppy's husband tossed the whip aside, covered the distance between him and Wartrace in two strides, and pummeled the other man's face and body with his fists. The beating was brutal and would have continued once he was down except for Brody's restraining hand on Logan's shoulder. "Enough. He's down and he's not getting back up soon."

"It's enough when I say it is. You didn't see what he did to Poppy's back." Logan shrugged off Brody's hold and would have continued his assault on the downed gunrunner if not for the entrance of a man and a woman dressed like Brody and Logan.

The man whistled. "Looks like we arrived at the party too late."

"Get her down," the woman said. "I need to check her quickly before we move her out of this place."

"I've got Wartrace," Brody said. "See to your wife, Logan. You're done here."

"I want him dead."

"Not your call. Priorities, buddy." When Brody was convinced Logan wouldn't lose control again, he stepped over to the lift controls for the chains and cuffs. "Coming down," he warned and activated the controls.

Gradually, the chains lowered, and Poppy's feet settled on the floor. Her legs gave out, and she sagged into Logan's embrace.

"I've got you."

She moaned as pain skyrocketed through her body.

"Hold, Brody. The pain will ease soon," the woman said to Poppy. "But it will spike when the chains are low enough for you to drop your arms. You've been suspended for a while and your joints are swollen, stiff, and sore. If you can, keep your arms above your head. We'll help you lower them a bit at a time. My name is Sam, by the way. The handsome guy talking to Brody is my husband, Joe. We're on loan from the Shadow unit until next week. I'm filling in for another medic, and Joe always goes where I go."

"I'm Poppy."

"Good to meet you, Poppy. I understand congratulations are in order. When did you and Logan get married?" Sam signaled Brody to lower the chains and cuffs again. This time, she and Logan kept Poppy's arms aloft for her.

"Yesterday morning."

"Nice work, both of you. I heard nothing about it, so you evaded the news media."

"Some feat," Joe said. "Especially given who your parents are."

"Ready, Poppy?" Sam looked her in the eyes. "This is going to hurt. No way around it, I'm afraid."

"Let's get this over with."

Sam massaged first one of Poppy's shoulders, then the other, warming the joints and encouraging blood flow to the swollen tissue.

Pain rocketed through her, leaving her feeling nauseated and light-headed.

"Still with me?"

"Unfortunately."

"Feeling ill?"

"Oh, yeah."

Sam said, "Joe, I need another hand."

Her husband crossed the distance between them in seconds. "How can I help?"

"Hold Poppy's arm aloft while I get something out of my mike bag." Once he took over for Sam, she thrust her hand in the bag, rummaged around a minute, then withdrew it with a round piece of candy. She unwrapped the treat and showed it to Poppy. "Peppermint. It will help settle your stomach. May I?"

She nodded, and Sam slipped the candy into Poppy's mouth. As the peppermint candy dissolved in her mouth, her nausea retreated to a manageable level.

"Better?"

"Yes. Miracle drug."

Sam smiled. "The best. My team loves them, too. I also keep a supply of suckers handy if you want one of those once your stomach settles down."

The medic sat back on her heels. "All right, Poppy. I've done what I can to do to prepare your joints. The next step is to lower your arms to their normal position. We'll do that as soon as your cuffs are removed."

"If you'll take over holding her arm for a minute, I'll pick the locks," Joe murmured.

They switched places, and Joe went to work on the iron cuffs around her wrists. Seconds later, the operative removed the cuffs.

"Poppy's not capable of standing on her own," Logan said. "You can't lay her down on her back. Wartrace did a number on her."

"We'll fix her up once she's safe. For now, we're going to lower her arms slowly, keeping them in line with her body. Ready? Go, Logan."

As soon as they began, Poppy's pain escalated to excruciating. Sweat broke out over her body as she fought the desire to scream. She couldn't. Logan was barely holding it together as it was. If she betrayed how bad the pain was, he'd lose all control and kill Wartrace. Personally, she wouldn't care if he was dead, but had no desire to visit her husband in prison.

Tears leaked from her eyes. She blinked to clear them and more tears fell.

"Hang in there, Poppy," Sam said. "You're doing great. We're almost finished. Tell me, where are you and Logan going on your honeymoon?"

A groan slipped out. Rats! No more. Logan looked ready to explode. "Um, I don't know. Logan is planning everything, and he's not talking."

"Oh, a secret, huh? I like it. Want some suggestions, Logan?"

"No."

"You're getting them anyway. No sand. Poppy's wounds need to heal before she hits the beach. When she does, she might want to consider a lightweight wrap to keep the questions down until the marks fade."

"No problem."

Sam glanced at Poppy and winked. "So, no beach, Poppy. Where does that leave for your honeymoon?"

"Mountains or overseas."

"Have a preference?"

She shook her head. "All I want is time with Logan without him being deployed or someone trying to kidnap me to trap my mother."

"Sounds like he has you covered. Do yourself a favor. Rest and enjoy yourself. Nothing strenuous, just pure fun with the man of your dreams."

"Is that what you did?"

"Oh, yeah, baby. I definitely did." Sam flashed a smile filled with love at her husband.

Finally, her hands rested against the sides of her body. "Thank God," she whispered shakily.

"Lean against your handsome husband. I'll take a quick look at you and see what we're dealing with."

Poppy rested her weight against Logan, her legs shaking with weakness. "Thank you."

"For what, baby?" he murmured.

"Rescuing me again. Nice to have a knight in shining armor on hand."

He kissed her forehead. "I love you, Poppy."

"I love you, too, Logan. I've never been so happy to see anyone in my life."

"Same here." He cast another glare toward Wartrace. "I should have killed him."

"You did a number on him. That will have to be enough. You owe me a super honeymoon, and I'm collecting on the debt, preferably with you."

"I hear you."

Sam said, "Turn for me, Poppy. I want to see the front of you." When she complied, Sam did a quick scan, going for a closer visual inspection of some areas. "I can treat some of these wounds in the SUV. The others will have to wait until we're in a safe location."

Brody said, "Josh, did you copy?" He listened a moment, the said, "Roger that. We're ready to move out with Poppy. Is the pick-up team still on standby? Good. Get them in here. We're in the basement. Wartrace goes to the black site. Don't care what happens to the rest of these clowns. An anonymous call to the cops is probably the best way to handle the bodies. Let them think a rival gun dealer took out the Holden compound and made off with the boss." He looked at Logan and the others. "We'll get out of here soon. The pick-up team is two minutes out."

Sam dug into her mike bag again. "I'll work on a few of Poppy's wounds while we wait."

Poppy endured the cleaning and bandaging process with only a few groans and gasps.

When the pick-up team arrived, Logan scooped Poppy carefully into his arms and cradled her against his chest. "Let's go, Brody. These guys can have the garbage on the floor."

As they left the room, Wartrace cursed the team securing him for transport, demanding to be taken to a hospital. Everyone ignored him.

Logan said, "Close your eyes, Poppy."

She blinked and glanced at him. "Why?"

"You don't want to see the results when the enemy opposes Fortress operatives."

Yeah, no problem. She was exhausted and hurting all over. Her strength had taken a nosedive from the moment Logan and Brody stepped into the room where she'd been held prisoner. Poppy nuzzled her face against Logan's neck and closed her eyes.

"Thanks," he whispered.

"Wake me when we get there, okay?"

"Sure, babe. Rest now."

The trip back to the safe house passed in a hazy blur thanks to some pain meds Jesse and Sam insisted she take. Between the two medics, they examined her wounds and decided all were treatable with the supplies they had on hand in their mike bags. A couple of slashes with Wartrace's whip had cut deep into the skin of her back and needed stitches. Jesse conceded Sam was better at fine stitching than he was, so he allowed her to take that part of the treatment plan once they reached the house.

Hours later, cleaned, stitched, and clad in soft, loose clothing, Poppy lay on her side, snuggled up against Logan, his arms wrapped around her, holding her close to his chest. "Logan?"

"What do you need?"

"You all to myself. When are we leaving for our honeymoon?"

He laughed. "As soon as the medics give us clearance and Brent approves my leave of absence."

She settled closer. "Good. I want as long as I can get with you. No company. No deadlines. Nothing but you."

"Excellent plan."

"I know what my next writing project is going to be."

Logan stilled. "Don't keep me in suspense."

"The Holden organization, specifically Ashley Holden, queen of the weapons trade."

"You sure you want to walk through those memories again?"

"It's the only way to expose the truth, and I think it will help me purge the memories plaguing me. After that, I think I'm going to look at cold cases instead of current true crime."

"All right. When you go on research trips, I want to go with you. If I'm out of the country and a deadline is looming, I'll send someone I trust to accompany you. Deal?"

"Deal." Whatever steps were necessary to help him be able to function in the field, she'd cooperate. An inattentive operative was a dead operative, and Poppy wanted her husband to come home in one piece, not in a body bag.

"Sleep, baby. Let your body heal. I've got you, and I'll never let you go."

Poppy let her mind shut down and her body drift into the depths of sleep securely, knowing that her husband stood between her and any danger lurking in the night.

Chapter Twenty-Eight

When Poppy entered the sitting room at the Reynolds estate, Beverly and Ivan surged to their feet and rushed to embrace her.

"Easy," Logan snapped. "Her injuries are still healing, and Poppy is sore all over." He knew they were relieved Poppy was free and elated to see her alive. However, he'd told them both of the injuries she'd received. Of all people, Beverly should be familiar with how painful the healing process would be.

Ivan stopped a foot from his daughter. "How bad?" he demanded.

"I'm fine, Dad. The medics told me exactly what to expect. I'm healing and following their instructions to the letter."

"Medics?" Beverly scowled. "You should have seen a doctor, not a medic. They aren't trained to the same skill level as a medical professional."

"These medics are trained to that level and beyond," Logan insisted. Did she believe he wouldn't demand the absolute best medical care for his most precious gift in this life? "They've also consulted with one of our trauma surgeons. Poppy has had the best medical care available. They all assure us she will recover fully with a couple of scars on her back that can be minimized with plastic surgery if she wants it done."

"I don't," Poppy said. "I don't care about a couple of scars. They're battle wounds and I'll wear them proudly."

Beverly's ice turned glacial. "How did you receive wounds deep enough to leave scars?"

"A whip," Logan said curtly.

"Show me. I want to see your back, sweetheart."

"Mom."

"No. I insist. If you don't want your father to see, he'll turn around or shut his eyes, but I want to see your back right now."

Poppy glanced at Logan and sighed. "Do you mind helping me with my shirt?"

"Of course not." He looked at Ivan in a silent demand for him to turn around. Poppy deserved as much privacy as he could provide, while satisfying her mother's desire to see the injuries to her daughter.

Ivan looked as though he'd protest.

"Don't." Logan glared at his father-in-law. "If you want to see for yourself, Beverly can take a picture with her phone to show you."

Although the vice president scowled, he complied with Logan's order.

Once his back was turned, Logan helped Poppy remove her shirt. He drew her against his chest and motioned for Beverly to look at the damage done to Poppy at the hands of Wartrace.

The woman circled behind her daughter and gasped. Before Logan's eyes, the mother disappeared and Lynx came to the forefront. "Wartrace did this to you, Poppy?"

"Yes. His guards did all the knife work, but Wartrace bragged about how skilled he was with a whip."

"He lied." Beverly laid a hand on Poppy's shoulder. "Thanks for showing me the marks. Your medic friends are correct. You will heal soon. A week, perhaps two, and the cuts will have healed. If you want plastic surgery, your father and I will pay for the bill." She flashed a look at Logan. "Nonnegotiable."

He inclined his head. The concession gave Lynx some way to assuage her guilt, though it was unnecessary. She'd done her duty, nothing less. Templeton had been bought, and he'd started the cascade of events that swept all of them into the flood.

Lynx would have to figure it out on her own, like Logan did. Of course, Poppy had helped him see he wasn't to blame for her being kidnapped twice. Sometimes in the dead of night, though, Logan wondered.

"What about Templeton and the Iron Outlaws?" Beverly asked. "What's their status?"

"Templeton is in the hands of the feds, heading for prison as soon as they're able to bring him to trial. In the meantime, he's in jail. No bond. The Outlaws are no more. We tied them up in a neat package and delivered them and all the evidence the ATF needed to put them away for a long time. They're all in the pokey, waiting for trial as well."

"And Wartrace?"

"Fortress black site undergoing intensive interrogation. When they're finished with him, he'll also be delivered to the ATF with a red ribbon around his neck."

His answers displeased Beverly and Ivan.

"That's the best you can do?" Ivan asked. "Send the men responsible for threatening my wife and hurting my daughter to jail?"

"I'm not a mercenary. We got what we needed. Now it's up to the law to lock the cell doors and throw away the keys."

"We'll see," Beverly murmured.

What did that mean? Logan watched her.

"So, what's next for you, Poppy?" Ivan asked. "When will you go home?"

"As soon as we leave here, we're flying home."

"For a couple of hours," Logan said. "We're going on our honeymoon as soon as the jet is fueled and ready."

Ivan's brows drew together. "Isn't that too soon? Poppy is still healing."

"We'll heal together over the next month."

"You were injured?"

"More cracked ribs. I'll be fine."

"I wish you'd wait until you're healed, Poppy," Beverly said. "Surely you can talk Logan into waiting for a few weeks so you can recover." She glared at him as though she was positive the trip was all his idea and not Poppy's.

"Mom, I want to go away with him. I asked him to take me as soon as possible."

"But what about the trials? Won't the prosecutors need your testimony to nail these men, especially Wartrace?"

"They know to contact Fortress if something comes up," Logan said. "However, the government won't be able to bring them to trial for a few months. They're still wrapping up loose ends."

"I see." Beverly stepped forward and gently hugged Poppy. "I love you, sweetheart. Call me when you get a chance, all right? I'd love to hear about where you went on your honeymoon. Enjoy yourself and rest."

"I will, Mom. I promise. Logan will make sure I do."

She and Ivan turned to Logan. Ivan was the first to hold out his hand. "Take care of my daughter."

"Yes, sir."

"I'm sorry, Logan," Beverly said. "I was unduly harsh on you, blaming you for things that were not in your control. I'll try to be a better mother-in-law but Poppy is our daughter. We loved her long before you did."

"Yes, ma'am."

"Am I forgiven?"

He gave a slight nod. "If there's nothing else, we need to go. The rest of the team is waiting for us."

After another round of hugs for Poppy, her parents sent them off with their well wishes for a safe and happy honeymoon.

Nevertheless, something didn't feel right to Logan. He wasn't sure what it was, but he knew something was off.

They joined the others in the SUVs and soon were at the airstrip. The same group of men who had met them with the vehicles when they arrived were waiting for them. After handing over the keys and unloading the bags, the Fortress group climbed the stairs to the cabin of the waiting Lear jet.

Logan stowed their bags and joined Poppy in the last row of seats. "You sure you don't want to sleep on the way back to Nashville?" he asked.

"What's the point? We won't be in the air that long. Besides, I'm too excited about the next leg of our journey."

His lips curved. "Is that right?"

"Will you tell me where we're going now?"

"Do you want the entire crew to know where we'll be honeymooning?"

She wrinkled her nose. "Now that you mention it, no, I don't want them anywhere in the area. I want you to myself."

"Excellent plan, Mrs. Fletcher." He leaned in and kissed her, slow and deep. When he drew back, her eyes were unfocused and her breathing ragged.

Logan threaded his fingers through hers. He couldn't wait until Poppy realized where they were going to be for the next month. A literary tour of the homes of her favorite authors in England, as well as museums associated with them. He'd planned for plenty of downtime, and if she wanted to go, he had reserved tickets for an Outlander Tour in Scotland. Since she loved the Outlander book series, Logan figured that was a sure bet as well.

One thing he knew. This honeymoon would be good for both of them. If anyone saw their bruises and cuts, they'd believe he and Poppy had been through a war. In a way, they had been and had come out victors in the end.

The next day, Logan escorted Poppy into the suite that would be their home away from home for the next month. "What do you think?" he asked as he set down their luggage near the door. He'd take everything into the bedroom soon.

"It's perfect." Eyes sparkling, Poppy glanced at the suite's living room on the way to the wide expanse of windows. "Oh, look at this. It's like everything I've seen in books, movies, and news reports. The double-decker buses, Big Ben, the bridges." She laughed. "The rain. I couldn't have asked for a better honeymoon destination, Logan. So, what's first?"

"Sleep. We need to adjust to this time zone. In London, it's bedtime. We'll start exploring tomorrow."

"What will we see?"

"The typical tourist sites plus a few special surprises I've arranged for you."

"Oh, I can't wait. I'm not sure I'll be able to sleep."

He chuckled. "We'll try. When the sun rises, we'll plan our first day together in London."

Poppy walked back to him and into his arms. "Logan?"

"Yeah, babe?"

"I trust you with everything. My heart, my mind, and my body."

He stilled. "Are you saying what I think you're saying?"

"Yes."

Logan wanted to rush her into the bedroom and lock the world out while he focused only on his wife. "Baby, there's no rush, no pressure. I meant what I said. I'll wait until you're ready."

Instead of replying verbally, Poppy stepped back, wrapped her hand around his, and tugged him toward the bedroom. Once inside, she locked the door.

Logan swept her up into his arms and carried the woman he adored to the bed.

Chapter Twenty-Nine

In the dead of night, Lynx stood over the man who had tortured and beaten her daughter. Soon, Wartrace would realize he was in serious trouble. Deadly trouble.

He was as evil as his wife had been. Although Lynx had only been doing her job, she didn't regret erasing Ashley Holden from existence. Her activities had led to the deaths of military personnel and civilian support staff overseas. Innocent deaths would have escalated without her intervention.

No, she didn't regret killing Ashley, just as she wouldn't regret killing her husband.

Right on schedule, Wartrace's eyelids flew up, and he pressed a hand to his throat as his breathing became more labored.

He stared at her as though he couldn't believe what he was seeing.

She smiled. "Hello, Noah. I thought we should meet in person before you exit this life. My name is Lynx."

His eyes widened, panic in their depths. Wartrace reached for the nurse's call button and pressed it frantically.

"You're wasting your time," Lynx said in a pleasant voice. "I disabled every device that would allow you to call for help. No one will come to your rescue."

He shook his head and tried to speak. Nothing came out.

"Don't bother. You won't be talking again until you meet your maker in about two minutes."

More head shaking.

"You shouldn't have touched my daughter, Noah. I would have left you alone, but you crossed the line when you went after my family. No one touches my family and lives. Your wife was evil incarnate, and so are you. No one will miss you after you're gone."

She leaned in closer to the man fighting to breathe. "My daughters and my husband will be safe from you and your organization, which no longer exists, by the way. My sons-in-law, Logan and Brody, saw to that. You will never harm my family again, Noah, or anyone else's family."

Lynx shook her head slowly. "You should never have come after what's mine. Now, you've lost it all, including your own life."

She glanced at her watch. "The poison will end your life in thirty seconds. Unlike you, I'll walk out of here in a minute. You'll be taken out of this room in a body bag."

Wartrace strained to breathe. One last slow, shallow breath, then no more.

Gone.

Lynx turned away from the bed and left the secured black site the same way she'd entered. Once clear of the compound, she melted into the shadows and disappeared.

#

About the Author

Rebecca Deel is a preacher's kid with a black belt in karate. She teaches business classes at a private four-year college in Nashville, Tennessee. She plays the piano for her church, writes freelance articles, and runs interference for the family dogs. She's married to an amazing husband and is the proud mom of two grown sons. She delivers occasional devotions to the women's group at her church and conducts seminars in personal safety, money management, and writing. Her articles have been published in *ONE Magazine*, *Contact*, and *Co-Laborer*, and she was profiled in the June 2010 Williamson edition of *Nashville Christian Family* magazine. Rebecca completed her Doctor of Arts degree in Economics and wears her favorite Dallas Cowboys sweatshirt when life turns ugly.

Read more at rebeccadeelbooks.com.